"NEW FOLKS' HO
Simak—Seeking she
very isolated house
doorway to opportur
his whole way of life

"HOT PLANET" by Hal Clement—It was
supposed to be a straightforward scientific
expedition to Mercury, at least until the volcanoes woke. . . .

"THE PAIN PEDDLERS" by Robert Silverberg—Even though the real pain was
someone else's, it still felt so good when it
stopped. . . .

"IF THERE WERE NO BENNY CEMOLI"
by Philip K. Dick—Earth just wasn't what
it used to be, and when the armada from Proxima Centauri arrived it was Benny who was
going to have to take the blame. . . .

Take a glimpse at our possible futures in these
masterful tales of the day after tomorrow.

ISAAC ASIMOV
PRESENTS
THE GREAT SF STORIES:
25

Watch for these exciting DAW anthologies:

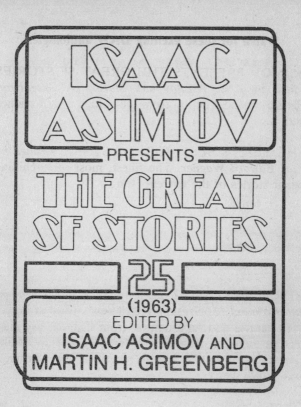

ISAAC ASIMOV

PRESENTS

THE GREAT SF STORIES

25

(1963)

EDITED BY
ISAAC ASIMOV AND
MARTIN H. GREENBERG

DAW BOOKS, INC.
DONALD A. WOLLHEIM, FOUNDER
375 Hudson Street, New York, NY 10014

ELIZABETH R. WOLLHEIM
SHEILA E. GILBERT
PUBLISHERS

First Printing, July 1992

1 2 3 4 5 6 7 8 9

DAW TRADEMARK REGISTERED
U.S. PAT. OFF. AND FOREIGN COUNTRIES
—MARCA REGISTRADA
HECHO EN U.S.A.

PRINTED IN THE U.S.A.

ACKNOWLEDGMENTS

CONTENTS

INTRODUCTION

All of us old enough to remember it know exactly where we were when we heard the news in the year outside reality—President John F. Kennedy had been assassinated in Dallas on November 22. That act and the events that followed so quickly—the arrest of Lee Harvey Oswald, the killing of Oswald by Jack Ruby—constitute one of the seminal events in the history of a generation.

The year also saw the establishment of the "Hot Line" between Washington and Moscow, an important event in those still Cold War years; the assassination of Ngo Diem in South Vietnam, an action tied to American intelligence and an important step on the road to American military involvement in that sad country; massive civil rights marches culminating in the march on Washington and the wonderful "I have a dream" speech by Dr. Martin Luther King, Jr. Sadly, the year was also marked by the death by bombing of four young Black schoolchildren in a church in Birmingham and severe brutality toward Black Americans and others asserting their human and civil rights. And Pope John XXIII, one of the most progressive men to fill the papacy, died in 1963.

That year Matthews and Sandage discovered the quasar, and Michael De Bakey made progress in the development of an artificial human heart. Outstanding or very popular books in 1963 included *Eichmann In Jerusalem* by Hannah Arendt; *The Spy Who Came In From The Cold* by John Le Carré; *The Bell Jar* by Sylvia Plath;

JFK: The Man And The Myth by Victor Lasky; *One Day In The Life Of Ivan Denisovich* by Alexander Solzhenitsyn; *Beyond The Melting Pot* by Nathan Glazer and Daniel P. Moynihan; *The Shoes Of The Fisherman* by Morris L. West; *The Fire Next Time* by James Baldwin; *The Group* by Mary McCarthy; *The American Way Of Death* by Jessica Mitford; *The Sand Pebbles* by our own Richard McKenna; *The Great Ascent* by Robert Heilbroner; and the most important book of the year, *The Feminine Mystique* by Betty Friedan.

Organs flew in 1963 as Hardy performed the first human lung transplant while Moore and Starzl did the honors with the first liver transplant. Valentina Tereshkova became the first woman to orbit the Earth, while insights into the shell structure of atomic nuclei won the Nobel Prize for Goppert-Mayer and Henson. Pop art reigned supreme as Roy Lichtenstein painted *Drowning Girl*, while Andy Warhol gave us his unique version of *Mona Lisa*.

Among the top songs of 1963 were "I Want to Hold Your Hand" by a new group called The Beatles; "Heatwave" by Martha and the Vandellas; "Surfin' U.S.A." by The Beach Boys; "Love's Gonna Live Here" by Buck Owens; "The Days of Wine and Roses" by Henry Mancini; "He's So Fine" by the Chiffons; Bob Dylan's "The Times They Are A-Changin'"; and "Puff the Magic Dragon" by Peter, Paul and Mary. Itzhak Perlman made his professional debut, as did The Amazing Spider Man and Weight Watchers.

Sandy Koufax had a great season, leading the Dodgers to victory over the hated Yankees in the World Series, making Marty a pleased twenty-two-year-old, while the Bears beat the Giants in the NFL Championship Game. Don Shula became the head coach of the Colts, Hank Aaron and Willie McCovey led the majors in homers with 44, Dick Butkus and Gale Sayers were college all-Americans, and Chateaugay won the Kentucky Derby. Top Broadway plays and musicals included *110 in the Shade, Barefoot in the Park, One Flew Over the Cuckoo's Nest, Enter Laughing*, and Lionel Bart's *Oliver!* Important films were *Hud, How the West Was Won*, Fellini's *8½, Tom Jones, Cleopatra*, and *Charade* with Cary Grant and the great Walter Matthau. Television offered us new shows like "General Hospital," David Janssen as "The Fugitive," "My Favorite Martian"; and Monty Hall said "Let's Make a Deal" for the first time.

Death took William Carlos Williams, Oliver La Farge, Edith Piaf, Adolphe Menjou, Jean Cocteau, Dick Powell, Robert Frost, Zasu Pitts, Rogers Hornsby, Aldous Huxley (one of ours), Clifford Odets, Estes Kefauver, and W.E.B. Du Bois.

In the real world things were much better, with the launch of two new magazines, *Worlds Of Tomorrow* from the *Galaxy* camp, and the feisty but hard to find *Gamma*, edited by Charles E. Fritch.

Important novels, collections, and anthologies included two good ones from Robert A. Heinlein, *Glory Road* and *Podkayne Of Mars; Planet Of The Apes* by Pierre Boulle; *Witch World* by Andre Norton; *Dune World* by Frank Herbert, serialized in *Analog; Fail-Safe* by Eugene L. Burdick and J.H. Wheeler; *Cat's Cradle* by Kurt Vonnegut, Jr.; the serialized *Here Gather The Stars* (later published as *Way Station*) by Clifford D. Simak; *The Star King* by Jack Vance, serialized in *Galaxy*; the excellent anthology *The Worlds Of Science Fiction*, edited by Robert P. Mills; *Who Fears The Devil?*, fine stories by Manly Wade Wellman; *The Reefs Of Space* by Frederik Pohl and Jack Williamson, serialized in *IF*; *The Unknown* and *The Unknown Five*, both edited by D.R. Benson; *I Love Galesburg In The Springtime* by Jack Finney; *First Flight*, edited by Damon Knight; *The Mile-Long Spaceship*, stories by Katherine MacLean; and the pioneering nonfiction book *Explorers Of The Infinite* by long-time fan-scholar Sam Moskowitz.

In the real world, more important people made their maiden voyages into reality: in January—Sonya Dorman with "The Putnam Tradition"; in February—Ted White with "Phoenix"; in April—Piers Anthony with "Possible to Rue"; in May—Norman Spinrad with "The Last of the Romany"; in June—Juanita Coulson with "Another Rib"; in July—Alexei Panshin with "Down to the Worlds of Men"; and in October—Hilary Bailey with "Breakdown."

On a grimmer note, death took the influential and underrated Mark Clifton along with C. S. Lewis and William Lindsay Gresham. Andrew Porter started his fanzine *Algol*.

It was a very weak year for fantastic films, saved only at the end of the year by the excellent *Children Of The Damned*. Other films included *Son Of Flubber, The Mouse On The Moon, The Nutty Professor* (not about Greenberg); the Soviet-produced *The Amphibious Man*, and *The Misadventures Of Merlin Jones*. On the other hand, two giant television series began—"Dr. Who" in Great Britain and "The Outer Limits" here in the U.S.A.

The Family gathered in Washington DC for the 21st World Science Fiction Convention—the Discon. Hugo Awards went to (awarded for achievements in 1962) Philip K. Dick for *The Man In The High Castle*; to Jack Vance for "The Dragon Masters"; to *The Magazine Of Fantasy And Science Fiction* for best magazine; to Roy G. Krenkel for Best Professional Artist; to Richard and Pat Lupoff for *Xero* as Best Fanzine; and Special Awards were given to P. Schuyler Miller for his book reviews and to our own Isaac Asimov for his science articles in *F&SF*.

Let us travel back to that honored but tragic year of 1963 and enjoy the best stories that the real world bequeathed to us.

FORTRESS SHIP

BY FRED SABERHAGEN (1930-   )

WORLDS OF IF
JANUARY

Fred Saberhagen is the creator of the very popular Berserker *and* Swords *series, and the author of more than
forty novels and short story collections. A native of Chicago, he worked as an electronics technician and as an
assistant editor at the* Encyclopaedia Britannica *before
turning to full-time writing in 1973. He collaborated with
Roger Zelazny on the excellent* Coils *(1980), and horror
readers should make it a point not to miss his* The Dracula
Tape *(1975) and* The Holmes-Dracula File *(1978). He
now resides in Albuquerque, New Mexico.*

"Fortress Ship" is the first of his Berserker *stories,
which constitute one of the most impressive treatments of
robotic spacecraft in the genre—and very nasty machines
they are.*

The machine was a vast fortress, containing no life, set
by its long-dead masters to destroy anything that lived.
It and many others like it were the inheritance of Earth
from some war fought between unknown interstellar
empires, in some time that could hardly be connected
with any Earthly calendar.

One such machine could hang over a planet colonized
by men and in two days pound the surface into a lifeless
cloud of dust and steam, a hundred miles deep. This
particular machine had already done just that.

It used no predictable tactics in its dedicated, unconscious war against life. The ancient, unknown gamesmen

had built it as a random factor, to be loosed in the enemy's territory to do what damage it might. Men thought its plan of battle was chosen by the random disintegrations of atoms in a block of some long-lived isotope buried deep inside it, and so was not even in theory predictable by opposing brains, human or electronic.

Men called it a berserker.

Del Murray, sometime computer specialist, had called it other names than that; but right now he was too busy to waste breath, as he moved in staggering lunges around the little cabin of his one-man fighter, plugging in replacement units for equipment damaged by the last near-miss of a berserker missile. An animal resembling a large dog with an ape's forelegs moved around the cabin too, carrying in its nearly human hands a supply of emergency sealing patches. The cabin air was full of haze. Wherever movement of the haze showed a leak to an unpressurized part of the hull, the dog-ape moved to apply a patch.

"Hello, Foxglove!" the man shouted, hoping that his radio was again in working order.

"Hello, Murray, this is Foxglove," said a sudden loud voice in the cabin. "How far did you get?"

Del was too weary to show much relief that his communications were open again. "I'll let you know in a minute. At least it's stopped shooting at me for a while. Move, Newton." The alien animal, pet and ally, called an *aiyan*, moved away from the man's feet and kept single-mindedly looking for leaks.

After another minute's work Del could strap his body into the deep-cushioned command chair again, with something like an operational panel before him. That last near-miss had sprayed the whole cabin with fine penetrating splinters. It was remarkable that man and *aiyan* had come through unwounded.

His radar working again, Del could say: "I'm about ninety miles out from it, Foxglove. On the opposite side from you." His present position was the one he had been trying to achieve since the battle had begun.

The two Earth ships and the berserker were half a light year from the nearest sun. The berserker could not leap out of normal space, toward the defenseless colonies on the planets of that sun, while the two ships stayed close to it. There were only two men aboard Foxglove. They had more machinery working for them than did Del, but both manned ships were mites compared to their opponent.

Del's radar showed him an ancient ruin of metal, not much smaller in cross section than New Jersey. Men had blown holes in it the size of Manhattan Island, and melted puddles of slag as big as lakes upon its surface.

But the berserker's power was still enormous. So far no man had fought it and survived. Now, it could squash Del's little ship like a mosquito; it was wasting its unpredictable subtlety on him. Yet there was a special taste of terror in the very indifference of it. Men could never frighten this enemy, as it frightened them.

Earthmen's tactics, worked out from bitter experience against other berserkers, called for a simultaneous attack by three ships. Foxglove and Murray made two. A third was supposedly on the way, but still about eight hours distant, moving at C-plus velocity, outside of normal space. Until it arrived, Foxglove and Murray must hold the berserker at bay, while it brooded unguessable schemes.

It might attack either ship at any moment, or it might seek to disengage. It might wait hours for them to make the first move—though it would certainly fight if the men attacked it. It had learned the language of Earth's spacemen—it might try to talk with them. But always, ultimately it would seek to destroy them and every other living thing it met. That was the basic command given it by the ancient warlords.

A thousand years ago, it would easily have swept ships of the type that now opposed it from its path, whether they carried fusion missiles or not. Now, it was in some electrical way conscious of its own weakening by accumulated damage. And perhaps in long centuries of fighting its way across the galaxy it had learned to be wary.

Now, quite suddenly, Del's detectors showed force fields forming in behind his ship. Like the encircling arms of a huge bear they blocked his path away from the enemy. He waited for some deadly blow, with his hand trembling over the red button that would salvo his atomic missiles at the berserker—but if he attacked alone, or even with Foxglove, the infernal machine would parry their missiles, crush their ships, and go on to destroy another helpless planet. Three ships were needed to attack. The red firing button was now only a last desperate resort.

Del was reporting the force field to Foxglove when he felt the first hint in his mind of another attack.

"Newton!" he called sharply, leaving the radio connection with Foxglove open. They would hear and understand what was going to happen.

The *aiyan* bounded instantly from its combat couch to stand before Del as if hypnotized, all attention riveted on the man. Del had sometimes bragged: "Show Newton a drawing of different-colored lights, convince him it represents a particular control panel, and he'll push buttons or whatever you tell him, until the real panel matches the drawing."

But no *aiyan* had the human ability to learn and to create on an abstract level; which was why Del was now going to put Newton in command of his ship.

He switched off the ship's computers—they were going to be as useless as his own brain under the attack he felt gathering—and said to Newton: "Situation Zombie."

The animal responded instantly as it had been trained, seizing Del's hands with firm insistence and dragging them one at a time down beside the command chair to where the fetters had been installed.

Hard experience had taught men something about the berserkers' mind weapon, although its principles of operation were still unknown. It was slow in its onslaught, and its effects could not be steadily maintained for more than about two hours, after which a berserker was evidently forced to turn it off for an equal time. But while in effect, it robbed any human or electronic brain of the ability to plan or to predict—and left it unconscious of its own incapacity.

It seemed to Del that all this had happened before, maybe more than once. Newton, that funny fellow, had gone too far with his pranks; he had abandoned the little boxes of colored beads that were his favorite toys, and was moving the controls around at the lighted panel. Unwilling to share the fun with Del, he had tied the man to his chair somehow. Such behavior was really intolerable, especially when there was supposed to be a battle in progress. Del tried to pull his hands free, and called to Newton.

Newton whined earnestly, and stayed at the panel.

"Newt, you dog, come lemme loose. I know what I have to say: Four score and seven . . . hey, Newt, where're your toys? Lemme see your pretty beads." There were hundreds of tiny boxes of varicolored beads, leftover trade goods that Newton loved to sort out and handle. Del peered around the cabin, chuckling a little at his own cleverness. He would get Newton distracted by the beads, and then . . . the vague idea faded into other crackbrained grotesqueries.

Newton whined now and then but stayed at the panel moving controls in the long sequence he had been taught, taking the ship through the feinting, evasive maneuvers that might fool a berserker into thinking it was still competently manned. Newton never put a hand near the big red button. Only if he felt deadly pain himself, or found a dead man in Del's chair, would he reach for that.

"Ah, roger, Murray," said the radio from time to time, as if acknowledging a message. Sometimes Foxglove added a few words or numbers that might have meant something. Del wondered what the talking was about.

At last he understood that Foxglove was trying to help maintain the illusion that there was still a competent brain in charge of Del's ship. The fear reaction came when he began to realize that he had once again lived through the effect of the mind weapon. The brooding berserker, half genius, half idiot, had forborne to press the attack when success would have been certain—perhaps deceived, perhaps following the strategy that avoided predictability at almost any cost.

"Newton." The animal turned, hearing a change in his voice. Now Del could say the words that would tell Newton it was safe to set his master free, a sequence too long for anyone under the mind weapon to recite.

"—shall not perish from the earth," he finished. With

a yelp of joy Newton pulled the fetters from Del's hands. Del turned instantly to the radio.

"Effect has evidently been turned off, Foxglove," said Del's voice through the speaker in the cabin of the larger ship.

The Commander let out a sigh. "He's back in control!"

The Second Officer—there was no third—said: "That means we've got some kind of fighting chance, for the next two hours. I say let's attack now!"

The Commander shook his head, slowly but without hesitation. "With two ships, we don't have any real chance. Less than four hours until Gizmo gets here. We have to stall until then, if we want to win."

"It'll attack the next time it gets Del's mind scrambled! I don't think we fooled it for a minute . . . we're out of range of the mind beam here, but Del can't withdraw now. And we can't expect that *aiyan* to fight his ship for him. We'll really have no chance, with Del gone."

The Commander's eyes moved ceaselessly over his panel. "We'll wait. We can't be sure it'll attack the next time it puts the beam on him. . . ."

The berserker spoke suddenly, its radioed voice plain in the cabins of both ships: "I have a proposition for you, little ship." Its voice had a cracking, adolescent quality, because it strung together words and syllables recorded from the voices of human prisoners of both sexes and different ages. Bits of human emotion, sorted and fixed like butterflies on pins, thought the Commander. There was no reason to think it had kept the prisoners alive after learning the language from them.

"Well?" Del's voice sounded tough and capable by comparison.

"I have invented a game which we will play," it said. "If you play well enough, I will not kill you right away."

"Now I've heard everything," murmured the Second Officer.

After three thoughtful seconds the Commander slammed a fist on the arm of his chair. "It means to test his learning ability, to run a continuous check on his brain while it turns up the power of the mind beam and tries different modulations. If it can make sure the mind beam is working, it'll attack instantly. I'll bet my life on it. That's the game it's playing this time."

"I will think over your proposition," said Del's voice coolly.

The Commander said: "It's in no hurry to start. It won't be able to turn on the mind beam again for almost two hours."

"But we need another two hours beyond that."

Del's voice said: "Describe the game you want to play."

"It is a simplified version of the human game called checkers."

The Commander and the Second looked at each other, neither able to imagine Newton able to play checkers. Nor could they doubt that Newton's failure would kill them within a few hours, and leave another planet open to destruction.

After a minute's silence, Del's voice asked: "What'll we use for a board?"

"We will radio our moves to one another," said the berserker equably. It went on to describe a checkers-like game, played on a smaller board with less than the normal number of pieces. There was nothing very profound about it; but, of course, playing would seem to require a functional brain, human or electronic, able to plan and to predict.

"If I agree to play," said Del slowly, "how'll we decide who gets to move first?"

"He's trying to stall," said the Commander, gnawing a thumbnail. "We won't be able to offer any advice, with that thing listening. Oh, stay sharp, Del boy!"

"To simplify matters," said the berserker, "I will move first in every game."

Del could look forward to another hour free of the mind weapon when he finished rigging the checkerboard. When the pegged pieces were moved, appropriate signals would be radioed to the berserker; lighted squares on the board would show him where its pieces were moved. If it spoke to him while the mind weapon was on, Del's voice would answer from a tape, which he had stocked with vaguely aggressive phrases, such as, "Get on with your game," or "Do you want to give up now?"

He hadn't told the enemy how far along he was with his preparations because he was still busy with something the enemy must not know—the system that was going to enable Newton to play a game of simplified checkers.

Del gave a soundless little laugh as he worked, and glanced over to where Newton was lounging on his couch, clutching toys in his hands as if he drew some comfort from them. This scheme was going to push the *aiyan* near the limit of his ability, but Del saw no reason why it should fail.

Del had completely analyzed the miniature checker game, and diagrammed every position that Newton could possibly face—playing only even-numbered moves, thank the random berserker for that specification!—on small cards. Del had discarded some lines of play that would arise from some poor early moves by Newton, further simplifying his job. Now, on a card showing each possible remaining position, Del indicated the best possible move with a drawn-in arrow. Now he could quickly teach Newton to play the game by looking at the appropriate card and making the move shown by the arrow—

"Oh, oh," said Del, as his hands stopped working and he stared into space. Newton whined at the tone of his voice.

Once Del had sat at one board in a simultaneous chess exhibition, one of sixty players opposing the world champion, Blankenship. Del had held his own into the middle game. Then, when the great man paused again opposite his board, Del had shoved a pawn forward, thinking he had reached an unassailable position and could begin a counter-attack. Blankenship had moved a rook to an innocent-looking square and strolled on to the next board—and then Del had seen the checkmate coming at him, four moves away but one move too late for him to do anything about it.

The Commander suddenly said a foul phrase in a loud distinct voice. Such conduct on his part was extremely rare, and the Second Officer looked round in surprise. "What?"

"I think we've had it." The Commander paused. "I hoped that Murray could set up some kind of a system over there, so that Newton could play the game—or appear to be playing it. But it won't work. Whatever system Newton plays by rote will always have him making the same move in the same position. It may be a perfect system—but a man doesn't play any game that way, damn it. He makes mistakes, he changes strategy. Even in a game this simple there'll be room for that. Most of all, a man *learns* a game as he plays it. He gets better as he goes along. That's what'll give Newton away, and that's what our bandit wants. It's probably heard about *aiyans*. Now as soon as it can be sure it's facing a dumb animal over there, and not a man or computer . . ."

After a little while the Second Officer said: "I'm getting signals of their moves. They've begun play. Maybe we should've rigged up a board so we could follow along with the game."

"We better just be ready to go at it when the time comes." The Commander looked hopelessly at his salvo button, and then at the clock that showed two hours must pass before Gizmo could reasonably be hoped for.

Soon the Second Officer said: "That seems to be the end of the first game; Del lost it, if I'm reading their scoreboard signal right." He paused. "Sir, here's that signal we picked up the last time it turned the mind beam on. Del must be starting to get it again."

There was nothing for the Commander to say. The two men waited silently for the enemy's attack, hoping only that they could damage it in the seconds before it would overwhelm them and kill them.

"He's playing the second game," said the Second Officer, puzzled. "And I just heard him say, 'Let's get on with it.' "

"His voice could be recorded. He must have made some plan of play for Newton to follow; but it won't fool the berserker for long. It can't."

Time crept unmeasurably past them.

The Second said: "He's lost the first four games. But he's *not* making the same moves every time. I wish we'd made a board. . . ."

"Shut up about the board! We'd be watching it instead of the panel. Now stay alert, Mister."

After what seemed a long time, the Second said: "Well, I'll be!"

"What?"

"Our side got a draw in that game."

"Then the beam can't be on him. Are you sure . . ."

"It is! Look, here, the same indication we got last time. It's been on him the better part of an hour now, and getting stronger."

The Commander stared in disbelief; but he knew and trusted his Second's ability. And the panel indications were convincing. He said: "Then someone—or something—with no functioning mind is learning how to play a game, over there. Ha, ha," he added, as if trying to remember how to laugh.

The berserker won another game. Another draw. Another win for the enemy. Then three drawn games in a row.

Once the Second Officer heard Del's voice ask coolly: "Do you want to give up now?" On the next move he lost another game. But the following game ended in another draw. Del was plainly taking more time than his opponent to move, but not enough to make the enemy impatient.

"It's trying different modulations on the mind beam," said the Second. "And it's got the power turned way up."

"Yeah," said the Commander. Several times he had almost tried to radio Del, to say something that might keep the man's spirits up—and also to relieve his own feverish inactivity, and to try to find out what could possibly be going on. But he could not take the chance. Any interference might upset the miracle.

He could not believe the inexplicable success could last, even when the checker match turned gradually into an endless succession of drawn games between two perfect players. Hours ago the Commander had said good-bye to life and hope, and he still waited for the fatal moment.

And he waited.

"—not perish from the earth!" said Del Murray, and Newton's eager hands flew to loose his right arm from its shackle.

A game, unfinished on the little board before him, had been abandoned seconds earlier. The mind beam had been turned off at the same time, when Gizmo had burst into normal space right in position and only five minutes late; and the berserker had been forced to turn all its energies to meet the immediate all-out attack of Gizmo and Foxglove.

Del saw his computers, recovering from the effect of the beam, lock his aiming screen onto the berserker's scarred and bulging midsection, as he shot his right arm forward, scattering pieces from the game board.

"Checkmate!" he roared out hoarsely, and brought his fist down on the big red button.

"I'm glad it didn't want to play chess," Del said later, talking to the Commander in Foxglove's cabin. "I could never have rigged that up."

The ports were cleared now, and the men could look out at the cloud of expanding gas, still faintly luminous, that had been a berserker; metal fire-purged of the legacy of ancient evil.

But the Commander was watching Del. "You got Newt to play by following diagrams, I see that. But how could he *learn* the game?"

Del grinned. "He couldn't, but his toys could. Now wait before you slug me." He called the *aiyan* to him and took a small box from the animal's hand. The box rattled faintly as he held it up. On the cover was pasted a diagram of one possible position in the simplified checker game, with a different-colored arrow indicating each possible move of Del's pieces.

"It took a couple of hundred of these boxes," said Del. "This one was in the group that Newt examined for the fourth move. When he found a box with a diagram matching the position on the board, he picked the box up, pulled out one of these beads from inside, without looking—that was the hardest part to teach him in a hurry, by the way," said Del, demonstrating. "Ah, this one's blue. That means, make the move indicated on the cover by a blue arrow. Now the orange arrow leads to a poor position, see?" Del shook all the beads out of the box into his hand. "No orange beads left; there were six of each color when we started. But every time Newton drew a bead, he had orders to leave it out of the box until the game was over. Then, if the scoreboard indicated a loss for our side, he went back and threw away all the beads he had used. All the bad moves were gradually eliminated. In a few hours, Newt and his boxes learned to play the game perfectly."

"Well," said the Commander. He thought for a moment, then reached down to scratch Newton behind the ears. "I never would have come up with that idea."

"I should have thought of it sooner. The basic idea's a couple of centuries old. And computers are supposed to be my business."

"This could be a big thing," said the Commander. "I mean your basic idea might be useful to any task force that has to face a berserker's mind beam."

"Yeah." Del grew reflective. "Also . . ."

"What?"

"I was thinking of a guy I met once. Named Blankenship. I wonder if I *could* rig something up. . . ."

NOT IN THE LITERATURE

BY CHRISTOPHER ANVIL
(HARRY C. CROSBY; DATE UNKNOWN)

ANALOG SCIENCE FICTION
MARCH

This is one of only two stories from Analog *in this year's retrospective of the best of 1963 (the other is the story by Cliff Simak). By 1963* Astounding/Analog *had big competition from not only* Galaxy *and* The Magazine of Fantasy and Science Fiction, *but also from* IF *and several of the "men's magazines," especially* Playboy. *Some of these paid better, but others were simply open to a wider variety of fiction than John W. Campbell was prepared to buy.* ANALOG *was still a good magazine, but it no longer got first look at everything that was written in sf.*

"Christopher Anvil" was one of Campbell's favorites, and with good reason. He wrote excellent puzzle stories, often with neat societal twists that came from some careful thinking about the impact of science on society—and isn't that what science fiction is supposed to be all about?

Alarik Kade had not spent fifty-eight years of his life on The Project without acquiring an instinct for a day that is really going to go sour.

Signs and portents a tyro would scarcely connect up often gave him the first powerful indications. Things like the hungry redjacket drill that droned down the ventilation pipe around 0266 the night before, popped through a rusty spot in the screen, then whined around the room, banging into concrete floor, ceiling, and walls at random till it picked up the heat radiation from Alarik, huddled under a light comforter with the pillow over his head.

The drill hit the comforter, and Alarik sprang out of bed in a rush. The ring of night-glow dots around the lamp base guided him quickly to the lamp, but where was the striker? As Alarik groped around the tabletop, he could hear behind him the *zzt-zzt* and half-hysterical whine as the drill got into the warm covers and stabbed around in all directions for some place to draw blood.

Cursing under his breath, Alarik felt the cold curving surface of a pewter water pitcher, the smooth back of a closed razor, a slim volume containing logarithms to the base eight, a handkerchief, a thick book of well-tested pragmatic formulas and their constants, an ashtray with gold-plated model of an early turbine plane, a glossy brochure telling why he should buy Koggik Steel, a progress report he should have read last night and hadn't, a .50 Special Service Revolver with all four barrels full of rust, a Lawyer Skeel mystery with three shapely girls on the cover, which he shouldn't have read last night but did— but no striker.

The whine of the drill was growing increasingly petulant. At any moment the thing might detect Alarik with its heat-sensitive nose and come for him. What would happen then, he thought, would be that in trying to hit the drill, he would knock the pitcher over and soak the book and papers on the table. With a sense of grim satisfaction in his foresight, Alarik set the pitcher on the floor, close to one of the table's massive cross-braced legs, and then felt of the tabletop again.

A little beyond where the pitcher had been, his three outstretched fingers felt the flaring squeeze-grip of the striker.

Just then, the whine grew suddenly louder. Alarik ducked, banged his head, and the striker clattered to the floor. The drill smacked into the wall behind him. Alarik groped for the striker. The drill took off in a new line and hit him squarely in the back.

The room seemed to take a somersault.

Alarik came to with his face in the concrete and the last dregs of the drill's knock-out poison fogging his mind. His head ached, he could hear a noise in his ears like the roar of a waterfall, and there was a throbbing bump on his back about half the size of his fist.

Dizzily he pulled himself to his feet.

The way things had happened so far assured him he was in for a rough day. Whether it would be a real record-breaker, he told himself, remained to be seen.

He took a step forward, and put his right foot squarely into the water pitcher. His foot slid in smoothly and tightly, and in clutching for support he knocked the razor off onto the floor. As he gripped the edge of the table, a muffled banging whine told him a fresh and hungry drill was blundering down the vent pipe.

Keeping a tight grip on his emotions, Alarik lowered himself to the floor and felt for the striker. His hand closed instead around the open blade of the razor. He gingerly shut the razor, slid it out of the way under the table, and heard it hit something with a metallic *clink*.

Alarik groped under the table, found the striker, stood up with his weight resting on his left foot, squeezed the striker once to see the cluttered tabletop by the light of the striker's sparks, managed to get the glass shade off the lamp without breaking anything, turned the knob of the rack-and-pinion mechanism to get the fragile mantle up out of the way, opened the gascock, and squeezed the handle of the striker. The flints scraped across the ridged steel, the gas lit with a *pop*, and Alarik triumphantly put on the chimney and lowered the mantle. The mantle lit up in a dazzling glare that showed a second redjacket drill, as big as Alarik's thumb, pushing in through the ventilator screen.

Alarik sprang forward to kill it, slipped, and landed on the floor. The drill streaked around overhead, Alarik's right arm and leg jerked up in a self-protective reflex, the water pitcher stuck to his right foot emptied itself in his face, and just then the drill detected the promising heat of the lamp. The drill whizzed around in tight circles, shot down the chimney, and whipped the mantle to bits. The room fell dark, and the gas jet settled down to incinerating the drill. A column of greasy smoke rose from the lamp chimney, and a powerful choking odor filled the room.

All this left Alarik Kade, Chairman-Director of the

Special Project, half-choked and with one foot in a pitcher, picking the smoldering remains of one drill out of the lamp while still dizzy from the bite of another, and with the muffled hopeful buzz of yet a third standing the hair on end all over his body.

That was how the day started.

And experience told Alarik that with a start like that, it was bound to be a day he would never forget—if he lived through it.

The sunlight, when Alarik came up into it, after finishing out the miserable night, lit up a day that, on its surface, at least, looked good.

For one thing, there was not a cloud in the sky. That meant reasonably good ground observation. He glanced up, and saw, far overhead, the glint of the shiny aluminum gondola of *Sunbird*. The name made him uneasy, reminding him of the hydrogen that had been substituted for helium in the hope of getting a little more precious lift for high-altitude observation. A brief dazzling flash told him that *Sunbird's* signal mirrors were working properly, and that in turn meant that the aggravating difficulties with the seals of the remote arm were taken care of, at least for the present.

Off over the flat bright sand to his right, at the end of the long runway, the big turbine plane was being slowly wheeled around. Judging from the slowness with which it was turned, it already had its load of fuel and water, and being perfectly reliable, no one was worried about it. Slung under its midsection like a babe clinging to its mother was one of his two big headaches.

To his left, like an upright giant dagger with nearly conical blade and an almost cylindrical haft, stood The Beast. This was his other, and much larger, headache. Contradictory emotions of love and hate welled up in Alarik as he looked at it. No one could work on The Project for all this time without feeling a little of both these emotions.

As Alarik gazed at the shiny form, a hurrying figure coming toward him from the base of The Beast drew his attention.

Alarik nodded in foreboding. Now it would start. He

had been allowed this moment of beautiful tranquillity in order to give a contrasting background against which the day's misfortunes would stand out to better effect. As a check, he glanced around toward the turbine plane. Sure enough, here came a second hurrying figure. To further test the auguries, he glanced up. A tiny cloud was materializing just about on a line between Observation 10 and the projected path of The Beast as it arced out over the ocean. That would foul up the whole launch, unless the cloud moved on.

But the cloud showed no sign of moving on. It seemed to be shredding away on one end, and forming again on the other end, and at the same time gliding steadily forward, so that the net result, fantastic as it might seem, was just the same as if it didn't move at all. But it was getting bigger, he was sure of that. Alarik squinted at the cloud, then shook his head. Even in this modern day, the only truly intelligent life form in the universe had no more control over the weather—or real basic understanding of it—than on that distant day when a remote ancestor peered out the burrow mouth and some spark of intelligence suggested that smoldering stubble from the grass could be put to use.

What had it been, thought Alarik, the fear of some digging enemy, or—

The chain of philosophical speculation was snapped as two hurrying pairs of feet arrived from opposite directions.

"Sir, the triggering clock is seventeen sixty-fourths off, halfway through the cycle, and the An. Comp. boys say she'll burn up on re-entry. We've tried resetting, but that throws the clock off on both ends, and Comp. tells us then she won't go into orbit. We've got a new clock checked out, but all the control wires have to be reset, and that's going to take the rest of the morning. If we lift off this afternoon, she'll land in the pick-up area at night, unless we reset the clock. But if we reset that clock, we won't be able to lift off till tonight."

"What about Ganner's magnesium flare?"

"Sir, we tried it out three times last week and it worked fine. We installed it last night and ran a test check on a Pup rocket. Nothing happened."

Alarik gripped his chin. "It came down with no signal?"

"Oh, the siren was on. And this morning the ocean was red for a hundred spans in all directions from where she hit. The underwater sound ship picked up a good solid *ping* from the noisemaker. But all that stuff is too slow and uncertain. When the boys got there, she was sunk."

"Scrub the flight. We'll try again tomorrow."

"Sir, Weather says—"

Alarik glanced at the cloud. There was now a smaller cloud trailing it, and the first cloud looked bigger. He looked away angrily.

"When did Weather ever know what it was talking about? If we don't get clear weather for a month, that's just so much more time to perfect our equipment. And get me the name of the contractor who sold us that clock."

"Yes, sir." He turned and sprinted back toward the gleaming shaft of The Beast.

Alarik considered that he had got off easy. What if the clock had gone sour after she took off? The odds were that with his luck the An. Comp. boys would be wrong and instead of burning up on re-entry, she would make a freak re-entry, and come down through the roof of a metropolitan temple with the chief priest in charge and the benches crammed with notables.

Someone cleared his throat, and Alarik realized he wasn't safe in the burrow yet. He looked up and waited.

"Sir, the Babe's got a malfunction."

"What is it this time?"

"The hydraulic columns that control the impact-fuse-igniters. There's an overflow for excess temperature. Well, somehow air worked back into the lines, and now they're spongy. As sure as anything, we're going to get up there, let her loose, and dig ourselves a crater."

Alarik could hear more feet approaching, this time from behind.

"How long," he said, "to bleed the lines?"

"Considering how cramped it is in there, it's an all day job. What we need is some simpler way to ignite the tubes."

"I know. We've got research teams working on it. But for now, we'll just have to put up with more delay."

"Yes, sir. We should be able to get off tomorrow for sure."

Alarik nodded, and turned to find his assistant, Kubic, holding a small earnest-looking man by the arm.

"Sir," said Kubic, "this fellow claims to have some reliable method of setting off fuses with constant-length wires."

Alarik shrugged. "It's been tried. I doubt that if our teams of trained chemists couldn't find the ideal solution, a lone researcher could."

Kubic nodded. "Yes, sir, I know. But we've had so much trouble—"

"No doubt about that," said Alarik with feeling. He glanced at the newcomer.

Kubic glanced at him, too, then cleared his throat. "Any hole in a hurry," he said.

The fellow certainly looked unprepossessing. But then, you could never tell with a chemist. Some of the best dispensed with appearance and pretense entirely. You just couldn't tell.

"All right," said Alarik. "Go ahead. What's your solution? Remember, these wires curl back through both hot and cold regions alike. The fuses don't ignite easily. It takes a sharp crack to ignite them. They aren't supposed to ignite one at a time, but a bunch together. And we don't want any fishnet of wires in there. The thing has to be reasonably simple. To keep your tension constant is no easy problem."

"I know." The newcomer beamed and nodded.

"We don't want any maze of springs and pulleys. The present system is bad enough, what with the need for special heat-resistant plastics, double-lines, heat-stable liquids, and so on. A terrific amount of the highest type of chemistry has gone into it."

"I realize that," said the newcomer. "I don't claim to be a true chemist. I just like to follow my interest. I've been sort of an amateur chemist since childhood, and . . . well, I got to playing around with strips of zinc and copper one day, and put them into some dilute sulfuric acid, and for some reason, I laid another strip of copper across the tops of the strips standing in the acid."

Alarik smiled. "And you got bubbles on the copper strip. It's a standard experiment."

"Yes, but I wondered about it. *Why* did I get bubbles?"

"It's a well known chemical fact. Immerse copper and zinc in acid, let there be contact, and bubbles form on the copper. The bubbles are hydrogen gas." Alarik smiled tolerantly. "Go ahead. What next?"

"I wondered, why must there be *contact*?"

Alarik blinked. "What's that?"

"Bubbles formed *when I joined zinc and copper strips*. Why did these strips *have to be joined*?"

Kubic glanced at Alarik's frown, and said hastily, "The Director's time is limited. Now, if you'll come to the practical aspect of your idea—"

"Wait," said Alarik. "He's got a point. Why *does* there have to be contact? I performed that experiment, too, but that question never occurred to me." He looked at the man with new respect. "I would say that you must be a natural-born chemist. You are, I suppose, associated with the university nearby, at Kerik Haven?"

"No, no." A stricken look crossed the visitor's face. "Please, I am nobody. All that matters is this discovery, which I happened across purely by accident."

Kubic cleared his throat, and said uncomfortably, "The fellow is a janitor at the University."

"Well, in that position, he could, I suppose, observe, experiment, learn—"

"In the Dance Workshop," said Kubic.

Alarik frowned.

Their guest hung his head. "I was thrown out of the Chemistry Program as a student. I hung on, got a job as a janitor, and they threw me out of that job, too. But I've got a friend in the stock room. He helps me get what I need."

Alarik considered the possibility that the man was a suppressed genius. It had happened often enough in the past, heaven knew. But in this enlightened age, such things were said to be impossible. Chemical talent was searched for eagerly, coaxed along with scholarships, rewarded lavishly with high pay.

Their visitor seemed to sense Alarik's line of thought. "Please," he said, "don't think that I am trying to present myself as a chemist of any kind. I think . . . I think I have some skill, some insight, but it is of a different type. At school, my teachers told me that I asked the wrong questions. I disagreed. I was more combative then." For a moment, he lifted his head. His eyes flashed. Then he shrugged, and looked down at the dirt. "It's all gone now." There was a bitterness in his voice. Then he smiled suddenly. "But I *can* solve your igniter problem for you."

"How does this wire of yours work?" said Alarik.

"Well, to explain it completely, I would have to describe to you a great deal of work I did with two strips of metal." A wary look crossed his face. "But I've found that it's better not to go into that."

Kubic said, "Just tell us the practical details."

"Well, essentially, it is this. You run a wire from the pilot's compartment back to the fuse. When the pilot wishes that particular fuse to ignite, he presses a button."

Alarik frowned. "This is a very stiff wire."

"No, not especially."

"Then it is a reasonably stiff wire enclosed within a casing?"

"No. Oh, well, yes. There is a fibrous sheath over the wire."

"How will that stiffen it?"

"It doesn't need to be stiff," the newcomer answered.

"Then what moves it?"

"It doesn't move."

Alarik scowled at him. Kubic frowned.

"Then," said Alarik, "why does the pilot punch the button?"

"Because—He does it to—Well, that's what I'm coming to."

"Wait a minute," said Alarik. "A push is communicated along this wire, is that right?"

"No, sir."

Alarik stared at him. Suddenly he snapped his fingers.

"It *twists*, is that it? You've found a way to convert a push into a twist, and then—"

"No. No, it *doesn't* twist. It doesn't move at all."

"Doesn't move at all?"

"That's the point. It *heats*."

Kubic groaned.

Alarik shook his head. "No good. No, it won't work."

"But why not? Heat will trigger off the fuse."

Alarik felt faintly sick. He glanced at Kubic, and jerked his head toward the gate. That, he thought, was the trouble with these unsung geniuses. They wanted to sing for an audience and they didn't even know the scale.

Kubic put his hand firmly on the man's arm.

"Ah, I see," said the fellow suddenly. "Not the *whole* wire. Just the *end*."

Alarik forced a smile. "It happens to be the *other* end we're interested in."

Kubic turned him around, and led him off forcibly.

Alarik could hear them in the distance. Kubic's voice was a series of low monosyllables. The other man's voice rose in loud complaint, and as the wind happened to be from that direction, he could hear him almost to the inner gate.

"But," the man cried, "it's the *fuse* end I'm talking about!"

Kubic muttered something or other.

"No, no, you don't understand! Friction has nothing to do with it! It's *not* heat conduction along the wire! That's not *it*!"

Kubic paused to take a better grip on his guest's sleeve.

Alarik frowned. If it wasn't friction, what *was* it? Here is a man who pushes a button attached to a wire. The wire is not stiff, but is enclosed in some kind of sleeve. The wire gets hot. Then it would burn the sleeve, wouldn't it? But wait a minute. Only the *end* gets hot. The rest of the wire doesn't move at all, doesn't twist— *How* does the end get hot?

"No! No! No! No!" came the voice, climbing higher. "It isn't that at all! I can show you!"

Alarik came to a sudden decision. He was hung around the neck with chemists of the most exalted rank. They all thought alike. They were the elite of the elite, but maybe he needed a fresh mind. What if the man's approach *wasn't* truly chemical? Just let it work, that's all. He cupped his hands to his mouth to shout to Kubic.

Abruptly the visitor ripped free of Kubic's grip. His voice carried in an almost hysterical shout:

"You're hidebound! You're blind as bats, the lot of you! I've begged for just a chance to *prove* there's such a thing as current, and there *is*! I can prove it! It's staring you in the face! But you won't listen! You fools! A *current* flows through that wire, and when it goes through the constricted end, *then* the end heats! No, it's not chemical! You can't argue against it because it's not chemical! It's potentially just as great as anything that *is* chemical! I try to tell you, *it's a whole new field of knowledge*!"

Alarik lowered his hands. He shook his head and shrugged. He glanced around at the towering evidences of chemistry in a chemical world. Chemistry was the study of matter, and matter was everywhere. Everything that was, was made of matter. There was nothing else, *could* be nothing else but matter. Oh, there was light, and sound, and lightning, but the best minds held that these were just disturbances in matter, or in finer forms of matter. There was the field of atmospheric chemistry, for instance, and the field of aetheric chemistry, but there was some doubt as to whether these fringe studies, particularly the latter, were really chemical at all.

How, all considered, could any other field of knowledge possibly *hope* ever to compare with the study of matter? Builders, mechanicians, physicians—all had important work to do, but they admitted they were only quasi-chemists, not truly chemical. Only the mathematicians held aloof, proclaiming a loftier discipline. But in actual practice, they were tied in knots. They couldn't accomplish a thing without a thousand trials, errors, and reservations. Matter just was not amenable to their theories, except in rare special cases.

He shrugged.

A last shout carried back on the wind:

"I'll show you! It's bound to come out some day. Current *does* flow!"

*   *   *

That decided it. What could flow through a solid metal wire? There was no space for anything to flow on the inside, and on the outside anything would fall off—or else ooze through the spaces in the fibrous sheath and drip out. Solid matter was largely incompressible. Therefore nothing could flow through it, because to flow, there must be space. And you couldn't have a current without something that flowed. And nothing could flow where there was no space.

Kubic came back, shaking his head.

"I'm sorry, sir. I didn't realize. The fellow's a fanatic."

"Well, it was worth a try. I thought for a minute there he had something."

"He acted plausible enough. But he blew up on the way out. Talked all kinds of gibberish."

"Yes, he didn't make much—Wait a minute!"

"Sir?"

"Listen. Suppose we use a stiff wire, inside a conduit of close spiral spring, and rotate the inner wire very fast, with pressure, against a narrow abrasive head applied to the fuse case?"

"Hm-m-m, you mean the friction will generate heat?"

"Sure it will. Now, of course, it isn't a very chemical procedure. It's just a piece of mechanism. But that's how we've progressed in The Project over the past hundred years or so. One little brick on top of another. In time, we'll get there."

"Yes, sir. But I don't know. Good mechanicians are as rare as shock-proof lamp mantles. You remember, twenty years ago, when we were using spring triggers on the fuses. That seemed pretty good till they complexified it up to the point where we couldn't recognize it any more. Then they got that hydraulic idea, and—Well, I don't know. One thing just seems to lead to another. It seems as if this is all taking too long. We go around in circles. Somehow, it's like trying to pull nails with a wrench. Where the devil do you take a hold? There's a tool missing from the kit somewhere."

"It's been a bad day," said Alarik, scowling. "Of course, over the long view, there *is* progress. And, occasionally, there's a real breakthrough. That new fuel, for instance. And, best of all, the superrefractive coating. Then, it was no small improvement when we hit on dissipation-cooling, and all the refinements of that. But I know, somehow these big advances don't make the dent they ought to.''

Kubic glanced around at various massive structures that stretched off to the north and west as far as the eye could see. "Well," he said, "it keeps unemployment down, I'll say that for it. But something tells me a lot of our effort here is at a tangent to the problem."

Alarik nodded. "I'll tell you what," he said. "We'll press this rotary-fire principle, and see what comes of it. We can send a routine payment check to this fellow you brought in. After all, he suggested the idea, whether he meant to or not. He, at least, *claims* to develop some new method. He may be a fanatic, but then, you look at some of the early chemists—"

Kubic nodded approval. "Good idea, sir. To tell the truth, *I* don't see why there has to be contact to evolve those bubbles, either."

"Take care of it now," said Alarik. "You never know when something will happen and we'll forget all about it."

Kubic's eyes widened. "Sir, look there—"

Alarik looked up.

"The devil with it. Get going, I'll take care of this."

Sprinting across the field from the bulk of The Beast came what looked like the whole maintenance crew. Alarik gave Kubic a shove, to start him in the right direction, and Kubic ran off to disappear behind a protecting buttress that led back to the Administration Building.

Alarik studied The Beast. Was that a wisp of smoke he saw, puffing out from under the drive ring?

Mechanicians, builders, brace men, clockers, supervisors, chemical technicians—the whole crew pounded across the field as if their lives were at stake.

That *was* smoke under the drive ring.

As he watched, a white plume billowed out, traveled slowly around the circumference, and wreathed the daggerlike base in smoke. Another plume joined the first, then another and another. The curving near-cylindrical top rode above the billowing clouds with no visible support.

Alarik held his arm out, stabbed his forefinger at the earth, and shouted, "*Ground*!"

All the workmen but the crew chief disappeared in a series of flying dives.

The crew chief, breathing hard, tears streaming out the corners of his eyes, ran to Alarik and saluted.

"Sir, I'll stay up and take my medicine. It was my fault. I—"

Thunder traveled across the field.

Alarik knocked the crew chief down the nearest hole and dove after him.

Pink brilliance reflected dimly on the sides of the tunnel.

"What happened?" said Alarik.

"The inside clocker—He's new. I shouldn't have let him down alone. We can't use any kind of lamps in there. He had to work with just a glow plate."

"What happened?"

The earth began to shake.

"Go on," shouted Alarik, "*what happened*?"

"He bumped the master pull wire, where it comes in out of the sheath from Control. The safety was pushed down, and by mistake, the tip must have been over the wire; the pin popped up out of the hole, the safety let go, the arming spring knocked the lever around, the safety came down and hit the taut wire, and that sprang the lever. We could hear it—Wham! Wham! Wham! Then she started."

Alarik swore.

The crew chief shouted above the roar. "He's still in there. *He's in there now!* The weight-savers dropped the ladders and weather covers loose. He couldn't get out. We just got down ourselves before the tower got jerked away."

The tunnel lit up in a pink glow, and they eased back around a corner.

"It's too complicated," the crew chief shouted. Then it was too loud to hear, and the uproar was too much to talk in anyway.

Alarik lay in the hole, his body one living ache. Gradually, awareness returned.

Well, he thought dully, there she goes. The faulty clock is still in her. The gliders and the *Sunbird* may get some data, but it's meaningless with that nonstandard clock in there. At intervals, The Beast will shoot out luminous vapor clouds, and that may help in the tracking—maybe. But where would she come down?

There must be some better way than this, he thought. It can't be this complicated. This was like trying to tie up a handful of marbles with a ball of string. When it got this complicated, it meant you were trying to do the job with tools or materials that weren't fitted to the work.

The roar was just about all gone now.

There was a thud, and Kubic came around the corner of the tunnel in a crouch.

"Sir, are you all right?"

"In a sense," growled Alarik. "How was it?"

"Beautiful. It looked beautiful. Actually, it was terrible, but it looked fine."

"Well, that's something."

"I got that pay voucher made out."

Alarik froze. Suddenly ignoring the staring crew chief, he jumped up and grabbed Kubic by the arm.

"The devil with all that," he said. "I'm sick of this stuff!"

"Sir? You want me to cancel it?"

"No, no! Go on out there! Go get him! Grab him! Bring him back!"

"Yes, sir!" said Kubic with alacrity.

He went up out of the hole in a rush.

Alarik climbed up into the open air. Far overhead was a small bright dot, gradually growing fainter.

As it disappeared, he could hear a determined voice carrying across the field, speaking of "currents" as something real, actual, and usable.

Alarik looked around. For a moment, he felt guilty. What he had in mind was unchemical. Therefore it was chicanery, fraud, quackery, unprofessional—

"The devil with it," growled Alarik. Years of accumulated frustration weighed on him like lead.

His hands opened and shut like those of a man badly in need of a hammer and he eyed the sky in supplication.

"Just give me," he said earnestly, "a tool to fit the job."

THE TOTALLY RICH

BY JOHN BRUNNER (1934-   )

WORLDS OF TOMORROW
JUNE

John Brunner is a resident of the United Kingdom whose huge, complex novels helped to set the tone for the "new" science fiction of the 1960s and early 1970s. His great dystopian works including Stand on Zanzibar *(1969),* The Sheep Look Up *(1972), and* The Shockwave Rider *(1975), are "awful warning" stories about overpopulation and pollution that derive from a deeply-felt concern for humanity and the preservation of our species. Among his scores of novels a personal favorite is* The Squares of the City *(1965) which is based on a famous chess match.*

"The Totally Rich" is about what is important in life.

They are the totally rich. You've never heard of them because they are the only people in the world rich enough to buy what they want: a completely private life. The lightning can strike into your life and mine:—you win a big prize or find yourself neighbor to an ax-murderer or buy a parrot suffering from psittacosis—and you are in the searchlight, blinking shyly and wishing to God you were dead.

They won their prizes by being born. They do not have neighbors, and if they require a murder they do not use so clumsy a means as an ax. They do not keep parrots. And if by some other million-to-one chance the searchlight does tend towards them, they buy it and instruct the man behind it to switch it off.

How many of them there are I don't know. I have

tried to estimate the total by adding together the gross national product of every country on earth and dividing by the amount necessary to buy a government of a major industrial power. It goes without saying that you cannot maintain privacy unless you can buy any two governments.

I think there may be one hundred of these people. I have met one, and very nearly another.

By and large they are night people. The purchase of light from darkness was the first economic advance. But you will not find them by going and looking at two o'clock in the morning, any more than at two in the afternoon. Not at the approved clubs; not at the Polo Grounds; not in the Royal Enclosure at Ascot nor on the White House lawn.

They are not on maps. Do you understand that? Literally, where they choose to live becomes a blank space in the atlases. They are not in census lists, *Who's Who*, or Burke's *Peerage*. They do not figure in tax collectors' files, and the post office has no record of their addresses. Think of all the places where your name appears—the yellowing school registers, the hospital case records, the duplicate receipt form in the store, the signature on letters. In *no single* such place is there one of their names.

How it is done . . . no, I don't know. I can only hazard a guess that to almost all human beings the promise of having more than everything they have ever conceived as desirable acts like a traumatic shock. It is instantaneous brainwashing; in the moment the promise is believed, the pattern of obedience is imprinted, as the psychologists say. But they take no chances. They are not absolute rulers—indeed, they are not rulers of anything except what directly belongs to them—but they have much in common with that caliph of Baghdad to whom a sculptor came, commissioned to make a fountain. This fountain was the most beautiful in the world, and the caliph approved it. Then he demanded of the sculptor whether anyone else could have made so lovely a fountain, and the sculptor proudly said no one but he in the whole world could have achieved it.

Pay him what was promised, said the caliph. And also—put out his eyes.

                        *   *   *

I wanted champagne that evening, dancing girls, bright
lights, music. All I had was a can of beer, but at least it
was cold. I went to fetch it, and when I came back stood
in the kitchen doorway looking at my . . . living room,
workshop, lab, whatever. It was a bit of all these.

All right, I didn't believe it. It was August 23rd, and
I had been here one year and one month, and the job
was done. I didn't believe it, and I wouldn't be able to
until I'd told people—called in my friends and handed
the beer around and made them drink a toast.

I raised the can. I said, "To the end of the job!" I
drank. That hadn't turned the trick. I said, "To the Cooper Effect!" That was a little more like it, but it still
wasn't quite complete.

So I frowned for a moment, thought I'd got it, and
said triumphantly, "To Santadora—the most wonderful
place on earth, without which such concentration would
never have been possible: may God bless her and all who
sail from her."

I was drinking this third toast with a sense of satisfaction when Naomi spoke from the shadows of the open
porch.

"Drink to me, Derek," she said. "You're coming
closer, but you aren't quite there."

I slammed the beer can down on a handy table, strode
across the room, and gave her a hug. She didn't respond;
she was like a beautiful doll displaying Paris creations in
a store window. I had never seen her wearing anything
but black, and tonight it was a black blouse of hand-spun
raw silk and tight black pants tapering down to black
espadrilles. Her hair, corn-pale, her eyes, sapphire-blue,
her skin, luminous under a glowing tan, had always been
so perfect they seemed unreal. I had never touched her
before. Sometimes, lying awake at night, I had wondered
why; she had no man. I had rationalized to myself that
I prized this haven of peace, and the concentration I
found possible here, too much to want to involve myself
with a woman who never demanded anything but who—
one knew it—would take nothing less than everything.

"It's done," I said, whirling and throwing out my arm.
"The millennium has arrived! Success at last!" I ran to

the haywire machine which I had never thought to see in real existence. "This calls for a celebration—I'm going out to collect everyone I can find and. . . ."

I heard my voice trail away. She had walked a pace forward and lifted a hand that had been hanging by her side, weighed down by something. Now it caught the light. A bottle of champagne.

"How—?" I said. And thought of something else, too. I had never been alone with Naomi before, in the thirteen months since coming to Santadora.

"Sit down, Derek," she said. She put the champagne bottle on the same table as the beer can. "It's no good going out to collect anyone. There isn't anybody here except you and me."

I didn't say anything.

She cocked a quizzical eyebrow. "You don't believe me? You will."

Turning, she went to the kitchen. I waited for her to return with a pair of the glasses I kept for company; I was leaning forward with my hands on the back of a chair, and it suddenly seemed to me that I had subconsciously intended to put the chair between myself and this improbable stranger.

Dexterously she untwisted the wire of the champagne bottle, caught the froth which followed the cork in the first glass, poured the second and held it out to me. I came—moving like a stupid, stolid animal—to take hold of it.

"Sit down," she said again.

"But—where is everybody else? Where's Tim? Where are Conrad and Ella? Where—?"

"They've gone," she said. She came, carrying her glass, to sit facing me in the only other chair not cluttered with broken bits of my equipment. "They went about an hour ago."

"But—Pedro! And—!"

"They put out to sea. They are going somewhere else." She made a casual gesture. "I don't know where, but they are provided for."

Raising her champagne, she added, "To you, Derek—and my compliments. I was never sure that you would do it, but it had to be tried."

I ran to the window which overlooked the sea, threw it open, and stared out into the gathering dark. I could see four or five fishing boats, their riding lights like shifting stars, moving out of the harbor. On the quay was a collection of abandoned furniture and some fishermen's gear. It *did* look as though they were making a permanent departure.

"Derek, *sit down*," Naomi said for the third time. "We're wasting time, and besides, your wine is getting flat."

"But how can they bring themselves to—?"

"Abandon their ancestral homes, dig up their roots, leave for fresh woods and pastures new?" Her tone was light and mocking. "They are doing nothing of the kind. They have no special attachment to Santadora. Santadora does not exist. Santadora was built eighteen months ago, and will be torn down next month."

I said after an eternal silence, "Naomi, are you—are you feeling quite well?"

"I feel wonderful." She smiled, and the light glistened on her white teeth. "Moreover, the fishermen were not fishermen and Father Francisco is not a priest and Conrad and Ella are not artists except in a very small way of business, as a hobby. Also my name is not Naomi, but since you're used to it—and so am I—it'll serve."

Now, I had to drink the champagne. It was superb. It was the most perfect wine I had ever tasted. I was sorry not to be in the mood to appreciate the fact.

"Are you making out that this entire village is a sham?" I demanded. "A sort of colossal—what—movie set?"

"In a way. A stage setting would be a more accurate term. Go out on the porch and reach up to the fretted decoration overhanging the step. Pull it hard. It will come away. Look at what you find on the exposed surface. Do the same to any other house in the village which has a similar porch—there are five of them. Then come back and we can talk seriously."

She crossed her exquisite legs and sipped her champagne. She knew beyond doubt that I was going to do precisely as she said.

Determinedly, though more to prevent myself feeling

foolish than for any better reason, I went on to the porch. I put on the light—a swinging yellow bulb, on a flex tacked amateurishly into place—and looked up at the fretted decoration on the edge of the overhang. The summer insects came buzzing in towards the attractive lamp.

I tugged at the piece of wood, and it came away. Holding it to the light, I read on the exposed surface, stamped in pale blue ink: *"Número 14,006—José Barcos, Barcelona."*

I had no ready-made reaction. Accordingly, holding the piece of wood like a talisman in front of me, I went back indoors and stood over Naomi in her chair. I was preparing to phrase some angry comment, but I never knew what it was to be, for at that moment my eye was caught by the label on the bottle. It was not champagne. The name of the firm was unknown to me.

"It is the best sparkling wine in the world," Naomi said. She had followed my gaze. "There is enough for about—oh—one dozen bottles a year."

My palate told me there was some truth at least in what she said. I made my way dizzily to my chair and sank into it at last. "I don't pretend to understand this. I—I haven't spent the last year in a place that doesn't exist!"

"But you have." Quite cool, she cradled her glass between her beautiful slim hands and set her elbows on the sides of the dirty chair. "By the way, have you noticed that there are never any mosquitoes among the insects that come to your lights? It was barely likely that you would have caught malaria, but the chance had to be guarded against."

I started. More than once I'd jokingly commented to Tim Hannigan that one of Santadora's greatest advantages was its freedom from mosquitoes. . . .

"Good. The facts are beginning to make an impression on you. Cast your mind back now to the winter before last. Do you recall making the acquaintance of a man going under the name of Roger Gurney, whom you subsequently met one other time?"

I nodded. Of course I remembered Roger Gurney. Often, since coming to Santadora, I'd thought that that first meeting with him had been one of the two crucial events that changed my life.

"You gave Gurney a lift one rather unpleasant November night—his car had broken down and there was no hope of getting a necessary spare part before the morning, and he had to be in London for an urgent appointment at ten next day. You found him very congenial and charming. You put him up in your flat; you had dinner together and talked until 4 A.M. about what has now taken concrete form here in this room. You talked about the Cooper Effect."

I felt incredibly cold, as though a finger of that bleak November night had reached through the window and traced a cold smear down my spine. I said, "Then, that very night, I mentioned to him that I only saw one way of doing the necessary experiments. I said I'd have to find a village somewhere, without outside distractions, with no telephone or newspapers, without even a radio. A place where living was so cheap that I could devote myself for two or three years to my work and not have to worry about earning my living."

My God! I put my hand to my forehead. It was as if memory was re-emerging like invisible ink exposed to a fire.

"That's right," Naomi nodded with an air of satisfaction. "And the second and only other time you met this delightful Roger Gurney was the weekend you were celebrating your small win on the football pools. Two thousand one hundred and four pounds, seventeen shillings, and a penny. And he told you of a certain small Spanish village, named Santadora, where the conditions for your research were perfectly fulfilled. He said he had visited some friends here, named Conrad and Ella Williams. The possibility of turning your dreams into facts had barely occurred to you, but by the time you'd had a few drinks with Gurney, it seemed strange that you hadn't already laid your plans."

I slammed my glass down so hard it might have broken. I said harshly, "Who are you? What game are you playing with me?"

"No game, Derek." She was leaning forward now, her blue jewel-hard eyes fixed on my face. "A very serious business. And one in which you also have a stake. Can you honestly say that but for meeting Roger Gurney, but for winning this modest sum of money, you would be here—or anywhere—with the Cooper Effect translated into reality?"

I said after a long moment in which I reviewed one whole year of my life, "No. No, I must be honest. I can't."

"Then there's your answer to the question you put a few moments ago." She laid her glass on the table and took out a small cigarette case from the pocket of her tight pants. "I am the only person in the world who wanted to have and *use* the Cooper Effect. Nobody else was eager enough to bring it about—not even Derek Cooper. Take one of these cigarettes."

She held out the case; the mere opening of it had filled the air with a fragrance I found startling. There was no name on the cigarette I took, the only clue to its origin being a faint striping of the paper, but when I drew the first smoke I knew that this, like the wine, was the best in the world.

She watched my reaction with amusement. I relaxed fractionally—smiling made her seem familiar. How many times had I seen her smile like that, here, or much more often at Tim's or at Conrad's?

"I wanted the Cooper Effect," she repeated. "And now I've got it."

I said, "Just a moment! I—"

"Then I want to rent it." She shrugged as though the matter were basically a trifling one. "After I've rented it, it is and will be forever yours. You have conceded yourself that but for—certain key interventions, let's call them—but for *me*, it would be a mere theory. An intellectual toy. I will not, even so, ask you to consider that a fair rental for it. For the use of your machine for one very specific purpose, I will pay you so much that for the rest of your life you may have anything *at all* your fancy turns to. Here!"

She tossed something—I didn't know where she had been hiding it—and I caught it reflexively. It was a long narrow wallet of soft, supple leather, zipped round the edge.

"Open it."

I obeyed. Inside I discovered one—two—three credit cards made out in my name, and a check book with my name printed ready on the checks. On each of the cards there was something I had never seen before: a single word overprinted in red. The word was UNLIMITED.

I put them back in the wallet. It had occurred to me to doubt that what she said was true, but the doubt had faded at once. Yes, Santadora had been created in order to permit me to work under ideal conditions. Yes, she had done it. After what she had said about Roger Gurney, I didn't have room to disbelieve.

Consequently I could go to Madrid, walk into a salesroom, and come out driving a Rolls-Royce; in it, I could drive to a bank and write the sum of one million pesetas on the first of those cheques and receive it—if the bank had that much in cash.

Still looking at the wallet, zipping and unzipping it mechanically, I said, "All right. You're the person who wanted the Effect. Who are you?"

"The person who could get it." She gave a little dry laugh and shook her head. Her hair waved around her face like wings. "Don't trouble me with more inquiries, Derek. I won't answer them because the answers would mean nothing."

I was silent for a little while. Then, finally, because I had no other comment to make, I said, "At least you must say why you wanted what I could give you. After all, I'm still the only person in the world who understands it."

"Yes." She studied me. "Yes, that is true. Pour more wine for us; I think you like it."

While I was doing so, and while I was feeling my body grow calm after the shock and storm of the past ten minutes, she said, looking at the air, "You *are* unique, you know. A genius without equal in your single field. That's why you're here, why I went to a little trouble for you. I can get everything I want, but for certain things I'm inevitably dependent on the *one* person who can provide them."

Her eyes roved to my new, ramshackle—but functioning—machine.

"I wanted that machine to get me back a man," she said. "He has been dead for three years."

The world seemed to stop in its tracks. I had been blind ever since the vision of unlimited money dazzled me. I had accepted that because Naomi could get everything she knew what it was she was getting. And, of course, she didn't.

A little imaginary pageant played itself out in my mind, in which faceless dolls moved in a world of shifting, rosy clouds. A doll clothed in black, with long pale hair, said "He's dead. I want him back. Don't argue. Find me a way."

The other dolls bowed and went away. Eventually one doll came back and said. "There is a man called Derek Cooper who has some unorthodox ideas. Nobody else in all the world is thinking about this problem at all."

"See that he gets what he needs," said the doll with pale hair.

I put down the bottle of wine. I hesitated—yes, I still did, I was still dazzled. But then I took up the soft leather wallet and tossed it into Naomi's lap. I said, "You've cheated yourself."

"What?" She didn't believe it. The wallet which had fallen in her lap was an apparition; she did not move to pick it up, as though touching it would turn it from a bad dream to a harsh fact.

I said, very thoughtfully because I was working out in my mind how it must be, "You talked about wanting my machine for a particular job. I was too dazed to wonder what the job might be—there *are* jobs which can be done with it, so I let it slide by. You are very rich, Naomi. You have been so rich all your life that you don't know about the one other thing that stands between the formulation of a problem and its solution. That's *time*, Naomi!"

I tapped the top of the machine. I was still proud of it. I had every right to be.

"You are like—like an empress of ancient China. Maybe she existed, I don't know. Imagine that one day she said, 'It has been revealed to me that my ancestors dwell in the moon. I wish to go there and pay the respects of a dutiful daughter. Find me a way.' So they hunted through the length and breadth of the empire, and one day a courtier came in with a poor and ragged man, and said to the empress, 'This man has invented a rocket.'

" 'Good,' said the empress. 'Perfect it so that I may go to the moon.' "

I had intended to tell the fable in a bantering tone—to laugh at the end of it. But I turned to glance at Naomi, and my laughter died.

Her face was as pale and still as a marble statue's, her lips a little parted, her eyes wide. On one cheek, like a diamond, glittered a tear.

All my levity evaporated. I had the sudden horrible impression that I had kicked at what seemed a stone and shattered a priceless bowl.

"No, Derek," she said after a while. "You don't have to tell me about time." She stirred, half turned in her chair, and looked at the table beside her. "Is this glass mine?" she added in a lighter tone, putting out her slim and beautiful hand to point. She did not wipe the tear; it remained on her cheek for some time, until the hot dry air of the night kissed it away.

Taking the glass at my nod, she stood up and came across to look at my machine. She regarded it without comment, then said, "I hadn't meant to tell you what I wanted. Time drove me to it."

She drank deeply. "Now," she went on, "I want to know exactly what your pilot model *can* do."

I hesitated. So much of it was not yet in words; I had kept my word-thinking separate from my work-thinking all during the past year, and lately I had talked of nothing except commonplaces when I relaxed in the company of my friends. The closer I came to success, the more superstitious I had grown about mentioning the purpose of this project.

And—height of absurdity—now that I knew what she wanted, I was faintly ashamed that my triumph reduced on close examination to such a little thing.

Sensing my mood, she glanced at me and gave a faint smile. " 'Yes, Mr. Faraday'—or was it Humphry Davy?—'but what is it *good* for?' I'm sorry."

A newborn baby. Well enough. Somehow the phrase

hit me—reached me emotionally—and I was suddenly not ashamed at all of anything; I was as proud as any father and much more so.

I pushed aside a stack of rough schematics on the corner of the table nearest the machine and perched where it had been. I held my glass between my palms, and it was so quiet I fancied I could hear the bubbles bursting as they surfaced in the wine.

I said, "It wasn't putting money in my way, or anything like that, which I owe you a debt of gratitude for. It was sending that persuasive and charming Roger Gurney after me. I had never met anyone else who was prepared to take my ideas except as an amusing talking point. I'd kicked the concept around with some of the finest intellects I know—people I knew at university, for instance, who've left me a long way behind since then." I hadn't thought of this before. I hadn't thought of a lot of things, apparently.

"But he could talk them real. What I said to him was much the same as what I'd said to others before then. I'd talked about the—the space a living organism defines around itself, by behaving as it does. A mobile does it. That's why I have one over there." I pointed, raising my arm, and as though by command a breeze came through the open window and stirred hanging metal panels in the half-shadowed far corner of the room. They squeaked a little as they turned; I'd been too busy to drop oil on the bearings lately.

I was frowning, and the frown was knotting my forehead muscles, and it was going to make my head ache, but I couldn't prevent myself.

"There must be a total interrelationship between the organism and its environment, including and especially its fellow organisms. Self-recognition was one of the first things they stumbled across in building mechanical simulacra of living creatures. They didn't plan for it—they built mechanical tortoises with little lights on top and a simple light-seeking urge, and if you showed this beast to a mirror, it would seem to recognize itself. . . . This is the path, not the deliberate step-by-step piecing together of a man, but the attempt to define the same shape as that which man himself defines in reacting with other people.

"Plain enough, that. But are you to process a trillion bits of information, store them, label them in time, translate them back for reproduction as—well, as what? I can't think of anything. What you want is. . . ."

I shrugged, emptied my glass, and stood up. "You want the Cooper Effect," I finished. "Here—take this."

From the little rack on top of my machine I took a flat translucent disk about the size of a penny but thicker. To handle it I used a key which plugged into a hole in the center so accurately that it held the weight by simple friction. I held it out to Naomi.

My voice shook, because this was the first random test I had ever made.

"Take hold of this. Handle it—rub your fingers over it, squeeze it gently on the flat sides, close your hand on it."

She obeyed. While it was in her hand, she looked at me.

"What is it?"

"It's an artificial piezoelectric crystal. All right, that should be enough. Put it back on the key—I don't want to confuse the readings by touching it myself."

It wasn't easy to slip the disk back on the key, and she made two false attempts before catching my hand to steady it. I felt a vibration coming through her fingers, as though her whole body were singing like a musical instrument.

"There," she said neutrally.

I carried the disk back to the machine. Gingerly I transferred it from the key to the little post on the top of the reader. It slid down like a record dropping to a turntable. A moment or two during which I didn't breathe. Then there was the reaction.

I studied the readings on the dials carefully. Not perfect. I was a little disappointed—I'd hoped for a perfect run this first time. Nonetheless, it was extraordinarily close, considering she had handled the disk for a bare ten seconds.

I said, "The machine tells me that you are female, slim, fair-haired and probably blue-eyed, potentially artistic, unaccustomed to manual labor, IQ in the range 120-140, under intense emotional stress—"

Her voice cut across mine like the lash of a whip. "How? How do I know the machine tells you this, not your own eyes?"

I didn't look up. I said, "The machine is telling me what changes were brought about in that little crystal disk when you touched it. I'm reading it as a kind of graph if you like—looking across the pattern of the dials and interpreting them into words."

"Does it tell you anything else?"

"Yes—but it must be in error somewhere, I'm afraid. The calibration has been rather makeshift, and would have to be completed with a proper statistical sample of say a thousand people from all walks of life." I forced a laugh as I turned away from the machine. "You see, it says that you're forty-eight to fifty years old, and this is ridiculous on the face of it."

She sat very still. I had moved all the way to the table beside her, intending to refill my glass, before I realized how still. My hand on the bottle's neck, I stared at her.

"Is something wrong?"

She shook herself and came back to life instantly. She said lightly, "No. No, nothing at all. Derek, you are the most amazing man in the world. I shall be fifty years old next week."

"You're joking." I licked my lips. I'd have said . . . oh, thirty-five and childless and extremely careful of her looks. But not more. Not a day more.

A trace of bitterness crossed her face as she nodded.

"It's true. I wanted to be beautiful—I don't think I have to explain why. I wanted to go on being beautiful because it was the only gift I could give to someone who had, as I have, everything he could conceivably want. So I—I saw to it."

"What happened to him?"

"I would prefer you not to know." The answer was cool and final. She relaxed deliberately, stretching her legs out before her, and gave a lazy smile. Her foot touched something on the floor as she moved, and she glanced down.

"What—? Oh, that!" She reached for the soft leather

wallet, which had fallen from her lap when she stood up
after I had tossed it back at her. Holding it out, she said,
"Take it, Derek. I know you've already earned it. By
accident—by mistake—whatever you call it, you've
proved that you can do what I was hoping for."

I did take it. But I didn't pocket it at first; I kept it
in my hands, absently turning it over.

I said, "I'm not so sure, Naomi. Listen." I picked up
my newly filled glass and returned to the chair facing
her. "What I ultimately envisage is being able to deduce
the individual from the traces he makes. You know that;
that was the dream I told to Roger Gurney. But between
now and then, between the simple superficial analysis of
a specially prepared material and going over, piece by
piece, ten thousand objects affected not merely by the
individual in question but by many others, some of whom
probably cannot be found in order to identify and rule
out their extraneous influence—and *then* processing the
results to make a coherent whole—there may be years,
decades, of work and study, a thousand false trails, a
thousand preliminary experiments with animals. . . .
Whole new techniques will have to be invented in order
to employ the data produced! Assuming you have your—
your analogue of a man: what are you going to do with
it? Are you going to try and *make* a man, artificially,
that fits the specifications?"

"Yes."

The simple word left me literally gasping; it was like
a blow to the stomach, driving my breath away. She bent
her brilliant gaze on me and once more smiled faintly.

"Don't worry, Derek. That's not your job. Work has
been going on in many places for a long time—they tell
me—on that problem. What nobody except yourself was
doing was struggling with the problem of the total
person."

I couldn't reply. She filled her own glass again before
continuing, in a tenser voice.

"There's a question I've got to put to you, Derek. It's
so crucial I'm afraid to hear the answer. But I can't
endure to wait any longer, either. I want to know how
long you think it will be before I can have what I want.
Assume—remember that you've *got* to assume—the best

men in the world can be set to work on the subsidiary problems; they'll probably make their reputations, they'll certainly make their fortunes. I want to hear what you think."

I said thickly, "Well, I find that pretty difficult! I've already mentioned the problem of isolating the traces from—"

"This man lived a different kind of existence from you, Derek. If you'd stop and think for a second, you'd guess that. I can take you to a place that was uniquely *his*, where his personality formed and molded and affected every grain of dust. Not a city where a million people have walked, not a house where a dozen families have lived."

It had to be true, incredible though I would have thought it a scant hour ago. I nodded.

"That's good. Well, I shall also have to work out ways of handling unprepared materials—calibrate the properties of every single substance. And there's the risk that the passage of time will have overlaid the traces with molecular noise and random movement. Moreover, the testing itself, before the actual readings, might disturb the traces."

"You are to assume"—she forced patience on the repetition—"that the best men in the world are going to tackle the side issues."

"It isn't a side issue, Naomi." I wished I didn't have to be honest. She was hurt by my insistence, and I was beginning to think that, for all the things one might envy her, she had been hurt very badly already. "It's simply a fact one has to face."

She drank down her wine and replaced the glass on the table. Musingly she said, "I guess it would be true to say that the—the object which a person affects most, and most directly, is his or her own body. If just handling your little disk reveals so much, how much more must be revealed by the hands themselves, the lips, the eyes!"

I said uncomfortably, "Yes, of course. But it's hardly practicable to process a human body."

She said, "I have his body."

*   *   *

This silence was a dreadful one. A stupid beetle, fat as a bullet, was battering its head on the shade of the lamp in the porch, and other insects were droning, too, and there was the sea distantly heard. The silence, nonetheless, was graveyard-deep.

But she went on at last. "Everything that could possibly be preserved is preserved, by every means that could be found. I had—" Her voice broke for a second. "I had it prepared. Only the thing which is *he*, the web in the brain, the little currents died. Curious that a person is so fragile." Briskening, she launched her question anew. "Derek, how long?"

I bit my lip and stared down at the floor by my feet. My mind churned as it considered, discarded relevant factors, envisaged problems, assumed them to be soluble, fined down everything to the simple irreducible of *time*. I might have said ten years and felt that I was being stupidly optimistic.

But in the end, I said nothing at all.

She waited. Then, quite unexpectedly, she gave a bright laugh and jumped to her feet. "Derek, it isn't fair!" she said. "You've achieved something fantastic, you want and deserve to relax and celebrate, and here I am plaguing you with questions and wanting answers out of the air. I know perfectly well that you're too honest to give me an estimate without time to think, maybe do a few calculations. And I'm keeping you shut up in your crowded room when probably what you most want is to get out of it for a while. Am I right?"

She put her hand out, her arm quite straight, as if to pull me from my chair. Her face was alight with what seemed pure pleasure, and to see it was to experience again the shock of hearing her say she was fifty years old. She looked—I can only say transformed. She looked like a girl at her first party.

But it lasted only a moment, this transformation. Her expression became grave and calm. She said, "I am sorry, Derek. I—I hate one thing about love. Have you ever thought how selfish it can make you?"

We wandered out of the house hand in hand, into the summer dark. There was a narrow slice of moon and the stars were like fierce hard lanterns. For the more than hundredth time I walked down the narrow ill-paved street leading from my temporary home towards the harbour; there was Conrad's house, and there was the grocery and wine shop; there was the church, its roof silvered by the moon; there were the little cottages all in a row facing the sea, where the families of fisherfolk lived. And here, abandoned, was the detritus of two hundred and seventy lives which had never actually existed— conjured up to order.

I said, when we had walked all the way to the quay, "Naomi, it's beyond belief, even though I know it's true. This village wasn't a sham, a showplace. It was real. I *know* it."

She looked around her. "Yes. It was intended to be real. But all it takes is thought and patience."

"What did you say? Did you tell—whoever it was— 'Go and build a real village'?"

"I didn't have to. They knew. Does it interest you, how it was done?" She turned a curious face to me, which I could barely see in the thin light.

"Of course," I said. "My God! To create real people and a real place—when I'm ordered to re-create a real person—should I not be interested?"

"If it were as easy to re-create as it is to create," she said emptily, "I would not be . . . lonely."

We stopped, close by the low stone wall which ran from the quay to the sharp rocks of the little headland sheltering the beach, and leaned on it. At our backs, the row of little houses; before us, nothing but the sea. She was resting on both her elbows, staring over the water. At less than arm's reach, I leaned on one elbow, my hands clasped before me, studying her as though I had never seen her before tonight. Of course, I hadn't.

I said, "Are you afraid of not being beautiful? Something is troubling you."

She shrugged. "There is no such word as 'forever'—is there?"

"You make it seem as though there were."

"No, no." She chuckled. "Thank you for saying it, Derek. Even if I know—even if I can see in the mirror— that I am still so, it's delightful to be reassured."

How had she achieved it, anyway? I wanted, and yet didn't want, to ask. Perhaps she didn't know; she had just said she wanted it so, and it was. So I asked a different question.

"Because it's—the thing that is most *yours*?"

Her eyes came back from the sea, rested on me, returned. "Yes. The *only* thing that is mine. You're a rare person; you have compassion. Thank you."

"How do you live?" I said. I fumbled out cigarettes from my pocket, rather crumpled; she refused one with a headshake, but I lit one for myself.

"How do I live?" she echoed. "Oh—many ways. As various people, of course, with various names. You see, I haven't even a name to call my own. Two women who look exactly like me exist for me, so that when I wish I can take their places in Switzerland or in Sweden or in South America. I borrow their lives, use them a while, give them back. I have seen them grow old, changed them for replacements—made into duplicates of me. But those are not persons; they are masks. I live behind masks. I suppose that's what you'd say."

"You can't do anything else," I said.

"No. No, of course I can't. And until this overtook me, I'd never conceived that I might want to."

I felt that I understood that. I tapped the first ash off my cigarette down towards the sea. Glancing around, I said irrelevantly, "You know, it seems like a shame to dismantle Santadora. It could be a charming little village. A real one, not a stage set."

"No," she said. And then, as she straightened and whirled around, "No! Look!" She ran wildly into the middle of the narrow street and pointed at the cobbles. "Don't you see? Already stones which weren't cracked are cracked! And the houses!" She flung up her arm and ran forward to the door of the nearest house. "The wood is warping! And that shutter—hanging loose on the hinges! And the step!" She dropped to her knees, felt along the low stone step giving directly on the street.

I was coming after her now, startled by her passion.

"Feel!" she commanded. "Feel it! It's been worn by people walking on it. And even the wall—don't you see the crack from the corner of the window is getting

wider?" Again she was on her feet, running her hand
over the rough wall. "Time is gnawing at it, like a dog
at a bone. God, no, Derek! Am I to leave it and know
that time is breaking it, breaking, *breaking* it?"

I couldn't find words.

"Listen!" she said. "Oh God! Listen!" She had tensed
like a frightened deer, head cocked.

"I don't hear anything," I said. I had to swallow hard.

"Like nails being driven into a coffin," she said. She
was at the house door, battering on it, pushing at it.
"You *must* hear it!"

Now, I did. From within the house there was a ticking
noise—a huge, majestic, slow rhythm, so faint I had not
noticed it until she commanded me to strain my ears. A
clock. Just a clock.

Alarmed at her frenzy, I caught her by the shoulder.
She turned and clung to me like a tearful child, burying
her head against my chest. "I can't stand it," she said,
her teeth set. I could feel her trembling.

"Come away," I murmured. "If it hurts you so much,
come away."

"No, that isn't what I want. I'd go on hearing it—don't
you understand?" She drew back a little and looked up
at me. "I'd go on hearing it!" Her eyes grew veiled,
her whole attention focusing towards the clock inside the
house. "Tick-tick-tick—God, it's like being buried
alive!"

I hesitated a moment. Then I said, "All right, I'll fix
it. Stand back."

She obeyed. I raised my foot and stamped it, sole and
heel together, on the door. Something cracked; my leg
stung all the way to the thigh with the impact. I did it
again, and the jamb split. The door flew open. At once
the ticking was loud and clear.

And visible in a shaft of moonlight opposite the door
was the clock itself: a tall old grandfather, bigger than
me, its pendulum glinting on every ponderous swing.

A snatch of an ancient and macabre Negro spiritual
came to my mind:

The hammer keeps ringing on somebody's coffin. . . .

Abruptly it was as doom-laden for me as for Naomi.
I strode across the room, tugged open the glass door of

the clock, and stopped the pendulum with a quick finger. The silence was a relief like cold water after long thirst.

She came warily into the room after me, staring at the face of the clock as though hypnotized. It struck me that she was not wearing a watch, and I had never seen her wear one.

"Get rid of it," she said. She was still trembling. "Please, Derek—get rid of it."

I whistled, taking another look at the old monster. I said, "That's not going to be so easy! These clocks are heavy!"

"Please, Derek!" The urgency in her voice was frightening. She turned her back, staring into a corner of the room. Like all these cramped, imitation-antique houses, this one had a mere three rooms, and the room we were in was crowded with furniture—a big bed, a table, chairs, a chest. But for that, I felt she would have run to the corner to hide.

Well, I could try.

I studied the problem and came to the conclusion that it would be best to take it in parts.

"Is there a lamp?" I said. "I'd work better if I could see."

She murmured something inaudible; then there was the sound of a lighter, and a yellow flicker grew to a steady glow which illumined the room. The smell of kerosene reached my nostrils. She put the lamp on a table where its light fell past me on the clock.

I unhitched the weights and pocketed them; then I unclipped a screwdriver from my breast pocket and attacked the screws at the corners of the face. As I had hoped, with those gone, it was possible to lift out the whole works, the chains following like umbilical cords, making little scraping sounds as they were dragged over the wooden ledge the movement had rested on.

"Here!" Naomi whispered, and snatched it from me. It was a surprisingly small porportion of the weight of the whole clock. She dashed out of the house and across the street. A moment, and there was a splash.

I felt a spasm of regret. And then was angry with myself. Quite likely this was no rare specimen of antique craftsmanship, but a fake. Like the whole village. I hugged the case to me and began to walk it on its front corners towards the door. I had been working with my cigarette in my mouth; now the smoke began to tease my eyes, and I spat it to the floor and ground it out.

Somehow I got the case out of the house, across the road, up on the seawall. I rested there for a second, wiping the sweat from my face, then got behind the thing and gave it the most violent push I could manage. It went over the wall, twisting once in the air, and splashed.

I looked down, and instantly wished that I hadn't. It looked exactly like a dark coffin floating off on the sea.

But I stayed there for a minute or so, unable to withdraw my gaze, because of an overwhelming impression that I had done some symbolic act, possessed of a meaning which could not be defined in logical terms, yet heavy, solid—real as that mass of wood drifting away.

I came back slowly, shaking my head, and found myself in the door of the house before I paid attention again to what was before my eyes. Then I stopped dead, one foot on the step which Naomi had cursed for being worn by passing feet. The flame of the yellow lamp was wavering a little in the wind, and it was too high—the smell of its smoke was strong, and the chimney was darkening.

Slowly, as though relishing each single movement, Naomi was unbuttoning the black shirt she wore, looking towards the lamp. She tugged it out of the waist of her pants and slipped it off. The brassiere she wore under it was black, too. I saw she had kicked away her espadrilles.

"Call it an act of defiance," she said in a musing tone—speaking more to herself, I thought, than to me. "I shall put off my mourning clothes." She unzipped her pants and let them fall. Her briefs also were black.

"Now I'm through with mourning. I believe it will be done. It will be done soon enough. Oh yes! Soon enough." Her slim golden arms reached up behind her back. She dropped the brassiere to the floor, but the last garment she caught up in her hand and hurled at the wall. For a moment she stood still; then seemed to become aware of my presence for the first time and turned slowly towards me.

"Am I beautiful?" she said.

My throat was very dry. I said, "God, yes. You're one of the most beautiful women I've ever seen."

She leaned over the lamp and blew it out. In the instant of falling darkness she said, "Show me."

And, a little later on the rough blanket of the bed, when I had said twice or three times, "Naomi—Naomi!" she spoke again. Her voice was cold and far away.

"I didn't mean to call myself Naomi. What I had in mind was Niobe, but I couldn't remember it."

And very much later, when she had drawn herself so close to me that it seemed she was clinging to comfort, to existence itself, with her arms around me and her legs locked with mine, under the blanket now because the night was chill, I felt her lips move against my ear.

"How long, Derek?"

I was almost lost; I had never before been so drained of myself, as though I had been cork-tossed on a stormy ocean and battered limp by rocks, I could barely open my eyes. I said in a blurred voice, "What?"

"How long?"

I fought a last statement from my wearying mind, neither knowing nor caring what it was. "With luck," I muttered, "it might not take ten years. Naomi, I don't know—" And in a burst of absolute effort, finished, "My God, you do this to me and expect me to be able to think afterwards?"

But that was the extraordinary thing. I had imagined myself about to go down into blackness, into coma to sleep like a corpse. Instead, while my body rested, my mind rose to the pitch beyond consciousness—to a vantage point where it could survey the future. I was aware of the thing I had done. From my crude, experimental machine I knew, would come a second and a third, and the third would be sufficient for the task. I saw and recognized the associated problems, and knew them to be soluble. I conceived names of men I wanted to work on those problems—some who were known to me and who, given the chance I had been given, could create in their various fields, such new techniques as I had created. Meshing like hand-matched cogs, the parts blended into the whole.

A calendar and a clock were in my mind all this while.

Not all of this was a dream; much of it was of the nature of inspiration, with the sole difference that I could feel it happening and that it was right. But towards the very end, I did have a dream—not in visual images but in a kind of emotional aura. I had a completely satisfying sensation, which derived from the fact that I was about to meet for the first time a man who was already my closest friend, whom I knew as minutely as any human being had ever known another.

I was waking. For a little while longer I wanted to bask in that fantastic warmth of emotion; I struggled not to wake while feeling that I was smiling and had been smiling for so long that my cheek muscles were cramped.

Also I had been crying, so that the pillow was damp.

I turned on my side and reached out gently for Naomi, already phrasing the wonderful gift-words I had for her. "Naomi! I know how long it will take now. It needn't take more than three years, perhaps as little as two and a half."

My hand, meeting nothing but the rough cloth, sought further. Then I opened my eyes and sat up with a start.

I was alone. Full daylight was pouring into the room; it was bright and sunny and very warm. Where was she? I must go in search of her and tell her the wonderful news.

My clothes were on the floor by the bed; I pulled them on, thrust my feet in my sandals, and padded to the door, pausing with one hand on the split jamb to accustom my eyes to the glare.

Just across the narrow street, leaning his elbows on the stone wall, was a man with his back to me. He gave not the slightest hint that he was aware of being watched. It was a man I knew at once, even though I'd met him no more than twice in my life. He called himself Roger Gurney.

I spoke his name, and he didn't turn around. He lifted one arm and made a kind of beckoning motion. I was sure then what had happened, but I walked forward to stand beside him, waiting for him to tell me.

Still he didn't look at me. He merely gestured towards the sharp rocks with which the end of the wall united. He said, "She came out at dawn and went up there. To the top. She was carrying her clothes in her hand. She threw them one by one into the sea. And then—" He turned his hand over, palm down, as though pouring away a little pile of sand.

I tried to say something, but my throat was choked.

"She couldn't swim," Gurney added after a moment. "Of course."

Now I could speak. I said, "But My God! Did you see it happen?"

He nodded.

"Didn't you go after her? Didn't you rescue her?"

"We recovered her body."

"Then—aritifical respiration! You must have been able to do something!"

"She lost her race against time," Gurney said after a pause. "She had admitted it."

"I—" I checked myself. It was becoming so clear that I cursed myself for a fool. Slowly I went on, "How much longer would she have been beautiful?"

"Yes." He expressed the word with form. "That was the thing she was running from. She wanted *him* to return and find her still lovely, and no one in the world would promise her more than another three years. After that, the doctors say, she would have—" He made an empty gesture. "Crumbled."

"She would always have been beautiful," I said. "My God! Even looking her real age, she'd have been beautiful!"

"We think so," Gurney said.

"And so stupid, so futile!" I slammed my fist into my palm. "You too, Gurney—do you realize what you've *done*, you fool?" My voice shook with anger, and for the first time he faced me.

"Why in hell didn't you revive her and send for me? It needn't have taken more than three years! Last night she demanded an answer and I told her ten, but it came clear to me during the night how it could be done in less than three!"

"I thought that was how it must have been." His face was white, but the tips of his ears were—absurdly—brilliant pink. "If you hadn't said that, Cooper; if you hadn't said that."

And then (I was still that wave-tossed cork, up one moment, down the next, up again the next) it came to me what my inspiration of the night really implied. I clapped my hand to my forehead.

"Idiot!" I said. "I don't know what I'm doing yet! Look, you have her body! Get it to—to wherever it is, with the other one, *quick*. What the hell else have I been doing but working to re-create a human being? And now I've seen how it can be done, I can do it—I can re-create her as well as him!" I was in a fever of excitement, having darted forward in my mind to that strange future I had visited in my sleep, and my barely visualized theories were solid fact.

He was regarding me strangely. I thought he hadn't understood, and went on, "What are you standing there for? I can do it, I tell you—I've seen how it can be done. It's going to take men and money, but those can be got."

"No," Gurney said.

"What?" I let my arms fall to my sides, blinking in the sunlight.

"No," he repeated. He stood up, stretching arms cramped by long resting on the rough top of the wall. "You see, it isn't hers any longer. Now she's dead, it belongs to somebody else."

Dazed, I drew back a pace. I said. "Who?"

"How can I tell you? And what would it mean to you if I did? You ought by now to know what kind of people you're dealing with."

I put my hand in my pocket, feeling for my cigarettes. I was trying to make it come clear to myself: now Naomi was dead she no longer controlled the resources which could bring her back. So my dream was—a dream. Oh, God!

I was staring stupidly at the thing which had met my hand; it wasn't my pack of cigarettes but the leather wallet she had given me.

"You can keep that," Gurney said. "I was told you could keep it."

I looked at him. And I *knew*.

Very slowly, I unzipped the wallet. I took out the three cards. They were sealed in plastic. I folded them in half, and the plastic cracked. I tore them across and let them fall to the ground. Then, one by one, I ripped the checks out of the book and let them drift confetti-wise over the wall, down to the sea.

He watched me, the color coming to his face until at last he was flushing red—with guilt, shame, I don't know. When I had finished, he said in a voice that was still level, "You're a fool, Cooper. You could still have bought your dreams with those."

I threw the wallet in his face and turned away. I had gone ten steps, blind with anger and sorrow, when I heard him speak my name and looked back. He was holding the wallet in both hands, and his mouth was working.

He said, "Damn you, Cooper. Oh, damn you to hell! I—I told myself I loved her, and I couldn't have done that. Why do you want to make me feel so *dirty*?"

"Because you are," I said. "And now you know it."

Three men I hadn't seen before came into my house as I was crating the machine. Silent as ghosts, impersonal as robots, they helped me put my belongings in my car. I welcomed their aid simply because I wanted to get to hell out of his mock village as fast as possible. I told them to throw the things I wanted to take with me in the passenger seats and the luggage compartment, without bothering to pack cases. While I was at it, I saw Gurney come to the side of the house and stand by the car as though trying to pluck up courage to speak to me again, but I ignored him, and when I went out he had gone. I didn't find the wallet until I was in Barcelona sorting through the jumbled belongings. It held, this time, thirty-five thousand pesetas in new notes. He had just thrown it on the back seat under a pile of clothes.

Listen. It wasn't a *long* span of time which defeated Naomi. It wasn't three years or ten years or any number of years. I worked it out later—too late. (So time defeated me, too, as it always defeats us.)

I don't know how her man died. But I'm sure I know why she wanted him back. Not because she loved him, as she herself believed. But because he loved her. And without him, she was afraid. It didn't need three years to re-create her. It didn't even need three hours. It needed *three words*.

And Gurney, the bastard, could have spoken them, long before I could—so long before that there was still time. He could have said, "I love you."

These are the totally rich. They inhabit the same planet, breathe the same air. But they are becoming, little by little, a different species, because what was most human in them is—well, this is my opinion—dead.

They keep apart, as I mentioned. And God! God! Aren't you grateful?

NO TRUCE WITH KINGS

BY POUL ANDERSON (1926-   )

THE MAGAZINE OF FANTASY AND SCIENCE FICTION
JUNE

Poul Anderson is a tall, gentle man who knows a great deal about fighting. A member of the Society for Creative Anachronism, which among other things stages fights with broadswords, maces, and other dainty items, he has been known to wield a pretty good killing weapon. "No Truce With Kings" is a war story, one of the best about fighting men and their work.

Poul Anderson is also one of the giants of speculative fiction, a multiple winner of the Hugo and Nebula Awards, and the recipient of the J.R.R. Tolkien Memorial Award, among others.

> *Ancient and Unteachable, abide—abide the Trumpets!*
> *Once, again the Trumpets, for the shuddering ground swell brings*
> *Clamour over ocean of the harsh, pursuing Trumpets—*
> *Trumpets of the Vanguard that have sworn no truce with Kings*—RUDYARD KIPLING

"Song, Charlie! Give's a song!"

"Yay, Charlie!"

The whole mess was drunk, and the junior officers at the far end of the table were only somewhat noisier than their seniors near the colonel. Rugs and hangings could not much muffle the racket, shouts, stamping boots, thump of fists on oak and clash of cups raised aloft, that rang from wall to stony wall. High up among shadows that hid the rafters they hung from, the regimental banners stirred in a draft, as if to join the chaos. Below, the light of bracketed lanterns and bellowing fireplace winked on trophies and weapons.

Autumn comes early on Echo Summit, and it was storming outside, wind-hoot past the watchtowers and rain-rush in the courtyards, an undertone that walked through the buildings and down all corridors, as if the story were true that the unit's dead came out of the cemetery each September Nineteenth night and tried to join the celebration but had forgotten how. No one let it bother him, here or in the enlisted barracks, except maybe the hex major. The Third Division, the Catamounts, was known as the most riotous gang in the Army of the Pacific States of America, and of its regiments the Rolling Stones who held Fort Nakamura were the wildest.

"Go on, boy! Lead off. You've got the closest thing to a voice in the whole goddamn Sierra," Colonel Mackenzie called. He loosened the collar of his black dress tunic and lounged back, legs asprawl, pipe in one hand and beaker of whisky in the other: a thickset man with blue wrinkle-meshed eyes in a battered face, his cropped hair turned gray but his mustache still arrogantly red.

"Charlie is my darlin', my darlin', my darlin'," sang Captain Hulse. He stopped as the noise abated a little. Young Lieutenant Amadeo got up, grinned, and launched into one they well knew.

> *"I am a Catamountain, I guard a border pass.*
> *And every time I venture out, the cold will freeze m—*

"Colonel, sir. Begging your pardon."

Mackenzie twisted around and looked into the face of Sergeant Irwin. The man's expression shocked him. "Yes?"

> *"I am a bloody hero, a decorated vet:*
> *The Order of the Purple Shaft, with pineapple clusters yet!"*

"Message just come in, sir. Major Speyer asks to see you right away."

Speyer, who didn't like being drunk, had volunteered for duty tonight; otherwise men drew lots for it on a holiday. Remembering the last word from San Francisco, Mackenzie grew chill.

The mess bawled forth the chorus, not noticing when the colonel knocked out his pipe and rose.

"The guns go boom! Hey, tiddley boom!
The rockets vroom, the arrows zoom.
From slug to slug is damn small room.
Get me out of here and back to the good old womb!
(Hey, doodle dee day!)"

All right-thinking Catamounts maintained that they could operate better with the booze sloshing up to their eardrums than any other outfit cold sober. Mackenzie ignored the tingle in his veins; forgot it. He walked a straight line to the door, automatically taking his sidearm off the rack as he passed by. The song pursued him into the hall.

"For maggots in the rations, we hardly ever lack.
You bite into a sandwich and the sandwich bites right
*   back.*
The coffee is the finest grade of Sacramento mud.
The ketchup's good in combat, though, for simulating
*   blood.*
(Cho-orus!)
The drums go bump! Ah-tumpty-tump!
The bugles make like Gabri'l's trump—'

Lanterns were far apart in the passage. Portraits of former commanders watched the colonel and the sergeant from eyes that were hidden in grotesque darknesses. Footfalls clattered too loudly here.

"I've got an arrow in my rump.
Right about and rearward, heroes, on the jump!
(Hey, doodle dee day!)"

*   *   *

Mackenzie went between a pair of fieldpieces flanking a stairway—they had been captured at Rock Springs during the Wyoming War, a generation ago—and upward. There was more distance between places in this keep than his legs liked at their present age. But it was old, had been added to decade by decade; and it needed to be massive, chiseled and mortared from Sierra granite, for it guarded a key to the nation. More than one army had broken against its revetments, before the Nevada marches were pacified, and more young men than Mackenzie wished to think about had gone from this base to die among angry strangers.

But she's never been attacked from the west. God, or whatever you are, you can spare her that, can't you?

The command office was lonesome at this hour. The room where Sergeant Irwin had his desk lay so silent: no clerks pushing pens, no messengers going in or out, no wives making a splash of color with their dresses as they waited to see the colonel about some problem down in the Village. When he opened the door to the inner room, though, Mackenzie heard the wind shriek around the angle of the wall. Rain slashed at the black windowpane and ran down in streams which the lanterns turned molten.

"Here the colonel is, sir," Irwin said in an uneven voice. He gulped and closed the door behind Mackenzie.

Speyer stood by the commander's desk. It was a beat-up old object with little upon it: an inkwell, a letterbasket, an interphone, a photograph of Nora, faded in these dozen years since her death. The major was a tall and gaunt man, hook-nosed, going bald on top. His uniform always looked unpressed, somehow. But he had the sharpest brain in the Cats, Mackenzie thought; and Christ, how could any man read as many books as Phil did! Officially he was the adjutant, in practice the chief advisor.

"Well?" Mackenzie said. The alcohol did not seem to numb him, rather make him too acutely aware of things: how the lanterns smelled hot (when would they get a big enough generator to run electric lights?), and the floor was hard under his feet, and a crack went through the plaster of the north wall, and the stove wasn't driving out much of the chill. He forced bravado, stuck thumbs in belt and rocked back on his heels. "Well, Phil, what's wrong now?"

"Wire from Frisco," Speyer said. He had been folding and unfolding a piece of paper, which he handed over.

"Huh? Why not a radio call?"

"Telegram's less likely to be intercepted. This one's in code, at that. Irwin decoded it for me."

"What the hell kind of nonsense is this?"

"Have a look, Jimbo, and you'll find out. It's for you, anyway. Direct from GHQ."

Mackenzie focused on Irwin's scrawl. The usual formalities of an order; then:

You are hereby notified that the Pacific States Senate has passed a bill of impeachment against Owen Brodsky, formerly Judge of the Pacific States of America, and deprived him of office. As of 2000 hours this date, former Vice Humphrey Fallon is Judge of the PSA in accordance with the Law of Succession. The existence of dissident elements constituting a public danger has made it necessary for Judge Fallon to put the entire nation under martial law, effective at 2100 hours this date. You are therefore issued the following instructions:

1. The above intelligence is to be held strictly confidential until an official proclamation is made. No person who has received knowledge in the course of transmitting this message shall divulge same to any other person whatsoever. Violators of this section and anyone thereby receiving information shall be placed immediately in solitary confinement to await courtmartial.

2. You will sequestrate all arms and ammunition except for ten percent of available stock, and keep same under heavy guard.

3. You will keep all men in the Fort Nakamura area until you are relieved. Your relief is Colonel Simon Hollis, who will start from San Francisco tomorrow morning with one battalion. They are expected to arrive at Fort Nakamura in five days, at which time you will surrender your command to him. Colonel Hollis will designate those officers and enlisted men who are to be replaced by members of his battalion, which will be integrated

into the regiment. You will lead the men replaced back to San Francisco and report to Brigadier General Mendoza at New Fort Baker. To avoid provocations, these men will be disarmed except for officers' sidearms.

4. For your private information, Captain Thomas Daniels has been appointed senior aide to Colonel Hollis.

5. You are again reminded that the Pacific States of America are under martial law because of a national emergency. Complete loyalty to the legal government is required. Any mutinous talk must be severely punished. Anyone giving aid or comfort to the Brodsky faction is guilty of treason and will be dealt with accordingly.

GERALD O'DONNELL,
GEN. APSA, CINC

Thunder went off in the mountains like artillery. It was a while before Mackenzie stirred, and then merely to lay the paper on his desk. He could only summon feeling slowly, up into a hollowness that filled his skin.

"They dared," Speyer said without tone. "They really did."

"Huh?" Mackenzie swiveled eyes around to the major's face. Speyer didn't meet that stare. He was concentrating his own gaze on his hands, which were now rolling a cigaret. But the words jerked from him, harsh and quick:

"I can guess what happened. The warhawks have been hollering for impeachment ever since Brodsky compromised the border dispute with West Canada. And Fallon, yeah, he's got ambitions of his own. But his partisans are a minority and he knows it. Electing him Vice helped soothe the warhawks some, but he'd never make Judge the regular way, because Brodsky isn't going to die of old age before Fallon does, and anyhow more than fifty percent of the Senate are sober, satisfied bossmen who don't agree that the PSA has a divine mandate to reunify the continent. I don't see how an impeachment could get through an honestly convened Senate. More likely they'd vote out Fallon."

"But a Senate had been called," Mackenzie said. The words sounded to him like someone else talking. "The newscasts told us."

"Sure. Called for yesterday 'to debate ratification of

the treaty with West Canada.' But the bossmen are scattered up and down the country, each at his own Station. They have to *get* to San Francisco. A couple of arranged delays—hell, if a bridge just happened to be blown on the Boise railroad, a round dozen of Brodsky's staunchest supporters wouldn't arrive on time—so the Senate has a quorum, all right, but every one of Fallon's supporters are there, and so many of the rest are missing that the warhawks have a clear majority. Then they meet on a holiday, when no cityman is paying attention. Presto, impeachment and a new Judge!" Speyer finished his cigaret and stuck it between his lips while he fumbled for a match.

"You sure?" Mackenzie mumbled. He thought dimly that this moment was like one time he'd visited Puget City and been invited for a sail on the Guardian's yacht, and a fog had closed in. Everything was cold and blind, with nothing you could catch in your hands.

"Of course I'm not sure!" Speyer snarled. "Nobody will be sure till it's too late." The matchbox shook in his grasp.

"They, uh, they got a new Cinc too, I noticed."

"Uh-huh. They'd want to replace everybody they can't trust, as fast as possible, and de Barros was a Brodsky appointee." The match flared with a hellish *scrit*. Speyer inhaled till his cheeks collapsed. "You and me included, naturally. The regiment reduced to minimum armament so that nobody will get ideas about resistance when the new colonel arrives. You'll note he's coming with a battalion at his heels just the same, just in case. Otherwise he could take a plane and be here tomorrow."

"Why not a train?" Mackenzie caught a whiff of smoke and felt for his pipe. The bowl was hot in his tunic pocket.

"Probably all rolling stock has to head north. Get troops among the bossmen there and forestall a revolt. The valleys are safe enough, peaceful ranchers and Esper colonies. None of them'll pot-shot Fallonite soldiers marching to garrison Echo and Donner outposts." A dreadful scorn weighted Speyer's words.

"What are we going to do?"

"I assume Fallon's take-over followed legal forms; that

there was a quorum," Speyer said. "Nobody will ever agree whether it was really Constitutional. . . . I've been reading this damned message over and over since Irwin decoded it. There's a lot between the lines. I think Brodsky's at large, for instance. If he were under arrest this would've said as much, and there'd have been less worry about rebellion. Maybe some of his household troops smuggled him away in time. He'll be hunted like a jackrabbit, of course."

Mackenzie took out his pipe but forgot he had done so. "Tom's coming with our replacements," he said thinly.

"Yeah. Your son-in-law. That was a smart touch, wasn't it? A kind of hostage for your good behavior, but also a backhand promise that you and yours won't suffer if you report in as ordered. Tom's a good kid. He'll stand by his own."

"This is his regiment too," Mackenzie said. He squared his shoulders. "He wanted to fight West Canada, sure. Young and . . . and a lot of Pacificans did get killed in the Idaho Panhandle during the skirmishes. Women and kids among 'em."

"Well," Speyer said, "you're the colonel, Jimbo. What do we do?"

"Oh, Jesus, I don't know. I'm nothing but a soldier." The pipestem broke in Mackenzie's fingers. "But we're not some bossman's personal militia here. We swore to support the Constitution."

"*I* can't see where Brodsky's yielding some of our claims in Idaho is grounds for impeachment. I think he was right."

"Well—"

"A *coup d'état* by any other name would stink as bad. You may not be much of a student of current events, Jimbo, but you know as well as I do what Fallon's Judgeship will mean. War with West Canada is almost the least of it. Fallon also stands for a strong central government. He'll find ways to grind down the old bossman families. A lot of their heads and scions will die in the front lines; that stunt goes back to David and Uriah. Others will be accused of collusion with the Brodsky people—not altogether falsely—and impoverished by fines. Esper communities will get nice big land grants, so their economic competition can bankrupt still other estates. Later wars will keep bossmen away for years at a time, unable to supervise their own affairs, which will therefore go to the devil. And thus we march toward the glorious goal of Reunification."

"If Esper Central favors him, what can we do? I've heard enough about psi blasts. I can't ask my men to face them."

"You could ask your men to face the Hellbomb itself, Jimbo, and they would. A Mackenzie has commanded the Rolling Stones for over fifty years."

"Yes. I thought Tom, someday—"

"We've watched this brewing for a long time. Remember the talk we had about it last week?"

"Uh-huh."

"I might also remind you that the Constitution was written explicitly 'to confirm the separate regions in their ancient liberties.' "

"Let me alone!" Mackenzie shouted. "I don't know what's right or wrong, I tell you! Let me alone!"

Speyer fell silent, watching him through a screen of foul smoke. Mackenzie walked back and forth a while, boots slamming the floor like drumbeats. Finally he threw the broken pipe across the room so it shattered.

"Okay." He must ram each word past the tension in his throat. "Irwin's a good man who can keep his lip buttoned. Send him out to cut the telegraph line a few miles downhill. Make it look as if the storm did it. The wire breaks often enough, heaven knows. Officially, then, we never got GHQ's message. That gives us a few days to contact Sierra Command HQ. I won't go against General Cruikshank . . . but I'm pretty sure which way he'll go if he sees a chance. Tomorrow we prepare for action. It'll be no trick to throw back Hollis' battalion, and they'll need a while to bring some real strength against us. Before then the first snow should be along, and we'll be shut off for the winter. Only we can use skis and snowshoes, ourselves, to keep in touch with the other units and organize something. By spring—we'll see what happens."

"Thanks, Jimbo." The wind almost drowned Speyer's words.

"I'd . . . I'd better go tell Laura."

"Yeah." Speyer squeezed Mackenzie's shoulder. There were tears in the major's eyes.

Mackenzie went out with parade-ground steps, ignoring Irwin: down the hall, down a stairway at its other end, past guarded doors where he returned salutes without really noticing, and so to his own quarters in the south wing.

His daughter had gone to sleep already. He took a lantern off its hook in his bleak little parlor, and entered her room. She had come back here while her husband was in San Francisco.

For a moment Mackenzie couldn't quite remember why he had sent Tom there. He passed a hand over his stubbly scalp, as if to squeeze something out . . . oh, yes, ostensibly to arrange for a new issue of uniforms; actually to get the boy out of the way until the political crisis had blown over. Tom was too honest for his own good, an admirer of Fallon and the Esper movement. His outspokenness had led to friction with his brother officers. They were mostly of bossman stock or from well-to-do protectee families. The existing social order had been good to them. But Tom Danielis began as a fisher lad in a poverty-stricken village on the Mendocino coast. In spare moments he'd learned the three R's from a local Esper; once literate, he joined the army and earned a commission by sheer guts and brains. He had never forgotten that the Espers helped the poor and that Fallon promised to help the Espers. . . . Then, too, battle, glory, Reunification Federal Democracy, those were heady dreams when you were young.

Laura's room was little changed since she left it to get married last year. And she had only been seventeen then. Objects survived which had belonged to a small person with pigtails and starched frocks—a teddy bear loved to shapelessness, a doll house her father had built, her mother's picture drawn by a corporal who stopped a bullet at Salt Lake. Oh, God, how much she had come to look like her mother.

Dark hair streamed over a pillow turned gold by the

light. Mackenzie shook her as gently as he was able. She
awoke instantly, and he saw the terror within her.

"Dad! Anything about Tom?"

"He's okay." Mackenzie set the lantern on the floor
and himself on the edge of the bed. Her fingers were
cold where they caught at his hand.

"He isn't," she said. "I know you too well."

"He's not been hurt yet. I hope he won't be."

Mackenzie braced himself. Because she was a soldier's
daughter, he told her the truth in a few words; but he
was not strong enough to look at her while he did. When
he had finished, he sat dully listening to the rain.

"You're going to revolt," she whispered.

"I'm going to consult with SCHQ and follow my com-
manding officer's orders," he said.

"You know what they'll be . . . once he knows you'll
back him."

Mackenzie shrugged. His head had begun to ache.
Hangover started already? He'd need a good deal more
booze before he could sleep tonight. No, no time for
sleep—yes, there would be. Tomorrow would do to
assemble the regiment in the courtyard and address them
from the breech of Black Hepzibah, as a Mackenzie of
the Rolling Stones always addressed his men, and—He
found himself ludicrously recalling a day when he and
Nora and this girl here had gone rowing on Lake Tahoe.
The water was the color of Nora's eyes, green and blue
and with sunlight flimmering across the surface, but so
clear you could see the rocks on the bottom; and Laura's
own little bottom had stuck straight in the air as she
trailed her hands astern.

She sat thinking for a space before saying flatly: "I
suppose you can't be talked out of it." He shook his
head. "Well, can I leave tomorrow early, then?"

"Yes. I'll get you a coach."

"T-t-to hell with that. I'm better in the saddle than
you are."

"Okay. A couple of men to escort you, though." Mackenzie drew a long breath. "Maybe you can persuade
Tom—"

"No. I can't. Please don't ask me to, Dad."

He gave her the last gift he could: "I wouldn't want

you to stay. That'd be shirking your own duty. Tell Tom
I still think he's the right man for you. Goodnight,
duck." It came out too fast, but he dared not delay.
When she began to cry he must unfold her arms from
his neck and depart the room.

"But I had not expected so much killing!"

*"Nor I . . . at this stage of things. There will be more
yet, I am afraid, before the immediate purpose is
achieved."*

"You told me—"

*"I told you our hopes, Mwyr. You know as well as I
that the Great Science is only exact on the broadest scale
of history. Individual events are subject to statistical
fluctuation."*

*"That is an easy way, is it not, to describe sentient
beings dying in the mud?"*

*"You are new here. Theory is one thing, adjustment to
practical necessities is another. Do you think it does not
hurt me to see that happen which I myself have helped
plan?"*

*"Oh, I know, I know. Which makes it no easier to live
with my guilt."*

"To live with your responsibilities, you mean."

"Your phrase."

*"No, this is not semantic trickery. The distinction is
real. You have read reports and seen films, but I was here
with the first expedition. And here I have been for more
than two centuries. Their agony is no abstraction to me."*

*"But it was different when we first discovered them. The
aftermath of their nuclear wars was still so horribly present. That was when they needed us—the poor starveling
anarchs—and we, we did nothing but observe."*

*"Now you are hysterical. Could we come in blindly,
ignorant of every last fact about them, and expect to be
anything but one more disruptive element? An element
whose effects we ourselves would not have been able to
predict. That would have been criminal indeed, like a surgeon who started to operate as soon as he met the patient,
without so much as taking a case history. We had to let
them go their own way while we studied in secret. You
have no idea how desperately hard we worked to gain*

*information and understanding. That work goes on. It was
only seventy years ago that we felt enough assurance to
introduce the first new factor into this one selected society.
As we continue to learn more, the plan will be adjusted.
It may take us a thousand years to complete our mission."*

*"But meanwhile they have pulled themselves back out
of the wreckage. They are finding their own answers to
their problems. What right have we to—"*

*"I begin to wonder, Mwyr, what right you have to claim
even the title of apprentice psychodynamician. Consider
what their 'answers' actually amount to. Most of the planet
is still in a state of barbarism. This continent has come
farthest toward recovery, because of having the widest dis-
tribution of technical skills and equipment before the
destruction. But what social structure has evolved? A jum-
ble of quarrelsome successor states. A feudalism where the
balance of political, military, and economic power lies
with a landed aristocracy, of all archaic things. A score
of languages and subcultures developing along their own
incompatible lines. A blind technology-worship inherited
from the ancestral society, that unchecked will lead them
in the end back to a machine civilization as demoniac as
the one that tore itself apart three centuries ago. Are you
distressed that a few hundred men have been killed,
because our agents promoted a revolution which did not
come off quite so smoothly as we hoped? Well, you have
the word of the Great Science itself that without our guid-
ance, the totaled misery of this race through the next five
thousand years would outweigh by three orders of magni-
tude whatever pain we are forced to inflict."*

*"—Yes. Of course. I realize I am being emotional. It is
difficult not to be at first, I suppose."*

*"You should be thankful that your initial exposure to
the hard necessities of the plan was so mild. There is worse
to come."*

"So I have been told."

*"In abstract terms. But consider the reality. A govern-
ment ambitious to restore the old nation will act aggres-
sively, thus embroiling itself in prolonged wars with
powerful neighbors. Both directly and indirectly, through
the operation of economic factors they are too naive to
control, the aristocrats and freeholders will be eroded*

*away by those wars. Anomic democracy will replace their
system, first dominated by a corrupt capitalism and later
by sheer force of whoever holds the central government.
But there will be no place for the vast displaced proletar-
iat, the one-time landowners and the foreigners incorporated by conquest. They will offer fertile soil to any
demagogue. The empire will undergo endless upheaval,
civil strife, despotism, decay, and outside invasion. Oh,
we will have much to answer for before we are done!"*

*"Do you think . . . when we see the final result . . .
will the blood wash off us?"*

"No. We pay the heaviest price of all."

Spring in the high Sierra is cold, wet, snowbanks melting away from forest floor and giant rocks, rivers in spate
until their canyons clang, a breeze ruffling puddles in
the road. The first green breath across the aspen seems
infinitely tender against pine and spruce, which gloom
into a brilliant sky. A raven swoops low, gruk, gruk, look
out for that damn hawk! But then you cross timberline
and the world becomes tumbled blue-gray immensity,
with the sun ablaze on what snows remain and the wind
sounding hollow in your ears.

Captain Thomas Danielis, Field Artillery, Loyalist
Army of the Pacific States, turned his horse aside. He
was a dark young man, slender and snubnosed. Behind
him a squad slipped and cursed, dripping mud from feet
to helmets, trying to get a gun carrier unstuck. Its alcohol
motor was too feeble to do more than spin the wheels.
The infantry squelched on past, stoop-shouldered, worn
down by altitude and a wet bivouac and pounds of mire
on each boot. Their line snaked from around a prowlike
crag, up the twisted road and over the ridge ahead. A
gust brought the smell of sweat to Danielis.

But they were good joes, he thought. Dirty, dogged,
they did their profane best. His own company, at least,
was going to get hot food tonight, if he had to cook the
quartermaster sergeant.

The horse's hoofs banged on a block of ancient concrete jutting from the muck. If this had been the old days
. . . but wishes weren't bullets. Beyond this part of the
range lay lands mostly desert, claimed by the Saints, who

were no longer a menace but with whom there was scant commerce. So the mountain highways had never been considered worth repaving, and the railroad ended at Hangtown. Therefore the expeditionary force to the Tahoe area must slog through unpeopled forests and icy uplands, God help the poor bastards.

God help them in Nakamura, too, Danielis thought. His mouth drew taut, he slapped his hands together and spurred the horse with needless violence. Sparks shot from iron shoes as the beast clattered off the road toward the highest point of the ridge. The man's saber banged his leg.

Reining in, he unlimbered his field glasses. From here he could look across a jumbled sweep of mountainscape, where cloud shadows sailed over cliffs and boulders, down into the gloom of a canyon and across to the other side. A few tufts of grass thrust out beneath him, mummy brown, and a marmot wakened early from winter sleep whistled somewhere in the stone confusion. He still couldn't see the castle. Nor had he expected to, as yet. He knew this country . . . how well he did!

There might be a glimpse of hostile activity, though. It had been eerie to march this far with no sign of the enemy, of anyone else whatsoever; to send out patrols in search of rebel units that could not be found, to ride with shoulder muscles tense against the sniper's arrow that never came. Old Jimbo Mackenzie was not one to sit passive behind walls, and the Rolling Stones had not been given their nickname in jest.

If Jimbo is alive. How do I know he is? That buzzard yonder may be the very one which hacked out his eyes.

Danielis bit his lip and made himself look steadily through the glasses. Don't think about Mackenzie, how he outroared and outdrank and outlaughed you and you never minded, how he sat knotting his brows over the chessboard where you could mop him up ten times out of ten and *he* never cared, how proud and happy he stood at the wedding . . . Nor think about Laura, who tried to keep you from knowing how often she wept at night, who now bore a grandchild beneath her heart and woke alone in the San Francisco house from the evil dreams of pregnancy. Every one of those dogfaces plodding toward the castle which has killed every army ever sent against it—every one of them has somebody at home and Hell rejoices at how many have somebody on the rebel side. Better look for hostile spoor and let it go at that.

Wait! Danielis stiffened. A rider—He focused. *One of our own.* Fallon's army added a blue band to the uniform. *Returning scout.* A tingle went along his spine. He decided to hear the report firsthand. But the fellow was still a mile off, perforce riding slowly over the hugger-mugger terrain. There was no hurry about intercepting him. Danielis continued to survey the land.

A reconnaissance plane appeared, an ungainly dragon-fly with sunlight flashing off a propellor head. Its drone bumbled among rock walls, where echoes threw the noise back and forth. Doubtless an auxiliary to the scouts, employing two-way radio communication. Later the plane would work as a spotter for artillery. There was no use making a bomber of it; Fort Nakamura was proof against anything that today's puny aircraft could drop, and might well shoot the thing down.

A shoe scraped behind Danielis. Horse and man whirled as one. His pistol jumped into his hand.

It lowered. "Oh. Excuse me, Philosopher."

The man in the blue robe nodded. A smile softened his stern face. He must be around sixty years old, hair white and skin lined, but he walked these heights like a wild goat. The Yang and Yin symbol burned gold on his breast.

"You're needlessly on edge, son," he said. A trace of Texas accent stretched out his words. The Espers obeyed the laws wherever they lived, but acknowledge no country their own: nothing less than mankind, perhaps ultimately all life through the space-time universe. Nevertheless, the Pacific States had gained enormously in prestige and influence when the Order's unenterable Central was established in San Francisco at the time when the city was being rebuilt in earnest. There had been no objection—on the contrary—to the Grand Seeker's desire that Philosopher Woodworth accompany the expedition as an observer. Not even from the chaplains;

the churches had finally gotten it straight that the Esper teachings were neutral with respect to religion.

Danielis managed a grin. "Can you blame me?"

"No blame. But advice. Your attitude isn't useful. Does nothin' but wear you out. You've been fightin' a battle for weeks before it began."

Danielis remembered the apostle who had visited his home in San Francisco—by invitation, in the hope that Laura might learn some peace. His simile had been still homelier: "You only need to wash one dish at a time." The memory brought a smart to Danielis' eyes, so that he said roughly:

"I might relax if you'd use your powers to tell me what's waiting for us."

"I'm no adept, son. Too much in the material world, I'm afraid. Somebody's got to do the practical work of the Order, and someday I'll get the chance to retire and explore the frontier inside me. But you need to start early, and stick to it a lifetime, to develop your full powers." Woodworth looked across the peaks, seemed almost to merge himself with their loneliness.

Danielis hesitated to break into that meditation. He wondered what practical purpose the Philosopher was serving on this trip. To bring back a report, more accurate than untrained senses and undisciplined emotions could prepare? Yes, that must be it. The Espers might yet decide to take a hand in this war. However reluctantly, Central had allowed the awesome psi powers to be released now and again, when the Order was seriously threatened, and Judge Fallon was a better friend to them than Brodsky or the earlier Senate of Bossmen and House of People's Deputies had been.

The horse stamped and blew out its breath in a snort. Woodworth glanced back at the rider. "If you ask me, though," he said, "I don't reckon you'll find much doin' around here. I was in the Rangers myself, back home, before I saw the Way. This country feels empty."

"If we could know!" Danielis exploded. "They've had the whole winter to do what they liked in the mountains, while the snow kept us out. What scouts we could get in reported a beehive—as late as two weeks ago. What have they planned?"

Woodworth made no reply.

It flooded from Danielis, he couldn't stop, he had to cover the recollection of Laura bidding him goodbye on his second expedition against her father, six months after the first one came home in bloody fragments:

"If we had the resources! A few wretched little railroads and motor cars; a handful of aircraft; most of our supply trains drawn by mules—what kind of mobility does that give us? And what really drives me crazy . . . we know how to make what they had in the old days. We've got the books, the information. More, maybe, than the ancestors. I've watched the electrosmith at Fort Nakamura turn out transistor units with enough bandwidth to carry television, no bigger than my fist. I've seen the scientific journals, the research labs, biology, chemistry, astronomy, mathematics. And all useless!"

"Not so," Woodworth answered mildly. "Like my own Order, the community of scholarship's becomin' supranational. Printin' presses, radiophones, telescribes—"

"I say useless. Useless to stop men killing each other because there's no authority strong enough to make them behave. Useless to take a farmer's hands off a horse-drawn plow and put them on the wheel of a tractor. We've got the knowledge, but we can't apply it."

"You do apply it, son, where too much power and industrial plant isn't required. Remember, the world's a lot poorer in natural resources than it was before the Hellbombs. I've seen the Black Lands myself, where the firestorm passed over the Texas oilfields." Woodworth's serenity cracked a little. He turned his eyes back to the peaks.

"There's oil elsewhere," Danielis insisted. "And coal, iron, uranium, everything we need. But the world hasn't got the organization to get at it. Not in any quantity. So we fill the Central Valley with crops that'll yield alcohol, to keep a few motors turning; and we import a dribble of other stuff along an unbelievably inefficient chain of middlemen; and most of it's eaten by the armies." He jerked his head toward that part of the sky which the handmade airplane had crossed. "That's one reason we've got to have Reunification. So we can rebuild."

"And the other?" Woodworth asked softly.

"Democracy—universal suffrage—" Danielis swallowed. "And so fathers and sons won't have to fight each other again."

"Those are better reasons," Woodworth said. "Good enough for the Espers to support. But as for that machinery you want—" He shook his head. "No, you're wrong there. That's no way for men to live."

"Maybe not," Danielis said. "Though my own father wouldn't have been crippled by overwork if he'd had some machines to help him. . . . Oh, I don't know. First things first. Let's get this war over with and argue later." He remembered the scout, now gone from view. "Pardon me, Philosopher, I've got an errand."

The Esper raised his hand in token of peace. Danielis cantered off.

Splashing along the roadside, he saw the man he wanted, halted by Major Jacobsen. The latter, who must have sent him out, sat mounted near the infantry line. The scout was a Klamath Indian, stocky in buckskins, a bow on his shoulder. Arrows were favored over guns by many of the men from the northern districts: cheaper than bullets, no noise, less range but as much firepower as a bolt-action rifle. In the bad old days before the Pacific States had formed their union, archers along forest trails had saved many a town from conquest; they still helped keep that union loose.

"Ah, Captain Danielis," Jacobsen hailed. "You're just in time. Lieutenant Smith was about to report what his detachment found out."

"And the plane," said Smith imperturbably. "What the pilot told us he'd seen from the air gave us the guts to go there and check for ourselves."

"Well?"

"Nobody around."

"What?"

"Fort's been evacuated. So's the settlement. Not a soul."

"But—but—" Jacobsen collected himself. "Go on."

"We studied the signs as best's we could. Looks like noncombatants left some time ago. By sledge and ski, I'd guess, maybe north to some strong point. I suppose the men shifted their own stuff at the same time, graduallike, what they couldn't carry with 'em at the last. Because the regiment and its support units, even field artillery, pulled out just three-four days ago. Ground's all tore up. They headed downslope, sort of west by northwest, far's we could tell from what we saw."

Jacobsen choked. "Where are they bound?"

A flaw of wind struck Danielis in the face and ruffled the horses' manes. At his back he heard the slow plop and squish of boots, groan of wheels, chuff of motors, rattle of wood and metal, yells and whipcracks of muleskinners. But it seemed very remote. A map grew before him, blotting out the world.

The loyalist army had had savage fighting the whole winter, from the Trinity Alps to Puget Sound—for Brodsky had managed to reach Mount Rainier, whose lord had furnished broadcasting facilities, and Rainier was too well fortified to take at once. The bossmen and the autonomous tribes rose in arms, persuaded that a usurper threatened their damned little local privileges. Their protectees fought beside them, if only because no rustic had been taught any higher loyalty than to his patron. West Canada, fearful of what Fallon might do when he got the chance, lent the rebels aid that was scarcely even clandestine.

Nonetheless, the national army was stronger: more matériel, better organization, above everything an ideal of the future. Cinc O'Donnel had outlined a strategy— concentrate the loyal forces at a few points, overwhelm resistance, restore order and establish bases in the region, then proceed to the next place—which worked. The government now controlled the entire coast, with naval units to keep an eye on the Canadians in Vancouver and guard the important Hawaii trade routes; the northern half of Washington almost to the Idaho line; the Columbia Valley; central California as far north as Redding. The remaining rebellious Stations and towns were isolated from each other in mountains, forests, desert. Bossdom after bossdom fell as the loyalists pressed on, defeating the enemy in detail, cutting him off from supplies and hope. The only real worry had been Cruikshank's Sierra Command, an army in its own right rather than a levy of yokels and citymen, big and tough and expertly led. This expedition against Fort Nakamura was only a small part of what had looked like a difficult campaign.

But now the Rolling Stones had pulled out. Offered no fight whatsoever. Which meant that their brother Catamounts must also have evacuated. You don't give up one anchor of a line you intend to hold. So?

"Down into the valleys," Danielis said; and there sounded in his ears, crazily, the voice of Laura as she used to sing. *Down in the valley, valley so low*.

"Judas!" the major exclaimed. Even the Indian grunted as if he had taken a belly blow. "No, they couldn't. We'd have known."

Hang your head over, hear the wind blow. It hooted across cold rocks.

"There are plenty of forest trails," Danielis said. "Infantry and cavalry could use them, if they're accustomed to such country. And the Cats are. Vehicles, wagons, big guns, that's slower and harder. But they only need to outflank us, then they can get back onto Forty and Fifty—and cut us to pieces if we attempt pursuit. I'm afraid they've got us boxed."

"The eastern slope—" said Jacobsen helplessly.

"What for? Want to occupy a lot of sagebrush? No, we're trapped here till they deploy in the flatlands." Danielis closed a hand on his saddlehorn so that the knuckles went bloodless. "I miss my guess if this isn't Colonel Mackenzie's idea. It's his style, for sure."

"But then they're between us and Frisco! With damn near our whole strength in the north—"

Between me and Laura, Danielis thought.

He said aloud: "I suggest, major, we get hold of the C.O. at once. And then we better get on the radio." From some well he drew the power to raise his head. The wind lashed his eyes. "This needn't be a disaster. They'll be easier to beat out in the open, actually, once we come to grips."

Roses love sunshine, violets love dew,
Angels in heaven know I love you.

The rains which fill the winter of the California lowlands were about ended. Northward along a highway whose pavement clopped under hoofs, Mackenzie rode through a tremendous greenness. Eucalyptus and live oak, flanking the road, exploded with new leaves. Beyond them on either side stretched a checkerboard of fields and vineyards, intricately hued, until the distant hills on the right and the higher, near ones on the left made walls. The freeholder houses that had been scattered across the land a ways back were no longer to be seen. This end of the Napa Valley belonged to the Esper community at St. Helena. Clouds banked like white mountains over the western ridge. The breeze bore to Mackenzie a smell of growth and turned earth.

Behind him it rumbled with men. The Rolling Stones were on the move. The regiment proper kept to the highway, three thousand boots slamming down at once with an earthquake noise, and so did the guns and wagons. There was no immediate danger of attack. But the cavalrymen attached to the force must needs spread out. The sun flashed off their helmets and lance heads.

Mackenzie's attention was directed forward. Amber walls and red tile roofs could be seen among plum trees that were a surf of pink and white blossoms. The community was big, several thousand people. The muscles tightened in his abdomen. "Think we can trust them?" he asked, not for the first time. "We've only got a radio agreement to a parley."

Speyer, riding beside him, nodded. "I expect they'll be honest. Particularly with our boys right outside. Espers believe in non-violence anyway."

"Yeah, but if it did come to fighting—I know there aren't very many adepts so far. The Order hasn't been around long enough for that. But when you get this many Espers together, there's bound to be a few who've gotten somewhere with their damned psionics. I don't want my men blasted, or lifted in the air and dropped, or any such nasty thing."

Speyer threw him a sidelong glance. "Are you scared of them, Jimbo?" he murmured.

'Hell, no!" Mackenzie wondered if he was a liar or not. "But I don't like 'em."

"They do a lot of good. Among the poor, especially."

"Sure, sure. Though any decent bossman looks after his own protectees, and we've got things like churches and hospices as well. I don't see where just being charitable—and they can afford it, with the profits they make on their holdings—I don't see where that gives any right to raise the orphans and pauper kids they take in, the way they do: so's to make the poor tikes unfit for life anywhere outside."

"The object of that, as you well know, is to orient them toward the so-called interior frontier. Which American civilization as a whole is not much interested in. Frankly, quite apart from the remarkable powers some Espers have developed, I often envy them."

"You, Phil?" Mackenzie goggled at his friend.

The lines drew deep in Speyer's face. "This winter I've helped shoot a lot of my fellow countrymen," he said low. "My mother and wife and kids are crowded with the rest of the Village in the Mount Lassen fort, and when we said goodbye we knew it was quite possibly permanent. And in the past I've helped shoot a lot of other men who never did me any personal harm." He sighed. "I've often wondered what it's like to know peace, inside as well as outside."

MacKenzie sent Laura and Tom out of his head.

"Of course," Speyer went on, "the fundamental reason you—and I for that matter—distrust the Espers is that they do represent something alien to us. Something that may eventually choke out the whole concept of life that we grew up with. You know, a couple weeks back in Sacramento I dropped in at the University research lab to see what was going on. Incredible! The ordinary soldier would swear it was witch work. It was certainly more weird than . . . than simply reading minds or moving objects by thinking at them. But to you or me it's a shiny new marvel. We'll wallow in it.

"Now why's that? Because the lab is scientific. Those men work with chemical, electronics, subviral particles. That fits into the educated American's world-view. But the mystic unity of creation . . . no, not our cup of tea. The only way we can hope to achieve Oneness is to renounce everything we've ever believed in. At your age or mine, Jimbo, a man is seldom ready to tear down his whole life and start from scratch."

"Maybe so." Mackenzie lost interest. The settlement was quite near now.

He turned around to Captain Hulse, riding a few paces behind. "Here we go," he said. "Give my compliments to Lieutenant Colonel Yamaguchi and tell him he's in charge till we get back. If anything seems suspicious, he's to act at his own discretion."

"Yes, sir." Hulse saluted and wheeled smartly about. There had been no practical need for Mackenzie to repeat what had long been agreed on; but he knew the value of ritual. He clicked his big sorrel gelding into a trot. At his back he heard bugles sound orders and sergeants howl at their platoons.

Speyer kept pace. Mackenzie had insisted on bringing an extra man to the discussion. His own wits were probably no match for a high-level Esper, but Phil's might be.

Not that there's any question of diplomacy or whatever. I hope. To ease himself, he concentrated on what was real and present—hoofbeats, the rise and fall of the saddle beneath him, the horse's muscles rippling between his thighs, creak and jingle of his saber belt, the clean odor of the animal—and suddenly remembered this was the sort of trick the Espers recommended.

None of their communities was walled, as most towns and every bossman's Station was. The officers turned off the highway and went down a street between colonnaded buildings. Side streets ran off in both directions. The settlement covered no great area, though, being composed of groups that lived together, sodalities or superfamilies or whatever you wanted to call them. Some hostility toward the Order and a great many dirty jokes stemmed from that practice. But Speyer, who should know, said there was no more sexual swapping around than in the outside world. The idea was simply to get away from possessiveness, thee versus me, and to raise children as part of a whole rather than an insular clan.

The kids were out, staring round-eyed from the porticos, hundreds of them. They looked healthy and, underneath a natural fear of the invaders, happy enough. But pretty solemn, Mackenzie thought; and all in the same blue garb. Adults stood among them, expressionless. Everybody had come in from the fields as the regiment neared. The silence was like barricades. Mackenzie felt sweat begin to trickle down his ribs. When he emerged on the central square, he let out his breath in a near gasp.

A fountain, the basin carved into a lotus, tinkled at the middle of the plaza. Flowing trees stood around it. The square was defined on three sides by massive buildings that must be for storage. On the fourth side rose a smaller temple-like structure with a graceful cupola, obviously headquarters and meeting house. On its lowest step were ranked half a dozen blue-robed men, five of them husky youths. The sixth was middle-aged, the Yang and Yin on his breast. His features held an implacable calm.

Mackenzie and Speyer drew rein. The colonel flipped a soft salute. "Philosopher Gaines? I'm Mackenzie, here's Major Speyer." He swore at himself for being so awkward about it and wondered what to do with his hands. The young fellows he understood, more or less; they watched him with badly concealed hostility. But he had some trouble meeting Gaines' eyes.

The settlement leader inclined his head. "Welcome, gentlemen. Won't you come in?"

Mackenzie dismounted, hitched his horse to a post and removed his helmet. His worn reddish-brown uniform felt shabbier yet in these surroundings. "Thanks. Uh, I'll have to make this quick."

"To be sure. Follow me, please."

Stiff-backed, the young men trailed after their elders, through an entry chamber and down a short hall. Speyer looked around at the mosaics. "Why, this is lovely," he murmured.

"Thank you," said Gaines. "Here's my office." He opened a door of superbly grained walnut and gestured the visitors through. When he closed it behind himself, the acolytes waited outside.

The room was austere, whitewashed walls enclosing little more than a desk, a shelf of books, and some back-less chairs. A window opened on a garden. Gaines sat down. Mackenzie and Speyer followed suit.

"We'd better get right to business," the colonel blurted.

Gaines said nothing. At last Mackenzie must plow ahead:

"Here's the situation. Our force is to occupy Calistoga, with detachments on either side of the hills. That way we'll control both the Napa Valley and the Valley of the Moon . . . from the northern ends, at least. The best place to station our eastern wing is here. We plan to establish a fortified camp in the field yonder. I'm sorry about the damage to your crops, but you'll be compensated once the proper government has been restored. And food, medicine—you understand this army has to requisition such items, but we won't let anybody suffer undue hardship and we'll give receipts. Uh, as a precaution we'll need to quarter a few men in this community, to sort of keep an eye on things. They'll interfere as little as possible. Okay?"

"The charter of the Order guarantees exemption from military requirements," Gaines answered evenly. "In fact, no armed man is supposed to cross the boundary of any land held by an Esper settlement. I cannot be party to a violation of the law, colonel."

"If you want to split legal hairs, Philosopher," Speyer said, "then I'll remind you that both Fallon and Judge Brodsky have declared martial law. Ordinary rules are suspended."

Gaines smiled. "Since only one government can be legitimate," he said, "the proclamations of the other are necessarily null and void. To a disinterested observer, it would appear that Judge Fallon's title is the stronger, especially when his side controls a large continuous area rather than some scattered bossdoms."

"Not any more, it doesn't," Mackenzie snapped.

Speyer gestured him back. "Perhaps you haven't followed the developments of the last few weeks, Philosopher," he said. "Allow me to recapitulate. The Sierra Command stole a march on the Fallonites and came down out of the mountains. There was almost nothing left in the middle part of California to oppose us, so we took over rapidly. By occupying Sacramento, we control river and rail traffic. Our bases extend south below Bakersfield, with Yosemite and King's Canyon not far away to provide sites for extremely strong positions. When we've consolidated this northern end of our gains, the Fallonite forces around Redding will be trapped between us and the powerful bossmen who still hold out in the Trinity, Shasta, and Lassen regions. The very fact of our being here has forced the enemy to evacuate the Columbia Valley, so that San Francisco may be defended. It's an open question which side today has the larger territory."

"What about the army that went into the Sierra against you?" Gaines inquired shrewdly. "Have you contained them?"

Mackenzie scowled. "No. That's no secret. They got out through the Mother Lode country and went around us. They're down in Los Angeles and San Diego now."

"A formidable host. Do you expect to stand them off indefinitely?"

"We're going to make a hell of a good try," Mackenzie said. "Where we are, we've got the advantage of interior communications. And most of the freeholders are glad to slip us word about whatever they observe. We can concentrate at any point the enemy starts to attack."

"Pity that this rich land must also be torn apart by war."

"Yeah. Isn't it?"

"Our strategic objective is obvious enough," Speyer said. "We have cut enemy communications across the middle, except by sea, which is not very satisfactory for troops operating far inland. We deny him access to a good part of his food and manufactured supplies, and most especially to the bulk of his fuel alcohol. The backbone of our own side is the bossdoms, which are almost self-contained economic and social units. Before long they'll be in better shape than the rootless army they face. I think Judge Brodsky will be back in San Francisco before fall."

"If your plans succeed," Gaines said.

"That's our worry." Mackenzie leaned forward, one fist doubled on his knee. "Okay, Philosopher. I know you'd rather see Fallon come out on top, but I expect you've got more sense than to sign up in a lost cause. Will you cooperate with us?"

"The Order takes no part in political affairs, colonel, except when its own existence is endangered."

"Oh, pipe down. By 'cooperate' I don't mean anything but keeping out from under our feet."

"I am afraid that would still count as cooperation. We cannot have military establishments on our lands."

Mackenzie stared at Gaines' face, which had set into granite lines, and wondered if he had heard aright. "Are you ordering us off?" a stranger asked with his voice.

"Yes," the Philosopher said.

"With our artillery zeroed in on your town?"

"Would you really shell women and children, colonel?"

O Nora—"We don't need to. Our men can walk right in."

"Against psi blasts? I beg you not to have those poor boys destroyed." Gaines paused, then: "I might also point out that by losing your regiment you imperil your whole cause. You are free to march around our holdings and proceed to Calistoga."

Leaving a Fallonite nest at my back, sprang across my communications southward. The teeth grated together in Mackenzie's mouth.

Gaines rose. "This discussion is at an end, gentlemen," he said. "You have one hour to get off our lands."

Mackenzie and Speyer stood up too. "We're not done yet," the major said. Sweat studded his forehead and the long nose. "I want to make some further explanations."

Gaines crossed the room and opened the door. "Show these gentlemen out," he said to the five acolytes.

"No, by God!" Mackenzie shouted. He clapped a hand to his sidearm.

"Inform the adepts," Gaines said.

One of the young men turned. Mackenzie heard the slap-slap of his sandals, running down the hall. Gaines nodded. "I think you had better go," he said.

Speyer grew rigid. His eyes shut. They flew open and he breathed, "*Inform* the adepts?"

Mackenzie saw the stiffness break in Gaines' countenance. There was no time for more than a second's bewilderment. His body acted for him. The gun clanked from his holster simultaneously with Speyer's.

"Get that messenger, Jimbo," the major rapped. "I'll keep these birds covered."

As he plunged forward, Mackenzie found himself worrying about the regimental honor. Was it right to open hostilities when you had come on a parley? But Gaines had cut the talk off himself—

"Stop him!" Gaines yelled.

The four remaining acolytes sprang into motion. Two of them barred the doorway, the other two moved in on either side. "Hold it or I'll shoot!" Speyer cried, and was ignored.

Mackenzie couldn't bring himself to fire on unarmed men. He gave the youngster before him the pistol barrel in his teeth. Bloody-faced, the Esper lurched back. Mackenzie stiff-armed the one coming in from the left. The third tried to fill the doorway. Mackenzie put a foot behind his ankles and pushed. As he went down, Mackenzie kicked him in the temple, hard enough to stun, and jumped over him.

The fourth was on his back. Mackenzie writhed about to face the man. Those arms that hugged him, pinioning his gun, were bear strong. Mackenzie put the butt of his free left hand under the fellow's nose, and pushed. The acolyte must let go. Mackenzie gave him a knee in the stomach, whirled, and ran.

There was not much further commotion behind him. Phil must have them under control. Mackenzie pelted along the hall, into the entry chamber. Where had that goddamn runner gone? He looked out the open entrance, onto the square. Sunlight hurt his eyes. His breath came in painful gulps, there was a stitch in his side, yeah, he was getting old.

Blue robes fluttered from a street. Mackenzie recognized the messenger. The youth pointed at this building. A gabble of his words drifted faintly through Mackenzie's pulse. There were seven or eight men with him—older men, nothing to mark their clothes . . . but Mackenzie knew a high-ranking officer when he saw one. The acolyte was dismissed. Those whom he had summoned crossed the square with long strides.

Terror knotted Mackenzie's bowels. He put it down. A Catamount didn't stampede, even from somebody who could turn him inside out with a look. He could do nothing about the wretchedness that followed, though. *If they clobber me, so much the better. I won't lie awake nights wondering how Laura is.*

The adepts were almost to the steps. Mackenzie trod forth. He swept his revolver in an arc. "Halt!" His voice sounded tiny in the stillness that brooded over the town.

They jarred to a stop and stood there in a group. He saw them enforce a catlike relaxation, and their faces became blank visors. None spoke. Finally Mackenzie was unable to keep silent.

"This place is hereby occupied under the laws of war," he said. "Go back to your quarters."

"What have you done with our leader?" asked a tall man. His voice was even but deeply resonant.

"Read my mind and find out," Mackenzie gibed. *No, you're being childish.* "He's okay, long's he keeps his nose clean. You too. Beat it."

"We do not wish to pervert psionics to violence," said the tall man. "Please do not force us."

"Your chief sent for you before we'd done anything," Mackenzie retorted. "Looks like violence was what he had in mind. On your way."

The Espers exchanged glances. The tall man nodded. His companions walked slowly off. "I would like to see Philosopher Gaines," the tall man said.

"You will pretty soon."

"Am I to understand that he is being held a prisoner?"

"Understand what you like." The other Espers were rounding the corner of the building. "I don't want to shoot. Go on back before I have to."

"An impasse of sorts," the tall man said. "Neither of us wishes to injure one whom he considers defenseless. Allow me to conduct you off these grounds."

Mackenzie wet his lips. Weather had chapped them rough. "If you can put a hex on me, go ahead," he challenged. "Otherwise scram."

"Well, I shall not hinder you from rejoining your men. It seems the easiest way of getting you to leave. But I most solemnly warn that any armed force which tries to enter will be annihilated."

Guess I had better go get the boys, at that. Phil can't mount guard on those guys forever.

The tall man went over to the hitching post. "Which of these horses is yours?" he asked blandly.

Almight eager to get rid of me, isn't he—Holy hellfire! There must be a rear door!

Mackenzie spun on his heel. The Esper shouted. Mackenzie dashed back through the entry chamber. His boots threw echoes at him. No, not to the left, there's only the office that way. Right . . . around this corner—

A long hall stretched before him. A stairway curved from the middle. The other Espers were already on it.

"Halt!" Mackenzie called. "Stop or I'll shoot!"

The two men in the lead sped onward. The rest turned and headed down again, toward him.

He fired with care, to disable rather than kill. The hall reverberated with the explosions. One after another they dropped, a bullet in leg or hip or shoulder. With such small targets, Mackenzie missed some shots. As the tall man, the last of them, closed in from behind, the hammer clicked on an empty chamber.

Mackenzie drew his saber and gave him the flat of it alongside the head. The Esper lurched. Mackenzie got past and bounded up the stair. It wound like something in a nightmare. He thought his heart was going to go to pieces.

At the end, an iron door opened on a landing. One man was fumbling with the lock. The other blue-robe attacked.

Mackenzie stuck his sword between the Esper's legs. As his opponent stumbled, the colonel threw a left hook to the jaw. The man sagged against the wall. Mackenzie grabbed the robe of the other and hurled him to the floor. "Get out," he rattled.

They pulled themselves together and glared at him. He thrust air with his blade. "From now on I aim to kill," he said.

"Get help, Dave," said the one who had been opening the door. "I'll watch him." The other went unevenly down the stairs. The first man stood out of saber reach. "Do you want to be destroyed?" he asked.

Mackenzie turned the knob at his back, but the door

was still locked. "I don't think you can do it. Not without what's here."

The Esper struggled for self-control. They waited through minutes that stretched. Then a noise began below. The Esper pointed. "We have nothing but agricultural implements," he said, "but you have only that blade. Will you surrender?"

Mackenzie spat on the floor. The Esper went on down.

Presently the attackers came into view. There might be a hundred, judging from the hubbub behind them, but because of the curve Mackenzie could see no more than ten or fifteen—burly fieldhands, their robes tucked high and sharp tools aloft. The landing was too wide for defense. He advanced to the stairway, where they could only come at him two at a time.

A couple of sawtoothed hay knives led the assault. Mackenzie parried one blow and chopped. His edge went into meat and struck bone. Blood ran out, impossibly red, even in the dim light here. The man fell to all fours with a shriek. Mackenzie dodged a cut from the companion. Metal clashed on metal. The weapons locked. Mackenzie's arm was forced back. He looked into a broad suntanned face. The side of his hand smote the young man's larynx. The Esper fell against the one behind and they went down together. It took a while to clear the tangle and resume action.

A pitchfork thrust for the colonel's belly. He managed to grab it with his left hand, divert the tines, and chop at the fingers on the shaft. A scythe gashed his right side. He saw his own blood but wasn't aware of pain. A flesh wound, no more. He swept his saber back and forth. The forefront retreated from its whistling menace. *But God, my knees are like rubber, I can't hold out another five minutes.*

A bugle sounded. There was a spatter of gunfire. The mob on the staircase congealed. Someone screamed.

Hoofs banged across the ground floor. A voice rasped: "Hold everything, there! Drop those weapons and come on down. First man tries anything gets shot."

Mackenzie leaned on his saber and fought for air. He hardly noticed the Espers melt away.

When he felt a little better, he went to one of the

small windows and looked out. Horsemen were in the plaza. Not yet in sight, but nearing, he heard infantry.

Speyer arrived, followed by a sergeant of engineers and several privates. The major hurried to Mackenzie. "You okay, Jimbo? You been hurt!"

"A scratch" Mackenzie said. He was getting back his strength, though no sense of victory accompanied it, only the knowledge of aloneness. The injury began to sting. "Not worth a fuss. Look."

'Yes, I suppose you'll live. Okay, men, get that door open."

The engineers took forth their tools and assailed the lock with a vigor that must spring half from fear. "How'd you guys show up so soon?" Mackenzie asked.

"I thought there'd be trouble," Speyer said, "so when I heard shots I jumped through the window and ran around to my horse. That was just before those clodhoppers attacked you; I saw them gathering as I rode out. Our cavalry got in almost at once, of course, and the dogfaces weren't far behind."

"Any resistance?"

"No, not after we fired a few rounds in the air." Speyer glanced outside. "We're in full possession now."

Mackenzie regarded the door. "Well," he said, "I feel better about our having pulled guns on them in the office. Looks like their adepts really depend on plain old weapons, huh? And Esper communities aren't supposed to have arms. Their charters say so. . . . That was a damn good guess of yours, Phil. How'd you do it?"

"I sort of wondered why the chief had to send a runner to fetch guys that claim to be telepaths. There we go!"

The lock jingled apart. The sergeant opened the door. Mackenzie and Speyer went into the great room under the dome.

They walked around for a long time, wordless, among shapes of metal and less identifiable substances. Nothing was familiar. Mackenzie paused at last before a helix which projected from a transparent cube. Formless darknesses swirled within the box, sparked as if with tiny stars.

"I figured maybe the Espers had found a cache of old-time stuff, from just before the Hellbombs," he said in a muffled voice. "Ultrasecret weapons that never got a chance to be used. But this doesn't look like it, think so?"

"No," Speyer said. "It doesn't look to me as if these things were made by human beings at all."

"But do you not understand? They occupied a settlement! That proves to the world that Espers are not invulnerable. And to complete the catastrophe, they seized its arsenal."

"Have no fears about that. No untrained person can activate those instruments. The circuits are locked except in the presence of certain encephalic rhythms which result from conditioning. That same conditioning makes it impossible for the so-called adepts to reveal any of their knowledge to the uninitiated, no matter what may be done to them."

"Yes, I know that much. But it is not what I had in mind. What frightens me is the fact that the revelation will spread. Everyone will know the Esper adepts do not plumb unknown depths of the psyche after all, but merely have access to an advanced physical science. Not only will this lift rebel spirits, but worse, it will cause many, perhaps most of the Order's members to break away in disillusionment."

"Not at once. News travels slowly under present conditions. Also, Mwyr, you underestimate the ability of the human mind to ignore data which conflict with cherished beliefs."

"But—"

"Well, let us assume the worst. Let us suppose that faith is lost and the Order disintegrates. That will be a serious setback to the plan, but not a fatal one. Psionics was merely one bit of folklore we found potent enough to serve as the motivator of a new orientation toward life. There are others, for example the widespread belief in magic among the less educated classes. We can begin again on a different basis, if we must. The exact form of the creed is not important. It is only scaffolding for the real structure: a communal, anti-materialistic social group, to which more and more people will turn for sheer lack of anything else, as the coming empire breaks up. In the end, the new

culture can and will discard whatever superstitions gave it the intial impetus."

"A hundred-year setback, at least."

"True. It would be much more difficult to introduce a radical alien element now, when the autochthonous society has developed strong institutions of its own, than it was in the past. I merely wish to reassure you that the task is not impossible. I do not actually propose to let matters go that far. The Espers can be salvaged."

"How?"

"We must intervene directly."

"Has that been computed as being unavoidable?"

"Yes. The matrix yields an unambigous answer. I do not like it any better than you. But direct action occurs oftener than we tell neophytes in the schools. The most elegant procedure would of course be to establish such initial conditions in a society that its evolution along desired lines becomes automatic. Furthermore, that would let us close our minds to the distressing fact of our own blood guilt. Unfortunately, the Great Science does not extend down to the details of day-to-day practicality.

"In the present instance, we shall help to smash the reactionaries. The government will then proceed so harshly against its conquered opponents that many of those who accept the story about what was found at St. Helena will not live to spread the tale. The rest . . . well, they will be discredited by their own defeat. Admittedly, the story will linger for lifetimes, whispered here and there. But what of that? Those who believe in the Way will, as a rule, simply be strengthened in their faith, by the very process of denying such ugly rumors. As more and more persons, common citizens as well as Espers, reject materialism, the legend will seem more and more fantastic. It will seem obvious that certain ancients invented the tale to account for a fact that they in their ignorance were unable to comprehend."

"I see. . . ."

"You are not happy here, are you, Mwyr?"

"I cannot quite say. Everything is so distorted."

"Be glad you were not sent to one of the really alien planets."

"I might almost prefer that. There would be a hostile

environment to think about. One could forget how far it is to home."

"Three years' travel."

"You say that so glibly. As if three shipboard years were not equal to fifty in cosmic time. As if we could expect a relief vessel daily, not once in a century. And . . . as if the region that our ships have explored amounts to one chip out of this one galaxy!"

"That region will grow until someday it engulfs the galaxy!"

"Yes, yes, yes. I know. Why do you think I chose to become a psychodynamician? Why am I here, learning how to meddle with the destiny of a world where I do not belong? 'To create the union of sentient beings, each member species a step toward life's mastery of the universe.' Brave slogan! But in practice, it seems, only a chosen few races are to be allowed the freedom of that universe."

"Not so, Mwyr. Consider these ones with whom we are, as you say, meddling. Consider what use they made of nuclear energy when they had it. At the rate they are going, they will have it again within a century or two. Not long after that they will be building spaceships. Even granted that time lag attenuates the effects of interstellar contact, those effects are cumulative. So do you wish such a band of carnivores turned loose on the galaxy?

"No, let them become inwardly civilized first; then we shall see if they can be trusted. If not, they will at least be happy on their own planet, in a mode of life designed for them by the Great Science. Remember, they have an immemorial aspiration toward peace on earth; but that is something they will never achieve by themselves. I do not pretend to be a very good person, Mwyr. Yet this work that we are doing makes me feel not altogether useless in the cosmos."

Promotion was fast that year, casualties being so high. Captain Thomas Danielis was raised to major for his conspicuous part in putting down the revolt of the Los Angeles citymen. Soon after occurred the Battle of Maricopa, when the loyalists failed bloodily to break the stranglehold of the Sierran rebels on the San Joaquin Valley, and he was brevetted lieutenant colonel. The army was ordered northward and moved warily under the coast ranges, half expecting attack from the east. But the Brodskyites seemed too busy consolidating their latest gains. The trouble came from guerrillas and the hedgehog resistance of bossman Stations. After one particularly stiff clash, they stopped near Pinnacles for a breather.

Danielis made his way through camp, where tents stood in tight rows between the guns and men lay about dozing, talking, gambling, staring at the blank blue sky. The air was hot, pungent with cookfire smoke, horses, mules, dung, sweat, boot oil; the green of the hills that lifted around the site was dulling toward summer brown. He was idle until time for the conference the general had called, but restlessness drove him. *By now I'm a father*, he thought, *and I've never seen my kid.*

At that, I'm lucky, he reminded himself. *I've got my life and limbs.* He remembered Jacobsen dying in his arms at Maricopa. You wouldn't have thought the human body could hold so much blood. Though maybe one was no longer human, when the pain was so great that one could do nothing but shriek until the darkness came.

And I used to think war was glamorous. Hunger, thirst, exhaustion, terror, mutilation, death, and forever the sameness, boredom grinding you down to an ox . . . I've had it. I'm going into business after the war. Economic integration, as the bossman system breaks up, yes, there'll be a lot of ways for a man to get ahead, but decently, without a weapon in his hand—Danielis realized he was repeating thoughts that were months old. What the hell else was there to think about, though?

The large tent where prisoners were interrogated lay near his path. A couple of privates were conducting a man inside. The fellow was blond, burly, and sullen. He wore a sergeant's stripes, but otherwise his only item of uniform was the badge of Warden Echevarry, bossman in this part of the coastal mountains. A lumberjack in peacetime, Danielis guessed from the look of him; a soldier in a private army whenever the interests of Echevarry were threatened; captured in yesterday's engagement.

On impulse, Danielis followed. He got into the tent as

Captain Lambert, chubby behind a portable desk, finished the preliminaries.

"Oh." The intelligence officer started to rise. "Yes, sir?"

"At ease," Danielis said. "Just thought I'd listen in."

"Well, I'll try to put on a good show for you." Lambert reseated himself and looked at the prisoner, who stood with hunched shoulders and widespread legs between his guards. "Now, sergeant, we'd like to know a few things."

"I don't have to say nothing except name, rank, and home town," the man growled. "You got those."

"Um-m-m, that's questionable. You aren't a foreign soldier, you're a rebel against the government of your own country."

"The hell I am! I'm an Echevarry man."

"So what?"

"So my Judge is whoever Echevarry says. He says Brodsky. That makes you the rebel."

"The law's been changed."

"Your mucking Fallon got no right to change any laws. Especially part of the Constitution. I'm no hillrunner, captain. I went to school some. And every year our Warden reads his people the Constitution."

"Times have changed since it was drawn," Lambert said. His tone sharpened. "But I'm not going to argue with you. How many riflemen and how many archers in your company?"

Silence.

"We can make things a lot easier for you," Lambert said. "I'm not asking you to do anything treasonable. All I want is to confirm some information I've already got."

The man shook his head angrily.

Lambert gestured. One of the privates stepped behind the captive, took his arm, and twisted a little.

"Echevarry wouldn't do that to me," he said through white lips.

"Of course not," Lambert said. "You're his man."

"Think I wanna be just a number on some list in Frisco? Damn right I'm my bossman's man!"

Lambert gestured again. The private twisted harder.

"Hold on, there," Danielis barked. "Stop that!"

The private let go, looking surprised. The prisoner drew a sobbing breath.

"I'm amazed at you, Captain Lambert," Danielis said. He felt his own face reddening. "If this has been your practice, there's going to be a courtmartial."

"No, sir," Lambert said in a small voice. "Honest. Only . . . they don't talk. Hardly any of them. What'm I supposed to do?"

"Follow the rules of war."

"With rebels?"

"Take that man away," Danielis ordered. The privates made haste to do so.

"Sorry, sir," Lambert muttered. "I guess . . . I guess I've lost too many buddies. I hate to lose more, simply for lack of information."

"Me too." A compassion rose in Danielis. He sat down on the table edge and began to roll a cigaret. "But you see, we aren't in a regular war. And so, by a curious paradox, we have to follow the conventions more carefully than ever before."

"I don't quite understand, sir."

Danielis finished the cigaret and gave it to Lambert: olive branch or something. He started another for himself. "The rebels aren't rebels by their own lights," he said. "They're being loyal to a tradition that we're trying to curb, eventually to destroy. Let's face it, the average bossman is a fairly good leader. He may be descended from some thug who grabbed power by strong-arm methods during the chaos, but by now his family's integrated itself with the region he rules. He knows it, and its people, inside out. He's there in the flesh, a symbol of the community and its achievements, its folkways and essential independence. If you're in trouble, you don't have to work through some impersonal bureaucracy, you go direct to your bossman. His duties are as clearly defined as your own, and a good deal more demanding, to balance his privileges. He leads you in battle and in the ceremonies that give color and meaning to life. Your fathers and his have worked and played together for two or three hundred years. The land is alive with the memories of them. You and he *belong*.

"Well, that has to be swept away, so we can go on to

a higher level. But we won't reach that level by alienating everyone. We're not a conquering army; we're more like the Householder Guard putting down a riot in some city. The opposition is part and parcel of our own society."

Lambert struck a match for him. He inhaled and finished: "On a practical plane, I might also remind you, captain, that the federal armed forces, Fallonite and Brodskyite together, are none too large. Little more than a cadre, in fact. We're a bunch of younger sons, countrymen who failed, poor citymen, adventurers, people who look to their regiment for that sense of wholeness they've grown up to expect and can't find in civilian life."

"You're too deep for me, sir, I'm afraid," Lambert said.

"Never mind," Danielis sighed. "Just bear in mind, there are a good many more fighting men outside the opposing armies than in. If the bossmen could establish a unified command, that'd be the end of the Fallon government. Luckily, there's too much provincial pride and too much geography between them for this to happen—unless we outrage them beyond endurance. What we want the ordinary freeholder, and even the ordinary bossman, to think, is: 'Well, those Fallonites aren't such bad guys, and if I keep on the right side of them I don't stand to lose much, and should even be able to gain something at the expense of those who fight them to a finish.' You see?"

"Y-yes. I guess so."

"You're a smart fellow, Lambert. You don't have to beat information out of prisoners. Trick it out."

"I'll try, sir."

"Good." Danielis glanced at the watch that had been given him as per tradition, together with a sidearm, when he was first commissioned. (Such items were much too expensive for the common man. They had not been so in the age of mass production; and perhaps in the coming age—) "I have to go. See you around."

He left the tent feeling somewhat more cheerful than before. *No doubt I am a natural-born preacher,* he admitted, *and I never could quite join in the horseplay at mess, and a lot of jokes go completely by me; but if I can get even a few ideas across where they count, that's pleasure enough.* A strain of music came to him, some men and a banjo under a tree, and he found himself whistling along. It was good that this much morale remained, after Maricopa and a northward march whose purpose had not been divulged to anybody.

The conference tent was big enough to be called a pavilion. Two sentries stood at the entrance. Danielis was nearly the last to arrive, and found himself at the end of the table, opposite Brigadier General Perez. Smoke hazed the air and there was a muted buzz of conversation, but faces were taut.

When the blue-robed figure with a Yang and Yin on the breast entered, silence fell like a curtain. Danielis was astonished to recognize Philosopher Woodworth. He'd last seen the man in Los Angeles, and assumed he would stay at the Esper center there. Must have come here by special conveyance, under special orders. . . .

Perez introduced him. Both remained standing, under the eyes of the officers. "I have some important news for you, gentlemen," Perez said most quietly. "You may consider it an honor to be here. It means that in my judgment you can be trusted, first, to keep absolute silence about what you are going to hear, and second, to execute a vital operation of extreme difficulty." Danielis was made shockingly aware that several men were not present whose rank indicated they should be.

"I repeat," Perez said, "any breach of secrecy and the whole plan is ruined. In that case, the war will drag on for months or years. You know how bad our position is. You also know it will grow still worse as our stocks of those supplies the enemy now denies us are consumed. We could even be beaten. I'm not defeatist to say that, only realistic. We could lose the war."

"On the other hand, if this new scheme pans out, we may break the enemy's back this very month."

He paused to let that sink in before continuing:

"The plan was worked out by GHQ in conjunction with Esper Central in San Francisco, some weeks ago. It's the reason we are headed north—" He let the gasp subside that ran through the stifling air. "Yes, you know that the Esper Order is neutral in political disputes. But you also know that it defends itself when attacked. And you probably know that an attack was made on it, by the rebels. They seized the Napa Valley settlement and have been spreading malicious rumors about the Order since then. Would you like to comment on that, Philosopher Woodworth?"

The man in blue nodded and said coolly: "We've our own ways of findin' out things—intelligence service, you might say—so I can give y'all a report of the facts. St. Helena was assaulted at a time when most of its adepts were away, helpin' a new community get started out in Montana." *How did they travel so fast?* Danielis wondered. *Teleport, or what?* "I don't know, myself, if the enemy knew about that or were just lucky. Anyhow, when the two or three adepts that were left came and warned them off, fightin' broke out and the adepts were killed before they could act." He smiled. "We don't claim to be immortal, except the way every livin' thing is immortal. Nor infallible, either. So now St. Helena's occupied. We don't figure to take any immediate steps about that, because a lot of people in the community might get hurt.

"As for the yarns the enemy command's been handin' out, well, I reckon I'd do the same, if I had a chance like that. Everybody knows an adept can do things that nobody else can. Troops that realize they've done wrong to the Order are goin' to be scared of supernatural revenge. You're educated men here, and know there's nothin' supernatural involved, just a way to use the powers latent in most of us. You also know the Order doesn't believe in revenge. But the ordinary foot soldier doesn't think your way. His officers have got to restore his spirit somehow. So they fake some equipment and tell him that's what the adepts were really usin'—an advanced technology, sure, but only a set of machines, that can be put out of action if you're brave, same as any other machine. That's what happened.

"Still, it is a threat to the Order; and we can't let an attack on our people go unpunished, either. So Esper Central has decided to help out your side. The sooner this war's over, the better."

A sigh gusted around the table, and a few exultant

oaths. The hair stirred on Danielis' neck. Perez lifted a hand.

"Not too fast, please," the general said. "The adepts are not going to go around blasting your opponents for you. It was one hell of a tough decision for them to do as much as they agreed to. I, uh, understand that the, uh, personal development of every Esper will be set back many years by this much violence. They're making a big sacrifice.

"By their charter, they can use psionics to defend an establishment against attack. Okay . . . an assault on San Francisco will be construed as one on Central, their world headquarters."

The realization of what was to come was blinding to Danielis. He scarcely heard Perez' carefully dry continuation:

"Let's review the strategic picture. By now the enemy holds more than half of California, all of Oregon and Idaho, and a good deal of Washington. We, this army, we're using the last land access to San Francisco that we've got. The enemy hasn't tried to pinch that off yet, because the troops we pulled out of the north—those that aren't in the field at present—make a strong city garrison that'd sally out. He's collecting too much profit elsewhere to accept the cost.

"Nor can he invest the city with any hope of success. We still hold Puget Sound and the southern California ports. Our ships bring in ample food and munitions. His own sea power is much inferior to ours: chiefly schooners donated by coastal bossmen, operating out of Portland. He might overwhelm an occasional convoy, but he hasn't tried that so far because it isn't worth his trouble; there would be others, more heavily escorted. And of course he can't enter the Bay, with artillery and rocket emplacements on both sides of the Golden Gate. No, about all he can do is maintain some water communication with Hawaii and Alaska.

"Nevertheless, his ultimate object is San Francisco. It has to be—the seat of government and industry, the heart of the nation.

"Well, then, here's the plan. Our army is to engage the Sierra Command and its militia auxiliaries again, striking out of San Jose. That's a perfectly logical maneuver. Successful, it would cut his California forces in two. We know, in fact, that he is already concentrating men in anticipation of precisely such an attempt.

"We aren't going to succeed. We'll give him a good stiff battle and be thrown back. That's the hardest part: to feign a serious defeat, even convincing our own troops, and still maintain good order. We'll have a lot of details to thresh out about that.

"We'll retreat northward, up the Peninsula toward Frisco. The enemy is bound to pursue. It will look like a God-given chance to destroy us and get to the city.

"When he is well into the Peninsula, with the ocean on his left and the Bay on his right, we will outflank him and attack from the rear. The Esper adepts will be there to help. Suddenly he'll be caught, between us and the capital's land defenses. What the adepts don't wipe out, we will. Nothing will remain of the Sierra Command but a few garrisons. The rest of the war will be a mopping up operation.

"It's a brilliant piece of strategy. Like all such, it's damn difficult to execute. Are you prepared to do the job?"

Danielis didn't raise his voice with the others. He was thinking too hard of Laura.

Northward and to the right there was some fighting. Cannon spoke occasionally, or a drumfire of rifles; smoke lay thin over the grass and the wind-gnarled live oaks which covered those hills. But down along the seacoast was only surf, blowing air, a hiss of sand across the dunes.

Mackenzie rode on the beach, where the footing was easiest and the view widest. Most of his regiment were inland. But that was a wilderness: rough ground, woods, the snags of ancient homes, making travel slow and hard. Once this area had been densely peopled, but the firestorm after the Hellbomb scrubbed it clean and today's reduced population could not make a go on such infertile soil. There didn't even seem to be any foemen near this left wing of the army.

The Rolling Stones had certainly not been given it for

that reason. They could have borne the brunt at the center as well as those outfits which actually were there, driving the enemy back toward San Francisco. They had been blooded often enough in this war, when they operated out of Calistoga to help expel the Fallonites from northern California. So thoroughly had that job been done that now only a skeleton force need remain in charge. Nearly the whole Sierra Command had gathered at Modesto, met the northward-moving opposition army that struck at them out of San Jose, and sent it in a shooting retreat. Another day or so, and the white city should appear before their eyes.

And there the enemy will be sure to make a stand, Mackenzie thought, *with the garrison to reinforce him. And his positions will have to be shelled; maybe we'll have to take the place street by street. Laura, kid, will you be alive at the end?*

Of course, maybe it won't happen that way. Maybe my scheme'll work and we'll win easy—What a horrible word "maybe" is! He slapped his hands together with a pistol sound.

Speyer threw him a glance. The major's people were safe; he'd even been able to visit them at Mount Lassen, after the northern campaign was over. "Rough," he said.

"Rough on everybody," Mackenzie said with a thick anger. "This is a filthy war."

Speyer shrugged. "No different from most, except that this time Pacificans are on the receiving as well as the giving end."

"You know damn well I never liked the business, anyplace."

"What man in his right mind does?"

"When I want a sermon I'll ask for one."

"Sorry," said Speyer, and meant it.

"I'm sorry too," said Mackenzie, instantly contrite. "Nerves on edge. Damnation! I could almost wish for some action."

"Wouldn't be surprised if we got some. This whole affair smells wrong to me."

Mackenzie looked around him. On the right the horizon was bounded by hills, beyond which the low but massive San Bruno range lifted. Here and there he spied one of his own squads, afoot or ahorse. Overhead sputtered a plane. But there was plenty of concealment for a redoubt. Hell could erupt at any minute . . . though necessarily a small hell, quickly reduced by howitzer or bayonet, casualties light. (Huh! Every one of those light casualties was a man dead, with women and children to weep for him, or a man staring at the fragment of his arm, or a man with eyes and face gone in a burst of shot, and what kind of unsoldierly thoughts were these?)

Seeking comfort, Mackenzie glanced left. The ocean rolled greenish gray, glittering far out, rising and breaking in a roar of white combers closer to land. He smelled salt and kelp. A few gulls mewed above dazzling sands. There was no sail or smokepuff—only emptiness. The convoys from Puget Sound to San Francisco, and the lean swift ships of the coastal bossmen, were miles beyond the curve of the world.

Which was as it should be. Maybe things were working out okay on the high waters. One could only try, and hope. And . . . it had been his suggestion, James Mackenzie speaking at the conference General Cruikshank held between the battles of Mariposa and San Jose; the same James Mackenzie who had first proposed that the Sierra Command come down out of the mountains, and who had exposed the gigantic fraud of Esperdom, and succeeded in playing down for his men the fact that behind the fraud lay a mystery one hardly dared think about. He would endure in the chronicles, that colonel, they would sing ballads about him for half a thousand years.

Only it didn't feel that way. James Mackenzie knew he was not much more than average bright under the best of conditions, now dull-minded with weariness and terrified of his daughter's fate. For himself he was haunted by the fear of certain crippling wounds. Often he had to drink himself to sleep. He was shaved, because an officer must maintain appearances, but realized very well that if he hadn't had an orderly to do the job for him he would be as shaggy as any buck private. His uniform was faded and threadbare, his body stank and itched, his mouth yearned for tobacco but there had been some trouble in the commissariat and they were lucky to eat. His achievements amounted to patchwork jobs carried out in utter confusion, or to slogging like this and wishing only for an end to the whole mess. One day, win or lose, his body would give out on him—he could feel the machinery wearing to pieces, arthritic twinges, shortness of breath, dozing off in the middle of things—and the termination of himself would be as undignified and lonely as that of every other human slob. Hero? What an all time laugh!

He yanked his mind back to the immediate situation. Behind him a core of the regiment accompanied the artillery along the beach, a thousand men with motorized gun carriages, caissons, mule-drawn wagons, a few trucks, one precious armored car. They were a dun mass topped with helmets, in loose formation, rifles or bows to hand. The sand deadened their footfalls, so that only the surf and the wind could be heard. But whenever the wind sank, Mackenzie caught the tune of the hex corps: a dozen leathery older men, mostly Indians, carrying the wands of power and whistling together the Song Against Witches. He took no stock in magic himself, yet when that sound came to him the skin crawled along his backbone.

Everything's in good order, he insisted. *We're doing fine.*

Then: *But Phil's right. This is a screwball business. The enemy should have fought through to a southward line of retreat, not let themselves be boxed.*

Captain Hulse galloped close. Sand spurted when he checked his horse. "Patrol report, sir."

"Well?" Mackenzie realized he had almost shouted. "Go ahead."

"Considerable activity observed about five miles northeast. Looks like a troop headed our way."

Mackenzie stiffened. "Haven't you anything more definite than that?"

"Not so far, with the ground so broken."

"Get some aerial reconnaissance there, for Pete's sake!"

"Yes, sir. I'll throw out more scouts, too."

"Carry on here, Phil." Mackenzie headed toward the radio truck. He carried a minicom in his saddlebag, of course, but San Francisco had been continuously jamming on all bands and you needed a powerful set to punch a signal even a few miles. Patrols must communicate by messenger.

He noticed that the firing inland had slacked off. There were decent roads in the interior Peninsula a ways further north, where some resettlement had taken place. The enemy, still in possession of that area, could use them to effect rapid movements.

If they withdrew their center and hit our flanks, where we're weakest—

A voice from field HQ, barely audible through the squeals and buzzes, took his report and gave back what had been seen elsewhere. Large maneuvers right and left, yes, it did seem as if the Fallonites were going to try a breakthrough. Could be a feint, though. The main body of the Sierrans must remain where it was until the situation became clearer. The Rolling Stones must hold out a while on their own.

"Will do." Mackenzie returned to the head of his columns. Speyer nodded grimly at the word.

"Better get prepared, hadn't we?"

"Uh-huh." Mackenzie lost himself in a welter of commands, as officer after officer rode to him. The outlying sections were to be pulled in. The beach was to be defended, with the high ground immediately above.

Men scurried, horses neighed, guns trundled about. The scout plane returned, flying low enough to get a transmission through: yes, definitely an attack on the way; hard to tell how big a force, through the damned tree cover and down in the damned arroyos, but it might well be at brigade strength.

Mackenzie established himself on a hilltop with his staff and runners. A line of artillery stretched beneath him, across the strand. Cavalry waited behind them, lances agleam, an infantry company for support. Otherwise the foot soldiers had faded into the landscape. The sea boomed its own cannonade, and gulls began to gather as if they knew there would be meat before long.

"Think we can hold them?" Speyer asked.

"Sure," Mackenzie said. "If they come down the beach, we'll enfilade them, as well as shooting up their front. If they come higher, well, that's a textbook example of defensible terrain. 'Course, if another troop punches through the lines further inland, we'll be cut off, but that isn't our worry right now."

"They must hope to get around our army and attack our rear."

"Guess so. Not too smart of them, though. We can approach Frisco just as easily fighting backwards as forwards."

"Unless the city garrison makes a sally."

"Even then. Total numerical strengths are about equal, and we've got more ammo and alky. Also a lot of bossman militia for auxiliaries, who're used to disorganized warfare in hilly ground."

"If we do whip them—" Speyer shut his lips together.

"Go on," Mackenzie said.

"Nothing."

"The hell it is. You were about to remind me of the next step: how do we take the city without too high a cost to both sides? Well, I happen to know we've got a hole card to play there, which might help."

Speyer turned pitying eyes away from Mackenzie. Silence fell on the hilltop.

It was an unconscionably long time before the enemy came in view, first a few outriders far down the dunes, then the body of him, pouring from the ridges and gullies and woods. Reports flickered about Mackenzie—a powerful force, nearly twice as big as ours, but with little artillery; by now badly short of fuel, they must depend far more than we on animals to move their equipment. They were evidently going to charge, accept losses in order to get sabers and bayonets among the Rolling Stones' cannon. Mackenzie issued his directions accordingly.

The hostiles formed up, a mile or so distant. Through his field glasses Mackenzie recognized them, red sashes of the Madera Horse, green and gold pennon of the Dagos, fluttering in the iodine wind. He'd campaigned with both outfits in the past. It was treacherous to remember that Ives favored a blunt wedge formation and use the fact against him. . . . One enemy armored car and some fieldpieces, light horse-drawn ones, gleamed wickedly in the sunlight.

Bugles blew shrill. The Fallonite cavalry laid lance in rest and started trotting. They gathered speed as they went, a canter, a gallop, until the earth trembled with them. Then their infantry got going, flanked by its guns. The car rolled along between the first and second line of foot. Oddly, it had no rocket launcher on top or repeater barrels thrust from the fire slits. Those were good troops, Mackenzie thought, advancing in close order with that ripple down the ranks which bespoke veterans. He hated what must happen.

His defense waited immobile on the sand. Fire crackled from the hillsides, where mortar squads and riflemen crouched. A rider toppled, a dogface clutched his belly and went to his knees, their companions behind moved forward to close the lines again. Mackenzie looked to his howitzers. Men stood tensed at sights and lanyards. Let the foe get well in range—There! Yamaguchi, mounted just rearward of the gunners, drew his saber and flashed the blade downward. Cannon bellowed. Fire spurted through smoke, and gouted up, shrapnel sleeted over the charging force. At once the gun crews fell into the rhythm of reloading, relaying, refiring, the steady three rounds per minute which conserved barrels and broke armies. Horses screamed in their own tangled red guts. But not many had been hit. The Madera cavalry continued in full gallop. Their lead was so close now that Mackenzie's glasses picked out a face, red, freckled, a ranch boy turned trooper, his mouth stretched out of shape as he yelled.

The archers behind the defending cannon let go. Arrows whistled skyward, flight after flight, curved past the gulls and down again. Flame and smoke ran ragged in the wiry hill grass, out of the ragged-leaved live oak copses. Men pitched to the sand, many still hideously astir, like insects that had been stepped on. The fieldpieces on the enemy left flank halted, swiveled about, and spat return fire. Futile . . . but God, their officer had courage! Mackenzie saw the advancing lines waver. An attack by his own horse and foot, down the beach, ought to crumple them. "Get ready to move," he said into his minicom. He saw his men poise.

The oncoming armored car slewed to a halt. Something within it chattered, loud enough to hear through the explosions.

A blue-white sheet ran over the nearest hill. Mackenzie shut half-blinded eyes. When he opened them again, he saw a grass fire through the crazy patterns of afterimage. A Rolling Stone burst from cover, howling, his clothes ablaze. The man hit the sand and rolled over. That part of the beach lifted in one monster wave, crested twenty feet high, and smashed across the hill. The burning soldier vanished in the avalanche that buried his comrades.

"*Psi blast!*" someone screamed, thin and horrible, through chaos and ground-shudder. "The Espers—"

Unbelievably, a bugle sounded and the Sierran cavalry lunged forward. Past their own guns, on against the scattering opposition . . . and horses and riders rose into the air, tumbled in a giant's invisible whirligig, crashed bonebreakingly to earth again. The second rank of lancers broke. Mounts reared, pawed the air, wheeled and fled in every direction.

A terrible deep hum filled the sky. Mackenzie saw the world as if through a haze, as if his brain were being dashed back and forth between the walls of his skull. Another glare ran across the hills, higher this time, burning men alive.

"They'll wipe us out," Speyer called, a dim voice that rose and fell on the air tides. "They'll reform as we stampede—"

"No!" Mackenzie shouted. "The adepts must be in that car. Come on!"

Most of his horse had recoiled on their own artillery, one squealing, trampling wreck. The infantry stood rigid, but about to bolt. A glance thrown to his right showed Mackenzie how the enemy themselves were in confusion, this had been a terrifying surprise to them too, but as soon as they got over the shock they'd advance and there'd be nothing left to stop them. . . . It was as if another man spurred his mount. The animal fought, foam-flecked with panic. He slugged its head around, brutally, and dug in spurs. They rushed down the hill toward the guns.

He needed all his strength to halt the gelding before the cannon mouths. A man slumped dead by his piece, though there was no mark on him. Mackenzie jumped to the ground. His steed bolted.

He hadn't time to worry about that. Where was help? "Come here!" His yell was lost in the riot. But suddenly another man was beside him, Speyer, snatching up a shell and slamming it into the breach. Mackenzie squinted through the telescope, took a bearing by guess and feel. He could see the Esper car where it squatted among dead and hurt. At this distance it looked too small to have blackened acres.

Speyer helped him lay the howitzer. He jerked the lanyard. The gun roared and sprang. The shell burst a few yards short of target, sand spurted and metal fragments whined.

Speyer had the next one loaded. Mackenzie aimed and fired. Overshot this time, but not by much. The car rocked. Concussion might have hurt the Espers inside; at least, the psi blasts had stopped. But it was necessary to strike before the foe got organized again.

He ran toward his own regimental car. The door gaped, the crew had fled. He threw himself into the driver's seat. Speyer clanged the door shut and stuck his face in the hood of the rocket launcher periscope. Mackenzie raced the machine forward. The banner on its rooftop snapped in the wind.

Speyer aimed the launcher and pressed the firing button. The missile burned across intervening yards and exploded. The other car lurched on its wheels. A hole opened in its side.

If the boys will only rally and advance—Well, if they don't, I'm done for anyway. Mackenzie squealed to a stop, flung open the door and leaped out. Curled, blackened metal framed his entry. He wriggled through, into murk and stenches.

Two Espers lay there. The driver was dead, a chunk of steel through his breast. The other one, the adept, whimpered among his unhuman instruments. His face was hidden by blood. Mackenzie pitched the corpse on its side and pulled off the robe. He snatched a curving tube of metal and tumbled back out.

Speyer was still in the undamaged car, firing repeaters at those hostiles who ventured near. Mackenzie jumped onto the ladder of the disabled machine, climbed to its roof and stood erect. He waved the blue robe in one hand and the weapon he did not understand in the other. "Come on, you sons!"he shouted, tiny against the sea wind. "We've knocked 'em out for you! Want your breakfast in bed too?"

One bullet buzzed past his ear. Nothing else. Most of the enemy, horse and foot, stayed frozen. In that immense stillness he could not tell if he heard surf or the blood in his own veins.

Then a bugle called. The hex corps whistled trumphantly; their tomtoms thuttered. A ragged line of his infantry began to move toward him. More followed. The cavalry joined them, man by man and unit by unit, on their flanks. Soldiers ran down the smoking hillsides.

Mackenzie sprang to sand again and into his car. "Let's get back," he told Speyer. "We got a battle to finish."

"Shut up!" Tom Danielis said.

Philosopher Woodworth stared at him. Fog swirled and dripped in the forest, hiding the land and the brigade, gray nothingness through which came a muffled noise of men and horses and wheels, an isolated and infinitely weary sound. The air was cold, and clothing hung heavy on the skin.

"Sir," protested Major Lescarbault, eyes wide and shocked.

"I dare tell a ranking Esper to stop quacking about a subject of which he's totally ignorant?" Danielis answered. "Well, it's past time that somebody did."

Woodworth recovered his poise. "All I said, son, was that we should consolidate our adepts and strike the Brodskyite center," he reproved. "What's wrong with that?"

Danielis clenched his fists. "Nothing," he said, "except it invites a worse disaster than you've brought on us yet."

"A setback or two," Lescarbault argued. "They did rout us on the west, but we turned their flank here by the Bay."

"With the net result that their main body pivoted, attacked, and split us in half," Danielis snapped. "The Espers have been scant use since then . . . now the rebels know they need vehicles to transport their weapons, and can be killed. Artillery zeroes in on their positions, or bands of woodsmen hit and run, leaving them dead, or the enemy simply goes around any spot where they're known to be. We haven't got enough adepts!"

"That's why I proposed gettin' them in one group, too big to withstand," Woodworth said.

"And too cumbersome to be of any value," Danielis replied. He felt more than a little sickened, knowing how the Order had cheated him his whole life; yes, he thought, that was the real bitterness, not the fact that the adepts had failed to defeat the rebels—by failing, essentially, to break their spirit—but the fact that the adepts were only someone else's cat's paws and every gentle, earnest soul in every Esper community was only someone's dupe.

Wildly he wanted to return to Laura—there'd been no chance thus far to see her—Laura and the kid, the last honest reality this fog-world had left him. He mastered himself and went on more evenly:

"The adepts, what few of them survive, will of course be helpful in defending San Francisco. An army free to move around in the field can deal with them, one way or another, but your . . . your weapons can repel an assault on the city walls. So that's where I'm going to take them."

Probably the best he could do. There was no word from the northern half of the loyalist army. Doubtless they'd withdrawn to the capital, suffering heavy losses en route. Radio jamming continued, hampering friendly and hostile communications alike. He had to take action, either retreat southward or fight his way through to the city. The latter course seemed wisest. He didn't believe that Laura had much to do with his choice.

"I'm not adept myself," Woodworth said. "I can't call them mind to mind."

"You mean you can't use their equivalent of radio," Danielis said brutally. "Well, you've got an adept in attendance. Have him pass the word."

Woodworth flinched. "I hope," he said, "I hope you understand this came as a surprise to me too."

"Oh, yes, certainly, Philosopher," Lescarbault said unbidden.

Woodworth swallowed. "I still hold with the Way and the Order," he said harshly. "There's nothin' else I can do. Is there? The Grand Seeker has promised a full explanation when this is over." He shook his head. "Okay, son, I'll do what I can."

A certain compassion touched Danielis as the blue robe disappeared into the fog. He rapped his orders the more severely.

Slowly his command got going. He was with the Second Brigade; the rest were strewn over the Peninsula in the fragments into which the rebels had knocked them. He hoped the equally scattered adepts, joining him on his march through the San Bruno range, would guide some of those units to him. But most, wandering demoralized, were sure to surrender to the first rebels they came upon.

He rode near the front, on a muddy road that snaked over the highlands. His helmet was a monstrous weight. The horse stumbled beneath him, exhausted by—how many days?—of march, counter-march, battle, skirmish, thin rations or none, heat and cold and fear, in an empty land. Poor beast, he'd see that it got proper treatment when they reached the city. That all those poor beasts behind him did, after trudging and fighting and trudging again until their eyes were filmed with fatigue.

There'll be chance enough for rest in San Francisco. We're impregnable there, walls and cannon and the Esper machines to landward, the sea that feeds us at our backs. We can recover our strength, regroup our forces, bring fresh troops down from Washington and up from the south by water. The war isn't decided yet . . . God help us.

I wonder if it will ever be.

And then, will Jimbo Mackenzie come to see us, sit by the fire and swap yarns about what we did? Or talk about something else, anything else? If not, that's too high a price for victory.

Maybe not too high a price for what we've learned,

*though. Strangers on this planet . . . what else could have
forged those weapons? The adepts will talk if I myself
have to torture them till they do.* But Danielis remembered tales muttered in the fisher huts of his boyhood,
after dark, when ghosts walked in old men's minds.
Before the holocaust there had been legends about the
stars, and the legends lived on. He didn't know if he
would be able to look again at the night sky without a
shiver.

This damned fog—

Hoofs thudded. Danielis half drew his sidearm. But
the rider was a scout of his own, who raised a drenched
sleeve in salute. "Colonel, an enemy force about ten
miles ahead by road. Big."

So we'll have to fight now. "Do they seem aware of
us?"

"No, sir. They're proceeding east along the ridge
there."

"Probably figure to occupy the Candlestick Park
ruins," Danielis murmured. His body was too tired for
excitement. "Good stronghold, that. Very well, Corporal." He turned to Lescarbault and issued instructions.

The brigade formed itself in the formlessness for combat. Patrols went out. Information began to flow back,
and Danielis sketched a plan that ought to work. He
didn't want to try for a decisive engagement, only brush
the enemy aside and discourage them from pursuit. His
men must be spared, as many as possible, for the city
defense and the eventual counter-offensive.

Lescarbault came back. "Sir! The radio jamming's
ended!"

"What?" Danielis blinked, not quite comprehending.

"Yes, sir. I've been using a minicom—" Lescarbault
lifted the wrist on which his tiny transceiver was
strapped— "for very short-range work, passing the battalion commanders their orders. The interference
stopped a couple of minutes ago. Clear as daylight."

Danielis pulled the wrist toward his own mouth.
"Hello, hello, radio wagon, this is the C.O. You read
me?"

"Yes, sir," said the voice.

"They turned off the jammer in the city for a reason. Get me the open military band."

"Yes, sir." Pause, while men mumbled and water runneled unseen in the arroyos. A wraith smoked past Danielis' eyes. Drops coursed off his helmet and down his collar. The horse's mane hung sodden.

Like the scream of an insect:

"—here at once! Every unit in the field, get to San Francisco at once! We're under attack by sea!"

Danielis let go Lescarbault's arm. He stared into emptiness while the voice wailed on and forever on.

"—bombarding Potrero Point. Decks jammed with troops. They must figure to make a landing there—"

Danielis' mind raced ahead of the words. It was as if Esp were no lie, as if he scanned the beloved city himself and felt her wounds in his own flesh. There was no fog around the Gate, of course, or so detailed a description could not have been given. Well, probably some streamers of it rolled in under the rusted remnants of the bridge, themselves like snowbanks against blue-green water and brilliant sky. But most of the Bay stood open to the sun. On the opposite shore lifted the Eastbay hills, green with gardens and agleam with villas; and Marin shouldered heavenward across the strait, looking to the roofs and walls and heights that were San Francisco. The convoy had gone between the coast defenses that could have smashed it, an unusually large convoy and not on time: but still the familiar big-bellied hulls, white sails, occasional fuming stacks, that kept the city fed. There had been an explanation about trouble with commerce raiders; and the fleet was passed on into the Bay, where San Francisco had no walls. Then the gun covers were taken off and the holds vomited armed men.

Yes, they did seize a convoy, those piratical schooners. Used radio jamming of their own; together with ours, that choked off any cry of warning. They threw our supplies overboard and embarked the bossman militia. Some spy or traitor gave them the recognition signals. Now the capital lies open to them, her garrison stripped, hardly an adept left in Esper Central, the Sierrans thrusting against her southern gates, and Laura without me.

"We're coming!" Danielis yelled. His brigade groaned

into speed behind him. They struck with a desperate ferocity that carried them deep into enemy positions and then stranded them in separated groups. It became knife and saber in the fog. But Danielis, because he led the charge, had already taken a grenade on his breast.

East and south, in the harbor district and at the wreck of the Peninsula wall, there was still some fighting. As he rode higher, Mackenzie saw how those parts were dimmed by smoke, which the wind scattered to show rubble that had been houses. The sound of firing drifted to him. But otherwise the city shone untouched, roofs and white walls in a web of streets, church spires raking the sky like masts, Federal House on Nob Hill and the Watchtower on Telegraph Hill as he remembered them from childhood visits. The Bay glittered insolently beautiful.

But he had no time for admiring the view, nor for wondering where Laura huddled. The attack on Twin Peaks must be swift, for surely Esper Central would defend itself.

On the avenue climbing the opposite side of those great humps, Speyer led half the Rolling Stones. (Yamaguchi lay dead on a pockmarked beach.) Mackenzie himself was taking this side. Horses clopped along Portola, between blankly shuttered mansions; guns trundled and creaked, boots knocked on pavement, moccasins slithered, weapons rattled, men breathed heavily and the hex corps whistled against unknown demons. But silence overwhelmed the noise, echoes trapped it and let it die. Mackenzie recollected nightmares when he fled down a corridor which had no end. *Even if they don't cut loose at us*, he thought bleakly, *we've got to seize their place before our nerve gives out.*

Twin Peaks Boulevard turned off Portola and wound steeply to the right. The houses ended; wild grasses alone covered the quasi-sacred hills, up to the tops where stood the buildings forbidden to all but adepts. Those two soaring, iridescent, fountainlike skyscrapers had been raised by night, within a matter of weeks. Something like a moan stirred at Mackenzie's back.

"Bugler, sound the advance. On the double!"

A child's jeering, the notes lifted and were lost. Sweat stung Mackenzie's eyes. If he failed and was killed, that didn't matter too much . . . after everything which had happened . . . but the regiment, the regiment—

Flame shot across the street, the color of hell. There went a hiss and a roar. The pavement lay trenched, molten, smoking and reeking. Mackenzie wrestled his horse to a standstill. *A warning only. But if they had enough adepts to handle us, would they bother trying to scare us off?* "Artillery, open fire!"

The field guns bellowed together, not only howitzers but motorized 75's taken along from Alemany Gate's emplacements. Shells went overhead with a locomotive sound. They burst on the walls above and the racket thundered back down the wind.

Mackenzie tensed himself for an Esper blast, but none came. Had they knocked out the final defensive post in their own first barrage? Smoke cleared from the heights and he saw that the colors which played in the tower were dead and that wounds gaped across loveliness, showing unbelievably thin framework. It was like seeing the bones of a woman murdered by his hand.

Quick, though! He issued a string of commands and led the horse and foot on. The battery stayed where it was, firing and firing with hysterical fury. The dry brown grass started to burn, as red-hot fragments scattered across the slope. Through mushroom bursts, Mackenzie saw the building crumble. Whole sheets of facing broke and fell to earth. The skeleton vibrated, took a direct hit and sang in metal agony.

What was that which stood within?

There were no separate rooms, no floors, nothing but girders, enigmatic machines, here and there a globe still aglow like a minor sun. The structure had enclosed something nearly as tall as itself, a finned and shining column, almost like a rocket shell but impossibly huge and fair.

Their spaceship, Mackenzie thought in the clamor. *Yes, of course, the ancients had begun making spaceships, and we always figured we would again someday. This, though—!*

The archers lifted a tribal screech. The riflemen and cavalry took it up, crazy, jubilant, the howl of a beast of prey. By Satan, we've whipped the stars themselves! As they burst onto the hillcrest, the shelling stopped, and their yells overrode the wind. Smoke was acrid as blood smell in their nostrils.

A few dead blue-robes could be seen in the debris. Some half dozen survivors milled toward the ship. A bowman let fly. His arrow glanced off the landing gear but brought the Espers to a halt. Troopers poured over the shards to capture them.

Mackenzie reined in. Something that was not human lay crushed near a machine. Its blood was deep violet color. *When the people have seen this, that's the end of the Order.* He felt no triumph. At St. Helena he had come to appreciate how fundamentally good the believers were.

But this was no moment for regret, or for wondering how harsh the future would be with man taken entirely off the leash. The building on the other peak was still intact. He had to consolidate his position here, then help Phil if need be.

However, the minicom said, "Come on and join me, Jimbo. The fracas is over," before he had completed his task. As he rode alone toward Speyer's place, he saw a Pacific States flag flutter up the mast on that skyscraper's top.

Guards stood awed and nervous at the portal. Mackenzie dismounted and walked inside. The entry chamber was a soaring, shimmering fantasy of colors and arches, through which men moved troll-like. A corporal led him down a hall. Evidently this building had been used for quarters, offices, storage, and less understandable purposes. . . . There was a room whose door had been blown down with dynamite. The fluid abstract murals were stilled, scarred, and sooted. Four ragged troopers pointed guns at the two beings whom Speyer was questioning.

One slumped at something that might answer to a desk. The avian face was buried in seven-fingered hands and the ridumentary wings quivered with sobs. *Are they able to cry, then?* Mackenzie thought, astonished, and had a sudden wish to take the being in his arms and offer what comfort he was able.

The other one stood erect in a robe of woven metal. Great topaz eyes met Speyer's from a seven-foot height, and the voice turned accented English into music.

"—a G-type star some fifty light-years hence. It is barely visible to the naked eye, though not in this hemisphere."

The major's fleshless, bristly countenance jutted forward as if to peck. "When do you expect reinforcements?"

"There will be no other ship for almost a century, and it will only bring personnel. We are isolated by space and time; few can come to work here, to seek to build a bridge of minds across that gulf—"

"Yeah," Speyer nodded prosaically. "The light-speed limit. I thought so. If you're telling the truth."

The being shuddered. "Nothing is left for us but to speak truth, and pray that you will understand and help. Revenge, conquest, any form of mass violence is impossible when so much space and time lies between. Our labor has been done in the mind and heart. It is not too late, even now. The most crucial facts can still be kept hidden—oh, listen to me, for the sake of your unborn!"

Speyer nodded to Mackenzie. "Everything okay?" he said. "We got us a full bag here. About twenty left alive, this fellow's the bossman. Seems like they're the only ones on Earth."

"We guessed there couldn't be many," the colonel said. His tone and his feelings were alike ashen. "When we talked it over, you and me, and tried to figure what our clues meant. They'd have to be few, or they'd've operated more openly."

"Listen, listen," the being pleaded. "We came in love. Our dream was to lead you—to make you lead yourselves—toward peace, fulfillment. . . . Oh, yes, we would also gain, gain yet another race with whom we could someday converse as brothers. But there are many races in the universe. It was chiefly for your own tortured sakes that we wished to guide your future."

"That controlled history notion isn't original with you," Speyer grunted. "We've invented it for ourselves, now and then on Earth. The last time it led to the Hellbombs. No, thanks!"

"But we *know*! The Great Science predicts with absolute certainty—"

"Predicted this?" Speyer waved a hand at the blackened room.

"There are fluctuations. We are too few to control so many savages in every detail. But do you not wish an end to war, to all your ancient sufferings? I offer you that for your help today."

"You succeeded in starting a pretty nasty war yourselves," Speyer said.

The being twisted its fingers together. "That was an error. The plan remains, the only way to lead your people toward peace. I, who have traveled between suns, will get down before your boots and beg you—"

"Stay put!" Speyer flung back. "If you'd come openly, like honest folk, you'd have found some to listen to you. Maybe enough, even. But no, your do-gooding had to be subtle and crafty. You knew what was right for us. We weren't entitled to any say in the matter. God in heaven, I've never heard anything so arrogant!"

The being lifted its head. "Do you tell children the whole truth?"

"As much as they're ready for."

"Your child-culture is not ready to hear these truths."

"Who qualified you to call us children—besides yourselves?"

"How do you know you are adult?"

"By trying adult jobs and finding out if I can handle them. Sure, we make some ghastly blunders, we humans. But they're our own. And we learn from them. You're the ones who won't learn, you and that damned psychological science you were bragging about, that wants to fit every living mind into the one frame it can understand.

"You wanted to re-establish the centralized state, didn't you? Did you ever stop to think that maybe feudalism is what suits man? Some one place to call our own, and belong to, and be part of; a community with traditions and honor; a chance for the individual to make decisions that count; a bulwark for liberty against the central overlords, who'll always want more and more power; a thousand different ways to live. We've always built super-countries, here on Earth, and we've always knocked them apart again. I think maybe the whole idea is wrong. And maybe this time we'll try something better. Why not a world of little states, too well rooted to dissolve in a nation, too small to do much harm—slowly rising above petty jealousies and spite, but keeping their identities—a thousand separate approaches to our problems. Maybe then we can solve a few of them . . . for ourselves!"

"You will never do so," the being said. "You will be torn in pieces all over again."

"That's what you think. I think otherwise. But whichever is right—and I bet this is too big a universe for either of us to predict—we'll have made a free choice on Earth. I'd rather be dead than domesticated.

"The people are going to learn about you as soon as Judge Brodsky's been reinstated. No, sooner. The regiment will hear today, the city tomorrow, just to make sure no one gets ideas about suppressing the truth again. By the time your next spaceship comes, we'll be ready for it: in our own way, whatever that is."

The being drew a fold of robe about its head. Speyer turned to Mackenzie. His face was wet. "Anything . . . you want to say . . . Jimbo?"

"No," Mackenzie mumbled. "Can't think of anything. Let's get our command organized here. I don't expect we'll have to fight any more, though. It seems to be about ended down there."

"Sure." Speyer drew an uneven breath. "The enemy troops elsewhere are bound to capitulate. They've got nothing left to fight for."

There was a house with a patio whose wall was covered by roses. The street outside had not yet come back to life, so that silence dwelt here under the yellow sunset. A maidservant showed Mackenzie through the back door and departed. He walked toward Laura, who sat on a bench beneath a willow. She watched him approach but did not rise. One hand rested on a cradle.

He stopped and knew not what to say. How thin she was!

Presently she told him, so low he could scarcely hear: "Tom's dead."

"Oh, no." Darkness came and went before his eyes.

"I learned the day before yesterday, when a few of his men straggled home. He was killed in the San Bruno."

Mackenzie did not dare join her, but his legs would not upbear him. He sat down on the flagstones and saw curious patterns in their arrangement. There was nothing else to look at.

Her voice ran on above him, toneless: "Was it worth it? Not only Tom, but so many others, killed for a point of politics?"

"More than that was at stake," he said.

"Yes, I heard on the radio. I still can't understand how it was worth it. I've tried very hard, but I can't."

He had no strength left to defend himself. "Maybe you're right, duck. I wouldn't know."

"I'm not sorry for myself," she said. "I still have Jimmy. But Tom was cheated out of so much."

He realized all at once that there was a baby, and he ought to take his grandchild to him and think thoughts about life going on into the future. But he was too empty.

"Tom wanted him named after you," she said.

Did you, Laura? he wondered. Aloud: "What are you going to do now?"

"I'll find something."

He made himself glance at her. The sunset burned on the willow leaves above and on her face, which was now turned toward the infant he could not see. "Come back to Nakamura," he said.

"No. Anywhere else."

"You always loved the mountains," he groped. "We—"

"No." She met his eyes. "It isn't you, Dad. Never you. But Jimmy is not going to grow up a soldier." She hesitated. "I'm sure some of the Espers will keep going, on a new basis, but with the same goals. I think we should join them. He ought to believe in something different from what killed his father, and work for it to become real. Don't you agree?"

Mackenzie climbed to his feet against Earth's hard pull. "I don't know," he said. "Never was a thinker. . . . Can I see him?"

"Oh, Dad—"

He went over and looked down at the small sleeping form. "If you marry again," he said, "and have a daughter, would you call her for her mother?" He saw Laura's head bend downward and her hands clench. Quickly he said, "I'll go now. I'd like to visit you some more, tomorrow or sometime, if you think you'll want to have me."

Then she came to his arms and wept. He stroked her hair and murmured, as he had done when she was a child. "You do want to return to the mountains, don't you? They're your country too, your people, where you belong."

"Y-you'll never know how much I want to."

"Then why not?" he cried.

His daughter straightened herself. "I can't," she said. "Your war is ended. Mine has just begun."

Because he had trained that will, he could only say, "I hope you win it."

"Perhaps in a thousand years—" She could not continue.

Night had fallen when he left her. Power was still out in the city, so the street lamps were dark and the stars stood forth above all roofs. The squad that waited to accompany their colonel to barracks looked wolfish by lantern light. They saluted him and rode at his back, rifles ready for trouble; but there was only the iron sound of horseshoes.

NEW FOLKS' HOME

BY CLIFFORD D. SIMAK (1904-1988)

ANALOG SCIENCE FICTION
JULY

Clifford D. Simak began publishing science fiction in 1931, and was one of a very small group of writers, which includes Murray Leinster and Jack Williamson, who debuted at the dawn of magazine science fiction yet who could adapt and grow and do important work in the field into the 1970s and 1980s. He is best known for works with rural settings and values, somewhat unique given the strong urban settings and biases present in modern science fiction. This is perhaps best illustrated in his fix-up novel City *(1952), for which he was awarded the World Fantasy Award, and which contains the impressive "Desertion," still my favorite short story.*

His illustrious career included the winning of Hugo Awards for "The Big Front Yard," Way Station, *and "The Grotto of the Dancing Deer," which also won the Nebula Award of the Science Fiction Writers of America, the organization that made him a Grand Master in 1977.*

His work is currently unavailable at my local chain stores—and possibly out-of-print—a major tragedy for this generation of readers.

The house was an absurdity. What is more, it was out of place. And it had no right to be there, Frederick Gray told himself. For this was his country, his and old Ben Lovell's. They had discovered it almost forty years before and had come here ever since and in all that time there had been no one else.

He knelt in the canoe and stroked idly with the paddle to keep the craft in place, with the bright, brown autumn water flowing past, bearing on its surface little curls of foam from the waterfall a half a mile ahead. He had heard the faint thunder of the falls when he had parked the car and lowered the canoe from its top and for the past hour he'd traveled toward it, listening to it and storing the sound of it away, as he was storing everything away, for this, he knew, was the last trip to this place he would ever make.

They could have waited, he told himself, with a strange mellow bitterness. They could have waited until he had made the trip. For it was all spoiled now. No longer could he ever think upon this stream without the house intruding. Not as he had known the stream for almost forty years, but now always with the house.

No one had ever lived here. No one would want to live here. No one ever came here. It had been his and Ben's alone.

But the house stood there, upon the little knoll above the flowing stream, framed in all its shiny whiteness against the greenness of the pines, and with a path leading from his old camping place up to where it sat.

He wielded the paddle savagely and drove the canoe to the shore. It grounded on the gravel and he stepped out and hauled it up the beach, where it would be safe from the tugging current.

Then he straightened and stared up at the house.

How would he tell Ben, he wondered. Or should he try to tell him? Might it not be better, when he talked with Ben, to disregard the house? You could not tell a man, lying in a hospital from which he had small chance of ever going home, that someone had robbed him of a segment of his past. For when a man is near the end, thought Gray, his past is somehow precious. And that, Gray admitted to himself, was the reason he himself resented the house upon the knoll.

Although, perhaps, he thought, he would not have resented it so much if it had not been so ridiculous. For it was not the kind of house for a place like this. If it had been a rustic structure, built of natural wood, with a great rock chimney, all built low against the ground, it would not have been so bad. For then it would have fitted, or would have tried to fit.

But this stark white structure, gleaming with the newness of its paint, was unforgivable. It was the sort of place that some junior executive might have built in some fashionable development, where all the other houses, sitting on the barren acres, would be of the same sleek architecture. There it would be quite all right and acceptable, but in this place of rock and pine it was an absurdity and an insult.

He bent stiffly and tugged the canoe farther up the beach. He lifted out his cased rod and laid it on the ground. He found the creel and strapped it on, and slung the pair of waders across his shoulders.

Then, picking up the rod, he made his way slowly up the path. For it was only dignified and proper that he make his presence known to these people on the knoll. It would not be right to go stalking past them up the river, without an explanation. But he would be very sure not to say anything that might imply he was asking their permission. Rather it might be quite fitting, he told himself, to make very clear to them the prior right that he held and to inform them stiffly that this would be the last time he was coming and that he would bother them no further.

The way was steep. It had seemed of late, he thought, that all little slopes were steep. His breath was shorter now and his breathing shallow and his knees were stiff and his muscles ached from kneeling and paddling the canoe.

Maybe it had been foolish to try the trip alone. With Ben it would have been all right, for there would have been the two of them, the one to help the other. He had told no one that he planned the trip, for if he had they would have attempted to dissuade him—or what might have been far worse, offered to go along with him. They would have pointed out that no man of almost seventy should try such a trip alone. Although, actually, it was not much of a trip, at all. Just a few hours' drive up from the city to the little town of Pineview and then four miles down the old logging road until he reached the river. And from there an hour of paddling up the river to the falls and the olden camping place just downstream from the falls.

Halfway up the slope he stopped to catch his breath and rest. From there he could see the falls, the white rush of the water and the little cloud of mist that, when the sun was right, held captive rainbows in it.

He stood looking at it all—the darkness of the pines, the barren face of rocky gorge, the flaming crimson and the goldenness of the hardwood trees, now turned into autumn bonfires by the touch of early frost.

How many times, he wondered—how many times had Ben and he fished above the falls? How many campfires had they lighted? How many times had they traveled up and down the river?

It had been a good life, a good way to spend their time together, two stodgy professors from a stodgy downstate college. But all things approach an end; nothing lasts forever. For Ben it had already ended. And after this one trip, it would be the end for him.

He stood and wondered once again, with a twinge of doubt, if he had made the right decision. The people of Wood's Rest seemed kind and competent and had shown him that he would be with the kind of people he could understand—retired teachers and ancient bankers and others from the genteel walks of life. But despite all this, the doubt kept creeping in.

It would have been so different, he thought, if only Clyde had lived. They had been closer than most sons and fathers. But now he had no one. Martha had been gone for many years and now Clyde was gone as well and there were no others.

On the face of it, from every practical consideration, Wood's Rest was the answer. He would be taken care of and he could live the kind of life, or at least an approximation of the kind of life, to which he was accustomed. It was all right now to keep on alone, but the time was coming when he would need someone. And Wood's Rest, while perhaps not the perfect answer, was at least an answer. A man must look ahead, he told himself, and that was why he had made the arrangements with Wood's Rest.

He was breathing easier now and he went on up the

path until he reached the little patch of level ground that lay before the house.

The house was new, he saw, newer than he had thought at first. From where he stood he imagined that he could smell the newness of the paint.

And how, he wondered, had the materials which had been used to build it been gotten to the site? There was no sign of any road. It might, he thought, have been trucked down the ancient logging road and brought up the river from where he had left his car. But if that had been the case, the logging road would have shown the signs of recent travel, and it hadn't. It still was no more than a rutted track, its center overgrown with grass, that snaked its way through a tunnel of encroaching second growth. And if it had been brought by boat, there should have been a skidway or a road leading from the river to the site, and there was nothing but the faint, scarcely worn path up which he'd made his way. There would not have been time, he knew, for the wilderness and weather to have wiped out the traces, for he and Ben had been here fishing in the spring and at that time there had been no house.

Slowly he crossed the level place and the patio that looked out upon the river and the falls. He reached the door and pressed the button and far in the house he could hear the sound of ringing. He waited and no one came. He pressed the bell again. He heard the ringing from within the house and listened for the sound of footsteps coming to the door, but there were no footsteps. He raised his hand and knocked upon the door and at the knock the door came open and swung wide into the hall.

He stood abashed at this invasion of another's privacy. He debated for a moment whether he should reach in and close the door and quietly go away. But that, he told himself, had a sense of sneaking that he did not like.

"Hello!" he called. "Is anybody home?"

He would explain, when someone came, that he had merely knocked upon the door, that he had not opened it.

But no one came.

For a moment he stood undecided, then stepped inside the hall to grasp the doorknob and pull it shut.

In that instant he saw the living room, newly carpeted and filled with furniture. Someone was living here, he thought, but they were not at home. They had gone somewhere for a little while and had not locked the door. Although, come to think of it, no one up here ever locked a door. There was no need to lock them.

He would forget it, he promised himself, forget this house, this blot upon the land, and spend his day fishing and in the afternoon go back downriver to the car and home. He would not let his day be spoiled.

Sturdily, he set out, tramping along the ridge that took him above the falls and to that stretch of water that he knew so well.

The day was calm and clear. The sun was shining brightly, but there was still a touch of chill. However, it was only ten o'clock. By noon it would be warm.

He jogged along, quite happily, and by the time he donned the waders and stepped into the water, a mile above the falls, the house no longer mattered.

It was early in the afternoon that the accident occurred.

He had waded ashore and found a medium-sized boulder that would serve as a chair while he ate the lunch he'd brought. He had laid the rod down carefully on the shingle of the little beach and had admired the three trout of keeping size that rested in the creel. And had noted, as he unwrapped his sandwich, that the sky was clouding over.

Perhaps, he told himself, he should start home a bit sooner than he had planned. There was no point in waiting if there were a chance the weather would turn bad. He had put in three good hours upon the stream and should be satisfied.

He finished the sandwich and sat quietly on the boulder, staring at the smooth flow of the water against the rampart of the pines that grew on the farther bank. It was a scene, he told himself, that he should fix into his memory, to keep and hold forever. It would be something to think upon in the days to come when there were no fishing trips.

He decided that he'd take another half hour before he left the stream. He'd fish down to the point where the fallen tree lay halfway across the water. There should be trout in there, underneath the tree, hiding there and waiting.

He got up stiffly and picked up the rod and creel and stepped into the stream. His foot slipped on a mossy boulder hidden by the water and he was thrown forward. A sharp pain slashed through his ankle and he hit the shallow water and lay there for a moment before he could move to right himself.

His foot, the one that had slipped, was caught between two chunks of rock, wedged into a crevice in the stream bed. Caught and twisted and throbbing with a steady and persistent pain.

His teeth clenched against an outcry, he slowly worked the foot free and dragged himself back onto the shore.

He tried to stand and found that the twisted ankle would not bear his weight. It turned under him when he tried and a red-hot streak of pain went shooting through his leg.

He sat down and carefully worked off his waders. The ankle already was becoming swollen and had a red and angry look.

He sat upon the shingle of the beach and carefully considered all that he must do.

He could not walk, so he would have to crawl. He'd leave the waders and the rod and creel, for he could not be encumbered by them. Once he got to the canoe, he could make it down the river to where he'd parked his car. But when he got there, he'd have to leave the canoe behind as well, for he could never load it on top the car.

Once he was in the car, he would be all right, for he could manage driving. He tried to remember if there were a doctor at Pineview. It seemed to him there was, but he could not be sure. But, in any case, he could arrange for someone to come back and pick up the rod and the canoe. Foolish, maybe, he thought, but he could not give up the rod. If it wasn't picked up soon, the porcupines would find and ruin it. And he could not allow a thing like that to happen. For the rod was a part of him.

He laid the three—the waders, the creel and rod—in a pile beside the river where they could be spotted easily by anyone who might be willing to come back for them. He looked for the last time at the river and began the crawl.

It was a slow and painful business. Try as he might, he could not protect the ankle from bumps along the way and every bump sent waves of pain surging through his body.

He considered fashioning a crutch, but gave it up as a bad idea when he realized that the only tool he had was a pocket knife, and not too sharp a one.

Slowly he inched his way along, making frequent stops to rest. He could see, when he examined it, that the ankle was more swollen than before and the redness of it was beginning to turn purple.

And suddenly the frightening realization came, somewhat belatedly, that he was on his own. No one knew that he was here, for he had told no one. It would be days, if he failed to make it, before anyone would think to hunt for him.

It was a foolish thought. For he could make it easily. The hardest part came first and that was for the best. Once he reached the beached canoe, he would have it made.

If only he could keep crawling longer. If he didn't have to rest so often. There had been a day when he could have made it without a single rest. But a man got old and weak, he thought. Weaker than he knew.

It was during one of his rests that he heard the rising wind whining in the treetops. It had a lonesome sound and was a little frightening. The sky, he saw, was entirely clouded over and a sort of ghostly twilight had settled on the land.

He tried to crawl the faster, spurred on by a vague uneasiness. But he only tired the quicker and banged the injured ankle cruelly. He settled down again to a slower pace.

He had passed the fall line and had the advantage of

a slightly downhill slope when the first drop of rain spattered on his outstretched hand.

And a moment after that the rain came in gusty sweeps of icy savagery.

He was soaked in the first few minutes and the wind was cold. The twilight deepened and the pines moaned in the rising gale and little rivulets of water ran along the ground.

Doggedly, he kept at his crawling. His teeth tried to chatter as the chill seeped in, but he kept his mouth clamped shut to stop the chattering.

He was better than halfway back to the canoe, but now the way seemed long. He was chilled to the bone and as the rain still came down it seemed to bear with it a great load of weariness.

The house, he thought I can find shelter at the house. They will let me in.

Not daring to admit that his earlier objective, to reach the canoe and float down the river to where he'd left his car, had now become impossible and unthinkable.

Ahead, through the murkiness of the storm, he saw the glow of light. That would be the house, he thought. They—whoever they might be—were now at home and had turned on the lights.

It took longer than he had thought it would, but he reached the house with what seemed to be the last shred of his strength. He crawled across the patio and managed to pull himself erect beside the door, leaning on the house, bracing on one leg. He thumbed the button and heard the ringing of the bell inside and waited for the footsteps.

There weren't any footsteps.

And it wasn't right, he told himself. There were lights within the house and there should be people there. And if that were the case, why should he get no answer?

Behind him the moaning in the pines seemed deeper and more fearsome and there was no doubt that it had grown darker. The rain still came hissing down in its chilling fury.

He balled his fist and pounded on the door and as it had that morning, the door swung open, to let the light spill out across the patio.

"Hello, in there!" he shouted. "Is anybody home?"

There was no answer and no stir, no sign of anything at all.

Hopping painfully, he crossed the threshold and stood within the hall. He called again and yet again and there was no response.

His leg gave out and he slumped upon the floor, catching himself and breaking the fall with his outstretched hands. Slowly, he inched his way along, crawling toward the living room.

He turned at the faint noise which came from behind his back and he saw that the door was closing—closing of its own accord and with no hand upon it. He watched in fascination as it closed, firm against the casing. The snick of the lock as it settled was loud in the stillness of the house.

Queer, he thought, fuzzily. Queer how the door came open as if to invite one in. And then when one was in, calmly closed itself.

But it did not matter what the door might do, he thought. The important thing was that he was inside and that the cold ferocity of the storm was shut in the outer dark. Already the warmth of the house was enfolding him and some of the chill was gone.

Careful not to bump the dragging ankle, he snaked himself along the carpeting until he reached a chair. He hauled himself upward and around and sat down in it, settling back into the cushions, with the twisted ankle thrust out in front of him.

Now, finally, he was safe. Now the cold and rain could no longer reach him, and in time someone would show up who could help him with the ankle.

He wondered where they were, these people to whom the house belonged. It was unlikely that they would stray far from it in a storm like this. And they must have been here not too long ago, because the lights were lit against the darkness of the storm.

He sat quietly, now only faintly aware of the dull throb of pain that was pulsing in the ankle. The house was warm and quiet and restful and he was glad for it.

Carefully he looked around, taking inventory.

There was a table in the dining room and it was set

for dinner, with the steaming silver coffee pot and the gleaming china tureen and a covered platter. He could smell the coffee and there was food as well, of that he felt quite sure. But there was only one place set, as if one person only had been meant to dine.

A door opened into another room that seemed to be a study. There was a painting on the wall and a massive desk set beneath the painting. There were floor to ceiling bookcases, but there were no books in them.

And a second door led into a bedroom. There was a bed turned down and a pair of pajamas were folded on the pillow. The lamp on the bedside table had been lit. As if the bed were waiting for someone to sleep in it, all turned down and ready.

But there was a strangeness, a fantastic something about the house that he could not quite put his finger on. Like a case at law, he thought, where there was a certain quality that eluded one, always with the feeling that this certain quality might be the very key to the case itself.

He sat and thought about it, and suddenly he knew.

The house was furnished, but the house was waiting. One could sense a feeling of expectancy, as if this were a house that was waiting for a tenant. It was set and ready, it was equipped and furnished. But there was no one living here. It had an unlived-in smell to it and a vague sort of emptiness.

But there was foolishness, he told himself. Of course there was someone living in it. Someone had turned on the lights, someone had cooked a dinner and set a place for one, someone had lit the bedside lamp and turned down the covers of the bed.

And yet, for all the evidence, he couldn't quite believe it. The house still persisted in its empty feeling.

He saw the trail of water he'd left in his crawl along the hall and across the carpeting to reach the chair. He saw the muddy handprints he'd left upon the wall where he had braced himself when he'd hobbled in.

It was no way to mess up a place, he thought. He'd do his best to explain it to the owner.

He sat and waited for the owner, nodding in the chair.

Seventy, he thought, or almost seventy, and this his last adventure. All his family gone and all his friends as well—all except old Ben, who was dying slowly and ungracefully in the alien and ungraceful atmosphere of a small hospital room.

He recalled that day of long ago when Ben and he had met, two young professors. Ben in astronomy and himself in law. They had been friends from the very first and it would be hard to have Ben go.

But perhaps he would not notice it, he thought, as much as he might have at one time. For he, himself, in another month, would be settled down at Wood's Rest. An old folks' home, he thought. Although now they didn't call them that. They called them fancy names like Wood's Rest, thinking that might take the sting away.

It didn't matter, though. There was no one left to whom it might matter now—except himself, of course. And he didn't care. Not very much, that is.

He snapped himself erect and looked at the mantle clock.

He'd dozed away, he thought, or been dreaming of the old days while no more than half awake. Almost an hour had passed since he'd last glanced at the clock and still the house was empty of anyone but he.

The dinner still was on the table, but it would be cold by now. Perhaps, he thought, the coffee still might be a little warm.

He pushed forward in the chair and rose carefully to his feet. And the ankle screamed at him. He fell back into the chair and weak tears of pain ran out of his eyes and dribbled down his cheeks.

Not the coffee, he thought. I don't want the coffee. If I can just make it to the bed.

He pulled himself tenderly from the chair and crawled into the bedroom. By slow and painful maneuver, he stripped off his sodden clothing and got into the pajamas that had been folded on the pillow.

There was a bathroom off the bedroom and by hopping from bed to chair to dresser he finally reached it.

Something to kill the pain, he told himself. Aspirin would be of some little help if he could only find one.

There was a medicine cabinet above the basin and he jerked it open, but the shelves were empty.

After a time he made it back to the bed again and crawled beneath the covers, switching off the bedside light.

Lying stiff and straight, shivering with the effort of getting into bed, he wondered dully what would happen when the owner should return and find a stranger in the bed.

But he didn't care. He was beyond all caring. His head was large and fuzzy and he guessed he had a fever.

He lay quietly, waiting for sleep to come to him, his body fitting itself by slow degrees into the strangeness of the bed.

He did not even notice when the lights throughout the house went out.

He awoke to the morning sun, streaming through the windows. There was the odor of frying bacon and of brewing coffee. And a telephone was ringing, loudly and insistently.

He threw off the covers and was halfway out of bed to answer the telephone when he remembered that this was not his house, that this was not his bed, that the ringing phone could not possibly be for him.

He sat upon the edge of the bed, bewildered, as the memory of the day before came crashing in upon him.

Good Lord, he thought, a phone! There can't be a phone. Way out here, there can't.

But still it kept on ringing.

In just a little while, he thought, someone would come to answer it. The someone who was frying bacon would come and answer it. And when they did, they'd go past the open door and he would be able to see them and know to whom the house belonged.

He got out of bed. The floor beneath his feet was cold and there might be slippers somewhere, but he didn't know where to look for them.

He was out in the living room before he remembered that he had a twisted ankle.

Stopping in amazement, he looked down at it and it looked as it had always looked, no longer red or purple, and no longer swollen. And most important, not hurting any more. He could walk on it as if nothing had ever been the matter with it.

The phone standing on the table in the hall pealed aloud at him.

"I'll be damned," said Frederick Gray, staring at his ankle.

The phone brayed at him again.

He hurried to the table and snatched the handpiece off the cradle.

"Hello," he said.

"Dr. Frederick Gray, perhaps."

"You are right. I am Frederick Gray."

"I trust you had a restful night."

"A very restful one. And thank you very much."

"Your clothes were wet and beyond repair. We disposed of them. I hope that you don't mind. The contents of the pockets are on the dressing table. There is other clothing in the closet that I am sure will fit you."

"Why," said Frederick Gray, "that was very thoughtful of you. But would you mind telling me—"

"Not at all," the caller said, "but perhaps you'd better hurry out and get your breakfast. It will be getting cold."

The phone went dead.

"Just a minute," Gray yelled at it. "Just hold on a minute—"

But the buzz of an empty line kept sounding in his ear.

He hung up and went into the bedroom, where he found a pair of slippers tucked beneath the bed.

We hope you had a restful night. Your clothes were wet, so we disposed of them. We put the contents of the pockets on the dressing table.

And who in the world were we?

Where was everyone?

And what happened, when he slept, to repair the ankle?

He had been right the night before, he thought. It was an empty house. There was no one here. But in some manner which he could not fathom, it still was tenanted.

He washed his hands and face, but did not bother with a shave, although when he looked into the medicine cabinet, it was no longer empty. It now held shaving tackle, a toothbrush and a tube of paste, a hairbrush and a comb.

Breakfast was on the table in the dining room and there was only one place set. There were bacon and eggs, hash brown potatoes, tomato juice, toast and a pot of coffee.

But there was no sign of anyone who might have prepared the food or placed it on the table.

Could there be, he wondered, a staff of invisible servants in the house who took care of guests?

And the electricity, he wondered. Was there a private power plant? Perhaps one that was powered by the waterfall? And what about the phone? Could it be a radiophone? He wondered if a radiophone would look different from just an ordinary phone. He could not recall that he had ever seen one.

And who had been the caller?

He stood and looked at the waiting breakfast.

"Whoever you are," he said, aloud, "I thank you. I wish that I could see you. That you would speak to me."

No one spoke to him.

He sat down and ate the breakfast, not realizing until he put the food into his mouth how hungry he had been.

After breakfast he went into the bedroom and found the clothes hanging in the closet. Not fancy clothes, but the kind of outfit a fisherman would wear.

Coming out of the bedroom, he saw that the breakfast things had been cleared off the table.

He stepped outside into the sunshine and the day was beautiful. The storm had blown itself out sometime in the night.

Now that he was all right, he told himself, perhaps he'd better go upstream and bring down the rod and the other stuff he'd left. The rest of it didn't amount to much, but the rod was much too good to leave.

It all was there, piled where he had left it, neatly on the shore. He bent down and picked up the rod and stood facing the river, with it in his hand.

Why not? he asked himself. There was no hurry to get back. As long as he was here he might as well get in a bit of fishing. He'd not have another chance. He'd not come back again.

He laid the rod aside and sat down to pull on the waders. He emptied the fish he'd caught the day before out of the creel and strapped it on his shoulder.

And why just this morning? he asked himself. Why just another day? There was no reason to get back and he had a house to stay in. There was no reason he shouldn't stay a while and make a real vacation of it.

He stood aghast at how easily he accepted the situation, how ready he found himself to take advantage of it. The house was a thing of mystery, and yet not terrifying. There was nothing in the house, strange as it might be, that a man need be afraid of.

He picked up the rod and stepped into the stream and whipped out the line. On the fifth cast a trout struck. The day had started fine.

He fished to the first break of the rapids just above the falls, then clambered out on shore. He had five fish in the creel and two of them were large.

He could fish the rapids from the shore, he thought, but perhaps he shouldn't. He should be getting back for a good look at the house. He had to settle in his mind the truth about the power source and the telephone and there might be a lot of other things that needed looking into.

He glanced down at his watch and it was later than he thought. He untied the fly and reeled in the line and disjointed the rod, then set off down the trail.

By the middle of the afternoon, he had finished his inspection of the house.

There were no power and no telephone lines coming to the house and there was no private power plant. The house was conventionally wired for electricity, but there was no source that he could find. The telephone plugged into a jack in the hall and there were other jacks in the bedroom and the study.

But there was another item: The night before, as he sat in the living room, he could see into the study. He had seen the painting and the desk and the empty book shelves. But now the shelves were no longer empty. They fairly bulged with books and the kind of books that he would have chosen if he had put them there himself—a law library that would have been the envy of any practicing attorney, and with a special section that he first took to be a joke.

But when he looked at the phone directory, it had seemed somewhat less a joke.

For it was no such directory as any man had ever seen before. It listed names and numbers, but the addresses ranged the galaxy!

Besur, Yar, Mekbuda V—FE 6-8731

Beten, Varmo, Polaris III—GR 7-3214

Beto, Elm, Rasalgethi IX—ST 1-9186

Star names, he thought, and the planet numbers. They could be nothing else.

And if it were a joke, it was pointless and expensive.

Star names listed in the pages of the directory and those other star names upon the books in that special section in the study!

The obvious conclusion, he told himself, rather plaintively, was too outrageous to be given even slight consideration. It was outrageous and ridiculous and it made no sense and he would not entertain it. There must be other answers and the one he did not like to think about was that he'd gone insane.

There might be a way, he thought, that it could be settled.

He flipped the directory closed and then opened the front cover and there it was: TELEPHONE SERVICE CALLS. He lifted the receiver and dialed for INFORMATION.

There were two ringing sounds and then a voice said:

"Good evening, Dr. Gray. We are glad you called. We hope everything's all right. There isn't any trouble?"

"You know my name," said Gray. "How do you know my name?"

"Sir," said Information, "it is a point of pride with us that we know the name of each of our subscribers."

"But I'm not a subscriber. I'm only—"

"Oh, but you are," insisted Information. "As soon as you took possession of the house—"

"Possession! I did not—"

"But, Dr. Gray, we thought you knew. We should

have told you at the start. We are very sorry. The house, you see, is yours."

"No," Gray said, weakly, "I did not understand."

"Yours," said Information, "so long as you may need it, so long as you may want to keep it. The house and everything that's in it. Plus all the services, naturally, that you may require."

"But it can't be mine," said Gray. "I have done nothing that would make it mine. How can I own a house for which I've given nothing?"

"There might be," said Information, "certain services that, from time to time, you might be willing to perform. Nothing strenuous, of course, and not required, you understand. If you would be willing to perform them, we would be the ones who would stand in debt. But the house is yours no matter what you may elect to do."

"Services?" asked Gray. "There are few services, I am afraid, that I could perform."

"It does not really matter," Information told him. "We are very glad you called. Call us again any time you wish."

The connection clicked and he was left, standing foolishly with the receiver in his hand.

He put it back into the cradle and went to the living room, sitting in the chair he'd sat in when he'd found his way into the house the night before.

While he'd been busy in the hall with the telephone, someone—or something, or some strange procedure—had laid wood in the fireplace and had lit it and the brass wood carrier that stood beside the hearth was filled with other wood against the need of it.

He watched the fire creeping up the logs, flickering as it climbed, with the cold wind outside growling in the chimney.

An Old Folks' Home, he thought.

For if he'd heard aright, that was what it was.

And a better one, by far, than the one he had planned to enter.

There was no reason in the world why anyone should give this house to him. He had done nothing he could think of that entitled him to have it.

An Old Folks' Home, all to himself, and on his favorite trout stream.

It would be wonderful, he thought, if he only could accept it.

He hitched the chair around so he could face the fire. He had always liked a fire.

Such a pleasant place, he thought, and such thoughtful service. He wished that he could stay.

And what was there to stop him? No one would mind if he did not return. In a day or two he could make his way out to Pineview and mail a couple of letters that would fix it so no one would hunt for him.

But it was madness, he thought. What if he got sick? What if he fell and hurt himself? He could not reach a doctor and there would be no one to help him.

Then he thought of how he'd hunted for an aspirin and there had been no aspirin. And how he'd crawled into bed with a twisted, swollen ankle that had been all right when he got up in the morning.

He had no worry, he realized, about ever being sick.

There had been no aspirin tablet because there had been no need of any.

This house was not a house alone. It was more than just a house. It was a shelter and a servant and a doctor. It was a safe and antiseptic house and it was compassionate.

It gave you everything you wanted. It fulfilled your every need. It gave you fire and food and comfort and a sense of being cared for.

There were the books, he thought. The rows and stacks of books, the very kind of books by which he'd lived for years.

Dr. Frederick Gray, dean of the school of law. Filled with honor and importance until he got too old, until his wife and son had died and all his friends were gone or incapacitated. Now no longer dean, now no longer scholar, but an old man with a name that was buried in the past.

He rose slowly from the chair and went into the study. He put out his hand and rubbed the palm of it along the leathery spines of a row of books.

These were the friends, he told himself, the friends a

man could count on. They always were in place and waiting for the time a man might need them.

He stopped in front of the section that had puzzled him at first, which he had thought of as a farfetched joke. But now he knew there was no joke.

He read the titles of a few of them: "Basic Statutes of Arcturus XXIV," "Comparison of the Legal Concepts of the Centaurian Systems," "Jurisprudence on Zubeneschamali III, VI, and VII," "The Practical Law of Canopus XII." And many others with the strange names in their titles.

Perhaps, he thought, he would not have recognized the names so readily had it not been for Ben. For years he had listened to him talk about his work, reeling off many of these very names as if they might be places no farther off than just down the street a ways.

And maybe, thought Frederick Gray, they were not so far, at that. All he had to do to talk to men—no, not men, perhaps, but beings—in all of these strange places was to walk out in the hall and dial their numbers on the phone.

A telephone directory, he thought, with numbers for the stars, and on all these shelves law books from the stars.

Perhaps there were, on those other solar systems, nothing like a telephone or a telephone directory; perhaps, on those other planets there weren't any law books. But here on Earth, he told himself, the means of communication had to be a telephone, the means of information books upon the shelf. For all of it had to be a matter of translation, twisting the unfamiliar into something that was familiar and that one could use. And translation not for Earth alone, but for all those other beings on all those other planets. On each of a dozen planets there might be a different means of communication, but in the case of a call to him from any of those planets, no matter what means the creature of the planet might employ, the telephone would ring.

And the names of those other stars would be translations, too. For the creatures who lived upon the planets circling Polaris would not call their sun Polaris. But here on Earth it had to be Polaris, for that was the only way a human had to identify the star.

The language would have to be translated, too. The creatures he had talked with on the phone could not have spoken English, and yet it had been English when it had reached his ear. And his replies, he knew, must have reached that other party in some language other than the tongue that he had used.

He stood aghast at the very thought of it, wondering how he could abide such an explanation. And yet there was no choice. It was the only explanation that would fit the situation.

Somewhere a bell rang sharply and he turned from the shelves of books.

He waited for it to ring again, but it did not ring.

He walked into the living room and saw that dinner had been set upon the table and was waiting for him.

So that was what it had been, he thought. A bell to summon him to dinner.

After dinner, he went back to the living room to sit before the fire and fight the whole thing out. He assembled the facts and evidence in his old lawyer's mind and gave full consideration to all possibilities.

He touched the edge of wonder and shoved it to one side, he erased it carefully—for in his consideration of this house there was no room for wonder and no place for magic.

Was it no more than illusion? That was the first question one must ask. Was this really happening, or was he just imagining that it was happening? Was he, perhaps, in all reality, sitting underneath a tree or squatting on the river bank, mumbling at nothing, scratching symbols in the dirt with his fingernails, and living the fantasy of this house, this fire, this room?

It was hard to believe that this might be the case. For there were too many details. Imagination formed a hazy framework and let it go at that.

There were here too many details and there was no haziness and he could move and think of his own volition; he still was the master of himself.

And if it were not imagination, if he could rule out insanity, then this house and all that happened must be, indeed, the truth. And if it were the truth, then here was a house built or shaped or somehow put into being by some outside agency that was as yet unsuspected in the mind of humankind.

But, he asked himself, why would they want to do it? What could be the motive?

With a view, perhaps, of studying him as a representative specimen of the creature, Man? Or with the idea that somehow they could make some use of him?

The thought struck him—was he the only man? Might there be others like him? Men who kept very silent about what was happening, for fear that human interference might spoil this good thing that they had?

He rose slowly from the chair and went out in the hall. He picked up the phone directory and brought it back with him. He threw another log upon the fire and sat down in the chair, with the phone book in his lap.

First himself, he thought; he would see if he was listed.

He had no trouble finding it: Gray, Frederick, Helios III—SU 6-2649.

He flipped the pages and started from the front, running his finger slowly down the column.

The book was thin, but it took him quite a while, going carefully so that he would not miss another man from Earth. But there was no other listed; not from Earth, not from the solar system. He was the only one.

Loneliness, he wondered. Or should it be just a touch of pride. To be the only one in the entire solar system.

He took the directory back to the table in the hall and lying in the place where he had gotten it was another one.

He stared at it and wondered if there were two of them, if there had been two of them all along and he had never noticed.

He bent to look the closer at it and when he did he saw that it was not another directory, but a file of some sort, with his name printed across the top of it.

He laid the directory down and took up the file. It was a bulky and a heavy thing, with great sheaves of papers enclosed between the covers.

*   *   *

It had not been there, he was certain, when he'd gotten the directory. It had been placed there, as the food was placed upon the table, as the books had been stacked upon the shelves, as the clothing that would fit him had been hung within the closet. By some agency that was unobtrusive, if not invisible.

Placement by remote control, he wondered. Could it be that somewhere this house was duplicated and that in that house certain agencies that were quite visible—and in their term of reference logical and ordinary—might place the food and hang the clothes and that at the moment of the action the same things happened in this house?

And if that were the case, not only space was mastered, but time as well. For they—whoever they might be—could not have known about the books that should be placed upon the shelves until the occupant of this house had appeared upon the scene. They could not have known that it would be Frederick Gray, that it would be a man who had made the law his business, who would blunder on this house. They had set a trap—a trap?—and there would have been no way for them to know what quarry they might catch.

It had taken time to print, by whatever process, the books upon the shelves. There would have been a searching for the proper books, and the translating and the editing. Was it possible, he wondered, that time could be so regulated that the finding and the translating and the editing, the printing and the placement, could have been compressed into no more than twenty-four hours as measured on the Earth? Could time be stretched out and, perhaps, foreshortened to accommodate the plans of those engineers who had built this house?

He flipped open the cover of the file and the printing on the first page struck him in the face.

SUMMARY & TRANSCRIPT
Valmatan vs. Mer El
Referral for Review
Under Universal Law

Panel for Review:

Vanz Kamis, Rasalgethi VI
Eta Nonskic, Thuban XXVIII
Frederick Gray, Helios III

Frozen, he stared at it.

His hands began to tremble and he laid it down, carefully on the tabletop, as if it might be something that would shatter if he dropped it.

Under universal law, he thought. Three students of the law, three experts (?), from three different solar systems!

And the facts at issue, and the law, more than likely, from yet another system.

Certain little services, the voice on the phone had told him.

Certain little services. To pass judgment under laws and jurisprudence he had never heard of!

And those others, he wondered—had they heard of them?

Swiftly he bent and leafed through the phone book. He found Kamis, Vanz. Deliberately, he dialed the number.

A pleasant voice said: "Vanz Kamis is not present at the moment. Is there any message?"

And it was not right, thought Gray. He should not have phoned. There was no point in it.

"Hello," said the pleasant voice. "Are you there?"

"Yes, I am here," said Gray.

"Vanz Kamis is not at home. Is there any message?"

"No," said Gray. "No, thanks. There isn't any message."

He should not have called, he thought. The act of phoning had been an act of weakness. This was a time when a man must rely upon himself. And he had to give an answer. It was not something that could be brushed off, it was not a thing that anyone could run from.

He got his cap and jacket from the closet in the hall and let himself outside.

A golden moon had risen, the lower half of it bearing on its face the dark silhouette of the jagged pines, growing on the ridge across the river. From somewhere in the forest an owl was muttering and down in the river a fish splashed as it jumped.

Here a man could think, Gray told himself. He stood and drew the freshness of the air deep into his lungs. Here on the earth that was his own. Better than in a house that was, at least by implication, the extension of many other worlds.

He went down the path to the landing where he had beached the canoe. The canoe was there and there was water in it from the storm of the night before. He tipped it on its edge so the water could run out.

To be reviewed, that first page had said, under universal law. And was there, he wondered, such a thing as universal law?

Law could be approached in many ways, he thought. As pure philosophy, as political theory, as a history of moral ideas, as a social system, or as a set of rules. But however it was viewed, however studied, no matter what the emphasis, it had one basic function, the providing of a framework that would solve all social conflict.

Law was no static thing; it must, and did, evolve. No matter how laggard it might be, still it followed in the footsteps of the society it served.

He grinned wryly in the darkness, staring at the foaming river, remembering how, for years, he had hammered on that viewpoint in seminar and lecture.

On one planet, given time and patience and the slow process of evolution, the law could be made to square with all social concepts and with the ordered knowledge of society at large.

But was there any chance to broaden this flexibility and this logic to include not one, but many planets. Did there exist somewhere a basis for a legal concept that would apply to society in the universal sense?

It could be true, he thought. Given wisdom and work, there was a bare chance of it.

And if this should be the case, then he might be of service, or more correctly, perhaps, the law of Earth might be of help. For Earth need not be ashamed of what it had to offer. The mind of Man had lent itself to law. For more than five thousand years there was a record of Man's concern with law and from that deep concern had come a legal evolution—or, more correctly, many evolutions. And in it might be found a point or two that could be incorporated in a universal code.

There was, throughout the universe, a common chemistry, and because of this there were those who thought that there was a common biochemistry as well.

Those other beings on those two other planets who had been named with him to review the issue set forth in the transcript could not be expected to be men, or even close to men. But given a common biochemistry, they would be basically the same sort of life as Man. They would be protoplasmic. They would make use of oxygen. The kind of things they were would be determined by nucleic acids. And their minds, while more than likely a far cry from a human mind, still would be based upon the same mechanism as the minds of Man.

If there were, he asked himself, a common chemistry and a common biochemistry, then did it not seem likely, as well, for there to exist a concept that would point toward common justice?

Not just yet, perhaps. But ten thousand years from now. Or a million years from now.

He started up the path again and his step was lighter than it had been for years, and the future brighter—not his future only, but the future of everything that was.

This was a thing he'd taught and preached for years—the hope that in some future time the law might represent some great and final truth.

It did a man's heart good, he thought, to find that there were others who felt the same as he, and who were at work on it.

No Old Folks' Home, he thought, and he was glad of that. For an Old Folks' Home was a dead end, and this was a bright beginning.

In a little while the phone would ring and there'd be a voice asking if he'd serve.

But he'd not wait for that. There was work to do—a great deal of work to do. There was the file to read and those strange books that he must study, and references that he would have to find and much thinking to be done.

He entered the house and shut the door behind him. He hung up his cap and coat.

Picking up the file, he went into the study and laid it on the desk.

He pulled out a drawer and took out pad and pencils and ranged them neatly, close at hand.

He sat down and entered upon the practice of interstellar law.

THE FACES OUTSIDE

BY BRUCE MCALLISTER (1946-   )

WORLDS OF IF
JULY

Bruce McAllister is certainly one of the least-known and greatest talents working in the science fiction field. His two novels, Humanity Prime *(1971) and* Dream Baby *(1991), are very different, exceptional works. His small output of published work, which includes more than forty short stories in a thirty year career, largely accounts for his relative neglect, although he is highly respected by his peers.*

"The Faces Outside," which forms the basis of Humanity Prime, *is a remarkable story as you will see, an accomplishment made all the more extraordinary by the fact that he was 16 when the story first appeared in* Worlds of If.

I wanted to call her Soft Breast, because she is soft when I hold her to me. But the Voice told me to call her Diane. When I call her Diane, I have a pleasant feeling, and she seems closer to me. She likes the name "Diane." The Voice knew what was best, of course, as it always does.

I must mate with her every day, when the water is brightest. The Voice says so. It also says that I am in a "tank," and that the water is brightest when the "sun" is over the "tank." I do not understand the meaning of "sun," but the Voice says that "noon" is when the "sun" is over the "tank." I must mate with Diane every "noon."

I *do* know what the "tank" is. It is a very large thing filled with water, and having four "corners," one of

160

which is the Cave where Diane and I sleep when the water is black like the ink of the squid and cold like dead fish. But we stay warm. There is the "floor" of the "tank," the "floor" being where all the rock and seaweed is, with all the crawling fish and crabs, where Diane and I walk and sleep. There are four "sides" "Sides" are smooth and blue walls, and have "view-ports"—round, transparent areas—on them. The Voice says that the things in the "view-ports" are Faces. I have a face, as does Diane. But the cracked, flat things with small lights circling about them are not pretty like Diane's face. The Voice says that the Faces have bodies, like myself, and Diane. No body could be like Diane's. I think I should be quite sick if I saw the bodies of the Faces.

The Voice then says that the Faces are watching us, as we sometimes watch the porpoises. It took a very long time to grow used to having the Faces watch us, as Diane and I came together, but we learned to do it as simply as we swim and sleep.

But Diane does not have babies. I am very sad when I see the porpoises and whales with their young. Diane and I sleep together in the Cave; Diane is very warm and soft. We sleep in happiness, but when we are awake, we are lonely. I question the Voice about a baby for Diane, but the Voice is always silent.

I grow to hate the Faces in the "view-ports." They are always watching, watching. The Voice says that they are enemies, and bad. The Faces have not tried to hurt me; but I must think of them as enemies because the Voice says so. I ask, bad, like the shark? The Voice says, no, worse than the sharks and eels. It says that the Faces are evil.

The "tank" must be high, because the water is high. I have gone once to the surface, and, although I could get used to it, the light was too much for my eyes. It took me two hundred and seventy kicks to the surface; it took me three thousand steps from our Cave to the opposite "side." The "tank" is very large, otherwise the whales would not be happy.

The fish are many, but the dangers are few. I have seen the sharks kill. But the shark does not come near me if I see it and am afraid. Sometimes I have caught it sneaking up behind me, but when I turn it leaves quickly. I have questioned the Voice about why the sharks leave. It does not know. It has no one to ask.

Today the "sun" must be very large, or powerful, or bright, because the water is brighter than most days.

When I awoke Diane was not beside me. The rock of the Cave is jagged, so as I make my way from our bed of cool and slick seaweed, toward the entrance, I scrape my leg on the fifth kick. Not much blood comes from the cut. That is fortunate, because when there is blood the sharks come.

Diane has grabbed the tail of a porpoise, and both are playing. Diane and I love the porpoises. Sometimes we can even hear their thoughts. They are different from the other fish; they are more like us. But they have babies and we do not.

Diane sees me and, wanting to play, swims behind a rock and looks back, beckoning. I make a grab at her as I sneak around the rock. But she darts upward, toward the surface, where her body is a shadow of beauty against the lighter water above her. I follow her, but she ducks and I sail past her. Diane pulls up her legs, knees under her chin, and puts her arms around them. She then drops like a rock toward the "floor."

I have caught a porpoise by his top fin. He knows my wish, so he speeds toward Diane, circles her and butts her soft thighs with his snout. She laughs, but continues to stay in a ball, her black hair waving. She is very beautiful.

I try to pry her arms from around her legs gently, but she resists. I must use force. Diane does not mind when I do: because she knows I love her.

I pull her arms away, and slip my arms under hers, kissing her on the lips for a long time. Struggling to free herself, laughing again, she pokes me sharply with her elbow and escapes my arms. I am surprised. She quickly puts her arms around my neck, pulls herself to my back and links her slim legs around my middle. She is pretending that I am a porpoise. I laugh. She pinches me to go ahead. I swim upward, but her thoughts tell me she wants to go to the Cave.

I understand. I carry her through the water very

slowly, feeling the warmth and nipples of her breasts pressed against my back as she rests her head on my shoulder and smiles.

The Faces continue to stare. Many times I have searched for a word to show my hatred for them. I shall find it somehow, though. Sooner or later.

"What count of planets had the Terrans infested?" The furry humanoid leaned over the desk and stared, unblinking, at the lesser humanoid in the only other chair in the room. His gaze was dropped as he scratched informally at the heavy fur at his wrist. He raised his gaze again.

"Forty-three is the count, *beush*," replied the other.

"And the count of planets destroyed?"

"Forty-three planetoid missiles were sent and detonated simultaneously without resistance or losses on our part, *beush*," the assistant *beush* answered indirectly.

The room was hot, so the *beush* lazily passed his hand over a faintly glowing panel.

The room was cooled, and a large-eyed female with silky, ochrous fur—very desirable to the majority of humanoids—entered with two flared glasses of an odorless transparent liquid—very desirable to the majority of humanoids. The lesser humanoid was being treated exceptionally well.

The room was momentarily silent as the two sipped at their drinks with black lips. The *beush*, as customary, spoke first. "Inform me of the pre-espionage intelligence accomplishments contra-Energi. I have not been previously informed. Do not spare the details."

"Of certainty, *beush*," began the assistant with all the grace of an informer. "The Light and Force Research of the Energi is executed in one center of one planet, the planet being Energa, as our intelligence service has conveniently listed it. The Energi have negative necessity for secrecy in their Light and Force Research, because, first, all centers are crusted and protected by Force Domes. Second, it is near impossibility that one could so self-disguise that he would negatively be detectable." He hesitated.

"And these Energi," queried the *beush*, "are semi-telepathic or empathic?"

"Affirmative," the assistant mumbled.

"Then you have there a third reason," offered the *beush*.

"Graces be given you, *beush*."

The *beush* nodded in approval. "Continue, but negatively hesitate frequently or it will be necessary to discuss this subject post-present."

His assistant trembled slightly. "Unequivocally affirmative. *Beush*, your memory relates that five periods antepresent, when there existed the Truce inter Energi, Terrans and ourselves, there was a certain period during which gifts of the three nucleus-planets were exchanged in friendship. The Terrans were self-contented to donate to the Energi an immense 'aquarium'—an 'aquarium' consisting of a partly transparent cell in which was placed a collection of Terran life-forms that breathed their oxygen from the dense atmosphere of Terran seas. But, as a warp-space message from the Terran Council indirectly proclaimed, the degenerate Terrans negatively possessed a ship of any Space type large or powerful enough to transport the 'aquarium' to Energa. Our ships being the largest of the Truce, we were petitioned by the Terrans to transport it. These events developed before the Terrans grew pestiferous to our cause. We obliged, but even our vastest ship was slow, because the physical power necessary to bring the weight of the cell through warp-space quickly was too great for the solitary four generators. It was imperative that the trip be on a longer trajectory arranged through norm-space. During the duration of the trip, feelings of suspicion arose inter Three Truce Races. As your memory also relates, the 'aquarium' was still in space when we found it necessary to obliterate the total race of Terrans. The message of the annihilation arrived in retard to the Energi, so Time permitted us to devise a contra-Energi intelligence plan, a necessity since it was realized that the Energi would be disturbed by our actions contra-Terrans and would, without doubt, take action, contra-ourselves.

"Unknown to you, *beush*, or to the masses and highers, an insignificant pleasure craft was extracted from Terran Space and negatively consumed with a planet when the bombs were detonated. The ship accommo-

dated two Terrans. Proper Terrans by birth, negatively
by reference. One was male, other female. The two had
been in their culture socially and religiously united in a
ceremony called 'matrimony.' Emotions of sex, protection and an emotion we have negatively been able to
analyze linked the two, and made them ideal for our
purpose."

The assistant looked at the *beush*, picked up his partially full glass and, before he could sip it, was dashed
to the floor beside the *beush* himself. The former helped
the higher to his unstable legs, and was commented to
by the same. "Assistant, proceed to the protecroom."

They entered the well-illuminated closet and immediately slipped into the unwieldy metallic suits. Once again
they took their seats, the *beush* reflecting and saying.
"As your memory relates, the explosion was a bomb-
drop concussion from the Rebellers. We must now wear
anti-radiation protection. For that reason, and the danger
of the Energi, you *do* see why we need the formulae of the
Force Domes, *immediately*."

There was menace in his voice. The assistant trembled
violently. Using the rare smile of that humanoid race, the
beush continued. "Do negatively self-preoccupy. Resume
your information, if contented."

"Contented," came the automatic reply, and the assistant began, "The two humans were perfect for the Plan.
I repeat. Before the Energi received the message of the
race destruction, it was imperative that we establish an
agent on Energa, near the Force Domes. We assumed
that the 'aquarium' would be placed on Energa, in the
greatest center. That was correct, but negatively yet
knowing for certainty, we perpetuated the Plan, with the
'aquarium' as the basis.

"One of our most competent protoplasmic computers
stabilized the final steps of the Plan. We were to subject
the two Terrans to radiation and have as a result two
Terrans who could breathe their normal oxygen from
H_2O—the atmosphere of the 'aquarium,' I repeat. We
were then to deprive them of memory, except of the
inter-attracting emotions, to allow them to live in har-
mony. Thirdly, we were to place them in the 'aquarium'
and have them forwarded under the reference of semi-

intelligent aqua-beings from Terran seas. A simple, but quite effective plan, your opinion, *beush?*"

"Quite," was the reply. "And concerning the method of info-interception?"

The assistant continued without hesitation, embarrassed by his incompetency, "A hyper-complex spheroid with radio interceptors, a-matter viewers and recorders and the general intelligence instruments of micro-size was placed in the cranium of the male mutant. The spheroid has negative direct control over the organism. Size was too scarce for use on trivialities. Then an agent was placed behind the larger controls at our end of the instruments."

"And you are the agent?"

"Hyper-contentedly affirmative."

I have done two things today. I have found the word for my hatred of the Faces. The Voice gave it to me. When I asked the Voice, it laughed and told me the word to use was "damn." So today I have thrice said, "Damn the Faces. Damn them."

Diane and I have decided that we *want* a baby. Maybe the other fish *wanted* them, so they got them. We *want* a baby.

"The two Terrans were so biologically mutated and are so nearly robotic, that it is physically impossible for reproduction on their part, *beush.*"

The *beush* ignored the assistant's words and said. "I have received copies of the thought-patterns and translations. There was something strange and very powerful about the meaning of the male's thought, 'want.' I query."

"Be assured without preoccupation that there exists negative danger of reproduction."

The name I wanted to call Diane was not good, because her breasts are hard and large, as is her stomach. I think she is sick.

I do not think Diane is sick. I think she is going to have a baby.

*   *   *

"Entities, assistant! On your oath-body you pro-claimed that there is negative danger of reproduction."

"Rest assured, peace, *beush*."

"But his thoughts!"

"Rest assured, peace, *beush*."

There is much blood in the water today. Diane is having a baby; sharks have come. I have never seen so many sharks, and as big as they are I have never seen. I am afraid, but still some sneak among us near Diane.

We love the porpoises, so they help us now. They are chasing the sharks away, injuring and killing some.

"Entities. Warp-spaced Entities! There has been reproduction."

"*Yorbeush*," cried the assistant in defense. "It is physically impossible. But they are mutants. It is negatively impossible that they possess Mind Force to a degree."

"To what degree? What degree could produce reproduction when it is physically impossible?" The *beush* was sarcastic. "How far can they go?"

"There is negatively great amount they can do. Negative danger, because we have studied their instincts and emotions and found that they will not leave the 'aquarium,' their 'home,' unless someone tells them to. But there is no one to do so."

Today, I damned the Faces nine times and finally *wanted* them to go away. The "view-ports" went black. It was like the sharks leaving when I wanted them to. I still do not understand.

There has been much useless noise and senseless talk from the Voice these days. It is annoying because I must concentrate on loving Diane and caring for the baby. So I *wanted* the Voice to leave. It left.

"Entities Be Simply Damned! The spheroid ceased to exist, assistant. How far can they go, assistant?" The *beush* rose, screamed hysterically for three seconds and then fired the hand weapon point-blank at the neck of his assistant.

                              *   *   *

The sharks come today, because Diane is having
another baby. Diane hurts, and there is more blood than
last time. Her face is not pretty when she hurts, as it is
pretty when she sleeps. So I *want* her to sleep. Her face
is pretty now with the smile on her lips.

"Fourteen thousand Energi ceased to exist, spheroid
ceased to exist, and another reproduction. Warp-space!
How far will they go?"

It has been hundreds of days. Faces keep appearing,
but I continue to *want* them to go away. Diane has had
eighteen babies. The oldest are swimming around and
playing with the porpoises. Diane and I spend most of
the time teaching the children by showing them things,
and by giving them our thoughts by touching them.

Today I found that none of the children have Voices.
I could *want* them to have Voices, but the children's
thoughts tell me that it is not right to have a Voice.

The eldest boy says that we should leave the tank, that
a greater "tank" is around us, and that it is easier to
move around in that greater tank. He also says that we
must guard ourselves against Faces outside. That is
strange, but the boy is a good boy. Many times he knows
that things will happen before they do. He is a good boy.

He is almost as tall as I am. The eldest girl is pretty like
Diane, her body very white and soft but, since I *wanted* it
so, her hair is golden, instead of dark. The boy likes her
very much, and I have seen them together, touching.

Tomorrow I will explain to him that if he *wants* something, he will get it. So he must *want* a baby.

"Query? The Energi will bomb-drop the 'aquarium'?
War declared against us? War declared? Entities be
wholly damned! Negative! Negativvv!" The disintegrator
was fired once more, this time into the orange eye of the
beush himself, by himself, and for the good of himself.

When, if I ever do *want* the Voice to come back, it
will be very surprised to know that Diane has had twenty-

four babies; that the three eldest boys have mated twice, once and twice, and have had four babies. The Voice will also be surprised to know that it took all twenty-nine of us to *want* all the Faces around the tank to die, as the eldest boy said to do. We could not tell, but the boy said that six million Faces were dead. That seems impossible to me, but the boy is always right.

Tomorrow we are leaving the tank. We will *want* to leave it; it is getting crowded. The boy says that beyond the greater tank, which we will also leave, there is enough space for all the babies Diane could have if she lived forever.

Forever, he said. It would be nice to live forever. I think I'll *want* . . .

HOT PLANET

BY HAL CLEMENT (HARRY STUBBS; 1922-   )

GALAXY SCIENCE FICTION
AUGUST

A science teacher by profession, Harry Stubbs in his "Hal Clement" persona has produced a substantial body of rigorous, inventive, logical science fiction for more than forty years. Such wonderful novels as Needle *(1950),* Mission of Gravity *(1954),* Cycle of Fire *(1957),* Close to Critical *(1964),* Nitrogen Fix *(1980), and* Still River *(1987) have made him one of the premier practictioners of what has become known as the "hard sf" story. Still going strong as author and fan, he was the Guest of Honor at the 1991 World Science Fiction Convention in Chicago.*

Harry can also write powerfully about people—witness "Hot Planet," one of the best stories about scientists and their work ever written.

The wind which had nearly turned the *Albireo*'s landing into a disaster instead of a mathematical exercise was still playing tunes about the fins and landing legs as Scholssberg made his way down to Deck Five.

The noise didn't bother him particularly, though the endless seismic tremors made him dislike the ladders. But just now he was able to ignore both. He was curious—though not hopeful.

"Is there anything at all obvious on the last sets of tapes, Joe?"

Mardikian, the geophysicist, shrugged. "Just what you'd expect . . . on a planet which has at least one quake in each fifty-mile-square area every five minutes.

You know yourself we had a nice seismic program set up, but when we touched down we found we couldn't carry it out. We've done our best with the natural tremors—incidentally stealing most of the record tapes the other projects would have used. We have a lot of nice information for the computers back home; but it will take all of them to make any sense out of it."

Schlossberg nodded; the words had not been necessary. His astronomical program had been one of those sabotaged by the transfer of tapes to the seismic survey.

"I just hoped," he said. "We each have an idea why Mercury developed an atmosphere during the last few decades, but I guess the high school kids on Earth will know whether it's right before we do. I'm resigned to living in a chess-type universe—few and simple rules, but infinite combinations of them. But it would be nice to know an answer sometime."

"So it would. As a matter of fact, I need to know a couple right now. From you. How close to finished are the other programs—or what's left of them?"

"I'm all set," replied Schlossberg. "I have a couple of instruments still monitoring the sun just in case, but everything in the revised program is on tape."

"Good. Tom, any use asking you?"

The biologist grimaced. "I've been shown two hundred and sixteen different samples of rock and dust. I have examined in detail twelve crystal growths which looked vaguely like vegetation. Nothing was alive or contained living things by any standards I could conscientiously set."

Mardikian's gesture might have meant sympathy.

"Camille?"

"I may as well stop now as any time. I'll never be through. Tape didn't make much difference to me, but I wish I knew what weight of specimens I could take home."

"Eileen?" Mardikian's glance at the stratigrapher took the place of the actual question.

"Cam speaks for me, except that I could have used any more tape you could have spared. What I have is gone."

"All right, that leaves me, the tape-thief. The last

spools are in the seismographs now, and will start running out in seventeen hours. The tractors will start out on their last rounds in sixteen, and should be back in roughly a week. Will, does that give you enough to figure the weights we rockhounds can have on the return trip?"

The *Albireo*'s captain nodded. "Close enough. There really hasn't been much question since it became evident we'd find nothing for the mass tanks here. I'll have a really precise check in an hour, but I can tell right now that you have about one and a half metric tons to split up among the three of you.

"Ideal departure time is three hundred ten hours away, as you all know. We can stay here until then, or go into a parking-and-survey orbit at almost any time before then. You have all the survey you need, I should think, from the other time. But suit yourselves."

"I'd just as soon be space-sick as seasick," remarked Camille Burkett. "I still hate to think that the entire planet is as shivery as the spot we picked."

Willard Rawson smiled. "You researchers told me where to land after ten days in orbit mapping this rockball. I set you just where you asked. If you'd found even five tons of juice we could use in the reaction tanks I could still take you to another one—if you could agree which one. I hate to say 'Don't blame me,' but I can't think of anything else that fits."

"So we sit until the last of the tractors is back with the precious seismo tapes, playing battleship while our back teeth are being shaken out by earthquakes—excuse the word. What a thrill! Glorious adventure!" Zaino, the communications specialist who had been out of a job almost constantly since the landing, spoke sourly. The captain was the only one who saw fit to answer.

"If you want adventure, you made a mistake exploring space. The only space adventures I've heard of are secondhand stories built on guesswork; the people who really had them weren't around to tell about it. Unless Dr. Marini discovers a set of Mercurian monsters at the last minute and they invade the ship or cut off one of the tractors, I'm afraid you'll have to do without adventures." Zaino grimaced.

"That sounds funny coming from a spaceman, Captain.

I didn't really mean adventure, though; all I want is something to do besides betting whether the next quake will come in one minute or five. I haven't even had to fix a suit-radio since we touched down. How about my going out with one of the tractors on this last trip, at least?"

"It's all right with me," replied Rowson, "but Dr. Mardikian runs the professional part of this operation. I require that Spurr, Trackman, Hargedon and Aiello go as drivers, since without them even a minor mechanical problem would be more than an adventure. As I recall it, Dr. Harmon, Dr. Schlossberg, Dr. Marini and Dr. Mardikian are scheduled to go; but if any one of them is willing to let you take his or her place, I certainly don't mind."

The radioman looked around hopefully. The geologists and the biologist shook their heads negatively, firmly and unanimously; but the astronomer pondered for a moment. Zaino watched tensely.

"It may be all right," Schlossberg said at last. "What I want to get is a set of wind, gas pressure, gas temperature and gas composition measures around the route. I didn't expect to be more meteorologist than astronomer when we left Earth, and didn't have exactly the right equipment. Hargedon and Aiello helped me improvise some, and this is the first chance to use it on Darkside. If you can learn what has to be done with it before starting time, though, you are welcome to my place."

The communicator got to his feet fast enough to leave the deck in Mercury's feeble gravity.

"Lead me to it, Doc. I guess I can learn to read a homemade weathervane!"

"Is that merely bragging or a challenge?" drawled a voice which had not previously joined the discussion. Zaino flushed a bit.

"Sorry, Luigi," he said hastily. "I didn't mean it just that way. But I still think I can run the stuff."

"Likely enough," Aiello replied. "Remember though, it wasn't made just for talking into." Schlossberg, now on his feet, cut in quickly.

"Come on, Arnie. We'll have to suit up to see the equipment; it's outside."

He shepherded the radioman to the hatch at one side of the deck and shooed him down toward the engine and air lock levels. Both were silent for some moments; but safely out of earshot of Deck Five the younger man looked up and spoke.

"You needn't push, Doc. I wasn't going to make anything of it. Luigi was right, and I asked for it." The astronomer slowed a bit in his descent.

"I wasn't really worried," he replied, "but we have several months yet before we can get away from each other, and I don't like talk that could set up grudges. Matter of fact, I'm even a little uneasy about having the girls along, though I'm no misogynist."

"Girls? They're not—"

"There goes your foot again. Even Harmon is about ten years older than you, I suppose. But they're girls to me. What's more important, they no doubt think of themselves as girls."

"Even Dr. Burkett? That is—I mean—"

"Even Dr. Burkett. Here, get into your suit. And maybe you'd better take out the mike. It'll be enough if you can listen for the next hour or two." Zaino made no answer, suspecting with some justice that anything he said would be wrong.

Each made final checks on the other's suit; then they descended one more level to the airlock. This occupied part of the same deck as the fusion plants, below the wings and reaction mass tanks but above the main engine. Its outer door was just barely big enough to admit a space-suited person. Even with the low air pressure carried by spaceships, a large door area meant large total force on jamb, hinges and locks. It opened onto a small balcony from which a ladder led to the ground. The two men paused on the balcony to look over the landscape.

This hadn't changed noticeably since the last time either had been out, though there might have been some small difference in the volcanic cones a couple of miles away to the northeast. The furrows down the sides of these, which looked as though they had been cut by water but were actually bone-dry ash slides, were always undergoing alteration as gas from below kept blowing fresh scoria fragments out of the craters.

The spines—steep, jagged fragments of rock which thrust upward from the plain beyond and to both sides of the cones—seemed dead as ever.

The level surface between the *Albireo* and the cones was more interesting. Mardikian and Schlossberg believed it to be a lava sheet dating from early in Mercury's history, when more volatile substances still existed in the surface rocks to cut down their viscosity when molten. They supposed that much—perhaps most—of the surface around the "twilight" belt had been flooded by this very liquid lava, which had cooled to a smoother surface than most Earthly lava flows.

How long it had stayed cool they didn't guess. But both men felt sure that Mercury must have periodic upheavals as heat accumulated inside it—heat coming not from radio-activity but from tidal energy. Mercury's orbit is highly eccentric. At perihelion, tidal force tries to pull it apart along the planet-to-sun line, while at aphelion the tidal force is less and the little world's own gravity tries to bring it back to a spherical shape. The real change in form is not great, but a large force working through even a small amount of distance can mean a good deal of energy.

If the energy can't leak out—and Mercury's rocks conduct heat no better than those of Earth—the temperature must rise.

Sooner or later, the men argued, deeply buried rock must fuse to magma. Its liquefaction would let the bulk of the planet give farther under tidal stress, so heat would be penetrated even faster. Eventually a girdle of magma would have to form far below the crust all around the twilight strip, where the tidal strain would be greatest. Sooner or later this would melt its way to the surface, giving the zone a period of intense volcanic activity and, incidentally, giving the planet a temporary atmosphere.

The idea was reasonable. It had, the astronomer admitted, been suggested long before to account for supposed vulcanism on the moon. It justified the careful examination that Schlossberg and Zaino gave the plain before they descended the ladder; for it made reasonable the occasional changes which were observed to occur in the pattern of cracks weaving over its surface.

No one was certain just how permanent the local surface was—though no one could really justify feeling safer on board the *Albireo* than outside on the lava. If anything really drastic happened, the ship would be no protection.

The sun, hanging just above the horizon slightly to the watcher's right, cast long shadows which made the cracks stand out clearly; as far as either man could see, nothing had changed recently. They descended the ladder carefully—even the best designed space suits are somewhat vulnerable—and made their way to the spot where the tractors were parked.

A sheet-metal fence a dozen feet high and four times as long provided shade, which was more than a luxury this close to the sun. The tractors were parked in this shadow, and beside and between them were piles of equipment and specimens. The apparatus Schlossberg had devised was beside the tractor at the north end of the line, just inside the shaded area.

It was still just inside the shade when they finished, four hours later. Hargedon had joined them during the final hour and helped pack the equipment in the tractor he was to drive. Zaino had had no trouble in learning to make the observations Schlossberg wanted, and the youngster was almost unbearably cocky. Schlossberg hoped, as they returned to the *Albireo*, that no one would murder the communications expert in the next twelve hours. There would be nothing to worry about after the trip started; Hargedon was quite able to keep anyone in his place without being nasty about it. If Zaino had been going with Aiello or Harmon—but he wasn't, and it was pointless to dream up trouble.

And no trouble developed all by itself.

Zaino was not only still alive but still reasonably popular when the first of the tractors set out, carrying Eileen Harmon and Eric Trackman, the *Albireo*'s nuclear engineer.

It started more than an hour before the others, since the stratigrapher's drilling program, "done" or not, took extra time. The tractor hummed off to the south, since both Darkside routes required a long detour to pass the chasm to the west. Routes had been worked out from the stereo-photos taken during the orbital survey. Even Darkside had been covered fairly well with Uniquantum film under Venus light.

The Harmon-Trackman vehicle was well out of sight when Mardikian and Aiello started out on one of the Brightside routes, and a few minutes later Marini set out on the other with the space-unit technician, Mary Spurr, driving.

Both vehicles disappeared quickly into a valley to the northeast, between the ash cones and a thousand-foot spine which rose just south of them. All the tractors were in good radio contact; Zaino made sure of that before he abandoned the radio watch to Rowson, suited up and joined Hargedon at the remaining one. They climbed in, and Hargedon set it in motion.

At about the same time, the first tractor came into view again, now traveling north on the farther side of the chasm. Hargedon took this as evidence that the route thus far was unchanged, and kicked in highest speed.

The cabin was pretty cramped, even though some of the equipment had been attached outside. The men could not expect much comfort for the next week.

Hargedon was used to the trips, however. He disapproved on principle of people who complained about minor inconveniences such as having to sleep in space suits; fortunately, Zaino's interest and excitement overrode any thought he might have had about discomfort.

This lasted through the time they spent doubling the vast crack in Mercury's crust, driving on a little to the north of the ship on the other side and then turning west toward the dark hemisphere. The route was identical to that of Harmon's machine for some time, though no trace of its passage showed on the hard surface. Then Hargedon angled off toward the southwest. He had driven this run often enough to know it well even without the markers which had been set out with the seismographs. The photographic maps were also aboard. With them, even Zaino had no trouble keeping track of their progress while they remained in sunlight.

However, the sun sank as they traveled west. In two hours its lower rim would have been on the horizon, had they been able to see the horizon; as it was, more of the "sea level" lava plain was in shadow than not even near the ship, and their route now lay in semidarkness.

The light came from peaks projecting into the sunlight, from scattered skylight which was growing rapidly fainter and from the brighter celestial objects such as Earth. Even with the tractor's lights it was getting harder to spot crevasses and seismometer markers. Zaino quickly found the fun wearing off . . . though his pride made him cover the fact as best he could.

If Hargedon saw this, he said nothing. He set Zaino to picking up every other instrument, as any partner would have, making no allowance for the work the youngster was doing for Schlossberg. This might, of course, have had the purpose of keeping the radioman too busy to think about discomfort. Or it might merely have been Hargedon's idea of normal procedure.

Whatever the cause, Zaino got little chance to use the radio once they had driven into the darkness. He managed only one or two brief talks with those left at the ship.

The talks might have helped his morale, since they certainly must have given the impression that nothing was going on in the ship while at least he had something to do in the tractor. However, this state of affairs did not last. Before the vehicle was four hours out of sight of the *Albireo*, a broadcast by Camille Burkett reached them.

The mineralogist's voice contained at least as much professional enthusiasm as alarm, but everyone listening must have thought promptly of the dubious stability of Mercury's crust. The call was intended for her fellow geologists Mardikian and Harmon. But it interested Zaino at least as much.

"Joe! Eileen! There's a column of what looks like black smoke rising over Northeast Spur. It can't be a real fire, of course; I can't see its point of origin, but if it's the convection current it seems to me the source must be pretty hot. It's the closest thing to a genuine volcano I've seen since we arrived; it's certainly not another of those ash mounds. I should think you'd still be close enough to make it out, Joe. Can you see anything?"

The reply from Mardikian's tractor was inaudible to Zaino and Hargedon, but Burkett's answer made its general tenor plain.

"I hadn't thought of that. Yes, I'd say it was pretty close to the Brightside route. It wouldn't be practical for you to stop your run now to come back to see. You couldn't do much about it anyway. I could go out to have a look and then report to you. If the way back is blocked there'll be plenty of time to work out another." Hargedon and Zaino passed questioning glances at each other during the shorter pause that followed.

"I know there aren't," the voice then went on, responding to the words they could not hear, "but it's only two or three miles, I'd say. Two to the spur and not much farther to where I could see the other side. Enough of the way is in shade so I could make it in a suit easily enough. I can't see calling back either of the Darkside tractors. Their work is just as important as the rest—anyway, Eileen is probably out of range. She hasn't answered yet."

Another pause.

"That's true. Still, it would mean sacrificing that set of seismic records—no, wait. We could go out later for those. And Mel could take his own weather measures on the later trip. There's plenty of time!"

Pause, longer this time.

"You're right, of course. I just wanted to get an early look at this volcano, if it is one. We'll let the others finish their runs, and when you get back you can check the thing from the other side yourself. If it is blocking your way there's time to find an alternate route. We could be doing that from the maps in the meantime, just in case."

Zaino looked at his companion.

"Isn't that just my luck!" he exclaimed. "I jump at the first chance to get away from being bored to death. The minute I'm safely away, the only interesting thing of the whole operation happens—back at the ship!"

"Who asked to come on this trip?"

"Oh, I'm not blaming anyone but myself. If I'd stayed back there the volcano would have popped out here somewhere, or else waited until we were gone."

"If it is a volcano. Dr. Burkett didn't seem quite sure."

"No, and I'll bet a nickel she's suiting up right now to go out and see. I hope she comes back with something while we're still near enough to hear about it."

Hargedon shrugged. "I suppose it was also just your luck that sent you on a Darkside trip? You know the radio stuff. You knew we couldn't reach as far this way with the radios. Didn't you think of that in advance?"

"I didn't think of it, any more than you would have. It was bad luck, but I'm not grousing about it. Let's get on with this job." Hargedon nodded with approval, and possibly with some surprise, and the tractor hummed on its way.

The darkness deepened around the patches of lava shown by the driving lights; the sky darkened toward a midnight hue, with stars showing ever brighter through it; and radio reception from the *Albireo* began to get spotty. Gas density at the low ion layer was high enough so that recombination of molecules with their radiation-freed electrons was rapid. Only occasional streamers of ionized gas reached far over Darkside. As these thinned out, so did radio reception. Camille Burkett's next broadcast came through very poorly.

There was enough in it, however, to seize the attention of the two men in the tractor.

She was saying: "—real all right, and dangerous. It's the . . . thing I ever saw . . . kinds of lava from what looks like . . . same vent. There's high viscosity stuff building a spatter cone to end all spatter cones, and some very thin fluid from somewhere at the bottom. The flow has already blocked the valley used by the Brightside routes and is coming along it. A new return route will have to be found for the tractors that . . . was spreading fast when I saw it. I can't tell how much will come. But unless it stops there's nothing at all to keep the flow away from the ship. It isn't coming fast, but it's coming. I'd advise all tractors to turn back. Captain Rowson reminds me that only one takeoff is possible. If we leave this site, we're committed to leaving Mercury. Arnie and Ren, do you hear me?"

Zaino responded at once. "We got most of it, Doctor. Do you really think the ship is in danger?"

"I don't know. I can only say that *if* this flow continues the ship will have to leave, because this area will sooner or later be covered. I can't guess how likely . . . check further to get some sort of estimate. It's different from any Earthly lava source—maybe you heard—should try to get Eileen and Eric back, too. I can't raise them. I suppose they're well out from under the ion layer by now. Maybe you're close enough to them to catch them with diffracted waves. Try, anyway. Whether you can raise them or not you'd better start back yourself."

Hargedon cut in at this point. "What does Dr. Mardikian say about that? We still have most of the seismometers on this route to visit."

"I think Captain Rowson has the deciding word here, but if it helps your decision Dr. Mardikian has already started back. He hasn't finished his route, either. So hop back here, Ren. And Arnie, put that technical skill you haven't had to use yet to work raising Eileen and Eric."

"What I can do, I will," replied Zaino, "but you'd better tape a recall message and keep it going out on—let's see—band F."

"All right. I'll be ready to check the volcano as soon as you get back. How long?"

"Seven hours—maybe six and a half," replied Hargedon. "We have to be careful."

"Very well. Stay outside when you arrive; I'll want to go right out in the tractor to get a closer look." She cut off.

"And *that* came through clearly enough!" remarked Hargedon as he swung the tractor around. "I've been awake for fourteen hours, driving off and on for ten of them. I'm about to drive for another six; and then I'm to stand by for more."

"Would you like me to do some of the driving?" asked Zaino.

"I guess you'll have to, whether I like it or not," was the rather lukewarm reply. "I'll keep on for a while though—until we're back in better light. You get at your radio job."

Zaino tried. Hour after hour he juggled from one band to another. Once he had Hargedon stop while he went

out to attach a makeshift antenna which, he hoped,
would change his output from broadcast to some sort of
beam; after this he kept probing the sky with the
"beam," first listening to the *Albireo*'s broadcast in an
effort to find projecting wisps of ionosphere and then,
whenever he thought he had one, switching on his transmitter and driving his own message at it.

Not once did he complain about lack of equipment or
remark how much better he could do once he was back
at the ship.

Hargedon's silence began to carry an undercurrent of
approval not usual in people who spent much time with
Zaino. The technician made no further reference to the
suggestion of switching drivers. They came in sight of the
Albireo and doubled the chasm with Hargedon still at
the wheel, Zaino still at his radio and both of them still
uncertain whether any of the calls had gotten through.

Both had to admit, even before they could see the
ship, that Burkett had had a right to be impressed.

The smoke column showed starkly against the sky,
blowing back over the tractor and blocking the sunlight
which would otherwise have glared into the driver's eyes.
Fine particles fell from it in a steady shower; looking
back, the men could see tracks left by their vehicle in
the deposit which had already fallen.

As they approached the ship the dark pillar grew
denser and narrower, while the particles raining from it
became coarser. In some places the ash was drifting into
fairly deep piles, giving Hargedon some anxiety about
possible concealed cracks. The last part of the trip, along
the edge of the great chasm and around its end, was
really dangerous, cracks running from its sides were definitely spreading. The two men reached the *Albireo* later
than Hargedon had promised, and found Burkett waiting
impatiently with a pile of apparatus beside her.

She didn't wait for them to get out before starting to
organize.

"There isn't much here. We'll take off just enough of
what you're carrying to make room for this. No—wait.
I'll have to check some of your equipment; I'm going to
need one of Milt Schlossberg's gadgets, I think, so leave
that on. We'll take—"

"Excuse me, Doctor," cut in Hargedon. "Our suits need servicing, or at least mine will if you want me to drive you. Perhaps Arnie can help you load for a while, if you don't think it's too important for him to get at the radio—"

"Of course. Excuse me. I should have had someone out here to help me with this. You two go on in. Ren, please get back as soon as you can. I can do the work here; none of this stuff is very heavy."

Zaino hesitated as he swung out of the cab. True, there wasn't too much to be moved, and it wasn't very heavy in Mercury's gravity, and he really should be at the radio; but the thirty-nine-year-old mineralogist was a middle-aged lady by his standards, and shouldn't be allowed to carry heavy packages. . . .

"Get along, Arnie!" the middle-aged lady interrupted this train of thought. "Eric and Eileen are getting farther away and harder to reach every second you dawdle!"

He got, though he couldn't help looking northeast as he went rather than where he was going.

The towering menace in that direction would have claimed anyone's attention. The pillar of sable ash was rising straighter, as though the wind were having less effect on it. An equally black cone had risen into sight beyond Northeast Spur—a cone that must have grown to some two thousand feet in roughly ten hours. It had far steeper sides than the cinder mounds near it; it couldn't be made of the same loose ash. Perhaps it consisted of half-melted particles which were fusing together as they fell—that might be what Burkett had meant by "spatter-cone." Still, if that were the case, the material fountaining from the cone's top should be lighting the plain with its incandescence rather than casting an inky shadow for its entire height.

Well, that was a problem for the geologists; Zaino climbed aboard and settled to his task.

The trouble was that he could do very little more here than he could in the tractor. He could have improvised longer-wave transmitting coils whose radiations would have diffracted a little more effectively beyond the horizon, but the receiver on the missing vehicle would not have detected them. He had more power at his disposal, but could only beam it into empty space with his better antennae. He had better equipment for locating any projecting wisps of charged gas which might reflect his waves, but he was already located under a solid roof of the stuff—the *Albireo* was technically on Brightside. Bouncing his beam from this layer still didn't give him the range he needed, as he had found both by calculation and trial.

What he really needed was a relay satellite. The target was simply too far around Mercury's sharp curve by now for anything less.

Zaino's final gesture was to set his transmission beam on the lowest frequency the tractor would pick up, aim it as close to the vehicle's direction as he could calculate from map and itinerary and set the recorded return message going. He told Rowson as much.

"Can't think of anything else?" the captain asked. "Well neither can I, but of course it's not my field. I'd give a year's pay if I could. How long before they should be back in range?"

"About four days. A hundred hours, give or take a few. They'll be heading back anyway by that time."

"Of course. Well, keep trying."

"I am—or rather, the equipment is. I don't see what else I can do unless a really bright idea should suddenly sprout. Is there anywhere else I could be useful? I'm as likely to have ideas working as just sitting."

"We can keep you busy, all right. But how about taking a transmitter up one of those mountains? That would get your wave farther."

"Not as far as it's going already. I'm bouncing it off the ion layer, which is higher than any mountain we've seen on Mercury even if it's nowhere near as high as Earth's."

"Hmph. All right."

"I could help Ren and Dr. Burkett, I could hang on outside the tractor—"

"They've already gone. You'd better call them, though, and keep a log of what they do."

"All right," Zaino turned back to his board and with no trouble raised the tractor carrying Hargedon and the mineralogist. The latter had been trying to call the *Al-*

bireo and had some acid comments about radio operators who slept on the job.

"There's only one of me, and I've been trying to get the Darkside team," he pointed out. "Have you found anything new about this lava flood?"

"Flow, not flood," corrected the professional automatically. "We're not in sight of it yet. We've just rounded the corner that takes us out of your sight. It's over a mile yet, and a couple of more corners, before we get to the spot where I left it. Of course, it will be closer than that by now. It was spreading at perhaps a hundred yards an hour then. That's one figure we must refine. . . . Of course, I'll try to get samples, too. I wish there were some way to get samples of the central cone. The whole thing is the queerest volcano I've ever heard of. Have you gotten Eileen started back?"

"Not as far as I can tell. As with your cone samples, there are practical difficulties," replied Zaino. "I haven't quit yet, though."

"I should think not. If some of us were paid by the idea we'd be pretty poor, but the perspiration part of genius is open to all of us."

"You mean I should charge a bonus for getting this call through?" retorted the operator.

Whatever Burkett's reply to this might have been was never learned; her attention was diverted at that point.

"We've just come in sight of the flow. It's about five hundred yards ahead. We'll get as close as seems safe, and I'll try to make sure whether it's really lava or just mud."

"Mud? Is that possible? I thought there wasn't—couldn't be—any water on this planet!"

"It is, and there probably isn't. The liquid phase of mud doesn't have to be water, even though it usually is on Earth. Here, for example, it might conceivably be sulfur."

"But if it's just mud, it wouldn't hurt the ship, would it?"

"Probably not."

"Then why all this fuss about getting the tractors back in a hurry?"

The voice which answered reminded him of another

lady in his past, who had kept him after school for drawing pictures in math class.

"Because in my judgment the flow is far more likely to be lava than mud, and if I must be wrong I'd rather my error were one that left us alive. I have no time at the moment to explain the basis of my judgment. I will be reporting our activities quite steadily from now on, and would prefer that you not interrupt unless a serious emergency demands it, or you get a call from Eileen.

"We are about three hundred yards away now. The front is moving about as fast as before, which suggests that the flow is coming only along this valley. It's only three or four feet high, so viscosity is very low or density very high. Probably the former, considering where we are. It's as black as the smoke column."

"Not glowing?" cut in Zaino thoughtlessly.

"*Black*, I said. Temperature will be easier to measure when we get closer. The front is nearly straight across the valley, with just a few lobes projecting ten or twelve yards and one notch where a small spine is being surrounded. By the way, I trust you're taping all this?" Again Zaino was reminded of the afternoon after school.

"Yes, Ma'am," he replied. "On my one and only monitor tape."

"Very well. We're stopping near the middle of the valley one hundred yards from the front. I am getting out, and will walk as close as I can with a sampler and a radiometer. I assume that the radio equipment will continue to relay my suit broadcast back to you." Zaino cringed a little, certain as he was that the tractor's electronic apparatus was in perfect order.

It struck him that Dr. Burkett was being more snappish than usual. It never crossed his mind that the woman might be afraid.

"Ren, don't get any closer with the tractor unless I call. I'll get a set of temperature readings as soon as I'm close enough. Then I'll try to get a sample. Then I'll come back with that to the tractor, leave it and the radiometer and get the markers to set out."

"Couldn't I be putting out the markers while you get the sample, Doctor!"

"You could, but I'd rather you stayed at the wheel."

Hargedon made no answer, and Burkett resumed her description for the record.

"I'm walking toward the front, a good deal faster than it's flowing toward me. I am now about twenty yards away, and am going to take a set of radiation-temperature measures." A brief pause. "Readings coming. Nine sixty. Nine eighty. Nine ninety—that's from the bottom edge near the spine that's being surrounded. Nine eighty-five—" The voice droned on until about two dozen readings had been taped. Then, "I'm going closer now. The sampler is just a ladle on a twelve-foot handle we improvised, so I'll have to get that close, The stuff is moving slowly; there should be no trouble. I'm in reach now. The lava is very liquid; there's no trouble getting the sampler in—or out again—it's not very dense, either. I'm heading back toward the tractor now. No, Ren, don't come to meet me."

There was a minute of silence, while Zaino pictured the space-suited figure with its awkwardly long burden, walking away from the creeping menace to the relative safety of the tractor. "It's frozen solid already; we needn't worry about spilling. The temperature is about—five eighty. Give me the markers, please."

Another pause, shorter this time. Zaino wondered how much of that could be laid to a faster walk without the ladle and how much to the lessening distance between flow and tractor. "I'm tossing the first marker close to the edge—it's landed less than a foot from the lava. They're all on a light cord at ten-foot intervals; I'm paying out the cord as I go back to the tractor. Now we'll stand by and time the arrival at each marker as well as we can."

"How close are you to the main cone?" asked Zaino.

"Not close enough to see its base, I'm afraid. Or to get a sample of it, which is worse. We—goodness, what was that?"

Zaino had just time to ask, "What was what?" when he found out.

For a moment, he thought that the *Albireo* had been flung bodily into the air. Then he decided that the great metal pillar had merely fallen over. Finally he realized that the ship was still erect, but the ground under it had just tried to leave.

Everyone in the group had become so used to the almost perpetual ground tremors that they had ceased to notice them; but this one demanded attention. Rowson, using language which suggested that his career might not have been completely free of adventure after all, flashed through the communication level on his way down to the power section. Schlossberg and Babineau followed, the medic pausing to ask Zaino if he were all right. The radioman merely nodded affirmatively; his attention was already back at his job. Burkett was speaking a good deal faster than before.

"Never mind if the sample isn't lashed tight yet—if it falls off there'll be plenty more. There isn't time! Arnie, get in touch with Dr. Mardikian and Dr. Marini. Tell them that this volcano is explosive, that all estimates of what the flow may do are off until we can make more measures, and in any case the whole situation is unpredictable. Everyone should get back as soon as possible. Remember, we decided that those big craters Eileen checked were not meteor pits. I don't know whether this thing will go in the next hour, the next year, or at all. Maybe what's happening now will act as a safety valve— but let's get out. Ren, that flow is speeding up and getting higher, and the ash rain is getting a lot worse. Can you see to drive?"

She fell silent, Zaino, in spite of her orders, left his set long enough to leap to the nearest port for a look at the volcano.

He never regretted it.

Across the riven plain, whose cracks were now nearly hidden under the new ash, the black cone towered above the nearer elevations. It was visibly taller than it had been only a few hours before. The fountain from its top was thicker, now jetting straight up as though wind no longer meant a thing to the fiercely driven column of gas and dust. The darkness was not so complete; patches of red and yellow incandescence showed briefly in the pillar, and glowing sparks rather than black cinders rained back on the steep slopes. Far above, a ring of smoke rolled and spread about the column, forming an ever-broaden-ing blanket of opaque cloud above a landscape which had never before been shaded from the sun. Streamers of lightning leaped between cloud and pillar, pillar and mountain, even cloud and ground. Any thunder there might have been was drowned in the howl of the escaping gas, a roar which seemed to combine every possible note from the shrillest possible whistle to a bass felt by the chest rather than heard by the ears. Rowson's language had become inaudible almost before he had disappeared down the hatch.

For long moments the radioman watched the spreading cloud, and wondered whether the *Albireo* could escape being struck by the flickering, ceaseless lightning. Far above the widening ring of cloud the smoke fountain drove, spreading slowly in the thinning atmosphere and beyond it. Zaino had had enough space experience to tell at a glance whether a smoke or dust cloud was in air or not. This wasn't, at least at the upper extremity. . . .

And then, quite calmly, he turned back to his desk, aimed the antenna straight up, and called Eileen Harmon. She answered promptly.

The stratigrapher listened without interruption to his report and the order to return. She conferred briefly with her companion, replied "We'll be back in twelve hours," and signed off. And that was that.

Zaino settled back with a sigh, and wondered whether it would be tactful to remind Rowson of his offer of a year's pay.

All four vehicles were now homeward bound; all one had to worry about was whether any of them would make it. Hargedon and Burkett were fighting their way through an ever-increasing ash rain a scant two miles away—ash which not only cut visibility but threatened to block the way with drifts too deep to negotiate. The wind, now blowing fiercely toward the volcano, blasted the gritty stuff against their front window as though it would erode through; and the lava flow, moving far faster than the gentle ooze they had never quite measured, surged—and glowed—grimly behind.

A hundred miles or more to the east, the tractors containing Mardikian, Marini and their drivers headed southwest along the alternate route their maps had suggested; but Mardikian, some three hours in the lead, reported that he could see four other smoke columns in that general direction.

Mercury seemed to be entering a new phase. The maps might well be out of date.

Harmon and Trackman were having no trouble at the moment, but they would have to pass the great chasm. This had been shooting out daughter cracks when Zaino and Hargedon passed it hours before. No one could say what it might be like now, and no one was going out to make sure.

"We can see you!" Burkett's voice came through suddenly. "Half a mile to go, and we're way ahead of the flow."

"But it's coming?" Rawson asked tensely. He had returned from the power level at Zaino's phoned report of success.

"It's coming."

"How fast? When will it get here? Do you know whether the ship can stand contact with it?"

"I don't know the speed exactly. There may be two hours, maybe five or six. The ship can't take it. Even the temperature measures I got were above the softening point of the alloys, and it's hotter and much deeper now. Anyway, if the others aren't back before the flow reaches the ship they won't get through. The tractor wheels would char away, and I doubt that the bodies would float. You certainly can't wade through the stuff in a space suit, either."

"And you think there can't be more than five or six hours before the flow arrives?"

"I'd say that was a very optimistic guess. I'll stop and get a better speed estimate if you want, but won't swear to it."

Rowson thought for a moment.

"No," he said finally, "don't bother. Get back here as soon as you can. We need the tractor and human muscles more than we need even expert guesses." He turned to the operator.

"Zaino, tell all the tractors there'll be no answer from

the ship for a while, because no one will be aboard. Then suit up and come outside." He was gone.

Ten minutes later, six human beings and a tractor were assembled in the flame-lit near-darkness outside the ship. The cloud had spread to the horizon, and the sun was gone. Burkett and Hargedon had arrived, but Rowson wasted no time on congratulations.

"We have work to do. It will be easy enough to keep the lava from the ship, since there seems to be a foot or more of ash on the ground and a touch of main drive would push it into a ringwall around us; but that's not the main problem. We have to keep it from reaching the chasm anywhere south of us, since that's the way the others will be coming. If they're cut off, they're dead. It will be brute work. We'll use the tractor any way we can think of. Unfortunately it has no plow attachment, and I can't think of anything aboard which could be turned into one. You have shovels, such as they are. The ash is light, especially here, but there's a mile and a half of dam to be built. I don't see how it can possibly be done . . . but it's going to be."

"Come on, Arnie! You're young and strong," came the voice of the mineralogist. "You should be able to lift as much of this stuff as I can. I understand you were lucky enough to get hold of Eileen—have you asked for the bonus yet?—but your work isn't done."

"It wasn't luck," Zaino retorted. Burkett, in spite of her voice, seemed much less of a schoolmistress when encased in a space suit and carrying a shovel, so he was able to talk back to her. "I was simply alert enough to make use of existing conditions, which I had to observe for myself in spite of all the scientists around. I'm charging the achievement to my regular salary. I saw—"

He stopped suddenly, both with tongue and shovel. Then, "Captain!"

"What is it?"

"The only reason we're starting this wall here is to keep well ahead of the flow so we can work as long as possible, isn't it?"

"Yes, I suppose so. I never thought of trying anywhere else. The valley would mean a much shorter dam, but if the flow isn't through it by now it would be before we could get there—oh! Wait a minute!"

"Yes, sir. You can put the main switch anywhere in a D. C. circuit. Where are the seismology stores we never had to use?"

Four minutes later the tractor set out from the *Albireo*, carrying Rowson and Zaino. Six minutes after that it stopped at the base of the ash cone which formed the north side of the valley from which the lava was coming. They parked a quarter of the way around the cone's base from the emerging flood and started to climb on foot, both carrying burdens.

Forty-seven minutes later they returned empty-handed to the vehicle, to find that it had been engulfed by the spreading liquid.

With noticeable haste they floundered through the loose ash a few yards above the base until they had outdistanced the glowing menace, descended and started back across the plain to where they knew the ship to be, though she was invisible through the falling detritus. Once they had to detour around a crack. Once they encountered one which widened toward the chasm on their right, and they knew a detour would be impossible. Leaping it seemed impossible, too, but they did it. Thirty seconds after this, forty minutes after finding the tractor destroyed, the landscape was bathed in a magnesium-white glare as the two one-and-a-half kiloton charges planted just inside the crater rim let go.

"Should we go back and see if it worked?" asked Zaino.

"What's the use? The only other charges we had were in the tractor. Thank goodness they were nuclear instead of H. E. If it didn't work we'd have more trouble to get back than we're having now."

"If it didn't work, is there any point in going back?"

"Stop quibbling and keep walking. Dr. Burkett, are you listening?"

"Yes, Captain."

"We're fresh out of tractors, but if you want to try it on foot you might start a set of flow measures on the lava. Arnie wants to know whether our landslide slid properly."

However, the two were able to tell for themselves before getting back to the *Albireo*.

The flow didn't stop all at once, of course; but with the valley feeding it blocked off by a pile of volcanic ash four hundred feet high on one side, nearly fifty on the other and more than a quarter of a mile long, its enthusiasm quickly subsided. It was thin, fluid stuff, as Burkett had noted; but as it spread it cooled, and as it cooled it thickened.

Six hours after the blast it had stopped with its nearest lobe almost a mile from the ship, less than two feet thick at the edge.

When Mardikian's tractor arrived, Burkett was happily trying to analyze samples of the flow, and less happily speculating on how long it would be before the entire area would be blown off the planet. When Marini's and Harmon's vehicles arrived, almost together, the specimens had been loaded and everything stowed for acceleration. Sixty seconds after the last person was aboard, the *Albireo* left Mercury's surface at two gravities.

The haste, it turned out, wasn't really necessary. She had been in parking orbit nearly forty-five hours before the first of the giant volcanoes reached its climax, and the one beside their former site was not the first. It was the fourth.

"And that seems to be that," said Camille Burkett rather tritely as they drifted a hundred miles above the little world's surface. "Just a belt of white-hot calderas all around the planet. Pretty, if you like symmetry."

"I like being able to see it from this distance," replied Zaino, floating weightless beside her. "By the way, how much bonus should I ask for getting that idea of putting the seismic charges to use after all?"

"I wouldn't mention it. Any one of us might have thought of that. We all knew about them."

"Anyone *might* have. Let's speculate on how long it would have been before anyone *did*."

"It's still not like the other idea, which involved your own specialty. I still don't see what made you suppose that the gas pillar from the volcano would be heavily charged enough to reflect your radio beam. How did that idea strike you?"

Zaino thought back, and smiled a little as the picture of lightning blazing around pillar, cloud and mountain rose before his eyes.

"You're not quite right," he said. "I was worried about it for a while, but it didn't actually strike me."

It fell rather flat; Camille Burkett, Ph.D., had to have it explained to her.

THE PAIN PEDDLERS

BY ROBERT SILVERBERG (1935-   )

GALAXY SCIENCE FICTION
AUGUST

*Robert Silverberg's first published story was "Gorgon
Planet" in* Nebula Science Fiction *in February, 1954.
Since then he has become one of the most accomplished
and distinguished writers in science fiction. A complete list
of his outstanding novels would take up more space than
we have here, but I should at least mention four favorites—*Hawksbill Station *(1968);* A Time of Changes
(1971); Dying Inside *(1974);* and Nightfall *(1990, written
with my esteemed co-editor).*

*"The Pain Peddlers" is a neat and scary story about a
possible form of entertainment, slightly reminiscent of
Robert Sheckley's more famous "The Prize of Peril." You
won't soon forget this one.*

The phone bleeped. Northrop nudged the cut-in switch
and heard Maurillo say, "We got a gangrene, chief.
They're amputating tonight."

Northrop's pulse quickened at the thought of action.
"What's the tab?" he asked.

"Five thousand for all rights."

"Anesthetic?"

"Natch," Maurillo said. "I tried it the other way."

"What did you offer?"

"Ten. It was no go."

Northrop sighed. "I'll have to handle it myself, I guess.
Where's the patient?"

"Clinton General. In the wards."

Northrop raised a heavy eyebrow and glowered into the screen. "In the *wards*?" he bellowed. "And you couldn't get them to agree?"

Maurillo seemed to shrink. "It was the relatives, chief. They were stubborn. The old man, he didn't seem to give a damn, but the relatives—"

"Okay. You stay there. I'm coming over to close the deal," Northrop snapped. He cut the phone out and pulled a couple of blank waiver forms out of his desk, just in case the relatives backed down. Gangrene was gangrene, but ten grand was ten grand. And business was business. The networks were yelling. He had to supply the goods or get out.

He thumbed the autosecretary. "I want my car ready in thirty seconds. South Street exit."

"Yes, Mr. Northrop."

"If anyone calls for me in the next half hour, record it. I'm going to Clinton General Hospital, but I don't want to be called there."

"Yes, Mr. Northrop."

"If Rayfield calls from the network office, tell him I'm getting him a dandy. Tell him—oh hell, tell him I'll call him back in an hour. That's all."

"Yes, Mr. Northrop."

Northrop scowled at the machine and left his office. The gravshaft took him down forty stories in almost literally no time flat. His car was waiting, as ordered, a long sleek '08 Frontenac with bubble top. Bulletproof, of course. Network producers were vulnerable to crackpot attacks.

He sat back, nestling into the plush upholstery. The car asked him where he was going, and he answered.

"Let's have a pep pill," he said.

A pill rolled out of the dispenser in front of him. He gulped it down. *Maurillo, you make me sick*, he thought. *Why can't you close a deal without me? Just once?*

He made a mental note: Maurillo had to go. The organization couldn't tolerate inefficiency.

The hospital was an old one. It was housed in one of the vulgar green-glass architectural monstrosities so popular sixty years before, a tasteless slab-sided thing without character or grace.

The main door irised and Northrop stepped through. The familiar hospital smell hit his nostrils. Most people found it unpleasant, but not Northrop. For him it was the smell of dollars.

The hospital was so old that it still had nurses and orderlies. Oh, plenty of mechanicals skittered up and down the corridors, but here and there a middle-aged nurse, smugly clinging to her tenure, pushed a tray of mush along, or a doddering orderly propelled a broom. In his early days on video Northrop had done a documentary on these living fossils of the hospital corridors. He had won an award for the film. He remembered it for its crosscuts from baggy-faced nurses to gleaming mechanicals, its vivid presentation of the inhumanity of the new hospitals. It was a long time since Northrop had done a documentary of that sort. A different kind of show was the order of the day now, ever since the intensifiers came in and telecasting medicine became an art.

A mechanical took him to Ward Seven. Maurillo was waiting there, a short, bouncy little man who wasn't bouncing much now. He knew he had fumbled. Maurillo grinned up at Northrop, a hollow grin, and said, "You sure made it fast, chief!"

"How long would it take for the competition to cut in?" Northrop countered. "Where's the patient?"

"Down by the end. You see where the curtain is? I had that put up. To get in good with the heirs. The relatives, I mean."

"Fill me in," Northrop said. "Who's in charge?"

"The oldest son, Harry. Watch out for him. Greedy."

"Who isn't?" Northrop sighed.

They were at the curtain now. Maurillo parted it. All through the long ward, patients were stirring. Potential subjects for taping, all of them, Northrop thought. The world was so full of different kinds of sickness—and one sickness fed on another.

He stepped through the curtain. There was a man in the bed, drawn and gaunt, his hollow face greenish, stubbly. A mechanical stood next to the bed, with an intravenous tube running across and under the covers.

The patient looked at least ninety. Knocking off ten

years for the effects of illness still made him pretty old,
Northrop thought.

He confronted the relatives.

There were eight of them. Five women, ranging from
middle age down to teens. Three men, the oldest about
fifty, the other two in their forties. Sons and nieces and
granddaughters, Northrop figured.

He said gravely. "I know what a terrible tragedy this
must be for all of you. A man in the prime of his life—
head of a happy family—" Northrop stared at the
patient. "But I know he'll pull through. I can see the
strength in him."

The oldest relative said, "I'm Harry Gardner. I'm his
son. You're from the network?"

"I'm the producer," Northrop said. "I don't ordinarily
come in person, but my assistant told me what a great
human situation there was here, what a brave person
your father was—"

The man in the bed slept on. He looked bad.

Harry Gardner said, "We made an arrangement. Five
thousand bucks. We wouldn't do it, except for the hospital bills. They can really wreck you."

"I understand perfectly," Northrop said in his most
unctuous tones. "That's why we're prepared to raise our
offer. We're well aware of the disastrous effects of hospitalization on a small family, even today, in these times
of protection. And so we can offer—"

"No! There's got to be anesthetic!" It was one of the
daughters, a round, drab woman with colorless thin lips.
"We ain't going to let you make him suffer!"

Northrop smiled. "It would only be a moment of pain
for him. Believe me. We'd begin the anesthesia immediately after the amputation. Just let us capture that single
instant of—"

"It ain't right! He's old, he's got to be given the best
treatment! The pain could kill him!"

"On the contrary," Northrop said blandly. "Scientific
research has shown that pain is often beneficial in amputation cases. It creates a nerve block, you see, that causes
a kind of anesthesia of its own, without the harmful side
effects of chemotherapy. And once the danger vectors
are controlled, the normal anesthetic procedures can be

invoked, and—" he took a deep breath, and went rolling glibly on to the crusher—"with the extra fee we'll provide, you can give your dear one the absolute finest in medical care. There'll be no reason to stint."

Wary glances were exchanged. Harry Gardner said, "How much are you offering for this absolute finest in medical care?"

"May I see the leg?" Northrop answered.

The coverlet was peeled back. Northrop stared.

It was a nasty case. Northrop was no doctor, but he had been in this line of work for five years, and that was long enough to give him an amateur acquaintance with disease. He knew the old man was in bad shape. It looked as though there had been a severe burn, high up along the calf, which had probably been treated only with first aid. Then, in happy proletarian ignorance, the family had let the old man rot until he was gangrenous. Now the leg was blackened, glossy, and swollen from mid-calf to the ends of the toes. Everything looked soft and decayed. Northrop had the feeling that he could reach out and break the puffy toes off, one at a time.

The patient wasn't going to survive.

Amputation or not, he was rotten to the core by this time. If the shock of amputation didn't do him in, general debilitation would. It was a good prospect for the show. It was the kind of stomach-turning vicarious suffering that millions of viewers gobbled up avidly.

Northrop looked up and said, "Fifteen thousand if you'll allow a network-approved surgeon to amputate under our conditions. And we'll pay the surgeon's fee besides."

"Well—"

"And we'll also underwrite the entire cost of postoperative care for your father," Northrop added smoothly. "Even if he stays in the hospital for six months, we'll pay every nickel, over and above the telecast fee."

He had them. He could see the greed shining in their eyes. They were faced with bankruptcy. He had come to rescue them; and did it matter all that much if the old man didn't have anesthetic when they sawed his leg off? Why, he was hardly conscious even now. He wouldn't really feel a thing. Not really.

Northrop produced the documents, the waivers, the contracts covering residuals and Latin-American reruns, the payment vouchers, all the paraphernalia. He sent Maurillo scuttling off for a secretary, and a few moments later a glistening mechanical was taking it all down.

"If you'll put your name here, Mr. Gardner—"

Northrop handed the pen to the eldest son. Signed, sealed, delivered.

"We'll operate tonight," Northrup said. "I'll send our surgeon over immediately. One of our best men. We'll give your father the care he deserves."

He pocketed the documents.

It was done. Maybe it was barbaric to operate on an old man that way, Northrop thought. But he didn't bear the responsibility, after all. He was just giving the public what it wanted. What the public wanted was spouting blood and tortured nerves.

And what did it matter to the old man, really? Any experienced medic could tell you he was as good as dead. The operation wouldn't save him. Anesthesia wouldn't save him. If the gangrene didn't get him, postoperative shock would do him in. At worst, he would suffer only a few minutes under the knife . . . but at least his family would be free from the fear of financial ruin.

On the way out, Maurillo said, "Don't you think it's a little risky, chief? Offering to pay the hospitalization expenses, I mean?"

"You've got to gamble a little sometimes to get what you want," Northrop said.

"Yeah, but that could run to fifty, sixty thousand! What'll that do to the budget?"

Northrop grinned. "We'll survive. Which is more than the old man will. He can't make it through the night. We haven't risked a penny, Maurillo. Not a stinking cent."

Returning to the office, Northrop turned the papers on the Gardner amputation over to his assistants, set the wheels in motion for the show and prepared to call it a day.

There was only one bit of dirty work left to do. He had to fire Maurillo.

It wasn't called firing, of course. Maurillo had tenure, just like the hospital orderlies and everyone else below

executive rank. It would have to be more a kick upstairs
than anything else.

Northrop had been increasingly dissatisfied with the
little man's work for months now. Today had been the
clincher. Maurillo had no imagination. He didn't know
how to close a deal. Why hadn't he thought of underwrit-
ing the hospitalization? *If I can't delegate responsibility
to him*, Northrop told himself, *I can't use him at all*.
There were plenty of other assistant producers in the
outfit who'd be glad to step in.

Northrop spoke to a couple of them. He made his
choice: A young fellow named Barton, who'd been working on documentaries all year. Barton had done the
plane-crash deal in London in the spring. He had a fine
touch for the gruesome. He had been on hand at the
Worlds' Fair fire last year at Juneau. Yes, Barton was
the man.

The next part was the sticky one. Things could go
wrong.

Northrop phoned Maurillo, even though Maurillo was
only two rooms away—these things were never done in
person—and said, "I've got some good news for you,
Ted. We're shifting you to a new program."

"Shifting—?"

"That's right. We had a talk in here this afternoon,
and we decided you were being wasted on the blood-
and-guts show. You need more scope for your talents.
So we're moving you over to *Kiddie Time*. We think
you'll really blossom there. You and Sam Kline and Ed
Bragan ought to make a terrific team."

Northrop saw Maurillo's pudgy face crumble. The
arithmetic was getting home; over here, Maurillo was
Number Two, and on the new show, a much less important one, he'd be Number Three. The pay meant nothing, of course; didn't Internal Revenue take it all
anyway? It was a thumping boot, and Maurillo knew it.

The mores of the situation called for Maurillo to pretend he was receiving a rare honor. He didn't play the
game. He squinted and said, "Just because I didn't sign
up that old man's amputation?"

"What makes you think—"

"Three years I've been with you! Three years, and you kick me out just like that!"

"I told you, Ted, we thought this would be a big opportunity for you. It's a step up the ladder. It's—"

Maurillo's fleshy face puffed up with rage. "It's getting junked," he said bitterly. "Well, never mind, huh? It so happens I've got another offer. I'm quitting before you can can me. You can take your tenure and—"

Northrop hastily blanked the screen.

The idiot, he thought. *The fat little idiot. Well, to hell with him!*

He cleared his desk, and cleared his mind of Ted Maurillo and his problems. Life was real, life was earnest. Maurillo just couldn't take the pace, that was all.

Northrop prepared to go home. It had been a long day.

At eight that evening came word that old Gardner was about to undergo the amputation. At ten, Northrop was phoned by the network's own head surgeon, Dr. Steele, with the news that the operation had failed.

"We lost him," Steele said in a flat, unconcerned voice. "We did our best, but he was a mess. Fibrillation set in, and his heart just ran away. Not a damned thing we could do."

"Did the leg come off?"

"Oh, sure. All this was after the operation."

"Did it get taped?"

"Processing it now."

"Okay," Northrop said. "Thanks for calling."

"Sorry about the patient."

"Don't worry yourself," Northrop said. "It happens to the best of us."

The next morning, Northrop had a look at the rushes. The screening was in the 23rd Floor studio, and a select audience was on hand—Northrop, his new assistant producer Barton, a handful of network executives, a couple of men from the cutting room. Slick, bosomy girls handed out intensifier helmets. No mechanicals doing the work here!

Northrop slipped the helmet on over his head. He felt the familiar surge of excitement as the electrodes descended and contact was made. He closed his eyes. There was a thrum of power somewhere in the room as the EEG-amplifier went into action. The screen brightened.

There was the old man. There was the gangrenous leg. There was Dr. Steele, crisp and rugged and dimple-chinned, the network's star surgeon, $250,000 a year's worth of talent. There was the scalpel, gleaming in Steele's hand.

Northrop began to sweat. The amplified brain waves were coming through the intensifier, and he felt the throbbing in the old man's leg, felt the dull haze of pain behind the old man's forehead, felt the weakness of being eighty years old and half dead.

Steele was checking out the electronic scalpel, now, while the nurses fussed around, preparing the man for the amputation. In the finished tape, there would be music, narration, all the trimmings, but now there was just a soundless series of images, and, of course, the tapped brain waves of the sick man.

The leg was bare.

The scalped descended.

Northrop winced as vicarious agony shot through him. He could feel the blazing pain, the brief searing hell as the scalpel slashed through diseased flesh and rotting bone. His whole body trembled, and he bit down hard on his lips and clenched his fists, and then it was over.

There was a cessation of pain. A catharsis. The leg no longer sent its pulsating messages to the weary brain. Now there was shock, the anesthesia of hyped-up pain, and with the shock came calmness. Steele went about the mop-up operation. He tidied the stump, bound it.

The rushes flickered on in anticlimax. Later, the production crew would tie up the program with interviews of the family, perhaps a shot of the funeral, a few observations on the problem of gangrene in the aged. Those things were the extras. What counted, what the viewers wanted, was the sheer nastiness of vicarious pain, and that they got in full measure. It was a gladiatorial contest without the gladiators, masochism concealed as medicine. It worked. It pulled in the viewers by the million.

Northrop patted sweat from his forehead.

"Looks like we got ourselves quite a little show here, boys," he said in satisfaction.

The mood of satisfaction was still on him as he left the building that day. All day he had worked hard, getting the show into its final shape, cutting and polishing. He enjoyed the element of craftsmanship. It helped him to forget some of the sordidness of the program.

Night had fallen when he left. He stepped out of the main entrance and a figure strode forward, a bulky figure, medium height, tired face. A hand reached out, thrusting him roughly back into the lobby of the building.

At first Northrop didn't recognize the face of the man. It was a blank face, a nothing face, a middle-aged empty face. Then he placed it.

Harry Gardner. The son of the dead man.

"Murderer!" Gardner shrilled. "You killed him! He would have lived if you'd used anesthetics! You phony, you murdered him so people would have thrills on television!"

Northrop glanced up the lobby. Someone was coming, around the bend. Northrop felt calm. He could stare this nobody down until he fled in fear.

"Listen," Northrop said, "we did the best medical science can do for your father. We gave him the ultimate in scientific care. We—"

"You murdered him!"

"No," Northrop said, and then he said no more, because he saw the sudden flicker of a slice gun in the blank-faced man's fat hand.

He backed away. But it didn't help, because Gardner punched the trigger and an incandescent bolt flared out, and sliced across Northrop's belly just as efficiently as the surgeon's scalpel had cut through the gangrenous leg.

Gardner raced away, feet clattering on the marble floor. Northrop dropped, clutching himself.

His suit was seared. There was a slash through his abdomen, a burn an eighth of an inch wide and perhaps four inches deep, cutting through intestines, through organs, through flesh. The pain hadn't begun yet. His nerves weren't getting the message through to his stunned brain.

But then they were; and Northrop coiled and twisted in agony that was anything but vicarious now.

Footsteps approached.

"Jeez," a voice said.

Northrop forced an eye open. Maurillo. Of all people, Maurillo.

"A doctor," Northrop wheezed. "Fast! Christ, the pain! Help me, Ted!"

Maurillo looked down, and smiled. Without a word, he stepped to the telephone booth six feet away, dropped in a token, punched out a call.

"Get a van over here, fast. I've got a subject, chief."

Northrop writhed in torment. Maurillo crouched next to him. "A doctor," Northrop murmured. "A needle, at least. Gimme a needle! The pain—"

"You want me to kill the pain?" Maurillo laughed. "Nothing doing. You just hang on. You stay alive till we get that hat on your head and tape the whole thing."

"But you don't work for me. You're off the program—"

"Sure," Maurillo said. "I'm with Transcontinental now. They're starting a blood-and-guts show too. Only they don't need waivers."

Northrop gaped. Transcontinental? The bootleg outfit that peddled tapes in Afghanistan and Mexico and Ghana and God knew where else? Not even a network show, he thought. No fee! Dying in agony for the benefit of a bunch of lousy tapeleggers. That was the worst part, Northrop thought. Only Maurillo would pull a deal like that.

"A needle! For God's sake, Maurillo, a needle!"

"Nothing doing. The van'll be here any minute. They'll sew you up, and we'll tape it nice."

Northrop closed his eyes. He felt the coiling intestines blazing within him. He willed himself to die, to cheat Maurillo.

But it was no use. He remained alive and suffering.

He lived for an hour. That was plenty of time to tape his dying agonies. The last thought he had was that it was a damned shame he couldn't star on his own show.

TURN OFF THE SKY

BY RAY NELSON (1931-   )

THE MAGAZINE OF FANTASY AND SCIENCE FICTION
AUGUST

Ray Nelson is a writer and artist who has produced a small number of excellent science fiction stories and novels since 1963. His most memorable works are the novels The Ganymede Takeover *(1967), written with Philip K. Dick; and* Timequest *(1985), which is a revision and expansion of his earlier novel* Blake's Progress, *itself notable as the (by far) best work to come out of the Laser Books program of novels of the mid-1970s. His notable short fiction includes such gems as "Time Travel for Pedestrians," "Nightfall on the Dead Sea," and "Eight O'Clock in the Morning."*

"Turn Off the Sky" is an excellent and bold work, and simply one of the finest first stories in the history of science fiction. It was brought to my attention—I don't remember reading it before—by a devoted reader of this series, whose letter I promptly lost. Please forgive me, as I wanted to thank you by name.

As usual, Abelard Rosenburg came to the party stark naked except for a briefcase full of left-wing propaganda and two coats of paint below. The paint was a beautiful ice blue, forming a striking contrast to his black skin and still blacker beard. He stood in the doorway of the little bookstore a moment, silhouetted against the blazing artificial aurora borealis in the sky; then when a few people had dutifully greeted him, he entered and opened his briefcase.

"Share my burden?" he asked a young ballet dancer, handing her a thick fistful of printed and mimeographed sheets.

"Thank you just the same," said the dancer, "but I don't read that sort of thing. I'm sure it's all very nice and all, but I am sort of anti-political."

"So am I," said Abelard. "Nobody could be more anti-political than me."

"Do you belong to the Anti-Political Party?"

"Worse than that. I am an anarchist."

The ballet dancer shook her head, purple pony tail swinging behind her.

"I'm sorry, honey, but I don't know that word. What's an anarchist?" she asked.

"It is someone who is opposed to the state."

"How can you be opposed to the state? If there wasn't any state to give us food, how could we eat? If there wasn't any state to build houses, where would we live? Gee, honey, you can't be serious." She turned her round vacant eyes on him and stuck out her lower lip.

"I define the state as an armed body of men," he said. "distinguished from other organizations by its four particular functions; cops, courts, jails and taxes. Society does not need to rely on coercion to function. All man's needs are supplied by cybernetic machines which function perfectly well without any human intervention, let alone government supervision."

"Well, perhaps that is true," she said, "but if there were no government, what would keep people from murdering each other and stealing each other's property?"

He raised a finger skyward. "The need to steal and murder no longer exists. There is more than enough of everything for everyone. Nobody needs to take from someone else."

She frowned, trying her best to think.

"Well, that's true enough of some things, like food and clothing and housing, but let's say I have a certain painting, a Boris Lee original, and someone else wants it," she postulated brightly.

"You could work out an arrangement with that person to lend the painting part time, or better yet, if you both liked the painting that much, you'd have enough in common to live together."

"Live together? What about that, now?" she considered, "What about crimes of passion?" She rolled the word "passion" off the tip of her tongue like a delicious drop of old French wine.

"That's the job of education. Passion is just an excuse the square gives to his conscience for enjoying the sexual pleasures he wants even though his religion tells him it is wrong." His grin was all teeth.

"Education? Honey, you know you can't change human nature." To her, this seemed beyond all dispute.

"That's not true. There was a time, long ago, when I would have been a social outcast—to be hunted, hated—even killed."

Her owl eyes grew wider still.

"You? Hated? Why it just wouldn't be possible to have a party without good old Abelard. Why would anyone hate you?" she asked, amazed.

"First of all, I am a Negro."

"So what?"

"Second, I am a Jew."

"You actually still go to church and all that stuff?"

"No, as a matter of fact, I am an atheist."

"What's that?"

"It means I don't believe in God."

"Oh." She frowned again and rubbed her nose with her purple fingernail.

"And being an anarchist alone might at one time have gotten me thrown in jail."

She crossed her arms on her chest and thrust out her chin.

"So what's the point?" she said.

"Just this . . . all those powerful forms of passion . . . hate, prejudice, religious and political intolerance, have been destroyed by education. Sexual passion is next to go."

"Somehow," said the little dancer, blinking her false eyelashes, "I think I'd rather keep the state than give up sex."

"You won't have to give up sex. Just the possessive forms of it, like marriage and the family. The race will be propogated by Universal Free Love." He spread his arms expansively.

She thought for a moment.

"Gee, that might be all right for the far distant future, but could we have free love right now?" she asked.

"Certainly. Right now!" he said.

The dancer closed her eyes, tilted back her head, and whispered huskily. "Show me!"

"Right here," said Abelard, thrusting a mimeographed pamphlet into her hand, "It tells all about it in here."

The conversation lagged a little after that, and the dancer wandered off with a bald, bitter Ancient Texts Translator, reputed to be familiar even with the forgotten language of Denmark. It seems that even he had finally become technologically unemployed.

Abelard followed half-heartedly, pushing his way through the crowd, until they went into the back room. As Abelard was about to go in he met the alcoholic poet, Dean Natkin, coming out.

"You don't want to go in there without a woman," said Dean drunkenly. "They are all making sex in there. Going at it like mad minks."

Dean took Abelard by the arm and led him toward an improvised bar in the part of the bookstore called the "Old Smokey Reading Room." A jazz fan was sprawled on the floor in one corner, idly picking out Anglo-Indian jazz riffs on an old sitar while another jazzman of the "cool" or 43-tones-to-the-octave school looked on with annoyance.

"It's not that I drink, mind you," said Dean, pouring himself a fresh drink, "but I *appreciate* liquor."

Abelard politely declined a drink and reached into his briefcase for a handful of literature.

"Share my burden?" he queried, handing a fistful of publications to the unimpressed Dean.

"You're the anarchist fellow, aren't you?"

"Yes."

"You are against being in the army, eh?"

"That's right."

"I can see why," Dean reflected, "All you get in the Army is a lot of little badges pinned all over you, and that might be painful to a fellow who dresses the way you do."

With that Dean downed another rum, drooling slightly on his black cape. The two jazzmen had begun to argue quite seriously the opposition of the spontaneous jazz of India vs. the intellectual 43-toned jazz of America.

"I read an interesting fact today," said Dean. "I say, do you know that what lice feed on is blood? I had an idea . . ."

He downed another glass and reached again for the bottle.

The argument in the corner was becoming quite violent. A small crowd had begun to gather to watch. The little ballet dancer came out of the back room buttoning up her blue jeans and joined the crowd.

"You think drink is bad," continued Dean. "You ought to see the chaps who take dope. There are quite a few here tonight. I wouldn't want to name names, but some of them play 'cool' jazz. They say even the President of the United World Government is on the needle. Nothing else to do, eh what? They had to make it legal when they found more than half the world's population were taking it. I heard one of them walk into a drug store the other day and say, 'Give me a bottle of Codeine, please. Don't bother to wrap it. I'll drink it here.' That's a hot one, what?—'I'll drink it here!' "

"Look, dad," screamed the cool jazzman. "Like that Raga sound is nowhere. It just don't make it. Like this open fifth drone is just too piercing, you know what I mean?"

"All the poets smoke marijuana, you know," continued Dean. "I heard a commercial on the feelies last night about it. 'For real, deep down inspiration, smoke POT, P-O-T, POT, the international joy smoke.' "

"This cookie has the word for you, dad," yelled the jazzman, "and you just better believe it."

The man with the sitar went on, idly whanging out his little riffs, with a swinging $5/7$ beat.

"The other day," said Dean quietly, "a fellow who was on the needle came into a United Buddhist-Christian church . . . they are very progressive, you know . . . they say they take the best from all the world faiths, but they really only believe in keeping their state subsidy . . . anyway, this junkie came into the church and told his story to the minister. The minister listened to the whole thing with his best bedside manner and when it was finished, you know what the minister said? He said, 'Do you really think this is the Best Approach to the Problems of Life?' "

"You want to make the scene, honey?" the cool jazzman snarled at the sitar player, who just kept on playing as if he were deaf. "You want to make some real sounds? Lemme show you where the real sounds come from!" He whipped out a leather case, opened it, and extracted a beautiful hypodermic needle, decorated with golden *Lingam* and *yoni* and precious jewels.

"There's a lot of queers here tonight, too, I suppose you noticed," Dean droned. "That one over there, that looks like a boy isn't queer, though, but she tries. She was taking Lesbianism One and Two at Yale, but never quite passed her finals."

Abelard could not take his eyes off the needle. He felt paralyzed, hypnotized, by the points of light dancing and leaping over its jewelled sides. The sitar player spoke softly.

"Put that thing away," he said.

"This take toooooo much for you, honey?"

"I don't like that stuff. It's habit-forming."

"No lie? Is that the true word?"

The little ballet dancer squealed, "Look, he's scared!" The crowd moved in closer, excited now.

"We go my way or we don't go at all. Isn't that right, cats?" said the cool jazzman.

The crowd was with him. If there was anyone present who didn't like dope or cool jazz, he was careful to keep it to himself.

"He's a coward," said the translator.

"A square," said an abstract painter.

"Hey," said Abelard, "what . . ."

"Shut up, friend," said Dean. "You want to get us both killed?"

"Why not try a little?" asked the jazzman, coaxingly. "Come on, the first time is hard but after that it's easy. It's so good you just can't put it down."

"No, thanks. I think I'll just run on home . . ." said the sitar player uncertainly.

The crowd was like a solid stone wall blocking his escape.

"Everyone said she was a real butch," said Dean, downing another rum, "but I knew better. 'She isn't gay,' I said, 'she's just neurotic.' "

"What are they going to do?" whispered Abelard.

"What else can they do but stick him? Sure you won't have a little drink?"

"No, I . . ."

The sitar player tried to get to his feet, but the balding translator shoved him back. Abelard tried to go to help him but found Dean holding him back with arms of iron. The ballet dancer giggled hysterically and put her sandaled foot through the sound-box of the sitar. The jazzman moved in like a cobra, poisoned fang poised to strike.

"Look," whispered Dean, "I thought you were a nonviolent anarchist! There's nothing you . . ."

The sitar player screamed in terror as the crowd moved in on him. He tried to struggle but a thousand fingers held him helpless.

"Hold him still, somebody," said the jazzman. "Here's mud in your eye."

And he carefully inserted the hypodermic needle and pushed the plunger.

Abelard broke free of Dean's grasp and bolted for the door, his ears torn by the player's screams. He ran into the street and almost without thinking made for the entrance of the nearest underground. "The trains . . ." he thought. "The trains . . ."

He dashed down the stairs, in too much of a hurry for the escalator, and emerged on the platform panting. There was nobody in the station but a lone security policeman. Abelard thought desperately.

"A cop. Maybe I can tell the cop what happened at the party . . . but how would that look to everyone? Me, an anarchist, calling the cops? The jazzman might not even be arrested, and it would throw a bad light on anarchists everywhere if it ever got out I had called the cops. I'd be laughed at . . . even more than now."

With a sinister hiss, the subway train swept in and Abelard stepped on board. It was bright and luxurious and airconditioned and soundproofed inside, but outside, through the windows, Abelard could see the rushing darkness, the two wires near the window weaving up and down as they swept by. The undergrounds were always the same, whether they slunk along on rubber tires and hydropneumatic suspension like this local, or hurtled through a vacuum, magnetically suspended and propelled, like the transcontinental and transoceanic tubes, at over a thousand miles an hour, cutting a chord through the depths of the earth, a straight line between two points on the curved surface of the globe. The basic idea of all underground trains is the same . . . to rush blindly through the blackness from one identical station to another, to burrow through the earth in a huge metal worm, to hide from the blinding brilliance of the never-darkened sky, deep in the womb of the earth.

The basic idea of all underground trains is the same. To sit and stare into the face of one's fellow man and never speak, never betray by the slightest movement of the eyes a recognition of his existence. During rush hours to be crushed against him, chest to chest, back to back, so tightly you cannot move, so close you can inspect the pimples on his face, the dandruff on his shoulders, smell his sweat and hear his breathing, yet never say hello, never know if he is married or single, if he has children, and if they are healthy. To stand pressed as close to a woman as if in the tenderest embrace of love, and yet think about the ball game or the latest programs on the feelies—then to part and never see her again. To stand, perhaps, crushed back to back against the one person who has the missing piece to the puzzle of your life and never know it.

Abelard sat and watched the two wires outside his window rise and fall, rise and fall . . . then suddenly they were in Greenwich Village Station. After the dimness, the station lights were blinding, but he could see the station had not changed. The same paintings on the walls, the same statues and mobiles. Only some of the names of the artists had been changed.

One person got on, a tall, pale, exotic Eurasian girl

with long black hair down to her waist—dressed in black leotard and tights and carrying a black purse with a lizard's claw clasp.

"Greenwich Village Station," thought Abelard. "That could just as easily be the name of any station in the world. Greenwich Village extends to meet and blend with the Near North Side of Chicago, with the Left Bank in Paris, with North Beach in San Francisco, with Taos, New Mexico and London and Tokyo and Leopoldville and Rio . . . all showing the same paintings and sculpture and mobiles and dancing the same dances to the same music."

The girl sat in the seat directly opposite from him and began to do her lips. Abelard noticed with a start that she wore a diamond tiara in her hair, an anti-democratic gesture if there ever was one. How did she dare? He felt sure, somehow, that the diamonds were real.

Some of the others in the car had noticed it, too, and stared at her openly with mingled surprise and resentment. Abelard hoped there would be no unfortunate incident like the one at the party, but, no, nothing would happen on the train. Rushing through darkness in temporary conjunction was not the same as being drunk at a party, a so-called social function.

"You were born in October," said the girl, "around the first of the month." It was a statement of fact.

"Why, yes," gasped Abelard, "that's true. October third, to be exact."

"Your mother was African, your father Black Jewish."

"How did you know?"

She snapped her purse and inspected her reflection in the window. The two wires outside leaped upward suddenly and slowly settled back.

"Your parents didn't get on. Your father probably killed himself or something. That's why you hate the world so much."

"No," said Abelard, "that's not true about my father. How do you know so much about me? Are you a cop? Do you know some of my friends?"

She shook her head.

"The truth of the matter is," she answered, "I never

saw or heard of you before in my life. If I am wrong about your father, what's the real story on him?"

"You're close, too close. If you never heard of me before, how do you know so much about me?" he said guardedly.

"Astrology, mixed with psychology, mixed with the methods of Sherlock Holmes, mixed with withcraft, mixed with woman's intuition . . . I've studied a lot, but the truth is, I haven't the faintest idea how I know. I just know."

Abelard was silent for a moment, examining her explanation with suspicion.

"Are those diamonds real?"

"Of course they are, boy. Now what's the real story on your father? Did you love him?"

Abelard had never spoken to anyone about his private life before. Never. He was speechless, tongue-tied. Desperately he wondered how he might steer the subject around to safe, normal ground like anarchism, or atheism, or free love. He fumbled with the clasps on his briefcase, trying to open it, but his hands were shaking too much.

"Don't ask me to share your burden," she said, "I know that line. You say 'share my burden' and hand me a fistful of meaningless trash, then we talk about Karl Marx or Robert Heinlein ad nauseum. You aren't the first red I've met, you know. Now about your father?"

"A-about my father?" stammered Abelard.

"Did you love him?"

"Yes, yes, sure I did."

"A lot?"

"God, I worshiped my old man. I worshiped him. He was always laughing, always bringing me presents," he said, running his hand through his beard.

"Yeah?" She leaned forward.

"Why should I tell you all this?"

"Don't you want me to share your burden?" she asked.

Abelard felt the ground drop from under him. The past rose in a wave, drowning him, throwing him around like a twig in its tide. He was only half aware of the girl before him when next he spoke.

"They were always fighting, always," he said, barely audible. "She would scream that he was running around with other women and he would scream that she was frigid. Sometimes I couldn't sleep all night for their fighting. Then there was a whole week they didn't fight. My mother seemed like a changed woman, she was so sweet and nice to daddy and me. When Sunday came my mother fixed a wonderful supper for us with all my father's favorite foods. Daddy and Mommy were laughing and kidding and kissing each other like newlyweds. I was so happy I ran out in the backyard singing like a mad canary bird and bouncing my little ball. Bounce, bounce, bounce. It was sunset, before the invention of the artificial northern lights. Everything was all red and peaceful and beautiful and I bounced my little ball around and sang little songs to myself. Then, all of a sudden I heard a loud bang in the house and my mother started calling to me, 'Abe! Abe! come here a minute.' I ran inside and there on the kitchen floor was my old man, with a little hole in the front of his head and a big hole in the back and everything was all over blood."

There was a sudden flash of light as they passed through a station, then darkness outside as they rushed onward. Abelard felt tears, rotted, ancient, painful tears clawing his eyes, rolling down his cheeks.

"Baby," whispered the girl.

He continued haltingly, "Mama had a gun in her hand and the air was full of smoke. I can still smell it. I cried, 'Mama, what did you do? What did you do?' 'Nothing,' she answered, 'that's all. Nothing.' Then she put the gun in my hand and called the cop in from the street and told him I did it. *I did it?* Oh, God, I was just a tiny little boy. I couldn't murder anybody. And I loved my father. I worshiped him! How could anyone believe I could murder my own father? They took me off to the reformatory and kept me there for five years and every day they came and asked me why I did it, but I never told on my mother. Never. If they took my Mama away I'd have nobody."

"Never mind, baby. Never mind," whispered the girl, taking his hand. "That's all past and gone. I'll take care of you. No matter what happens, you'll always have me."

"You? You? Who are you?" he demanded.

"We'll go off somewhere together and be alone," she comforted him.

"There's no place in the world where we can be alone," he cried, "Where there were once deserts, now there are crowded cities. The polar regions are busy cybernetic farms, even the sea is one big algae and sea-food farm—and darkness? . . . God, they never turn off the sky! Not for one second. Not anywhere."

"But under the sea," she persisted. "What about the trans-Atlantic tube? It's dim in the tube cars and black as outer space outside the windows. Nobody is riding the tube at this time of night. Look, we're almost to Grand Central Station. Let's go. What do you say?"

"All right," he agreed.

They got off at Grand Central, picked up a meal and a bottle of wine from the free vending machines, then rode down the interminable escalator to the subterranean departure station.

The crowds moved heedlessly this way and that . . . the station seemed busy, but actually, compared with other seasons and other times of day, it was all but empty. If the trains had been run for profit, they probably would not be running at all. As it was, they left once every five minutes for Chicago, San Francisco, South America, Africa, France, England, wherever anyone could wish.

"Let's go to France," said Abelard.

"No, England," said the girl. "There's something there I want you to see."

They crossed a crystal bridge and emerged on the Trans-Atlantic tube platform. It was deserted. The feelies were playing to a host of empty chairs. Abelard tried to keep his eyes away from the screen. He always resented the power the feelies had over him, the way they could manipulate and control his emotions through control of the ionization of the air and the calculated use of sounds above the audible range. The way they could convince him that he was receiving a blow on the jaw or a kiss, or was drowning or flying. Some people who did nothing but watch them during their every waking hour, had no

other thoughts than those impressed on them by the feelies, no other feelings, no other lives.

With a hiss, the airlock opened and a recorded voice
said, "Train leaving for London. Please watch your step
upon entering and remain seated during the first part of
your journey. You will feel a slight pressure pulling you
toward the back of the train during the first part of the
trip, but do not worry. It is only inertia force resulting
from acceleration. Thank you."

They entered the dimly lit corridor, turned right, and
passed a long line of compartments, entering the last one
and closing the door behind them. Abelard switched the
lights to dim and turned to the girl. She clasped her
hands around his face and kissed him once, on the lips,
very gently. The train began to move.

The wall outside the window melted into a gray blur
and the acceleration force pressed them gently but firmly
into the deep, soft seat. Abelard took her in his arms
and held her, the tension draining from him, the sadness
drifting away. Gently, her tongue touched his lips, his
ears, his neck. He nipped her lightly on the ear lobe,
nibbled her lip. She returned his love-bites, softly at first,
then so they hurt just enough.

"I love you," she said softly. "You know that, don't
you?"

"And I love you, too," he answered, "I don't know
why or how, but I do."

She sighed and kissed him on the lips. His hand
moved, feeling the flesh of her beautiful young body
through the thin leotard.

Outside the movies painted on the walls flashed by
unnoticed, casting a flickering multicolored glow into the
compartment. The acceleration increased slightly.

"I tried to kill myself, a few months ago," she said.
"Have you ever tried that?"

"No."

"I guess you wouldn't," she mused. "You aren't the
type. I couldn't do it either. I went for a swim in the
Pacific Ocean near the Golden Gate Bridge. I took off
my clothes and waded into the surf. My plan was to swim
out a little ways, then a little ways more, then a little
ways more, until at last I was too far out to get back. I

figured that way I could trick my survival instinct into letting me die. I knew it had to be some accident or impersonal force that finally finished me off. Otherwise I would chicken out at the last minute."

"What happened then?" asked Abelard.

"I couldn't do it. The water was too cold."

Another movie flashed in through a window. A huge eye, watching, watching. On the screen outside appeared the words. "See it!" Then a huge hand appeared reaching, clutching.

"Darling, darling!" she gasped. Outside danced the words, "Touch it!" A huge mouth appeared, opening and closing. A gigantic tongue licked its lips. Breathing deep, sobbing breaths, Abelard and the girl kissed each other.

"Oh, darling, oh, darling," she whispered.

The movie outside flickered, "United Nations Hams are real meat, a treat that can't be beat!" A huge ham appeared at the window, dripping with juice. A knife appeared from the left hand side of the screen and sank deep, deep into it.

For a moment afterward, he was unconcious. Then he woke again, drenched in sweat, burning with fever. They lay a long time side by side, now and then kissing, now and then shifting slightly.

"Tell me something," she asked at last.

"What?"

She whispered in his ear.

"I don't think so," he said. "Why?"

"Because I feel sort of bluish inside," she said.

They were silent again for a while. The acceleration gradually stopped. Another ad flashed on outside.

"We're going pretty fast now, eh?" she asked.

"Over a thousand miles an hour," he answered.

They were silent a while longer.

"What do you expect from me?" she asked.

"Nothing," said Abelard.

"You'd better not say that. People generally get just what they expect."

"What do you expect from me?" he asked.

"Oh, plenty, plenty."

"What?"

"I want everything you have," she said. "I want your mind and soul and body, your every waking thought and all your dreams."

When they reached London they switched to a local, then another local, and finally emerged above ground at Angel Station, in one of the nearest things to a slum that still existed in London. Angel Station!

As they walked down the shadowless street, the name "Angel Station" echoed in Abelard's mind like the sound of two hands clapped in a huge empty auditorium. On the other side of Torrens Street a line of students with their arms around each other's shoulders danced the grapevine sideways down the walk, singing, "Boom chicka boom chicka boom chicka boom." That reminded Abelard of the thousand-leggers, frightful little bugs which he had, when a little boy, delighted in killing with a burning glass. He remembered his delight when he managed to catch one of them with a point of concentrated sunlight, how it twisted in agony and then lay still, slowly turning black.

They turned another corner and stood before a building that looked as old as civilization itself. A sign in ancient, faded, cracking paint said, "Collin's Music Hall."

"It's still there, thank God," said the girl. "They have been on the verge of closing for the last two hundred years."

"What is this, anyway?"

It was an old-fashioned British pub and music hall, the only place left in the world that still had professional entertainers outside of the feelies. "Have you got any money?" she demanded.

"Why, no, I never use it," he replied. "It's taxable, and if I were to use it I would be helping to support the government."

She laughed at him.

"But you don't hate the government enough to turn down its free food and housing, do you? Here, I'll pay."

She bought tickets at the box office and they went in. The seats were mostly empty, and the theatre was dark except for the stage, where an old woman dressed in gold

and spangles was singing, accompanied by an old man at
the piano. The tune fell on Abelard's ears like a blow. It
was in the hauntingly simple chromatic scale, a folksong,
probably, from the distant past. "Oh, it's a long, long
time, from May to December . . ."

He had not heard one of the old songs since he was a
child. His ear, trained by now to think of the chromatic
scale as a single, consonant chord, was charmed and
seduced by the monotonous wave-like repetition of major
triads, sevenths, and sixths . . . he seemed to relax and
stretch out in the vast distances between the chordal
tones. No longer was the ear lost in a gray continuum of
relative dissonance . . . a chord was either a triad and
consonant, or it was not black and white, and even the
most intense dissonance of the scale was milder than
most of the consonances his ear was trained to accept.
Anglo-Indian jazz was condemned as primitive . . . what
if one of those 43-tone purists could hear this?

The woman, as nearly as Abelard could tell, was about
two hundred and fifty to three hundred years old . . .
the man at the piano even older. Even so, she was able
to make herself clearly heard and understood in the farthest corners of the theatre without benefit of electronic
amplification. Few, if any, of the modern ultrarefined
crooners could say the same, and Abelard realized with
a start that she was putting across the emotional impact
of the song without benefit of ultra-high frequency jabs
in the audience's ribs.

"These precious days, I'll spend with you," she sang.

When the old woman had finished her song she bowed
stiffly, first to the right, then to the left, then straight
ahead of her. Abelard was startled. People just didn't
bow these days. It was undemocratic! There was scattered applause as the woman left the stage, followed by
the piano player. Suddenly there was only one person in
the theatre applauding, the strange Eruasian girl at his
side. She was clapping wildly, hysterically, tears running
down her cheeks. "Encore!" she shouted, "Encore!"

"People are looking at you," whispered Abelard.

"I don't care! I don't care! More! Encore! Encore!"

She stood up, but Abelard pulled her down again,
afraid someone would notice her diamonds and start a

riot. Finally she was silent, staring into space with her lips half parted, humming the final bars of the song in a barely audible whisper. The next act came on immediately; another old man, doing imitations of famous people. The audience roared when he did one of the World President giving a speech while high on H.

"It seems I've forgotten my speech," said the comic. "Ah, here it is." He drew out of his coat a huge hypodermic needle, the kind used to give injections to horses, pretended to jab it into the main artery of his arm, staggered, rolled his eyes, steadied himself and said, "As I was saying, before I was so rudely interrupted . . ."

The audience roared with laughter.

Next he produced an old beat-up sitar and gave a startlingly good imitation of Aga Carlson, the idol of the young and the central figure in the world of Anglo-Indian jazz, complete with a sexy Hindu dance at the end.

Everyone laughed but the Eurasian girl, who was still lost in the spell of the ancient folksong.

The rest of the show went by unseen by Abelard. His eyes were fixed on the profile of the girl beside him, studying her curiously theatrical makeup, the long black hair that hung to her waist, the diamonds above her forehead, hanging from her ears, and in rings on her fingers. He looked down at her sandaled feet and saw, even there, diamond rings on her toes. He was sure that they were real. Anyone could buy artificial diamonds which only an electronic microscope could tell from real ones, but only someone who had a job could afford real ones, and no one had jobs but soldiers, policemen, techmen, and politicians. She was not a soldier and was too young to be either a techman or a politician. She must be a cop, he reasoned, a plainclotheswoman. Perhaps now, on the eve of an election, the government had finally decided to crack down on anarchists, to make an example of them. Perhaps she was a feelies star, but no, the feelies had been manned by volunteer workers for a good ten years. And how did she know his birthday? Only a cop could know his birthday. But then, if she was a cop, sent to spy on him, why did she give herself away by wearing diamonds? There was only one thing he was sure of. She frightened him.

"Let's get out of here," she whispered.

He followed her out of the theatre and into the pub next door. They sat down at a table near the door and looked around at the other patrons. They were mostly quite old . . . there were a few soldiers and one table of techmen, but not one of the artists, poets, chessplayers, dancers, philosophers, etc., Abelard was used to seeing in pubs. One of the old men strolled over to their table and, to Abelard's intense surprise, asked, "Sir and Madam, what can I do for you?"

Abelard was speechless, but the girl said, "Two glasses of half and half."

"Very good, Madam," said the man, and walked quickly away.

"I see you're surprised," chuckled the girl. "This is the first time you've ever been called *Sir*?"

"Why, yes, it is, as a matter of fact."

"That's not the worst of it, baby. When he comes back we are going to have to tip him."

"Tip?" He was astounded.

"That's right," she chuckled. "The beer we will drink is, of course, free, but we are going to have to pay hard cash to have it brought to our table by a human being instead of a machine. We are going to have to pay hard cash to have a fellow human being call us Sir and Madam."

"What's going on here?" he demanded. "What kind of a place is this you've dragged me into?"

She gestured at the crowd.

"This is nothing but one of the last outposts of capitalism," she said. "That man who just called you Sir is the last of a class of men who once literally owned the world. What you buy from him is nothing different than what has always been bought from him. In the days when he owned the world, the issue was confused by the difficulty in procuring and processing raw materials, but really there never was in all the history of man and never will be anything at all for sale but the privilege of having another fellow human being call you *Sir*."

Just then the old man returned with two beers on a tray and carefully set them on the table. Abelard noticed that the old man, too, wore diamond rings on his fingers and diamond earrings in his ears . . . and even in his nose. The girl laid a coin on the tray as great as an average man's pension for a year.

"Thank you, Madam," said the capitalist with a deep bow, and strode away.

"Try the beer," she said. "It's something different from what you might expect."

Abelard sipped it.

"Ugh! It's warm, and it's gone flat!" he snorted.

"That's the way it's supposed to taste. You'll get used to it."

"I don't like this place," Abelard grumbled. "How can you stand to see a fellow human being degrade himself in front of you the way that so-called capitalist just did?"

"Watch what you say," she said, eyes flashing. "I'm a capitalist too, *Sir*."

"You?"

"Of course. How else do you suppose I can afford these diamonds, *Sir*?"

Abelard laid a hesitant hand on her arm.

"But what do you sell?" he asked.

"The same thing that fellow who brought us our drinks sells. The only thing anyone has ever sold since the beginning of time. Myself!"

"What are you saying? Are you a . . ."

"A prostitute? A whore? That's right, *Sir*, that's what I am."

He was really confused now.

"I don't understand. Why? Why do you do it? Everything you need is given you. For the sake of a few diamonds you . . . I can't believe it! How can anyone sink so low?"

She drew herself up proudly.

"How can anyone be so useless as *you* are! You dare to preach to me? I work. I earn my money. I give something to somebody and receive something in return! What do you do? Hang on to the metal hand of the state and call yourself an anarchist! Paint pictures and try to give them to people who can paint pictures of their own, write poems that people only read in hopes that you will read theirs, pass out your mimeographed rubbish that people only use to blow their noses on. If the Anti-Political Party is elected there won't be any government any more. There won't be any more army, there won't be any more cops, courts, jails and taxes. What will you protest about then, eh? What will you write about then in your mimeographed throw-away sheets? What will you march around with signs and demonstrate against then? What will you fast about, what will you strike about? What will you passively resist? I don't give a damn what party is elected. It doesn't effect me in the slightest. I'm a working girl, *Sir*. I have no time for politics. I'm a capitalist. I wear diamonds. Why shouldn't I wear diamonds? People throw rocks at me in the streets, children follow me and call me every foul name in the language, but I know this. If I take my diamonds off I'm dead.

"There are men, and women, too, all over the world in little bars and pubs . . . they go there every night, night after night, for only one reason. There is an outside chance they might run into me. I might drop by, maybe, and sit with them an hour or two and listen to them talk and let them give me presents and money and, maybe, if I feel like it, kiss them a few times or maybe even sleep with them. I just might. Sure, they could go to a government sexhouse and sleep with a beautiful robot . . . twice as beautiful as me, twice as soft to the touch, twice as tender, and responsive, with a voice that says, 'I love you' so you almost believe it.

"Funny, isn't it, how you never quite get around to going. Funny how some men still get married, or live with real flesh and blood women, or wander into bars every night looking for me. Who cares whether *you* live or die? Who would weep if the whole anarchistic movement were to pass away some night? If I die and the people who love me hear about it they will cry and get drunk and kill themselves and go on the needle. You try going to those robots once or twice. The illusion is absolutely convincing except for one thing; you know ahead of time that under that flawless flesh there is nothing but wires and tubes and gears, and you never forget it.

"But I'm a real woman, *Sir*, with a real womb and real breasts and a real liver and even a real bellybutton. Do you know that I even have real periods? I bleed like a wounded animal, I lie in bed moaning with the pain of my cramps . . . and right within arm's reach are the anti-menstrual pills that almost every woman but me takes these days. I have them right there, on my bedstand, all the time, but I have never taken one. Those are wonderful little pills, baby. You take one a month and you never need worry again about menstruation or pregnancy. I sleep with a man almost every night . . . always a different one, and every time I think maybe this one will make me pregnant.

"I'm only 23 years old and I've had two children already. I don't go to the big, beautiful government hospitals to have my babies. They would say I wasn't a fit mother and put my children in those damn, big, perfect, beautiful kindergartens. I go down into the trans-Atlantic tube and go into a little compartment and lock the door and dim the lights and lie down on the seat and let the contractions come. Have you ever watched a woman have a baby? Of course not. Nobody watches childbirth any more but the impersonal eyes of the surgical machines. It isn't pretty. I go down into the trans-Atlantic tube in a little sound-proof compartment deep down under the sea, deep down under the earth, and have my baby. Do you know I scream with pain? Do you know I squat in that little room all by myself and scream at the top of my voice? The contractions are slow at first, then a little faster and a little more painful, a little faster and more painful still, faster, faster, still faster. I'm rushing through the darkness at over a thousand miles an hour and nobody is watching me but the big eye of the UN Ham movie, sweating and screaming and wiggling and shoving down with all my strength, and all of a sudden the baby comes and I hit it and it cries and I cut the umbilical cord with my jacknife or my fingernail file and put the baby on the breast and come up in London or New York or maybe Paris with one of those big black capes around me and the kid on my breast, hoping the security police won't hear it cry. I'm a real woman. I'm a working girl. I work for my diamonds."

Abelard sat stunned as the torrent of words rushed over him. All this time the girl had hardly raised her voice, but her words were charged with an intensity that drove every other thought from his mind. She was lean-ing forward, staring into his eyes with the unwinking hyp-notic gaze of a snake. Impulsively, she took his hand.

"Look, buy me something, will you?" she whispered.

"I have no money. You know that."

"I'll lend you some. Buy me a flower. There's an old woman here who sells flowers. She grows them in her own windowbox. Here," she slipped him some money under the table, "you can pay me back later. She's sitting by the bar, back by the lavatory. See her? Call her over and buy me a flower."

Abelard was still too stunned by the strange mono-logue he had heard to refuse. He signaled the old woman to come over.

"Flower, sir? A pretty flower for the lady?" said the old woman as she came up to the table.

"What kind do you want?" asked Abelard.

"A white one. I need a white one."

"Here you are," said the old woman. "It's called a gardenia. Maybe it ain't as nice as what you can get from the government nurseries, but I grew it myself, sir. There's love went into the growing of that flower."

Abelard paid the woman, and she bowed and went away.

The pale, intense Eurasian girl sat a long time, silent, holding the gardenia in her hand and studying it.

"You're a beautiful thing, little flower," she said at last. "Beautiful and imperfect. There's a wonderful, beautiful spot on one of your petals. You're dying, poor thing, the same as I am, the same as everybody is, and that's what makes you so beautiful. It's the promise of death, and decay, and rebirth, and growth again. Isn't it beautiful, black baby?"

"Yes. Very beautiful," he murmured.

"Don't spoil it by trying to call it 'very beautiful' as if you were trying to make words mean more than they really do. It's just beautiful, that's all. Don't talk about it. Just look at it. Look!"

Abelard looked. The girl turned the flower around and around in the tips of her fantastically long, thin fingers.

"This flower is mine, you know," she said, "I think it's really mine."

"Of course," said Abelard softly.

"No. Not, of course. Maybe it doesn't belong to me at all. Maybe it belongs to God. Maybe I belong to God and you belong to God, too, whether you believe in Him or not. Maybe there's nothing in the world that really belongs to a person. Not even his own life." Her voice was gentle and far away. "I could die now, you know. Some day I will surely die and lie quietly in the earth, slowly rotting away. Will I still be beautiful then, baby? You don't like to think about my flesh turning gray and black and hanging off my bones, do you? You don't like to think about the little white worms that will burrow into my brain, my breasts, my womb, do you? I do. I like to think about it. I think everybody should think about it often. Perhaps when my body rots away it will turn into beautiful little blades of grass or perhaps a white, white flower like this. I wouldn't mind dying if I could become a flower."

She bowed her head ever so slightly before the flower and said reverently, "Sir."

Then she gently pulled one of the petals from its blossom and began to nibble on it. She ate it slowly, and when she had finished, she broke off another petal and ate it too.

"Can I have some?" asked Abelard.

"Here, darling," said the girl, and placed a petal in his mouth. It was soft and nearly tasteless, but he ate it anyway. She gave him another. Quietly, petal by petal, they finished off the gardenia and sat a long time, looking at each other without tension, without thought. While he was eating it, he had tasted little or nothing. It left a bitter aftertaste, however. He washed it down with beer.

"Darling," said the girl, "if anything ever happens to me, try to get along without me. Don't forget me, but, you know, go on doing whatever it is you are doing. I won't always be around to watch out for you. Even when I'm not with you, remember that I still love you, I still care about you. Keep warm, baby, and don't take dope. Okay? Promise?"

"I promise."

"And try and get some money and give it to that woman with the flowers. She takes care of my children, you know. And maybe, some day, one of my children will be yours. Promise?"

"I promise."

Abelard felt a sudden need to go to the lavatory. It was not the moment for such a thing, but it seldom is. It was probably the beer. Quickly he excused himself and made his way back to the men's room.

It was an old, old lavatory. The walls writhed with inscriptions on inscriptions on inscriptions . . . Faded names and addresses of homosexuals, drawings, dirty jokes. "Make date." "Tourists, please do not eat the rock candy in the urinal." "Do not throw cigarettes in the toilet. It makes them soggy and hard to light." "Donald Duck is a Jew."

There were even a few half-oblitered remarks in lipstick dating from that fantastic period just after the World Civil War when men had taken to wearing makeup. When he had finished and washed his hands, Abelard was still reluctant to leave the safety of the lavatory. "What will that girl do next?" he wondered, but he braced himself and went out.

She was gone.

He rushed to the table but found nothing there but a note saying, "I will always be with you. You will see me again the next time you need me."

It was signed "Reva."

"Where is she?" he shouted at the old flower woman. "Where did she go?"

"I don't know, sir. She comes and she goes as she pleases."

"When will she be back?"

"I don't know that either, sir. All I know is when she does she'll have her arms full of things for the kids. Most likely she'll have two or three men with her, all loaded down with presents. It's like an old fashioned Christmas whenever Reva comes home."

Desperately Abelard dashed out into the night shouting, "Reva! Reva! Come back! You can't just leave me like this! REVA!"

There was no answer.

He ran all the way to Angel Station.

"REVA!" he shouted again.

Silence.

He went down the stairs three steps at a time and emerged onto the platform.

"REVA!"

Only the echo of the tunnel answered him.

With a rush and a hiss, the train pulled in and opened its doors. Abelard got on board in a daze. The doors closed behind him and the train was moving again, with no perceptible jerk. At each station he searched in vain for some glimpse of a tall, thin figure in black with black hair to her waist . . . some glimpse of a glittering diamond. There were people on the train now, a few at first, then more and more until they were packed in solid. Once or twice Abelard thought he saw Reva in the crowd and struggled through the packed bodies only to find that he was wrong. Once or twice he thought he saw her in a station as the train pulled out. He had no idea how long he had searched by the time he fell asleep in the seat. He only knew, as he slept, that he was being watched over, protected. He awoke, looked through the window, and saw her standing on the platform, not three feet away from him, smiling gently. Before he could rise the train doors shut, and Reva slipped away behind. He was asleep again before the next station, asleep and at peace. In a trance he boarded the trans-Atlantic tube for New York and fell asleep again. As he staggered into his little apartment in Brooklyn, his roommate stared at him amazed. It was the first time Abelard had ever been seen without his briefcase.

"Where's your burden?"

"I don't know," said Abelard. "I guess I lost it somewhere. Not important."

Some months later, Abelard strolled into Miss Smith's Tea Room on Grant Avenue in San Francisco with a new briefcase and a new supply of left-wing propaganda. It was possible to obtain a great many things in Miss Smith's Tea Room, none of them tea. The legends of the place had it that it was originally a hang-out for lesbians in some dim and distant period in the past, that there had once been a real Miss Smith who owned it and several other businesses in the Bay Area. It seems the "tea room" had gradually become infiltrated by heterosexuals until at last Miss Smith sold it in disgust. After passing through many hands and many different types of clientele it had at last become a meeting-place for the non-voting minority of anarchists in the area; that is, those who had not been swallowed up in the Anti-Political Party.

"Comrade Abelard!" said George, sitting in the front booth by the window. George was a permanent fixture in the window. It was said that he slept under the bar.

"Comrade George!" cried Abelard, sitting down and pouring himself a beer from the wall tap. "Share my burden?"

"Certainly. Certainly."

"Still on the job?"

"That's right. My job is just to sit here in the window of Miss Smith's and talk to whoever wants to talk to me on any level he wants to talk. Like I told them, when the time comes to move, I'll move; up, down, backwards, forwards, or sideways. They say, why don't you go somewhere, George, and I say, Man, there's really no place to go. You want to go to London and see the Collin's Music Hall? This is a music hall right here, if you look at it from the right angle. You want to go to the Mistral Bookstore in Paris and buy some dirty books? Listen, any book is a dirty book if you read it right. I can get aroused reading the telephone book or the dictionary. That's what I told them. There's only one direction that's worth going and that's inward. That's all I'm saying. Inward. They say, George, haven't you got anything better to do than talk, and I say I'm working, what about you? I look around at all these poor fools who want me to do this and do that and there's only one thing I can say about them, no wonder the ship sank—look at the crew! Now I can tell you are thinking about getting married. You've even got pants on to show what a faithful husband you can be. There's no such thing as a marriage with your pants on. You've got to love the person you are with. That's all I'm saying. Right now I'm your wife. And your kids, and your mama and papa, but don't get an electra complex. You're here, that's what I told them, so you're married to me. I can be anything you like to you. I can be a bird if you really want me to and fly to

Mars and back, and never get up from this table. We can go together. Just don't get hung up, that's all I'm saying don't get hung up on any one special thing or you're hooked. People say, George, what are you hooked on, and I say Life, man, Life, that's all. I just can't put it down. You think 200 or 300 years old is old. I don't look it, but I'm older than that. I was here before this place was built. I helped build the pyramids. Ever heard of Caligari? That was me. I'm in the Bible two or three times. Ever heard of Judas? That was me. Don't give me a bad time about it. I was under orders. Ever heard of Cain? That was me. Doomed to walk the earth forever and never die. In the Bible it neglects to mention that the earth is a beautiful place, that there's enough beauty in one hair of your beard to last all eternity. I don't want to go to Heaven. Man, I'm there! That bridge out there has been remodeled three times, but they still call it The Golden Gate. I've crossed over it hundreds of times. I could cross over every day if I wanted to. Who are you marrying?"

"Her name is Reva," said Abelard, looking away. "She's a prostitute."

"The Reva with the diamonds?"

"You know her?"

"Sure I know her," laughed George. "We lived together once, a few years back. Everybody knows Reva, or has heard of her. They call her Reva, the Witch."

"Reva, the Witch? Why?" asked Abelard, leaning forward.

"If you don't know she's a witch, you don't know her at all. I'm a witch, too."

"You?"

George grinned proudly.

"How do you think I know what you're thinking of all the time, eh? You've got eyes, but they're for decoration only. Sure she's a witch. Anyone can be a witch if they just open their eyes a fraction of an inch more. She's a saint, too. The first authentic saint in two thousand years. She'd even be a martyr, except that there isn't anything left worth dying for."

"You say you lived together?" Abelard was amazed.

"That's right," said George. "I had a place across the

bay in Berkeley, just off Telegraph Avenue. I got up about noon one morning as usual and opened my front door and there she was, curled up on my doorstep, fast asleep. I woke her up and she looked at me with no more recognition than if she'd just been born, and said, 'I feel very ethereal this morning.' She pulled my face into her hair and I sniffed and she was reeking of ether. She had spent all the previous night on the fourth floor of Cowell Hospital with some student medical techmen, sniffing ether to see what is was like. And when she has menstrual cramps, she won't even take an aspirin. Well, she walked in and looked around my place and finally she said, 'How do you like your eggs?' and I said 'Scrambled,' so she scrambled some eggs and we had breakfast and went to bed together. Two months later I came home and there was a note on the table saying, 'Darling, I have to go to Tibet, love, Reva!' I never saw her again. Do you see her very often?"

Abelard shook his head sadly.

"I've only seen her once, months ago," he said.

"And you're in love with her? You want to marry her? Isn't marriage against your principles?" demanded George, thrusting a quivering finger under Abelard's nose.

"I know, I know. It's just this damned insomnia. I can't sleep. I've tried pills, I've tried booze, but nothing helps. I just keep thinking about her and thinking about her, carrying on imaginary conversations with her, trying to clearly visualize her face. When I get her face into focus, there is a moment of wonderful peace. She's smiling at me! She loves me! Then I think of some key phrase, some particular sentence, like 'years and years' or just 'somewhere' and my eyes fill with tears and I cry and cry and cry, and can't stop crying. Whenever I don't get enough sleep it's bad for my complexion. Look at my face, all over pimples, painful ones. There's more on my back."

"What about your principles?" said George. "I can see your pimples."

"Those mimeographed 'Principles' in my briefcase?" snorted Abelard. "I used to read them by the hour, but now I start one and pretty soon I find I've read the first sentence over ten or eleven times without getting a mote of meaning out of it."

The Tearoom door burst open and Little Brother Ivanovitch strode in, short, stocky, unkempt, with shaggy, matted red hair and a bushy mustache. He was carrying a heavy package.

"Comrade Ivanovitch!" cried Abelard. "Share my burden?"

"Don't comrade me, you yellow-bellied pacifist! You can share *my* burden!" and with that he plunked the package down on the table.

"What's that?" asked Abelard.

"It's a bomb," said Little Brother.

"A *bomb!*"

"I'm an anarchist of the old school. The bomb-throwing kind!"

"Sit down and have a beer, Little Brother," said George. "How is the Destruction of Civilization coming along?"

"Go ahead and laugh, you Capitalistic Dog, you Lackey of the Ruling Class. After the revolution you'll be laughing through the holes in your chest."

"So, it's Brother Ivanovitch's turn to throw the bomb, eh?" chuckled George. "You'd better hurry up, comrade. If the Anti-Political Party wins the next election, there won't be any government for you to throw bombs at. You'll be out of a job."

"The State will never voluntarily give up its powers!" roared Little Brother. "Don't you know any history? Social progress can only come through violent revolution! The old order must be washed away in a bath of blood."

"Sometimes," said George, "I think you are more interested in the bath of blood than in the social progress that is supposed to come out of it."

"Never mind," growled Little Brother, "you'll see. Nothing can alter the inevitable tides of history. The new social order will come and at its head will be the professional revolutionaries, like Lenin, Trotsky, and me."

"If you want to destroy civilization," said Abelard, "why don't you become a Feelies techman? Those hi-fi feelies can broadcast a tone above the audio range called the 'death whisper' that can kill a man."

"That's right," said George. "Just picture it, Little Brother. All over the world everyone is listening to the feelies. Maybe the President is giving a speech."

"His inaugural address," said Abelard.

"Everybody is listening," continued George, "except for the revolutionary elite. You are in the control room. You throw a switch, turn up the gain a little."

"People feel uncomfortable and they don't know why," said Abelard.

"You turn up the gain a little more. A few high-strung people go nuts and fall on the floor, kicking and screaming. You turn up the gain a little more and everybody craps out. A little more and it starts to work on the tissues of their bodies."

"They go deaf," said Abelard.

"They start bleeding from every pore," added George. "They scream and thrash around in their blood, a bath of blood, just like you want. Then you turn up the gain just a hair more and they stop moving. All over the world they stop moving. They're dead, Little Brother, and all because of a musical tone, a little musical tone they can't even hear, because of you, Little Brother. Doesn't that make your mouth water?"

"You know I don't know anything about electronics. It would take me fifty years of study to become a feelies techman!" shouted Ivanovitch, pounding on the table with his fist.

"You are only worried about the practical angle, eh?" said George. "Suppose I could smuggle you into the control room while the President is speaking. Suppose I pointed out to you which switch to throw, which knob to turn? What then?"

"Could you do it, really?" asked Little Brother, eyes glowing; then he saw that George was laughing at him. "PIG!" screamed Ivanovitch, "COUNTER-REVOLUTIONARY SCAB! you are only trying to trick me! You are trying to make fun of me! You'll see!"

"Oh, shut up!" snapped Abelard.

Ivanovitch was stunned.

"Who are you telling to shut up, you yellow-bellied pacifist? Who do you think you are, *me?*"

"Excuse Brother Abelard," said George. "He is not himself. He is in love."

"Oh, he is, is he?"

"He wants to get married."

"Oh, he does, does he? And who, may I ask, is the poor, stupid, misguided, idiotic, bad-smelling female?"

"Reva, the Witch."

"If only I knew where she was," moaned Abelard.

"I know where she is, pig," said Little Brother.

"WHERE?"

"Right outside the Tearoom in my car, waiting for me."

George and Abelard leaped to their feet, as one man. "If you're lying . . ." growled Abelard, as he dashed past Little Brother and out the door, with George right behind him. Sure enough, there she was, sitting in the sky-car, reading a dogeared copy of "Capital."

"Reva!" shouted Abelard.

Carefully Reva marked her place and closed the book. "Black Baby!" she said, "and George! Hello, boys!"

She opened the door and got out. She was very, very pregnant.

"I've been looking for you, Black Boy," she said. "You know, I don't even know your name?"

"Reva, the Witch," said George. "Let me introduce you to Abelard Rosenburg."

"How do you do, Abelard?" said Reva, shaking his hand. "Haven't I seen you somewhere before?"

"Reva," cried Abelard. "I've searched and searched for you! Where did you go?"

"To Chicago," answered Reva. "You didn't have to search for me. I told you I'd turn up when you needed me."

"I was in Jimmy's Tavern, near the University of Chicago," said Little Brother, "when Reva came up to me and said, 'You're an anarchist, aren't you?' and I said, 'That's right. I'm the only true anarchist left. The rest are all fakes. You're a prostitute, aren't you?' and she said, 'Yes, I'm the only true prostitute left. The rest are all amateurs.' She wanted to know all about anarchism and she kept pumping and pumping me, so finally I said, 'Look, I can't possibly teach you all about anarchism in one night. Why don't you come and live with me for a while and we can exchange services?' She said, 'All right,' and we went home together."

"You went home with . . . him?" gasped Abelard to Reva.

"Why not?" she answered, "He said he would teach me about anarchism, and I really wanted to know."

"I did teach you about anarchism, didn't I?" said Little Brother.

"Frankly, no, but you were a barrel of fun anyway. All we ever did was make love and work on the bomb and play games."

"What games?" asked George.

"Different games," answered Reva. "Believe me, there was never a dull moment with Little Brother Ivanovitch."

Abelard felt sick. Suddenly all he wanted to do was to leave, to run, to get away. He turned and took a few steps.

"Hey," said Reva, and he stopped. "Come back here," she said, and he slowly returned. "You shouldn't be so touchy. You may be seeing a lot of me for the rest of your life."

"What-what do you mean?" Abelard stammered.

"Well, not marriage exactly," answered Reva, looking away. "But you know, when I found out I was pregnant I thought maybe the child might be yours. If it's white, it might be anybody's, but if it's black, it can't be anyone's but yours. You know how these things go. You'll know it's yours and I'll know it's yours, and you'll always be coming around to see it. Well, pretty soon it will start to think of you as daddy and my other kids will get used to seeing you around too. I'll keep running into you all the time when you're there and have to make supper for you and lunch and if you stay overnight even breakfast. We'll be all the time playing with the kids together and we'll get to be really good friends, not just lovers. I know how these things snowball. All the time sitting around and talking and doing the dishes together and listening to music together and reading the books we recommend to each other. Do you play chess? I do."

"I play chess a little," said Abelard.

"I play the guitar, too," said Reva. "I like to sing the old songs, the simple ones like we heard that night in the music hall. Do you sing?"

"I could learn."

"It's not hard with these songs. I know how it will go. We'll be all the time sitting around the kitchen table singing together and when the kids get older they'll be singing too. It will seem silly to us to go anywhere, to leave, so you'll move in. I can just see you moving in now. You may not want to, but lives are so Goddamn long now, sooner or later you will. The way I am it won't be long before there are other black babies . . . we'll have to educate them all ourselves because I'd rather die than let my kids go to public school and learn to appreciate the feelies. I don't know if that's marriage, but that's what will happen if the baby is yours."

"What if it isn't?" asked Abelard.

"Maybe we'll be together for a while. I'm in love with you, you know, because that story you told me about your childhood was so sad it made me cry. I thought I'd forgotten how. You're in love with me, too, I can see, but being in love doesn't last very long. A week, a month, a year, then it will go stale and we'll both start looking again, riding undergrounds alone and looking for someone to pick up. That's what will happen if it isn't."

"I have to be getting back," said George, "Somebody might come into the Tearoom looking for me."

"Goodbye, George," said Little Brother. "We won't miss you."

George strolled away leaving the two anarchists jealously glowering at each other.

"Well," growled Little Brother to Reva, "are you going with me or staying with Abelard?"

"Why do you have to be so anti-social?" asked Reva, "I thought we might all go somewhere together. I'm too far along to have sex anyway, so there's no reason to be jealous."

Little Brother put the bomb in the car and considered a moment. "But it's him you love?" he muttered.

"I love everybody," said Reva, with a toss of her head.

"Well, perhaps," said Little Brother. He turned to

Abelard. "Is that all right with you, comrade? Let's shake hands and call it a truce."

"All right with me. Here, shake."

As they extended their hands to each other, a happy, peaceful smile came over Little Brother's face. It remained there, as fixed as if it had been painted on, as Little Brother took hold of Abelard's thumb and bent it over backwards until it broke with an audible snap.

"He won't fight back," said Little Brother, turning to Reva. "He's a non-violent, pacifistic anarchist." Still smiling, Little Brother brought his elbow up suddenly into Abelard's face, then, in a single efficient gesture, kneed him in the groin and swung the blade of his hand down on Abelard's neck in a perfect rabbit punch.

"This is called passive resistance," explained Little Brother as he straight-armed Abelard's head against the side of the car. As Abelard staggered forward, blood streaming from his nose and mouth, Little Brother tripped him up and threw him flat on his face on the concrete sidewalk, then aimed a vicious kick at his head. Abelard grabbed Little Brother's foot with his good hand and hung on.

"So you're going to fight, eh?" crowed Little Brother. "What will it be? Knives? Guns? Or bombs?" Abelard released the foot. Little Brother took out a switchblade knife, popped it open, and began cleaning his nails. "Well, Reva, you wanted to learn all about anarchism. You have just witnessed a demonstration of the difference between violent and non-violent anarchism. Note that Abelard did not once cry out in pain, even when I broke his thumb, but nevertheless I am standing up and he," he spat in Abelard's face, "is lying down." He folded the knife up and put it back in his pocket. "I hope you two will be very, very happy."

With that, Little Brother climbed into the sky-car, kicked it abruptly into the air, then swung east and was soon out of sight.

"Come on," said Reva, helping Abelard to his feet, "we've got to get you to a hospital."

In about a week the thumb was healed enough so Abelard could remove the splint and bandages, but he still had to use it with care. Reva and Abelard settled down for a trial run at marriage. The best part of it was the long, long talks together in bed. Sometimes these lasted until the early hours of the morning, and touched on every subject conceivable. They talked about love, and politics, and religion, and children, and astrology, and their childhoods, and history, and music, and every other thing man has ever thought about. Sometimes Reva would get out her guitar and sit cross-legged on the bed, playing it and singing old folksongs like "Stormy Weather," "Stardust," and "White Christmas," for hours. Sometimes they would lie dozing for ten minutes or so between sentences, then start talking again on an entirely different tack.

"Abe," she would say, soft and drowsy.

"Yeah?"

"Why don't you believe in God?"

"I'd hate to think that anyone would make a world like this on purpose," he answered.

"What do you mean?"

"If there is a God, he would have to be a monster, creating only to destroy, giving life only to kill. God made every living thing with a hunger for something. He made the world so that every living thing must kill to live, then be killed in turn. Include me out!" he said, with a gesture of contempt.

"What you say is true, black baby, except the part where you try to include yourself out. You are mad at God because you don't agree with the way he put the world together. You think you might do a better job if you had the chance. Maybe leave death out. Maybe make a few other alterations here and there to make it more to your taste. I think if you understood a little better how the whole thing works, you'd change your mind. Like death, for instance. You don't understand death at all. It isn't so bad. You think it is like losing a game of cards. Man, you don't lose! It is just that every once in a while they reshuffle the cards and deal out a new hand. You think you are a player, but you are really more like a hand of cards. One combination of cards makes a man, another hand of cards makes a cow, another a flower, but they keep using the same cards over and over. You are always dying, but you never really die. Nothing dies. There's nothing to be afraid of. No reason to feel sorry for yourself and give God a bad time."

He raised his hand to stem the torrent of words.

"I don't care what happens to the atoms in my body, Reva. They can turn into snakes, spiders and poison ivy for all I care. That isn't me. That isn't the real me."

"What is the real you?" she asked, tickling his nose.

He thought a moment.

"A mathematical point. The point of consciousness," he said. "The inner eye that can see everything but itself. I speak of *my* body, *my* thoughts, *my* feelings. They are all my belongings, my possessions, but they are not me. I am the owner of these things but separate from them. The Hindus call the 'I' thing the Atman. That Atman eye opens when I am born, slowly at first, without understanding, then watches, watches, watches as my life passes through time. It doesn't miss a thing, Reva. It doesn't miss a thing. Even if I go insane, the Atman eye that is me will go on quietly watching my delusions and hallucinations. Then I die, and the inner eye closes, never to open again. That is death. Don't try to make it pretty. Don't try to pretend it doesn't exist. When that inner eye closes, you're dead, dead, deadly dead as if you had never lived."

She ran her fingers through his kinky steel-wool hair.

"You're top-heavy, Abe," she said. "You're trying to live all in your head and ignore your body. You're trying to make out like one small part of you is the whole works. A woman has a harder time than a man pretending she hasn't got a body. Once a month she gets a little reminder from the body that it is still there, and if she gets pregnant all the thinking in the world won't stop the baby from coming. I know all about that inner eye, baby, but I also know that everything in life that is real is of the body. You eat with your mouth and stomach, you have sex largely with your genitals, you carry a child in your womb. When you are angry or afraid, you do it with your glands. Some of the most intense moments of pleasure come when that Atman eye is temporarily closed. A wild drinking binge that you can't remember in the morning, a dream that is too beautiful to see with that eye, that evaporates in the daylight like a mirage. And actually, honey, you don't know for sure that that inner eye ever closes. Maybe just when you think it is closing, it really opens for the first time. Just when you think you are going to sleep forever, you really wake up as never before. A mathematical point has no physical dimensions . . . it needs no physical body to give it reality. Your Hindu friends thought the Atman, that point of consciousness, just got shuffled and re-dealt like all the rest of the cards in the deck, at least until it reached a state of oneness with God called Nirvana. I ask you, when you die, where do you think that thing goes, that Atman, that mathematical point, that soul-thing? Where does it go?"

"Well, Reva, when you blow out a candle, where does the flame go? I guess they both go about the same place." He laughed.

"You're too much, black baby. You're too much."

She rolled over and gave him up for lost, for the moment.

One day there was a rainstorm and Reva and Abelard went out naked into the children's playground and danced primitive African dances and sang primitive improvised African chants amid the dark skeletons of slides and swings and see-saws as the lightning flashed and the rain poured down. They waded through mud-puddles, splashing and shrieking, their feet sinking up to the ankle in warm mud. Abelard found a slick spot, took a running start, and slid on it, falling headlong at the end of the slick. Reva got into a swing and started swinging, higher and higher into the sheets of rain. Lightning made cracks in the roof of the sky and thunder beat its fists on the floor of the earth and in between the skyscrapers swam in gray and dirty yellow light and the sidewalks were glazed like pottery. Reva got on the Merry-Go-Round and Abelard pushed it, slowly at first, then faster and faster, until Reva's mop of hair stood out horizontally with centrifugal force. Reva hooked her legs around the seat and leaned back on empty space until her head almost touched the ground, laughing like a madwoman. Suddenly a single beam of sunlight broke through the clouds and came down directly onto the little merry-go-round, blindingly bright. Reva, hanging by the crooks of her legs and lying on the air, stared straight up into the turning sky and the savage, unsheathed sun, unblinking, until the clouds covered its face again, turning it first into a moon, then hiding it altogether.

"Abe," yelled Reva, "Stop this thing, will you?"

"What's wrong?"

"The baby is starting to dance, too. I want to go home."

They went home arm in arm, singing "Careless Love" at the top of their voices.

As they slopped up the hallway, covered with mud, one of the other tenants, a dignified old spinster, stared at them as if they were visitors from Mars. When they got into their apartment they went straight to the bathroom, turned on the shower, got into the shower, together, and with many a grunt and ticklish giggle, proceeded to wash each other clean.

As the day when the baby was due drew near, Reva became less and less active. She was sick a lot, and had pains . . . particularly in her back. Abelard spent a good deal of time rubbing her back, fixing her meals, reading to her and talking to her. She liked poetry, and though Abelard had never been much interested in it before, except for the social protest type of poem, he became, in the hours of reading aloud, intoxicated with the written and spoken word. One day, while Reva was taking a nap, he sat down, his head buzzing with the "hipster" poetry of the late twentieth century, and began to scribble a poem of his own. A few lines came easily . . . the tough part was the "filler" lines between the ones supplied him by inspiration. He had written pounds of prose on political subjects before . . . but such writing is mostly a matter of lining up a few well-worn cliches in a slightly different order. The trouble with poetry, real poetry, was that it had to "ring true"—to reflect, if not reality, at least a recognizable delusion. He had rewritten it five times when Reva awoke and asked him what he was doing.

"Oh, nothing," he answered, trying to hide the paper.

"Here, let's see that."

"No, no, it's something private."

"Then, I really *must* see it."

"It's just a sort-of-poem."

"Read it aloud to me."

"No, it's too awful."

"Here, give it to me. I'll read it aloud. Don't worry, I won't expect too much," she said.

Reluctantly he handed it to her. She cleared her throat and in a low, husky voice, began to read.

"To Reva.

"And thus it begins,

> Singing and dancing and drinking and laughing and standing,
> Suddenly silent, in each other's eyes.
> It is the moment of touching.
> It is the day of the Revelation of the Body.
> It is the month of Obsession, the year of sleep-dancing.
> The end of the some questions,
> 'What is Right and Wrong?'
> 'Is there a God?'
> 'If a tree falls with no one to hear it, does it make a sound?'
> The beginning of others.
> 'Do you really love me?'
> 'What are you thinking?'
> 'Where are you going?'
> 'How could you hurt me so much?'

"And thus it begins,

> With pleasure, and the pleasure of giving pleasure.
> With moist lips, warm thighs, and tongues and hands and bodies,
> And words, and silences,
> The compulsion to submit, to serve,
> The proud examination of the tooth's brand
> By the bedlamp.

"And thus, and thus it begins,

> With the wonder of this small hand thrust into mine,
> So fierce, so commanding,

So timid, so pleading.
It is the hand of a young girl's love,

A young girl,
Still fleeing the phantoms of childhood,
Still trusting to the fortuitous intervention of elves,
Loving small animals and large gestures.
Lovely girl, sweet creature,
I would walk a ways with you.
I would protect you and catch your tears in my hands
    to save.
We will hide together in a little room,
And sleep,
And when you wake you will dress slowly as I
    watch
As I watch you don the purple vestments and robes
    of Woman.

"Thus begins—the always beginning—without end."

After she had finished, Reva was silent for some time,
staring at the paper. Finally she set it gently on the bedta-
ble and looked at Abelard. Then she smiled, and Abelard sat down on the edge of the bed, took her in his
arms, and kissed her. He lay down beside her and she
put her head on his shoulder. A train rumbled by, far
away. The wind moved the light white curtains at the
window. Some children outside sang, 'Nya-nya, nya-nya,
Peggy's got a boy friend. Peggy's got a boy friend." A
rocket scratched the white enamel surface of the sky, one
straight hairline dividing the never-darkened heaven into
two nearly equal halves. The ghost of the crescent moon
lay low near the horizon, tangled in feelies antennae.
Abelard kissed Reva's earlobe and she sighed softly, tan-
gling her fingers in his beard.
    "You're beginning to see now," said Reva.
    "Yes," whispered Abelard.
    Then the phone rang.
    Abelard reached over and turned it on. The screen
glowed milky and vague for a moment, then the face of
Little Brother Ivanovitch snapped into focus.

"Comrade!" said Little Brother, with an attempt at a friendly grin.

"What do you want?" growled Abelard in answer.

"Nothing much," said Little Brother. "I just want to borrow your woman for a few hours. All she has to do is appear with me on the speaker's platform at a political meeting. I think it will show that we Nichivist Anarchists are interested in the future if I show up with a pregnant woman."

"You're crazy," said Abelard, "She can't go anywhere now. The baby is due in a few days."

"Never mind," said Reva, then turned to the screen. "Greetings, Comrade. What kind of games do you want to play with me, now? Can't they wait?"

Little Brother shook his head.

"No, the world election is tomorrow. We have only a matter of hours to convince the people not to vote. I need your help, Reva, badly. Our movement has been branded as the Minority in favor of Death by the Anti-Political Party. Unless we can in some way identify ourselves with Life there will be an Anti-Political landslide. The APP has dug up proof positive that the World President is a dope addict."

"It will take more than my bulging stomach to sway the people," said Reva.

Little Brother nervously tugged at his mustache.

"No, no, Reva. The APP revelations have swapped people just a little too much. There are strong indications that a great number of people will not vote at all out of sheer disgust with all politics. That a crazy party like the APP could gain such power in the first place is strong evidence that people have had just about all they can take of government. If we can bring about a general voters' strike, the whole structure of Government will come down with a crash."

"What's that to me?" asked Reva.

"We've got some time on the feelies in a few hours. How we look means a lot more than what we say on the feelies, you know."

Reva thought a moment.

"How long will I be on?" she asked.

"Just a few minutes."

"Okay, I might just as well. It will do me good to get out."

Abelard was alarmed. "What if . . ." he began.

"You want to come along, Abe?" asked Reva.

"No, and I don't think you should go either."

"Nonsense," said Reva. "You worry too much."

"I'll pick you up in a half an hour," said Little Brother, and the screen went blank. Half an hour later Little Brother arrived, carrying his bomb, as usual, under his arm. For a moment the two anarchists glared at each other; then Abelard turned to Reva and said, "For God's sake, be reasonable. A feelies studio is no place for a woman in your condition."

"What do you know about it?" asked Reva. "Have you ever had a baby? I've had two, and I know what I'm doing."

With that she slipped on her jacket, took Little Brother's arm, and started for the door.

"I'll meet you after the broadcast at Angel Station in London," she shouted over her shoulder. Then the door closed and Abelard was alone with his growing apprehension. Restlessly he wandered around the apartment, nervous fingers toying with his beard, then he sat down beside the bed and drummed a few Anglo-Indian flams on the nighttable. "Obviously," he thought, "it won't do me any good to hang around here. Must be some place I can go to kill some time."

Then he thought of the Tivoli Gardens in Denmark. It was a gigantic amusement park, covering the entire area of what had once been the city of Copenhagen. The Age of Leisure had created an insatiable hunger for amusement that had caused many other amusement parks to devour the cities around them, but the Tivoli was the world's largest and, to Abelard's mind, the best of them all. Without further thought, he left the apartment and headed for the subway.

After the broadcast, Little Brother stormed out of the studio, mumbling curses and obscenities and glaring balefully at everyone in sight. Reva trotted behind him, trying to conceal her amusement.

"They didn't even listen," he snarled, as they went

down in the elevator. "They laughed at me, as if I was just some kind of a comic trying to amuse them."

"They only laughed when you threw your script at the audience," Reva reminded him.

"I couldn't stand their goddamn polite silence! They were just tolerating me. Just humoring me, as if I was a madman!"

The elevator opened and they emerged onto the ground floor, a long corridor lined with small shops and feelies screens showing every imaginable kind of show. A large crowd was gathered before the one showing the Deva Dasi Show. The crowd gazed in rapt admiration as two seemingly double-jointed Hindus illustrated seemingly impossible positions for making love.

"Look at that!" screamed Little Brother. "Just look at that! Are those the mindless sheep, the stupid, dirty-minded, worthless, no-good pigs of a dog that I am devoting my whole life to freeing? All they want is bread and circuses! Some new way of overpopulating the already overpopulated planet! I should just let them sink in their comfortable, smothering mud. They don't care. I am prepared to die for them and they don't even care enough to listen to me without laughing."

Reva took his arm and patted him comfortingly.

"Why don't you come to Collin's Music Hall in London and drown your sorrows in Half and Half with the rest of us anarchists, capitalists, prostitutes and other semi-extinct dinosaurs?" she asked.

"I might as well, for all they care."

When they boarded the Trans-Atlantic Tube, Little Brother was still in a foul mood. As they went down the corridor to their compartment, a fat old matron temporarily blocked their way. Little Brother screamed, "Pig!" and raised his bomb as if to strike her with it. Reva restrained him and gently guided him onward. She managed to get him settled in the compartment and sat holding his hand and saying soothing, comforting, and meaningless things to him until the train got under way. Then she left him, carefully closing the door behind her, and made her way to the lavatory. An old man with a bottle of whiskey in his hand was just coming out. Reva recognized him.

"Hello, Sanders," she said, "still riding the trains, eh?"

"That's right," chuckled the old man. Since they put in the free whiskey vending machines ten years ago, I haven't been above ground once. I've been around the world, more times in more ways than I can count, and I expect I'll go around it a few hundred times more before I'm done."

She smiled and touched his lips with her finger, silencing him.

"I know Sanders. You told me all about it before, a couple of years ago."

"I don't see why anyone ever bothers to go above ground, Reva. The seats in these tubes are as comfortable as any bed, and you can get anything you want from the machines . . ."

"Look, Sanders, I'll see you around. Okay? I gotta go now."

Sanders reached out a shaking claw of a hand to grab her arm, but Reva stepped back, turned, and had pushed through the door to the lavatory when the first contraction came. Gritting her teeth against the pain, she staggered out of the lavatory and down the corridor to her compartment. When she tried the door, she found it was locked. She knocked, lightly at first, then harder.

"It's Reva!" she shouted. "Let me in.

There was no answer. She pounded again, this time with all her strength.

"Open up, damn you! My contractions have begun! You want me to have pups all over the corridor floor?"

There was no answer.

Reva kicked the door.

"I know you're in there! Open up, you crazy bastard!" she screamed.

The door opened a crack and Little Brother peeped out.

"Go somewhere else to have your lousy baby. I'm busy in here," he growled.

"What are you up to anyway? Let me in, for God's sake." She threw her full weight against the door and it opened enough for her to see that the seat was strewn with wrapping paper. The box in which Little Brother kept his bomb lay empty on the floor. Wedging her foot in the door she forced her head in far enough so she could see the window. There was the bomb, black and sinister, stuck to the window with some sort of suction disks.

"You put that thing away," she said. "You might hurt somebody with it."

"No, I will not put it away. I'll show them I mean business. I'll show them I am not a harmless crackpot. The time has come for some Propaganda of the Act."

"Look, you make propaganda some other time. I'm making a baby now, and it won't wait."

"Even *you* don't believe I'm serious! Even *you* don't believe I have the guts to give my life for freedom!" he shouted.

"You aren't the only one on this train. You can give your life for freedom if you want to, but I need my life. I am a mother and I've got kids to watch out for."

"It is for your kids that I am doing this. Yes, and for all the other kids in the world today, and in all the centuries to come."

Suddenly he released his hold on the door and Reva fell inward. While she was still off balance, he gave her a terrific shove that landed her flat on her bottom in the corridor, then slammed and locked the door.

Reva sat staring at the door a moment, then pulled herself to her feet and began to run. An old folksong beat time for her steps.

"Run, sinnerman, where will you run to . . ."

She came to an open compartment door. Inside, Sanders was just tipping up the bottle. The bald top of his head glistened in the indirect lighting, the white hair at the back hung down his neck as he tilted his head back, trying to squeeze the last drop.

"Hello," said Reva, stepping in.

Sanders jumped to his feet.

"Hello, Reva," he said. "Sit down and talk a bit."

"Hello," she repeated tonelessly, taking his outstretched hand.

"What's wrong?" His watery bloodshot eyes widened.

"Hello," she repeated softly, "hello, hello, hello."

Somewhere in her mind a door began to open and a tired voice said. "Well, here it finally is. Hello, death!"

There was a dull, deep thud that sent a shudder through the whole train. "No," whispered Reva, throwing her arms around Sanders. "No!" She kissed his toothless mouth, drawing the stink of his alcoholic breath into her lungs until she could hold no more. With a long weary sigh the air left the train through the flowerlike hole in its side, pouring into the vacuum of the tunnel in swirling, glittering clouds of snow crystals. Inside, compartment doors bulged and burst open, and the passengers, like deep-sea fish brought too quickly to the surface, exploded, spattering the luxurious walls and upholstery with blood and flesh and bits of sticky cloth. The blood froze before it had a chance to run, and the train rushed on at a thousand miles an hour in absolute silence. The United Nations Ham movie cast a fantastic multi-colored light into the compartment containing what had once been an old man and what had once been a young woman. There was another being in the compartment, lying half in and half out of the torn stomach of the woman. Enough remained of it so that at least you could see its skin was dark, very dark, and it was a boy.

The Trans-Atlantic Tube arrived in London exactly on time.

Abelard waited at Angel Station, growing more and more restless and worried as the hours rolled by. He picked up some algae candy at the vending machines, but he couldn't seem to swallow it. For a while he would sit on the platform, watching the trains come and go and the people hurry about almost as if they had something important to do. Then he would go upstairs and loaf around on the street level. The window of a nearby house was open, and Abelard could hear the feelies playing inside. They were reporting the returns of the world elections.

Abelard listened with half an ear, shifting nervously from one foot to the other. He listened more for the time announcements than for the election returns; the time announcements that came and kept on coming while Abelard waited.

The Election results were no surprise.

It was a landslide victory for the Anti-Political Party.

There was a lot of cheering as the feelies focused on one city after another, a few minor bigwigs spoke briefly, then . . . "and now we take you to the World Capital at Antarctica for the acceptance speech of Gerald Davis, president of the Anti-Political Party and now President of the World!"

"Thank you, thank you," came a trained feelies voice, deep and convincing. "Thank you for the applause and thank you for your votes. I think you all realize that this has been not just another election, but an election to end, literally to end, all elections. For the first time in history a group of men has come into power for the sole purpose of putting an end to power. The behavior of my predecessor in this office has clearly demonstrated what wise men have always known, that is—power tends to corrupt, and absolute power to corrupt absolutely. I and my party are pledged to a unique platform . . . a program for our own removal from office. Yes, we are going to abdicate and there will be, we hope, no successors to our offices, ever again."

"Where is that bitch?" wondered Abelard. "What happened to her? Do you suppose she ran off with Little Brother? Maybe the baby was born, and it was white. Then she'll stay with Little Brother. Then she'll kiss him and play his filthy perverted games . . . and love him. Then she might never see me again!"

"My first act in office," said the President of the World, "will be the dissolution of the army and security police. They have long since ceased to have any real reason for existence. The few regulatory functions still exercised by the police will be taken over by automatic machines. My second act in office will be to abandon the money system. In an age when automation provides plenty for all, free, money is only the worthless plaything of people who want to live in the past."

"What does it matter," thought Abelard, "who is the biological father of Reva's child? If it wasn't mine, I'd still love it. I'd still bring it up just as if it were my own."

"No more cops, courts, jails and taxes," said the President of the World. "No more armed bodies of men, no more monopoly on the use of force, no more coercism of man by man, no more tyranny of the majority over the minorities. Today marks the beginning of a new era . . . the era of freedom! Mankind has conquered nature, overthrown the tyrant of economic necessity! Now mankind overthrows the last tyrant of all, the tyrant of government! The world that men have dreamed of since the dawn of time at last is here, a world of peace, and unlimited plenty, and unlimited freedom . . . the last barrier to happiness is destroyed!"

"That crazy bitch! How can she do this to me?" whispered Abelard, sitting down on the curb and holding his head in his hands. "I love her, I love her! How can she just wander away and never come back? Wander away and never find her way home . . ."

"The last barrier to Happiness is destroyed, my friends, and I, your elected President, have only one command for you. Seize it!"

Abelard reached into the gutter and picked up a rock and hurled it through the window with a crash of breaking glass.

"She's not coming," he whispered. "She's not coming, ever." A head appeared at the window.

"Hurrah for freedom!" shouted the head.

Abelard wove drunkenly down the steps into the subway.

The sky shone a blank and shadowless white, and continued to shine night and day throughout his long and vacant life.

THEY DON'T MAKE LIFE LIKE THEY USED TO

BY ALFRED BESTER (1913-1987)

THE MAGAZINE OF FANTASY AND SCIENCE FICTION
OCTOBER

I haven't seen Alfred Bester's two monumental novels The
Demolished Man *(1953) and* The Stars My Destination
*(1959) on the shelves of bookstores or in the racks at
newstands for several years. The reduction in the amount
of backlist books seems like an ominous development for
a writer like Bester, who produced fewer than ten books
in his long career. His short stories, which number less
than forty, are still reprinted, which is fortunate, since he
is arguably one of the five finest science fiction writers at
the shorter lengths.* Starlight: The Great Short Fiction Of
Alfred Bester *(1976) belongs in the collection of everyone
at all interested in this field.*

*"They Don't Make Life Like They Used To" is one of
the great post-holocaust stories of the 1960s.*

The girl driving the jeep was very fair and very Nordic.
Her blonde hair was pulled back in a pony tail, but it
was so long that it was more a mare's tail. She wore
sandals, a pair of soiled bluejeans, and nothing else. She
was nicely tanned. As she turned the jeep off Fifth Avenue and drove bouncing up the steps of the library, her
bosom danced enchantingly.

She parked in front of the library entrance, stepped
out, and was about to enter when her attention was
attracted by something across the street. She peered, hesitated, then glanced down at her jeans and made a face.
She pulled off the pants and hurled them at the pigeons

eternally cooing and courting on the library steps. As they clattered up in fright, she ran down to Fifth Avenue, crossed, and stopped before a shop window. There was a plum-colored wool dress on display. It had a high waist, a full skirt, and not too many moth holes. The price was $79.90.

The girl rummaged through old cars skewed on the avenue until she found a loose fender. She smashed the plate-glass shop door, carefully stepped across the splinters, entered, and sorted through the dusty dress racks. She was a big girl and had trouble fitting herself. Finally she abandoned the plum-colored wool and compromised on a dark tartan, size 12, $120 reduced to $99.90. She located a salesbook and pencil, blew the dust off, and carefully wrote: *I.O.U. $99.90. Linda Nielsen.*

She returned to the library and went through the main doors which had taken her a week to batter in with a sledge hammer. She ran across the great hall, filthied with five years of droppings from the pigeons roosting there. As she ran, she clapped her arms over her head to shield her hair from stray shots. She climbed the stairs to the third floor and entered the Print Room. As always, she signed the register: *Date—June 20, 1981. Name— Linda Nielsen. Address—Central Park Model Boat Pond. Business or Firm—Last Man on Earth.*

She had had a long debate with herself about *Business or Firm* the first time she broke into the library. Strictly speaking, she was the last woman on earth, but she had felt that if she wrote that it would seem chauvinistic; and "Last Person on Earth" sounded silly, like calling a drink a beverage.

She pulled portfolios out of racks and leafed through them. She knew exactly what she wanted; something warm with blue accents to fit a twenty by thirty frame for her bedroom. In a priceless collection of Hiroshige prints she found a lovely landscape. She filled out a slip, placed it carefully on the librarian's desk, and left with the print.

Downstairs, she stopped off in the main circulation room, went to the back shelves, and selected two Italian grammars and an Italian dictionary. Then she back-tracked through the main hall, went out to the jeep, and placed the books and print on the front seat alongside her companion, an exquisite Dresden China doll. She picked up a list that read:

> Jap. print
> Italian
> 20 × 30 pict. fr.
> Lobster bisque
> Brass polish
> Detergent
> Furn. polish
> Wet mop

She crossed off the first two items, replaced the list on the dashboard, got into the jeep, and bounced down the library steps. She drove up Fifth Avenue, threading her way through crumbling wreckage. As she was passing the ruins of St. Patrick's Cathedral at 50th Street, a man appeared from nowhere.

He stepped out of the rubble and, without looking left or right, started crossing the avenue just in front of her. She exclaimed, banged on the horn which remained mute, and braked so sharply that the jeep slewed and slammed into the remains of a No. 3 bus. The man let out a squawk, jumped ten feet, and then stood frozen, staring at her.

"You crazy jaywalker," she yelled. "Why don't you look where you're going? D'you think you own the whole city?"

He stared and stammered. He was a big man, with thick, grizzled hair, a red beard, and weathered skin. He was wearing army fatigues, heavy ski boots, and had a bursting knapsack and blanket roll on his back. He carried a battered shotgun, and his pockets were crammed with odds and ends. He looked like a prospector.

"My God," he whispered in a rusty voice. "Somebody at last. I knew it. I always knew I'd find someone." Then, as he noticed her long, fair hair, his face fell. "But a woman," he muttered. "Just my goddam lousy luck."

"What are you, some kind of nut?" she demanded. "Don't you know better than to cross against the lights?"

He looked around in bewilderment. "What lights?"

"So all right, there aren't any lights, but couldn't you look where you were going?"

"I'm sorry, lady. To tell the truth, I wasn't expecting any traffic."

"Just plain common sense," she grumbled, backing the jeep off the bus.

"Hey lady, wait a minute."

"Yes?"

"Listen, you know anything about TV? Electronics, how they say . . ."

"Are you trying to be funny?"

"No, this is straight. Honest."

She snorted and tried to continue driving up Fifth Avenue, but he wouldn't get out of the way.

"Please, lady," he persisted. "I got a reason for asking. Do you know?"

"No."

"Damn! I never get a break. Lady, excuse me, no offense, but you got any guys in this town?"

"There's nobody but me. I'm the last man on earth."

"That's funny. I always thought I was."

"So all right, I'm the last woman on earth."

He shook his head. "There's got to be other people; there just has to. Stands to reason. South, maybe you think? I'm down from New Haven, and I figured if I headed where the climate was like warmer, there'd be some guys I could ask something."

"Ask what?"

"Aw, a woman wouldn't understand. No offense."

"Well, if you want to head south you're going the wrong way."

"That's south, ain't it?" he asked, pointing down Fifth Avenue.

"Yes, but you'll just come to a dead end. Manhattan's an island. What you have to do is go uptown and cross the George Washington bridge to Jersey."

"Uptown? Which way is that?"

"Go straight up Fifth to Cathedral Parkway, then over to the West Side and up Riverside. You can't miss it."

He looked at her helplessly.

"Stranger in town?"

He nodded.

"Oh, all right," she said. "Hop in. I'll give you a lift."

She transferred the books and the china doll to the back seat, and he squeezed in alongside her. As she started the jeep she looked down at his worn ski boots.

"Hiking?"

"Yeah."

"Why don't you drive? You can get a car working, and there's plenty of gas and oil."

"I don't know how to drive," he said despondently. "It's the story of my life."

He heaved a sigh, and that made his knapsack jolt massively against her shoulder. She examined him out of the corner of her eye. He had a powerful chest, a long, thick back, and strong legs. His hands were big and hard, and his neck was corded with muscles. She thought for a moment, then nodded to herself and stopped the jeep.

"What's the matter?" he asked. "Won't it go?"

"What's your name?"

"Mayo. Jim Mayo."

"I'm Linda Nielsen."

"Yeah. Nice meeting you. Why don't it go?"

"Jim, I've got a proposition for you."

"Oh?" He looked at her doubtfully. "I'll be glad to listen, lady—I mean Linda, but I ought to tell you, I got something on my mind that's going to keep me pretty busy for a long t . . ." His voice trailed off as he turned away from her intense gaze.

"Jim, if you'll do something for me, I'll do something for you."

"Like what, for instance?"

"Well, I get terribly lonesome, nights. It isn't so bad during the day—there's always a lot of chores to keep you busy—but at night it's just awful."

"Yeah, I know," he muttered.

"I've got to do something about it."

"But how do I come into this?" he asked nervously.

"Why don't you stay in New York for a while? If you do, I'll teach you how to drive, and find you a car so you don't have to hike south."

"Say, that's an idea. Is it hard, driving?"

"I could teach you in a couple of days."

"I don't learn things so quick."

"All right, a couple of weeks, but think of how much time you'll save in the long run."

"Gee," he said, "that sounds great." Then he turned away again. "But what do I have to do for you?"

Her face lit up with excitement. "Jim, I want you to help me move a piano."

"A piano? What piano?"

"A rosewood grand from Steinway's on Fifty-seventh Street. I'm dying to have it in my place. The living room is just crying for it."

"Oh, you mean you're furnishing, huh?"

"Yes, but I want to play after dinner, too. You can't listen to records all the time. I've got it all planned; books on how to play, and books on how to tune a piano. . . . I've been able to figure everything except how to move the piano in."

"Yeah, but . . . but there's apartments all over this town with pianos in them," he objected. "There must be hundreds, at least. Stands to reason. Why don't you live in one of them?"

"Never! I love my place. I've spent five years decorating it, and it's beautiful. Besides, there's the problem of water."

He nodded. "Water's always a headache. How do you handle it?"

"I'm living in the house in Central Park where they used to keep the model yachts. It faces the boat pond. It's a darling place, and I've got it all fixed up. We could get the piano in together, Jim. It wouldn't be hard."

"Well, I don't know, Lena . . ."

"Linda."

"Excuse me. Linda. I—"

"You look strong enough. What'd you do, before?"

"I used to be a pro rassler."

"There! I knew you were strong."

"Oh, I'm not a rassler anymore. I became a bartender and went into the restaurant business. I opened 'The Body Slam' up in New Haven. Maybe you heard of it?"

"I'm sorry."

"It was sort of famous with the sports crowd. What'd you do before?"

"I was a researcher for BBDO."

"What's that?"

"An advertising agency," she explained impatiently. "We can talk about that later, if you'll stick around. And I'll teach you how to drive, and we can move in the piano, and there's a few other things that I—but that can wait. Afterward you can drive south."

"Gee, Linda, I don't know . . ."

She took Mayo's hands. "Come on, Jim, be a sport. You can stay with me. I'm a wonderful cook, and I've got a lovely guest room . . ."

"What for? I mean, thinking you was the last man on earth."

"That's a silly question. A proper house has to have a guest room. You'll love my place. I turned the lawns into a farm and gardens, and you can swim in the pond, and we'll get you a new Jag . . . I know where there's a beauty up on blocks."

"I think I'd rather have a Caddy."

"You can have anything you like. So what do you say, Jim? Is it a deal?"

"All right, Linda," he muttered reluctantly. "You've a deal."

It was indeed a lovely house with its pagoda roof of copper weathered to verdigris green, fieldstone walls, and deep recessed windows. The oval pond before it glittered blue in the soft June sunlight, and Mallard ducks paddled and quacked busily. The sloping lawns that formed a bowl around the pond were terraced and cultivated. The house faced west, and Central Park stretched out beyond like an unkempt estate.

Mayo looked at the pond wistfully. "It ought to have boats."

"The house was full of them when I moved in," Linda said.

"I always wanted a model boat when I was a kid. Once I even—" Mayo broke off. A penetrating pounding sounded somewhere; an irregular sequence of heavy knocks that sounded like the dint of stones under water. It stopped as suddenly as it had begun. "What was that?" Mayo asked.

Linda shrugged. "I don't know for sure. I think it's

the city falling apart. You'll see buildings coming down every now and then. You get used to it." Her enthusiasm rekindled. "Now come inside. I want to show you everything."

She was bursting with pride and overflowing with decorating details that bewildered Mayo, but he was impressed by her Victorian living room, *Empire* bedroom, and Country Kitchen with a working kerosene cooking stove. The Colonial guest room, with four-poster bed, hooked rug, and Tole lamps, worried him.

"This is kind of girlie-girlie, huh?"

"Naturally. I'm a girl."

"Yeah. Sure. I mean . . ." Mayo looked around doubtfully. "Well, a guy is used to stuff that ain't so delicate. No offense."

"Don't worry, that bed's strong enough. Now remember, Jim, no feet on the spread, and remove it at night. If your shoes are dirty, take them off before you come in. I got that rug from the museum and I don't want it messed up. Have you got a change of clothes?"

"Only what I got on."

"We'll have to get you new things tomorrow. What you're wearing is so filthy it's not worth laundering."

"Listen," he said desperately, "I think maybe I better camp out in the park."

"Why on earth?"

"Well, I'm like more used to it than houses. But you don't have to worry, Linda. I'll be around in case you need me."

"Why should I need you?"

"All you have to do is holler."

"Nonsense," Linda said firmly. "You're my guest and you're staying here. Now get cleaned up; I'm going to start dinner. Oh damn! I forgot to pick up the lobster bisque."

She gave him a dinner cleverly contrived from canned goods and served on exquisite Fornisetti china with Danish silver flatware. It was a typical girl's meal, and Mayo was still hungry when it was finished, but too polite to mention it. He was too tired to fabricate an excuse to go out and forage for something substantial. He lurched off to bed, remembering to remove his shoes but forgetting all about the spread.

He was awakened next morning by a loud honking and clattering of wings. He rolled out of bed and went to the windows just in time to see the Mallards dispossessed from the pond by what appeared to be a red balloon. When he got his eyes working properly, he saw that it was a bathing cap. He wandered out to the pond, stretching and groaning. Linda yelled cheerfully and swam toward him. She heaved herself up out of the pond onto the curbing. The bathing cap was all that she wore. Mayo backed away from the splash and spatter.

"Good morning," Linda said. "Sleep well?"

"Good morning," Mayo said. "I don't know. The bed put kinks in my back. Gee, that water must be cold. You're all gooseflesh."

"No, it's marvelous." She pulled off the cap and shook her hair down. "Where's that towel? Oh, here. Go on in, Jim. You'll feel wonderful."

"I don't like it when it's cold."

"Don't be a sissy."

A crack of thunder split the quiet morning. Mayo looked up at the clear sky in astonishment. "What the hell was that?" he exclaimed.

"Watch," Linda ordered.

"It sounded like a sonic boom."

"There!" she cried, pointing west. "See?"

One of the West Side skyscrapers crumbled majestically, sinking into itself like a collapsible cup and raining masses of cornice and brick. The flayed girders twisted and contorted. Moments later they could hear the roar of the collapse.

"Man, that's a sight," Mayo muttered in awe.

"The decline and fall of the Empire City. You get used to it. Now take a dip, Jim. I'll get you a towel."

She ran into the house. He dropped his shorts and took off his socks, but was still standing on the curb, unhappily dipping his toe into the water when she returned with a huge bath towel.

"It's awful cold, Linda," he complained.

"Didn't you take cold showers when you were a wrestler?"

"Not me. Boiling hot."

"Jim, if you just stand there, you'll never go in. Look at you, you're starting to shiver. Is that a tattoo around your waist?"

"What? Oh, yeah. It's a python, in five colors. It goes all the way around. See?" He revolved proudly. "Got it when I was with the Army in Saigon back in '64. It's a Oriental-type python. Elegant, huh?"

"Did it hurt?"

"To tell the truth, no. Some guys try to make out like it's Chinese torture to get tattooed, but they're just showin' off. It itches more than anything else."

"You were a soldier in '64?"

"That's right."

"How old were you?"

"Twenty."

"You're thirty-seven now?"

"Thirty-six going on thirty-seven."

"Then you're prematurely gray?"

"I guess so."

She contemplated him thoughtfully. "I tell you what, if you do go in, don't get your head wet."

She ran back into the house. Mayo, ashamed of his vacillation, forced himself to jump feet first into the pond. He was standing, chest deep, splashing his face and shoulders with water when Linda returned. She carried a stool, a pair of scissors, and a comb.

"Doesn't it feel wonderful?" she called.

"No."

She laughed. "Well, come out. I'm going to give you a haircut."

He climbed out of the pond, dried himself, and obediently sat on the stool while she cut his hair. "The beard, too," Linda insisted. "I want to see what you really look like." She trimmed him close enough for shaving, inspected him, and nodded with satisfaction. "Very handsome."

"Aw, go on," he blushed.

"There's a bucket of hot water on the stove. Go and shave. Don't bother to dress. We're going to get you new clothes after breakfast, and then . . . the Piano."

"I couldn't walk around the streets naked," he said, shocked.

"Don't be silly. Who's going to see? Now hurry."

They drove down to Abercrombie & Fitch on Madison and 45th Street, Mayo wrapped modestly in his towel. Linda told him she'd been a customer for years, and showed him the pile of sales slips she had accumulated. Mayo examined them curiously while she took his measurements and went off in search of clothes. He was almost indignant when she returned with her arms laden.

"Jim, I've got some lovely elk moccasins, and a Safari suit, and wool socks, and Shipboard shirts, and—"

"Listen," he interrupted, "do you know what your whole tab comes to? Nearly fourteen hundred dollars."

"Really? Put on the shorts first. They're drip-dry."

"You must have been out of your mind, Linda. What'd you want all that junk for?"

"Are the socks big enough? What junk? I needed everything."

"Yeah? Like . . ." He shuffled the signed sales slips. "Like one Underwater Viewer with Plexiglass Lens, nine ninety-five? What for?"

"So I could see to clean the bottom of the pond."

"What about this Stainless Steel Service for Four, thirty-nine fifty?"

"For when I'm lazy and don't feel like heating water. You can wash stainless steel in cold water." She admired him. "Oh, Jim, come look in the mirror. You're real romantic, like the big-game hunter in that Hemingway story."

He shook his head. "I don't see how you're ever going to get out of hock. You got to watch your spending, Linda. Maybe we better forget about that piano, huh?"

"Never," Linda said adamantly. "I don't care how much it costs. A piano is a lifetime investment, and it's worth it."

She was frantic with excitement as they drove uptown to the Steinway showroom, and helpful and underfoot by turns. After a long afternoon of muscle-cracking and critical engineering involving makeshift gantries and an agonizing dollie-haul up Fifth Avenue, they had the piano in place in Linda's living room. Mayo gave it one last shake to make sure it was firmly on its legs and then sank down, exhausted. "Je-zuz!" he groaned. "Hiking south would've been easier."

"Jim!" Linda ran to him and threw herself on him with a fervent hug. "Jim, you're an angel. Are you all right?"

"I'm okay." He grunted. "Get off me, Linda. I can't breathe."

"I just can't thank you enough. I've been dreaming about this for ages. I don't know what I can do to repay you. Anything you want, just name it."

"Aw," he said, "you already cut my hair."

"I'm serious."

"Ain't you teaching me how to drive?"

"Of course. As quickly as possible. That's the least I can do." Linda backed to a chair and sat down, her eyes fixed on the piano.

"Don't make such a fuss over nothing," he said, climbing to his feet. He sat down before the keyboard, shot an embarrassed grin at her over his shoulder, then reached out and began stumbling through *The Minuet in G*.

Linda gasped and sat bolt upright. "You play," she whispered.

"Naw. I took piano when I was a kid."

"Can you read music?"

"I used to."

"Could you teach me?"

"I guess so; it's kind of hard. Hey, here's another piece I had to take." He began mutilating *The Rustle of Spring*. What with the piano out of tune and his mistakes, it was ghastly.

"Beautiful," Linda breathed. "Just beautiful!" She stared at his back while an expression of decision and determination stole across her face. She arose, slowly crossed to Mayo, and put her hands on his shoulders.

He glanced up. "Something?" he asked.

"Nothing," she answered. "You practice the piano. I'll get dinner."

But she was so preoccupied for the rest of the evening that she made Mayo nervous. He stole off to bed early.

It wasn't until three o'clock the following afternoon that they finally got a car working, and it wasn't a Caddy,

but a Chevy—a hardtop because Mayo didn't like the
idea of being exposed to the weather in a convertible.
They drove out of the Tenth Avenue garage and back to
the East Side, where Linda felt more at home. She con-
fessed that the boundaries of her world were from Fifth
Avenue to Third, and from 42nd Street to 86th. She was
uncomfortable outside this pale.

She turned the wheel over to Mayo and let him creep
up and down Fifth and Madison, practicing starts and
stops. He sideswiped five wrecks, stalled eleven times,
and reversed through a storefront which, fortunately, was
devoid of glass. He was trembling with nervousness.

"It's real hard," he complained.

"It's just a question of practice," she reassured him.
"Don't worry. I promise you'll be an expert if it takes
us a month."

"A whole month!"

"You said you were a slow learner, didn't you? Don't
blame me. Stop here a minute."

He jolted the Chevy to a halt. Linda got out.

"Wait for me."

"What's up?"

"A surprise."

She ran into a shop and was gone for half an hour.
When she reappeared she was wearing a pencil-thin black
sheath, pearls, and high heeled opera pumps. She had
twisted her hair into a coronet. Mayo regarded her with
amazement as she got into the car.

"What's all this?" he asked.

"Part of the surprise. Turn east on Fifty-second
Street."

He labored, started the car, and drove east. "Why'd
you get all dressed up in an evening gown?"

"It's a cocktail dress."

"What for?"

"So I'll be dressed for where we're going. Watch out,
Jim!" Linda wrenched the wheel and sheered off the
stern of a shattered sanitation truck. "I'm taking you to
a famous restaurant."

"To eat?"

"No, silly, for drinks. You're my visiting fireman, and

I have to entertain you. That's it on the left. See if you can park somewhere."

He parked abominably. As they got out of the car, Mayo stopped and began to sniff curiously.

"Smell that?" he asked.

"Smell what?"

"That sort of sweet smell."

"It's my perfume."

"No, it's something in the air, kind of sweet and chokey. I know that smell from somewhere, but I can't remember."

"Never mind. Come inside." She led him into the restaurant. "You ought to be wearing a tie," she whispered, "but maybe we can get away with it."

Mayo was not impressed by the restaurant decor, but was fascinated by the portraits of celebrities hung in the bar. He spent rapt minutes burning his fingers with matches, gazing at Mel Allen, Red Barber, Casey Stengel, Frank Gifford, and Rocky Marciano. When Linda finally came back from the kitchen with a lighted candle, he turned to her eagerly.

"You ever see any of them TV stars in here?" he asked.

"I suppose so. How about a drink?"

"Sure. Sure. But I want to talk more about them TV stars."

He escorted her to a bar stool, blew the dust off, and helped her up most gallantly. Then he vaulted over the bar, whipped out his handkerchief, and polished the mahogany professionally. "This is my specialty," he grinned. He assumed the impersonally friendly attitude of the bartender. "Evening, ma'am. Nice night. What's your pleasure?"

"God, I had a rough day in the shop! Dry martini on the rocks. Better make it a double."

"Certainly, ma'am. Twist or olive?"

"Onion."

"Double-dry Gibson on the rocks. Right." Mayo searched behind the bar and finally produced whiskey, gin, and several bottles of soda, as yet only partially evaporated through their sealed caps. "Afraid we're fresh out of martinis, ma'am. What's your second pleasure?"

"Oh, I like that. Scotch, please."

"This soda'll be flat," he warned, "and there's no ice."

"Never mind."

He rinsed a glass with soda and poured her a drink.

"Thank you. Have one on me, bartender. What's your name?"

"They call me Jim, ma'am. No thanks. Never drink on duty."

"Then come off duty and join me."

"Never drink off duty, ma'am."

"You can call me Linda."

"Thank you, Miss Linda."

"Are you serious about never drinking, Jim?"

"Yeah."

"Well, Happy Days."

"And Long Nights."

"I like that, too. Is it your own?"

"Gee, I don't know. It's sort of the usual bartender's routine, a specially with guys. You know? Suggestive. No offense."

"None taken."

"Bees!" Mayo burst out.

Linda was startled. "Bees what?"

"That smell. Like inside beehives."

"Oh? I wouldn't know," she said indifferently. "I'll have another, please."

"Coming right up. Now listen, about them TV celebrities, you actually saw them here? In person?"

"Why of course. Happy Days, Jim."

"May they all be Saturdays."

Linda pondered. "Why Saturdays?"

"Day off."

"Oh."

"Which TV stars did you see?"

"You name 'em, I saw 'em." She laughed. "You remind me of the kid next door. I always had to tell him the celebrities I'd seen. One day I told him I saw Jean Arthur in here, and he said, 'With his horse?' "

Mayo couldn't see the point, but was wounded nevertheless. Just as Linda was about to soothe his feelings, the bar began a gentle quivering, and at the same time a faint subterranean rumbling commenced. It came from a distance, seemed to approach slowly, and then faded away. The vibration stopped. Mayo stared at Linda.

"Je-zus! You think maybe this building's going to go?"

She shook her head. "No. When they go, it's always with that boom. You know what that sounded like? The Lexington Avenue subway."

"The subway?"

"Uh-huh. The local train."

"That's crazy. How could the subway be running?"

"I didn't say it *was*. I said it *sounded* like. I'll have another, please."

"We need more soda." Mayo explored and reappeared with bottles and a large menu. He was pale. "You better take it easy, Linda," he said. "You know what they're charging per drink? A dollar seventy-five. Look."

"To hell with expense. Let's live a little. Make it a double, bartender. You know something, Jim? If you stayed in town, I could show you where all your heroes lived. Thank you. Happy Days. I could take you up to BBDO and show you their tapes and films. How about that? Stars like . . . like Red . . . Who?"

"Barber."

"Red Barber, and Rocky Gifford, and Rocky Casey, and Rocky, the Flying Squirrel."

"You're putting me on," Mayo said, offended again.

"Me, sir? Putting you on?" Linda said with dignity. "Why would I do a thing like that? Just trying to be pleasant. Just trying to give you a good time. My mother told me, Linda, she told me, just remember this about a man, wear what he wants and say what he likes, is what she told me. You want this dress?" she demanded.

"I like it, if that's what you mean."

"Know what I paid for it? Ninety-nine fifty."

"What? A hundred dollars for a skinny black thing like that?"

"It is not a skinny black thing like that. It is a basic black cocktail frock. And I paid twenty dollars for the pearls. Simulated," she explained. "And sixty for the opera pumps. And forty for the perfume. Two hundred and twenty dollars to give you a good time. You having a good time?"

"Sure."

"Want to smell me?"

"I already have."

"Bartender, give me another."

"Afraid I can't serve you, ma'am."

"Why not?"

"You've had enough already."

"I have not had enough already," Linda said indignantly. "Where's your manners?" She grabbed the whiskey bottle. "Come on, let's have a few drinks and talk up a storm about TV stars. Happy Days. I could take you up to BBDO and show you their tapes and films. How about that?"

"You just asked me."

"You didn't answer. I could show you movies, too. You like movies? I hate 'em, but I can't knock 'em anymore. Movies saved my life when the big bang came."

"How was that?"

"This is a secret, understand? Just between you and me. If any other agency ever found out . . ." Linda looked around and then lowered her voice. "BBDO located this big cache of silent films. Lost films, see? Nobody knew the prints were around. Make a great TV series. So they sent me to this abandoned mine in Jersey to take inventory."

"In a mine?"

"That's right. Happy Days."

"Why were they in a mine?"

"Old prints. Nitrate. Catch fire. Also rot. Have to be stored like wine. That's why. So took two of my assistants with me to spend weekend down there, checking."

"You stayed in the mine a whole weekend?"

"Uh-huh. Three girls. Friday to Monday. That was the plan. Thought it would be a fun deal. Happy Days. So. . . . Where was I? Oh. So, took lights, blankets, linen, plenty of picnic, the whole schmeer, and went to work. I remember exact moment when blast came. Was looking for third reel of an UFA film, *Gekronter Blumenorden an der Pegnitz*. Had reel one, two, four, five, six. No three. Bang! Happy Days."

"Jesus. Then what?"

"My girls panicked. Couldn't keep 'em down there. Never saw them again. But I knew. I knew. Stretched

that picnic forever. Then starved even longer. Finally
came up, and for what? For who? Whom?" She began
to weep. "For nobody. Nobody left. Nothing." She took
Mayo's hands. "Why won't you stay?"

"Stay? Where?"

"Here."

"I am staying."

"I mean for a long time. Why not? Haven't I got lovely
home? And there's all New York for supplies. And farm
for flowers and vegetables. We could keep cows and
chickens. Go fishing. Drive cars. Go to museums. Art gal-
leries. Entertain . . ."

"You're doing all that right now. You don't need me."

"But I do. I do."

"For what?"

"For piano lessons."

After a long pause he said, "You're drunk."

"Not wounded, sire, but dead."

She lay her head on the bar, beamed up at him rogu-
ishly, and then closed her eyes. An instant later, Mayo
knew she had passed out. He compressed his lips. Then
he climbed out of the bar, computed the tab, and left
fifteen dollars under the whiskey bottle.

He took Linda's shoulder and shook her gently. She
collapsed into his arms, and her hair came tumbling
down. He blew out the candle, picked Linda up, and
carried her to the Chevy. Then, with anguished concentration, he drove through the dark to the boat pond. It
took him forty minutes.

He carried Linda into her bedroom and sat her down
on the bed, which was decorated with an elaborate
arrangement of dolls. Immediately she rolled over and
curled up with a doll in her arms, crooning to it. Mayo
lit a lamp and tried to prop her upright. She went over
again, giggling.

"Linda," he said, "you got to get that dress off."

"Mf."

"You can't sleep in it. It cost a hundred dollars."

"Nine'nine-fif'y."

"Now come on, honey."

"Fm."

He rolled his eyes in exasperation and then undressed

her, carefully hanging up the basic black cocktail frock, and standing the sixty-dollar pumps in a corner. He could not manage the clasp of the pearls (simulated), so he put her to bed still wearing them. Lying on the pale blue sheets, nude except for the necklace, she looked like a Nordic odalisque.

"Did you muss my dolls?" she mumbled.

"No. They're all around you."

"Tha's right. Never sleep without 'em." She reached out and petted them lovingly. "Happy Days. Long Nights."

"Women!" Mayo snorted. He extinguished the lamp and tramped out, slamming the door behind him.

Next morning Mayo was again awakened by the clatter of dispossessed ducks. The red balloon was sailing on the surface of the pond, bright in the warm June sunshine. Mayo wished it was a model boat instead of the kind of girl who got drunk in bars. He stalked out and jumped into the water as far from Linda as possible. He was sluicing his chest when something seized his ankle and nipped him. He let out a yell, and was confronted by Linda's beaming face bursting out of the water before him.

"Good morning," she laughed.

"Very funny," he muttered.

"You look mad this morning."

He grunted.

"And I don't blame you. I did an awful thing last night. I didn't give you any dinner, and I want to apologize."

"I wasn't thinking about dinner," he said with baleful dignity.

"No? Then what on earth are you mad about?"

"I can't stand women who get drunk."

"Who was drunk?"

"You."

"I was not," she said indignantly.

"No? Who had to be undressed and put to bed like a kid?"

"Who was too dumb to take off my pearls?" she countered. "They broke and I slept on pebbles all night. I'm covered with black and blue marks. Look. Here and here and—"

"Linda," he interrupted sternly, "I'm just a plain guy from New Haven. I got no use for spoiled girls who run up charge accounts and all the time decorate theirselves and hang around society-type saloons getting loaded."

"If you don't like my company, why do you stay?"

"I'm going," he said. He climbed out and began drying himself. "I'm starting south this morning."

"Enjoy your hike."

"I'm driving."

"What? A kiddie-kar?"

"The Chevy."

"Jim, you're not serious?" She climbed out of the pond, looking alarmed. "You really don't know how to drive yet."

"No? Didn't I drive you home falling-down drunk last night?"

"You'll get into awful trouble."

"Nothing I can't get out of. Anyway, I can't hang around here forever. You're a party girl; you just want to play. I got serious things on my mind. I got to go south and find guys who know about TV."

"Jim, you've got me wrong. I'm not like that at all. Why, look at the way I fixed up my house. Could I have done that if I'd been going to parties all the time?"

"You done a nice job," he admitted.

"Please don't leave today. You're not ready yet."

"Aw, you just want me to hang around and teach you music."

"Who said that?"

"You did. Last night."

She frowned, pulled off her cap, then picked up her towel and began drying herself. At last she said, "Jim, I'll be honest with you. Sure, I want you to stay a while. I won't deny it. But I wouldn't want you around permanently. After all, what have we got in common?"

"You're so damn uptown," he growled.

"No, no, it's nothing like that. It's simply that you're a guy and I'm a girl, and we've got nothing to offer each other. We're different. We've got different tastes and interests. Fact?"

"Absolutely."

"But you're not ready to leave yet. So I tell you what; we'll spend the whole morning practicing driving, and then we'll have some fun. What would you like to do? Go window-shopping? Buy more clothes? Visit the Modern Museum? Have a picnic?"

His face brightened. "Gee, you know something? I was never to a picnic in my whole life. Once I was bartender at a clambake, but that's not the same thing; not like when you're a kid."

She was delighted. "Then we'll have a real kid-type picnic."

And she brought her dolls. She carried them in her arms while Mayo toted the picnic basket to the Alice in Wonderland monument. The statue perplexed Mayo, who had never heard of Lewis Carroll. While Linda seated her pets and unpacked the picnic, she gave Mayo a summary of the story, and described how the bronze heads of Alice, the Mad Hatter, and the March Hare had been polished bright by the swarms of kids playing King of the Mountain.

"Funny, I never heard of that story," he said.

"I don't think you had much of a childhood, Jim."

"Why would you say a—" He stopped, cocked his head, and listened intently.

"What's the matter?" Linda asked.

"You hear that bluejay?"

"No."

"Listen. He's making a funny sound; like steel."

"Steel?"

"Yeah. Like . . . like swords in a duel."

"You're kidding."

"No. Honest."

"But birds sing; they don't make noises."

"Not always. Bluejays imitate noises a lot. Starlings, too. And parrots. Now why would he be imitating a sword fight? Where'd he hear it?"

"You're a real country boy, aren't you, Jim? Bees and bluejays and starlings and all that . . ."

"I guess so. I was going to ask; why would you say a thing like that, me not having any childhood?"

"Oh, things like not knowing Alice, and never going

on a picnic, and always wanting a model yacht." Linda opened a dark bottle. "Like to try some wine?"

"You better go easy," he warned.

"Now stop it, Jim. I'm not a drunk."

"Did you or didn't you get smashed last night?"

She capitulated. "All right, I did; but only because it was my first drink in years."

He was pleased by her surrender. "Sure. Sure. That figures."

"So? Join me?"

"What the hell, why not?" He grinned. "Let's live a little. Say, this is one swingin' picnic, and I like the plates, too. Where'd you get them?"

"Abercrombie & Fitch," Linda said, deadpan. "Stainless Steel Service for Four, thirty-nine fifty. Skoal."

Mayo burst out laughing. "I sure goofed, didn't I, kicking up all that fuss? Here's looking at you."

"Here's looking right back."

They drank and continued eating in warm silence, smiling companionably at each other. Linda removed her Madres silk shirt in order to tan in the blazing afternoon sun, and Mayo politely hung it up on a branch. Suddenly Linda asked, "Why didn't you have a childhood, Jim?"

"Gee, I don't know." He thought it over. "I guess because my mother died when I was a kid. And something else, too; I had to work a lot."

"Why?"

"My father was a schoolteacher. You know how they get paid."

"Oh, so that's why you're anti-egghead."

"I am?"

"Of course. No offense."

"Maybe I am," he conceded. "It sure was a letdown for my old man, me playing fullback in high school and him wanting like an Einstein in the house."

"Was football fun?"

"Not like playing games. Football's a business. Hey, remember when we were kids how we used to choose up sides? *Ibbety, bibbety, zibbety, zab?*"

"We used to say, *Eenie, meenie, miney, mo.*"

"Remember: *April Fool, go to school, tell your teacher you're a fool?*"

"I love coffee, I love tea, I love the boys, and the boys love me."

"I bet they did at that," Mayo said solemnly.

"Not me."

"Why not?"

"I was always too big."

He was astonished. "But you're not big," he assured her. "You're just the right size. Perfect. And really built. I noticed when we moved the piano in. You got muscle, for a girl. A specially in the legs, and that's where it counts."

She blushed. "Stop it, Jim."

"No. Honest."

"More wine?"

"Thanks. You have some, too."

"All right."

A crack of thunder split the sky with its sonic boom, and was followed by the roar of collapsing masonry.

"There goes another skyscraper," Linda said. "What were we talking about?"

"Games," Mayo said promptly. "Excuse me for talking with my mouth full."

"Oh yes. Jim did you play *Drop the Handkerchief* up in New Haven?" Linda sang. *"A tisket, a tasket, a green and yellow basket. I sent a letter to my love, and on the way I dropped it . . ."*

"Gee," he said, much impressed. "You sing real good."

"Oh, go on!"

"Yes you do. You got a swell voice. Now don't argue with me. Keep quiet a minute. I got to figure something out." He thought intently for a long time, finishing his wine and absently accepting another glass. Finally he delivered himself of a decision. "You got to learn music."

"You know I'm dying to, Jim."

"So I'm going to stay a while and teach you; as much as I know. Now hold it! Hold it!" he added hastily, cutting off her excitement. "I'm not going to stay in your house. I want a place of my own."

"Of course, Jim. Anything you say."

"And I'm still headed south."

"I'll teach you to drive, Jim. I'll keep my word."

"And no strings, Linda."

"Of course not. What kind of strings?"

"You know. Like the last minute you all of a sudden got a Looey Cans couch you want me to move in."

"*Louis Quinze!*" Linda's jaw dropped. "Wherever did you learn that?"

"Not in the Army, that's for sure."

They laughed, clinked glasses, and finished their wine. Suddenly Mayo leaped up, pulled Linda's hair, and ran to the Wonderland monument. In an instant he had climbed to the top of Alice's head.

"I'm King of the Mountain," he shouted, looking around in imperial survey. "I'm King of the—" He cut himself off and stared down behind the statue.

"Jim, what's the matter?"

Without a word, Mayo climbed down and strode to a pile of debris half-hidden inside overgrown Forsythia bushes. He knelt and began turning over the wreckage with gentle hands. Linda ran to him.

"Jim, what's wrong?"

"These used to be model boats," he muttered.

"That's right. My God, is that all? I thought you were sick or something."

"How come they're here?"

"Why, I dumped them, of course."

"You?"

"Yes. I told you. I had to clear out the boathouse when I moved in. That was ages ago."

"You did this?"

"Yes. I—"

"You're a murderer," he growled. He stood up and glared at her. "You're a killer. You're like all women, you got no heart and soul. To do a thing like this!"

He turned and stalked toward the boat pond. Linda followed him, completely bewildered.

"Jim, I don't understand. Why are you so mad?"

"You ought to be ashamed of yourself."

"But I had to have house room. You wouldn't expect me to live with a lot of model boats."

"Just forget everything I said. I'm going to pack and go south, I wouldn't stay with you if you was the last person on earth."

Linda gathered herself and suddenly darted ahead of Mayo. When he tramped into the boathouse, she was standing before the door of the guest room. She held up a heavy iron key.

"I found it," she panted. "Your door's locked."

"Gimmie that key, Linda."

"No."

He stepped toward her, but she faced him defiantly and stood her ground.

"Go ahead," she challenged. "Hit me."

He stopped. "Aw, I wouldn't pick on anybody that wasn't my own size."

They continued to face each other, at a complete impasse.

"I don't need my gear," Mayo muttered at last. "I can get more stuff somewheres."

"Oh, go ahead and pack," Linda answered. She tossed him the key and stood aside. Then Mayo discovered there was no lock in the bedroom door. He opened the door, looked inside, closed it, and looked at Linda. She kept her face straight but began to sputter. He grinned. Then they both burst out laughing.

"Gee," Mayo said, "you sure made a monkey out of me. I'd hate to play poker against you."

"You're a pretty good bluffer yourself, Jim. I was scared to death you were going to knock me down."

"You ought to know I wouldn't hurt nobody."

"I guess I do. Now, let's sit down and talk this over sensibly."

"Aw, forget it, Linda. I kind of lost my head over them boats, and I—"

"I don't mean the boats; I mean going south. Every time you get mad you start south again. Why?"

"I told you, to find guys who know about TV."

"Why?"

"You wouldn't understand."

"I can try. Why don't you explain what you're after—specifically? Maybe I can help you."

"You can't do nothing for me; you're a girl."

"We have our uses. At least I can listen. You can trust me, Jim. Aren't we chums? Tell me about it."

Well, when the blast come (Mayo said) I was up in the Berkshires with Gil Watkins. Gil was my buddy, a real nice guy and a real bright guy. He took two years from M.I.T. before he quit college. He was like chief engineer or something at WNHA, the TV station in New Haven. Gil had a million hobbies. One of them was spee—speel—I can't remember. It meant exploring caves.

So anyway we were up in this flume in the Berkshires, spending the weekend inside, exploring and trying to map everything and figure out where the underground river come from. We brought food and stuff along, and bed rolls. The compass we were using went crazy for like twenty minutes, and that should have give us a clue, but Gil talked about magnetic ores and stuff. Only when we come out Sunday night, I tell you it was pretty scarey. Gil knew right off what happened.

"By Christ, Jim," he said, "they up and done it like everybody always knew they would. They've blew and gassed and poisoned and radiated themselves straight to hell, and we're going back to that goddamn cave until it all blows over."

So me and Gil went back and rationed the food and stayed as long as we could. Finally we come out again and drove back to New Haven. It was dead like all the rest. Gil put together some radio stuff and tried to pick up broadcasts. Nothing. Then we packed some canned goods and drove all around; Bridgeport, Waterbury, Hartford, Springfield, Providence, New London . . . a big circle. Nobody. Nothing. So we come back to New Haven and settled down, and it was a pretty good life.

Daytime, we'd get in supplies and stuff, and tinker with the house to keep it working right. Nights, after supper, Gil would go off to WNHA around seven o'clock and start the station. He was running it on the emergency generators. I'd go down to "The Body Slam," open it up, sweep it out, and then start the bar TV set. Gil fixed me a generator for it to run on.

It was a lot of fun watching the shows Gil was broadcasting. He'd start with the news and weather, which he always got wrong. All he had was some Farmer's Almanacs and a sort of antique barometer that looked like that clock you got there on the wall. I don't think it worked so good, or maybe Gil never took weather at M.I.T. Then he'd broadcast the evening show.

I had my shotgun in the bar in case of holdups. Anytime I saw something that bugged me, I just up with the gun and let loose at the set. Then I'd take it and throw it out the front door and put another one in its place. I must have had hundreds waiting in the back. I spent two days a week just collecting reserves.

Midnight, Gil would turn off WNHA, I'd lock up the restaurant, and we'd meet home for coffee. Gil would ask how many sets I shot, and laugh when I told him. He said I was the most accurate TV poll ever invented. I'd ask him about what shows were coming up next week and argue with him about . . . oh . . . about like what movies or football games WNHA was scheduling. I didn't like Westerns much, and I hated them high-minded panel discussions.

But the luck had to turn lousy; it's the story of my life. After a couple of years, I found out I was down to my last set, and then I was in trouble. This night Gil run one of them icky commercials where this smart-aleck woman saves a marriage with the right laundry soap. Naturally I reached for my gun, and only at the last minute remembered not to shoot. Then he run an awful movie about a misunderstood composer, and the same thing happened. When we met back at the house, I was all shook up.

"What's the matter?" Gil asked.

I told him.

"I thought you liked watching the shows," he said.

"Only when I could shoot 'em."

"You poor bastard," he laughed, "you're a captive audience now."

"Gil, could you maybe change the programs, seeing the spot I'm in?"

"Be reasonable, Jim. WNHA has to broadcast variety. We operate on the cafeteria basis; something for everybody. If you don't like a show, why don't you switch channels?"

"Now that's silly. You know damn well we only got one channel in New Haven."

"Then turn your set off."

"I can't turn the bar set off, it's part of the entertainment. I'd lose my whole clientele. Gil, do you *have* to show them awful movies, like that army musical last night, singing and dancing and kissing on top of Sherman tanks, for Jezus sake!"

"The women love uniform pictures."

"And those commercials; women always sneering at somebody's girdle, and fairies smoking cigarettes, and—"

"Aw," Gil said, "write a letter to the station."

So I did, and a week later I got an answer. It said: *Dear Mr. Mayo: We are very glad to learn that you are a regular viewer of WNHA, and thank you for your interest in our programming. We hope you will continue to enjoy our broadcasts. Sincerely yours, Gilbert O. Watkins, Station Manager.* A couple of tickets for an interview show were enclosed. I showed the letter to Gil, and he just shrugged.

"You see what you're up against, Jim," he said. "They don't care about what you like or don't like. All they want to know is if you are watching."

I tell you, the next couple of months were hell for me. I couldn't keep the set turned off, and I couldn't watch it without reaching for my gun a dozen times a night. It took all my willpower to keep from pulling the trigger. I got so nervous and jumpy that I knew I had to do something about it before I went off my rocker. So one night I brought the gun home and shot Gil.

Next day I felt a lot better, and when I went down to "The Body Slam" at seven o'clock to clean up, I was whistling kind of cheerful. I swept out the restaurant, polished the bar, and then turned on the TV to get the news and weather. You wouldn't believe it, but the set was busted. I couldn't get a picture. I couldn't even get a sound. My last set, busted.

So you see, that's why I have to head south (Mayo explained)—I got to locate a TV repairman.

There was a long pause after Mayo finished his story. Linda examined him keenly, trying to conceal the gleam in her eye. At last she asked with studied carelessness, "Where did he get the barometer?"

"Who? What?"

"Your friend, Gil. His antique barometer. Where did he get it?"

"Gee, I don't know. Antiquing was another one of his hobbies."

"And it looked like that clock?"

"Just like it."

"French?"

"I couldn't say."

"Bronze?"

"I guess so. Like your clock. Is that bronze?"

"Yes. Shaped like a sunburst?"

"No, just like yours."

"That's a sunburst. The same size?"

"Exactly."

"Where was it?"

"Didn't I tell you? In our house."

"Where's the house?"

"On Grant Street."

"What number?"

"Three fifteen. Say, what is all this?"

"Nothing, Jim. Just curious. No offense. Now I think I'd better get our picnic things."

"You wouldn't mind if I took a walk by myself?"

She cocked an eye at him. "Don't try driving alone. Garage mechanics are scarcer than TV repairmen."

He grinned and disappeared; but after dinner the true purpose of his disappearance was revealed when he produced a sheaf of sheet music, placed it on the piano rack, and led Linda to the piano bench. She was delighted and touched.

"Jim, you angel! Wherever did you find it?"

"In the apartment house across the street. Fourth floor, rear. Name of Horowitz. They got a lot of records, too. Boy, I can' tell you it was pretty spooky snooping around in the dark with only matches. You know something funny, the whole top of the house is full of glop."

"Glop?"

"Yeah. Sort of white jelly, only it's hard. Like clear concrete. Now look, see this note? It's C. Middle C. It stands for this white key here. We better sit together. Move over . . ."

The lesson continued for two hours of painful concentration and left them both so exhausted that they tottered to their rooms with only perfunctory good nights.

"Jim," Linda called.

"Yeah?" he yawned.

"Would you like one of my dolls for your bed?"

"Gee, no. Thanks a lot, Linda, but guys really ain't interested in dolls."

"I suppose not. Never mind. Tomorrow I'll have something for you that really interests guys."

Mayo was awakened next morning by a rap on his door. He heaved up in bed and tried to open his eyes.

"Yeah? Who is it?" he called.

"It's me. Linda. May I come in?"

He glanced around hastily. The room was neat. The hooked rug was clean. The precious candlewick bedspread was neatly folded on top of the dresser.

"Okay. Come on in."

Linda entered, wearing a crisp seersucker dress. She sat down on the edge of the four-poster and gave Mayo a friendly pat. "Good morning," she said. "Now listen. I'll have to leave you alone for a few hours. I've got things to do. There's breakfast on the table, but I'll be back in time for lunch. All right?"

"Sure."

"You won't be lonesome?"

"Where you going?"

"Tell you when I get back." She reached out and tousled his head. "Be a good boy and don't get into mischief. Oh, one other thing. Don't go into my bedroom."

"Why should I?"

"Just don't anyway."

She smiled and was gone. Moments later, Mayo heard the jeep start and drive off. He got up at once, went into Linda's bedroom, and looked around. The room was neat, as ever. The bed was made, and her pet dolls were lovingly arranged on the coverlet. Then he saw it.

"Gee," he breathed.

It was a model of a full-rigged clipper ship. The spars

and rigging were intact, but the hull was peeling, and the sails were shredded. It stood before Linda's closet, and alongside it was her sewing basket. She had already cut out a fresh set of white linen sails. Mayo knelt down before the model and touched it tenderly.

"I'll paint her black with a gold line around her," he murmured, "and I'll name her the *Linda N.*"

He was so deeply moved that he hardly touched his breakfast. He bathed, dressed, took his shotgun and a handful of shells, and went out to wander through the park. He circled south, passed the playing fields, the decaying carousel, and the crumbling skating rink, and at last left the park and loafed down Seventh Avenue.

He turned east on Fiftieth Street and spent a long time trying to decipher the tattered posters advertising the last performance at Radio City Music Hall. Then he turned south again. He was jolted to a halt by the sudden clash of steel. It sounded like giant sword blades in a titanic duel. A small herd of stunted horses burst out of a side street, terrified by the clangor. Their shoeless hooves thudded bluntly on the pavement. The sound of steel stopped.

"That's where that bluejay got it from," Mayo muttered. "But what the hell is it?"

He drifted eastward to investigate, but forgot the mystery when he came to the diamond center. He was dazzled by the blue-white stones glittering in the showcases. The door on one jewel mart had sagged open, and Mayo tiptoed in. When he emerged it was with a strand of genuine matched pearls which had cost him an I.O.U. worth a year's rent on "The Body Slam."

His tour took him to Madison Avenue where he found himself before Abercrombie & Fitch. He went in to explore and came at last to the gun racks. There he lost all sense of time, and when he recovered his senses, he was walking up Fifth Avenue toward the boat pond. An Italian Cosmi automatic rifle was cradled in his arms, guilt was in his heart, and a sales slip in the store read: *I.O.U. 1 Cosmi Rifle, $750.00. 6 Boxes Ammo. $18.00. James Mayo.*

It was past three o'clock when he got back to the boat-house. He eased in, trying to appear casual, hoping the extra gun he was carrying would go unnoticed. Linda was sitting on the piano bench with her back to him.

"Hi," Mayo said nervously. "Sorry I'm late. I . . . I brought you a present. They're real." He pulled the pearls from his pocket and held them out. Then he saw she was crying.

"Hey, what's the matter?"

She didn't answer.

"You wasn't scared I'd run out on you? I mean, well, all my gear is here. The car, too. You only had to look."

She turned. "I hate you!" she cried.

He dropped the pearls and recoiled, startled by her vehemence. "What's the matter?"

"You're a lousy, rotten liar!"

"Who? Me?"

"I drove up to New Haven this morning." Her voice trembled with passion. "There's no house standing on Grant Street. It's all wiped out. There's no Station WNHA. The whole building's gone."

"No."

"Yes. And I went to your restaurant. There's no pile of TV sets out in the street. There's only one set, over the bar. It's rusted to pieces. The rest of the restaurant is a pigsty. You were living there all the time. Alone. There was only one bed in back. It was lies! All lies!"

"Why would I lie about a thing like that?"

"You never shot any Gil Watkins."

"I sure did. Both barrels. He had it coming."

"And you haven't got any TV set to repair."

"Yes I do."

"And even if it is repaired, there's no station to broadcast."

"Talk sense," he said angrily. "Why would I shoot Gil if there wasn't any broadcast."

"If he's dead, how can he broadcast?"

"See? And you just now said I didn't shoot him."

"Oh, you're mad! You're insane!" she sobbed. "You just described that barometer because you happened to be looking at my clock. And I believed your crazy lies. I had my heart set on a barometer to match my clock. I've been looking for years." She ran to the wall arrangement and hammered her fist alongside the clock. "It belongs right here. Here. But you lied, you lunatic. There never was a barometer."

"If there's a lunatic around here, it's you," he shouted. "You're so crazy to get this house decorated that nothing's real for you anymore."

She ran across the room, snatched up his old shotgun, and pointed it at him. "You get out of here. Right this minute. Get out or I'll kill you. I never want to see you again."

The shotgun kicked off in her hands, knocking her backward, and spraying shot over Mayo's head into a corner bracket. China shattered and clattered down. Linda's face went white.

"Jim! My God, are you all right? I didn't mean to . . . it just went off . . ."

He stepped forward, too furious to speak. Then, as he raised his hand to cuff her, the sound of distant reports came, BLAM-BLAM-BLAM. Mayo froze.

"Did you hear that?" he whispered.

Linda nodded.

"That wasn't any accident. It was a signal."

Mayo grabbed the shotgun, ran outside, and fired the second barrel into the air. There was a pause. Then again came the distant explosions in a stately triplet, BLAM-BLAM-BLAM. They had an odd sucking sound, as though they were implosions rather than explosions. Far up the park, a canopy of frightened birds mounted into the sky.

"There's somebody," Mayo exulted. "By God, I told you I'd find somebody. Come on."

They ran north, Mayo digging into his pockets for more shells to reload and signal again.

"I got to thank you for taking that shot at me, Linda."

"I didn't shoot at you," she protested. "It was an accident."

"The luckiest accident in the world. They could be passing through and never know about us. But what the hell kind of guns are they using? I never heard no shot like that before, and I heard 'em all. Wait a minute."

On the little piazza before the Wonderland monument, Mayo halted and raised the shotgun to fire. Then he slowly lowered it. He took a deep breath. In a harsh voice he said, "Turn around. We're going back to the house." He pulled her around and faced her south.

Linda stared at him. In an instant he had become transformed from a gentle teddy bear into a panther.

"Jim, what's wrong?"

"I'm scared," he growled. "I'm goddam scared, and I don't want you to be, too." The triple salvo sounded again. "Don't pay any attention," he ordered. "We're going back to the house. Come on!"

She refused to move. "But why? Why?"

"We don't want any part of them. Take my word for it."

"How do you know? You've got to tell me."

"Christ! You won't let it alone until you find out, huh? All right. You want the explanation for that bee smell, and them buildings falling down, and all the rest?" He turned Linda around with a hand on her neck, and directed her gaze at the Wonderland monument. "Go ahead. Look."

A consummate craftsman had removed the heads of Alice, the Mad Hatter, and the March Hare, and replaced them with towering mantis heads, all saber mandibles, antenna, and faceted eyes. They were of a burnished steel and gleamed with unspeakable ferocity. Linda let out a sick whimper and sagged against Mayo. The triple report signaled once more.

Mayo caught Linda, heaved her over his shoulder, and loped back toward the pond. She recovered consciousness in a moment and began to moan. "Shut up," he growled. "Whining won't help." He set her on her feet before the boathouse. She was shaking but trying to control herself. "Did this place have shutters when you moved in? Where are they?"

"Stacked." She had to squeeze the words out. "Behind the trellis."

"I'll put 'em up. You fill buckets with water and stash 'em in the kitchen. Go!"

"Is it going to be a siege?"

"We'll talk later. Go!"

She filled buckets and then helped Mayo jam the last of the shutters into the window embrasures. "All right, inside," he ordered. They went into the house and shut

and barred the door. Faint shafts of the late afternoon
sun filtered through the louvers of the shutters. Mayo
began unpacking the cartridges for the Cosmi rifle. "You
got any kind of gun?"

"A .22 revolver somewhere."

"Ammo?"

"I think so."

"Get it ready."

"Is it going to be a siege?" she repeated.

"I don't know. I don't know who they are, or what
they are, or where they come from. All I know is, we
got to be prepared for the worst."

The distant implosions sounded. Mayo looked up
alertly, listening. Linda could make him out in the dimness now. His face looked carved. His chest gleamed
with sweat. He exuded the musky odor of caged lions.
Linda had an overpowering impulse to touch him. Mayo
loaded the rifle, stood it alongside the shotgun, and
began padding from shutter to shutter, peering out vigi-
lantly, waiting with massive patience.

"Will they find us?" Linda asked.

"Maybe."

"Could they be friendly?"

"Maybe."

"Those heads looked so horrible."

"Yeah."

"Jim, I'm scared. I've never been so scared in my life."

"I don't blame you."

"How long before we know?"

"An hour, if they're friendly; two or three, if they're
not."

"W-Why longer?"

"If they're looking for trouble, they'll he more
cautious."

"Jim, what do you really think?"

"About what?"

"Our chances."

"You really want to know?"

"Please."

"We're dead."

She began to sob. He shook her savagely. "Stop that.
Go get your gun ready."

She lurched across the living room, noticed the pearls Mayo had dropped, and picked them up. She was so dazed that she put them on automatically. Then she went into her darkened bedroom and pulled Mayo's model yacht away from the closet door. She located the .22 in a hatbox on the closet floor and removed it along with a small carton of cartridges.

She realized that a dress was unsuited to this emergency. She got a turtleneck sweater, jodhpurs, and boots from the closet. Then she stripped naked to change. Just as she raised her arms to unclasp the pearls, Mayo entered, paced to the shuttered south window, and peered out. When he turned back from the window, he saw her.

He stopped short. She couldn't move. Their eyes locked, and she began to tremble, trying to conceal herself with her arms. He stepped forward, stumbled on the model yacht, and kicked it out of the way. The next instant he had taken possession of her body, and the pearls went flying, too. As she pulled him down on the bed, fiercely tearing the shirt from his back, her pet dolls also went into the discard heap along with the yacht, the pearls, and the rest of the world.

BERNIE THE FAUST

BY WILLIAM TENN (PHILIP KLASS; 1920-   )

PLAYBOY
NOVEMBER

I first met Phil Klass some sixteen years ago at a meeting of the Science Fiction Research Association at Penn State University, the fine institution where he taught English. His teaching and administrative duties have seriously eroded his writing time, and I wish he had more time to produce more of the acerbic, intelligent stories that made him one of the very best of the "social science fiction" writers of the 1950s and 1960s. If you newcomers to science fiction want a real treat, all you need do is pick up a copy of The Human Angle *(1956),* The Square Root of Man *(1968), or* The Wooden Star *(also 1968) and start reading. I still remember reading his excellent anthology* Children of Wonder *(1953) in 1955 and thinking that some of those kids were just like me.*

"Bernie the Faust" shows him at the top of his form.

That's what Ricardo calls me. I don't know what I am.

Here I am, I'm sitting in my little nine-by-six office. I'm reading notices of government surplus sales. I'm trying to decide where lies a possible buck and where lies nothing but more headaches.

So the office door opens. This little guy with a dirty face, wearing a very dirty, very wrinkled Palm Beach suit, he walks into my office, and he coughs a bit and he says:

"Would you be interested in buying a twenty for a five?"

That was it. I mean, that's all I had to go on.

290

I looked him over and I said, *"Wha-at?"*

He shuffled his feet and coughed some more. "A twenty," he mumbled. "A twenty for a five."

I made him drop his eyes and stare at his shoes. They were lousy, cracked shoes, lousy and dirty like the rest of him. Every once in a while, his left shoulder hitched up in a kind of tic. "I give you twenty," he explained to his shoes, "and I buy a five from you with it. I wind up with five, you wind up with twenty."

"How did you get into the building?"

"I just came in," he said, a little mixed up.

"You just *came in*," I put a nasty, mimicking note in my voice. "Now you just go right back downstairs and come the hell out. There's a sign in the lobby—NO BEGGARS ALLOWED."

"I'm not begging." He tugged at the bottom of his jacket. It was like a guy trying to straighten out his slept-in pajamas. "I want to sell you something. A twenty for a five. I give you . . ."

"You want me to call a cop?"

He looked very scared. "No. Why should you call a cop? I haven't done anything to make you call a cop!"

"I'll call a cop in just a second. I'm giving you fair warning. I just phone down to the lobby and they'll have a cop up here fast. They don't want beggars in this building. This is a building for business."

He rubbed his hand against his face, taking a little dirt off, then he rubbed the hand against the lapel of his jacket and left the dirt there. "No deal?" he asked. "A twenty for a five? You buy and sell things. What's the matter with my deal?"

I picked up the phone.

"All right," he said, holding up the streaky palm of his hand. "I'll go. I'll go."

"You better. And shut the door behind you."

"Just in case you change your mind." He reached into his dirty, wrinkled pants pocket and pulled out a card. "You can get in touch with me here. Almost any time during the day."

"Blow," I told him.

He reached over, dropped the card on my desk, on top of all the surplus notices, coughed once or twice, looked at me to see if maybe I was biting. No? No. He trudged out.

I picked the card up between the nails of my thumb and forefinger and started to drop it into the wastebasket.

Then I stopped. A card. It was just so damned out of the ordinary—a slob like that with a card. A card, yet.

For that matter, the whole play was out of the ordinary. I began to be a little sorry I hadn't let him run through the whole thing. Listening to a panhandler isn't going to kill me. After all, what was he trying to do but give me an off-beat sales pitch? I can always use an off-beat sales pitch. I work out of a small office, I buy and sell, but half my stock is good ideas. I'll use ideas, even from a bum.

The card was clean and white, except where the smudge from his fingers made a brown blot. Written across it in a kind of ornate handwriting were the words *Mr. Ogo Eksar*. Under that was the name and the telephone number of a hotel in the Times Square area, not far from my office. I knew that hotel: not expensive, but not a fleabag either—somewhere just under the middle line.

There was a room number in one corner of the card. I stared at it and I felt kind of funny. I really didn't know.

Although come to think of it, why couldn't a panhandler be registered at a hotel? "Don't be a snob, Bernie," I told myself.

A twenty for a five, he'd offered. Man, I'd love to have seen his face if I'd said: Okay, give me the twenty, you take the five, and now get the hell out of here.

The government surplus notices caught my eye. I flipped the card into the wastebasket and tried to go back to business.

Twenty for five. What kind of panhandling pitch would follow it? I couldn't get it out of my mind!

There was only one thing to do. Ask somebody about it. Ricardo? A big college professor, after all. One of my best contacts.

He'd thrown a lot my way—a tip on the college building program that was worth a painless fifteen hundred, an office equipment disposal from the United Nations, stuff like that. And any time I had any questions that needed a college education, he was on tap. All for the couple, three hundred, he got out of me in commissions.

I looked at my watch. Ricardo would be in his office now, marking papers or whatever it is he does there. I dialed his number.

"Ogo Eksar?" he repeated after me. "Sounds like a Finnish name. Or maybe Estonian. From the eastern Baltic, I'd say."

"Forget that part," I said. "This is all I care about." And I told him about the twenty-for-five offer.

He laughed. "That thing again!"

"Some old hustle that the Greeks pulled on the Egyptians?"

"No. Something the Americans pulled. And not a con game. During the depression, a New York newspaper sent a reporter around the city with a twenty-dollar bill which he offered to sell for exactly one dollar. There were no takers. The point being, that even with people out of work and on the verge of starvation, they were so intent on not being suckers that they turned down an easy profit of nineteen hundred per cent."

"Twenty for one? This was twenty for five."

"Oh, well, you know, Bernie, inflation," he said, laughing again. "And these days it's more likely to be a television show."

"Television? You should have seen the way the guy was dressed!"

"Just an extra, logical touch to make people refuse to take the offer seriously. University research people operate much the same way. A few years back, a group of sociologists began an investigation of the public's reaction to sidewalk solicitors in charity drives. You know, those people who jingle little boxes on street corners: *Help the Two-Headed Children, Relief for Flood-Ravaged Atlantis?* Well, they dressed up some of their students . . ."

"You think he was on the level, then, this guy?"

"I think there is a good chance that he was. I don't see why he would have left his card with you, though."

"That I can figure—now. If it's a TV stunt, there must

be a lot of other angles wrapped up in it. A giveaway show with cars, refrigerators, a castle in Scotland, all kinds of loot."

"A giveaway show? Well, yes—it could be."

I hung up, took a deep breath, and called Eksar's hotel. He was registered there all right. And he'd just come in.

I went downstairs fast and took a cab. Who knew what other connections he'd made by now?

Going up in the elevator, I kept wondering. How did I go from the twenty-dollar bill to the real big stuff, the TV giveaway stuff, without letting Eksar know that I was on to what it was all about? Well, maybe I'd be lucky. Maybe he'd give me an opening.

I knocked on the door. When he said, "Come in," I came in. But for a second or two I couldn't see a thing.

It was a little room, like all the rooms in that hotel, little and smelly and stuffy. But he didn't have the lights on, any electric lights. The window shade was pulled all the way down.

When my eyes got used to the dark, I was able to pick out this Ogo Eksar character. He was sitting on the bed, on the side nearest me. He was still wearing that crazy rumpled Palm Beach suit.

And you know what? He was watching a program on a funny little portable TV set that he had on the bureau. Color TV. Only it wasn't working right. There were no faces, no pictures, nothing but colors chasing around. A big blob of red, a big blob of orange, and a wiggly border of blue and green and black. A voice was talking from it, but all the words were fouled up. *"Wah-wah, de-wah, de-wah."*

Just as I came in, he turned it off. "Times Square is a bad neighborhood for TV," I told him. "Too much interference."

"Yes," he said. "Too much interference." He closed up the set and put it away. I wished I'd seen it when it was working right.

Funny thing, you know? I would have expected a smell of liquor in the room, I would have expected to see a couple of empties in the tin trash basket near the bureau. Not a sign.

The only smell in the room was a smell I couldn't recognize. I guess it was the smell of Eksar himself, concentrated.

"Hi," I said, feeling a little uncomfortable because of the way I'd been with him back in the office. So rough I'd been.

He stayed on the bed. "I've got the twenty," he said. "You've got the five?"

"Oh, I guess I've got the five, all right," I said, looking in my wallet hard and trying to be funny. He didn't say a word, didn't even invite me to sit down. I pulled out a bill. "Okay?"

He leaned forward and stared, as if he could see—in all that dimness—what kind of a bill it was. "Okay," he said. "But I'll want a receipt. A notarized receipt."

Well, what the hell, I thought, a notarized receipt. "Then we'll have to go down. There's a druggist on forty-fifth."

"Okay," he said, getting to his feet with a couple of small coughs that came one, two, three, four, right after one another. "The bathroom's out in the hall. Let me wash up and we'll go down."

I waited for him outside the bathroom, thinking that he'd grown a whole hell of a lot more sanitary all of a sudden.

I could have saved my worries. I don't know what he did in the bathroom, but one thing I knew for sure when he came out: soap and water had nothing to do with it. His face, his neck, his clothes, his hands—they were all as dirty as ever. He still looked like he'd been crawling over a garbage dump all night long.

On the way to the druggist, I stopped in a stationery store and bought a book of blank receipts. I filled out most of it right there. *New York, N. Y.* and the date. *Received from Mr. Ogo Eksar the sum of twenty dollars for a five-dollar bill bearing the serial number* . . . . "That okay?" I asked him. "I'm putting in the serial number to make it look as if you want that particular bill, you know, what the lawyers call the value-received angle."

He screwed his head around and read the receipt.

Then he checked the serial number of the bill I was holding. He nodded.

We had to wait for the druggist to get through with a couple of customers. When I signed the receipt, he read it to himself, shrugged and went ahead and stamped it with his seal.

I paid him the two bits: I was the one making the profit.

Eksar slid a crisp new twenty to me along the glass of the counter. He watched while I held it up to the light, first one side, then the other.

"Good bill?" he asked.

"Yes. You understand: I don't know you, I don't know your money."

"Sure. I'd do it myself with a stranger." He put the receipt and my five-dollar bill in his pocket and started to walk away.

"Hey," I said. "You in a hurry?"

"No." He stopped, looking puzzled. "No hurry. But you've got the twenty for a five. We made the deal. It's all over."

"All right, so we made the deal. How about a cup of coffee?"

He hesitated.

"It's on me," I told him. "I'll be a big shot for a dime. Come on, let's have a cup of coffee."

Now he looked worried. "You don't want to back out? I've got the receipt. It's all notarized. I gave you a twenty, you gave me a five. We made a deal."

"It's a deal, it's a deal," I said, shoving him into an empty booth. "It's a deal, it's all signed, sealed and delivered. Nobody's backing out. I just want to buy you a cup of coffee."

His faced cleared up, all the way through that dirt. "No coffee. Soup. I'll have some mushroom soup."

"Fine, fine. Soup, coffee, I don't care. I'll have coffee."

I sat there and studied him. He hunched over the soup and dragged it into his mouth, spoonful after spoonful, the living picture of a bum who hadn't eaten all day. But pure essence of bum, triple-distilled, the label of a fine old firm.

A guy like this should be living in a doorway trying to say no to a cop's nightstick, he should be coughing his alcoholic guts out. He shouldn't be living in a real honest-to-God hotel, or giving me a twenty for a five, or swallowing anything as respectable as mushroom soup.

But it made sense. A TV giveaway show, they want to do this, they hire a damn good actor, the best money can buy, to toss their dough away. A guy who'll be so good a bum that people'll just laugh in his face when he tries to give them a deal with a profit.

"You don't want to buy anything else?" I asked him.

He held the spoon halfway to his mouth and stared at me suspiciously. "Like what?"

"Oh, I don't know. Like maybe you want to buy a ten for a fifty. Or a twenty for a hundred dollars?"

He thought about it, Eksar did. Then he went back to his soup, shoveling away. "That's no deal," he said contemptuously. "What kind of a deal is that?"

"Excuse me for living. I just thought I'd ask. I wasn't trying to take advantage of you." I lit a cigarette and waited.

My friend with the dirty face finished the soup and reached for a paper napkin. He wiped his lips. I watched him: he didn't smudge a spot of the grime around his mouth. He just blotted the drops of soup up. He was dainty in his own special way.

"Nothing else you want to buy? I'm here, I've got time right now. Anything else on your mind, we might as well look into it."

He balled up the paper napkin and dropped it into the soup plate. It got wet. He'd eaten all the mushrooms and left the soup.

"The Golden Gate Bridge," he said all of a sudden.

I dropped the cigarette. "What?"

"The Golden Gate Bridge. The one in San Francisco. I'll buy that. I'll buy it for . . ." he lifted his eyes to the fluorescent fixtures in the ceiling and thought for a couple of seconds ". . . say a hundred and a quarter. A hundred and twenty-five dollars. Cash on the barrel."

"Why the Golden Gate Bridge?" I asked him like an idiot.

"That's the one I want. You asked me what else I

want to buy—well, that's what else. The Golden Gate Bridge."

"What's the matter with the George Washington Bridge? It's right here in New York, it's across the Hudson River. It's a newer bridge. Why buy something all the way out on the coast?"

He grinned at me as if he admired my cleverness. "Oh, no," he said, twitching his left shoulder hard. Up, down, up, down. "I know what I want. The Golden Gate Bridge in San Francisco. A hundred and a quarter. Take it or leave it."

"The *George Washington* Bridge," I argued, talking my head off just so I'd have a chance to think, "has a nice toll set-up, fifty cents a throw, and lots of traffic, plenty of traffic. I don't know what the tolls are on the Golden Gate, but I'm damn sure you don't have anywhere near the kind of traffic that New York can draw. And then there's maintenance. The Golden Gate's one of the longest bridges in the world, you'll go broke trying to keep it in shape. Dollar for dollar, location for location, I'd say the George Washington's a better deal for a man who's buying a bridge."

"The Golden Gate," he said, slamming the table with his open hand and letting a whole series of tics tumble through his face. "I want the Golden Gate and nothing but the Golden Gate. Don't give me a hard time again. Do you want to sell or don't you?"

I'd had a chance to think it through. And I knew that Ricardo's angle had been the angle. I was in.

"Sure I'll sell. If that's what you want, you're the doctor. But look—all I can sell you is my share of the Golden Gate Bridge, whatever equity in it I may happen to own."

He nodded. "I want a receipt. Put that down on the receipt."

I put it down on the receipt. And back we went. The druggist notarized the receipt, shoved the stamping outfit in the drawer under the counter and turned his back on us. Eksar counted out six twenties and one five from a big roll of bills, all of them starchy new. He put the roll back into his pants pocket and started away again.

"More coffee?" I said, catching up. "A refill on the soup?"

He turned a very puzzled look at me and kind of twitched all over. "Why? What do you want to sell now?"

I shrugged. "What do you want to buy? You name it. Let's see what other deals we can work out."

This was all taking one hell of a lot of time, but I had no complaints. I'd made a hundred and forty dollars in fifteen minutes. Say a hundred and thirty-eight fifty, if you deducted expenses like notary fees, coffee, soup—all legitimate expenses, all low. I had no complaints.

But I was waiting for the big one. There had to be a big one.

Of course, it could maybe wait until the TV program itself. They'd be asking me what was on my mind when I was selling Eksar all that crap, and I'd be explaining, and they'd start handing out refrigerators and gift certificates at Tiffany's and . . .

Eksar had said something while I was away in cloudland. Something damn unfamiliar. I asked him to say it again.

"The Sea of Azov," he told me. "In Russia. I'll give you three hundred and eighty dollars for it."

I'd never heard of the place. I pursed my lips and thought for a second. A funny amount—three hundred and eighty. And for a whole damn sea. I tried an angle.

"Make it four hundred and you've got a deal."

He began coughing his head off, and he looked mad. "What's the matter," he said between coughs, "three hundred and eighty is a bad price? It's a small sea, one of the smallest. It's only 14,000 square miles. And do you know what the maximum depth is?"

I looked wise. "It's deep enough."

"Forty-nine feet," Eksar shouted. "That's all, forty-nine feet! Where are you going to do better than three hundred and eighty dollars for a sea like that?"

"Take it easy," I said, patting his dirty shoulder. "Let's split the difference. You say three eighty, I want four hundred. How about leaving it at three ninety?" I didn't really care: ten bucks more, ten bucks less. But I wanted to see what would happen.

He calmed down. "Three hundred and ninety dollars for the Sea of Azov," he muttered to himself, a little sore at being a sucker, at being taken. "All I want is the sea itself; it's not as if I'm asking you to throw in the Kerch Strait, or maybe a port like Taganrog or Osipenko . . ."

"Tell you what." I held up my hands. "I don't want to be hard. Give me my three ninety and I'll throw in the Kerch Strait as a bonus. Now how about that?"

He studied the idea. He sniffled. He wiped his nose with the back of his hand. "All right," he said, finally. "It's a deal. Azov *and* the Kerch Strait for three hundred ninety."

Bang! went the druggist's stamp. The bangs were getting louder.

Eksar paid me with six fifties, four twenties and a ten, all new-looking bills from that thick roll in his pants pocket.

I thought about the fifties still on the roll, and I felt the spit start to ball up in my mouth.

"Okay," I said. "Now what?"

"You still selling?"

"For the right price, sure. You name it."

"There's lots of stuff I could use," he sighed. "But do I need it right now? That's what I have to ask myself."

"Right now is when you've got a chance to buy it. Later—who knows? I may not be around, there may be other guys bidding against you, all kinds of things can happen." I waited a while, but he just kept scowling and coughing. "How about Australia?" I suggested. "Could you use Australia for, say, five hundred bucks? Or Antarctica? I could give you a real nice deal on Antarctica."

He looked interested. "Antarctica? What would you want for it? No—I'm not getting anywhere. A little piece here, a little piece there. It all costs so much."

"You're getting damn favorable prices, buddy, and you know it. You couldn't do better buying at wholesale."

"Then how about wholesale? How much for the whole thing?"

I shook my head. "I don't know what you're talking about. What whole thing?"

He looked impatient. "The whole thing. The world. Earth."

"Hey," I said. "That's a lot."

"Well, I'm tired of buying a piece at a time. Will you give me a wholesale price if I buy it all?"

I shook my head, kind of in and out, not yes, not no. Money was coming up, the big money. This was where I was supposed to laugh in his face and walk away. I didn't even crack a smile. "For the whole planet—sure, you're entitled to a wholesale price. But what is it, I mean, exactly *what* do you want to buy?"

"Earth," he said, moving close to me so that I could smell his stinking breath. "I want to buy Earth. Lock, stock and barrel."

"It's got to be a good price. I'll be selling out completely."

"I'll make it a good price. But this is the deal. I pay two thousand dollars, cash. I get Earth, the whole planet, and you have to throw in some stuff on the Moon. Fishing rights, mineral rights and rights to Moon buried treasure. How about it?"

"It's a hell of a lot."

"I know it's a lot," he agreed. "But I'm paying a lot."

"Not for what you're asking. Let me think about it."

This was the big deal, the big giveaway. I didn't know how much money the TV people had given him to fool around with, but I was pretty sure two thousand was just a starting point. Only what was a sensible, businesslike price for the whole world?

I mustn't be made to look like a penny-ante chiseler on TV. There was a top figure Eksar had been given by the program director.

"You really want the whole thing," I said, turning back to him, "the Earth and the Moon?"

He held up a dirty hand. "Not all the Moon. Just those rights on it. The rest of the Moon you can keep."

"It's still a lot. You've got to go a hell of a lot higher than two thousand dollars for any hunk of real estate that big."

Eksar began wrinkling and twitching. "How—how much higher?"

"Well, let's not kid each other. This is the big time

now! We're not talking about bridges or rivers or seas. This is a whole world and part of another that you're buying. It takes dough. You've got to be prepared to spend dough."

"How much?" He looked as if he were jumping up and down inside his dirty Palm Beach suit. People going in and out of the store kept staring at us. "How *much*?" he whispered.

"Fifty thousand. It's a damn low price. And you know it."

Eksar went limp all over. Even his weird eyes seemed to sag. "You're crazy," he said in a low, hopeless voice. "You're out of your head."

He turned and started for the revolving door, walking in a kind of used-up way that told me I'd really gone over the line. He didn't look back once. He just wanted to get far, far away.

I went through the door after him. I grabbed the bottom of his filthy jacket and held on tight.

"Look, Eksar," I said, fast, as he pulled. "I went over your budget, way over, I can see that. But you know you can do better than two thousand. I want as much as I can get. What the hell, I'm taking time out to bother with you. How many other guys would?"

That got him. He cocked his head, then began nodding. I let go of his jacket as he came around. We were connecting again!

"Good. You level with me, and I'll level with you. Go up a little higher. What's your best price? What's the best you can do?"

He stared down the street, thinking, and his tongue came out and licked at the side of his dirty mouth. His tongue was dirty, too. I mean that! Some kind of black stuff, grease or grime, was all over his tongue.

"How about," he said, after a while, "how about twenty-five hundred? That's as high as I can go. I don't have another cent."

I didn't think so. I've got a feeling when a guy says this is as high as he can go that actually he's prepared to go a little higher. Eksar wanted to make the deal real bad, but he couldn't resist pulling back just a little. He was the kind of guy, he could be absolutely dying of

thirst, ready to kick off in a second if he didn't get something to drink. You offer him a glass of water, and you
say you want a buck for it. He looks at it with his eyes
popping and his tongue all swollen, and he asks will you
take ninety-five cents?

He was like me: he was a natural bargainer.

"You can go to three thousand," I urged. "How much
is three thousand? Only another five hundred. Look what
you get for it. Earth, the whole planet, and fishing and
mineral rights and buried treasure, all that stuff on the
Moon. How's about it?"

"I can't. I just can't. I wish I could." He shook his
head as if to shake loose all those tics and twitches.
"Maybe this way. I'll go as high as twenty-six hundred.
For that, will you give me Earth and just fishing rights
and buried treasure rights on the Moon? You keep the
mineral rights. I'll do without them."

"Make it twenty-eight hundred, and you can have the
mineral rights, too. You want them, I can tell you do.
Treat yourself. Just two hundred bucks more, and you
can have them."

"I can't have everything. Some things cost too much.
How about twenty-six fifty, without the mineral rights
and without the buried treasure rights?"

We were both really swinging now. I could feel it.

"This is my absolutely last offer," I told him. "I can't
spend all day on this. I'll go down to twenty-seven hundred and fifty, and not a penny less. For that, I'll give
you Earth, and just fishing rights on the Moon. Or just
buried treasure rights. You pick whichever one you
want."

"All right," he said. "You're a hard man: we'll do it
your way."

"Twenty-seven fifty for the Earth, and either fishing
or buried treasure rights on the Moon?"

"No, twenty-seven even, and no rights on the Moon.
I'll forget about that. Twenty-seven even, and all I get
is the Earth."

"Deal!" I sang out, and we struck hands. We shook
on it.

Then, with my arm around his shoulder—what did I
care about the dirt on his clothes when the guy was worth

twenty-seven hundred dollars to me?—we marched back to the drug store.

"I want a receipt," he reminded me.

"Right," I said. "But I put the same stuff on it: that I'm selling you whatever equity I own or have a right to sell. You're getting a lot for your money."

"You're getting a lot of money for what you're selling," he came right back. I liked him. Twitches and dirt or not, he was my kind of guy.

We got back to the druggist for notarization, and, honest, I've never seen a man look more disgusted in my life. "Business is good, huh?" he said. "You two are sure hotting it up."

"Listen you," I told him. "You just notarize." I showed the receipt to Eksar. "This the way you want it?"

He studied it, coughing. "Whatever equity you own or have a right to sell. All right. And put in, you know, in your capacity as sales agent, your professional capacity."

I changed the receipt and signed it. The druggist notarized.

Eksar brought that lump of money out of his pants pocket. He counted out fifty-four crisp new fifties and laid them on the glass counter. Then he picked up the receipt, folded it and put it away. He started for the door.

I grabbed the money up and went with him. "Anything else?"

"Nothing else," he said. "It's all over. We made our deal."

"I know, but we might find something else, another item."

"There's nothing else to find. We made our deal." And his voice told me he really meant it. It didn't have a trace of the tell-me-more whine that you've got to hear before there's business.

I came to a stop and watched him push out through the revolving door. He went right out into the street and turned left and kept moving, all fast, as if he was in a hell of a hurry.

There was no more business. Okay. I had thirty-two

hundred and thirty dollars in my wallet that I'd made in one morning.

But how good had I really been? I mean, what was the top figure in the show's budget? How close had I come to it?

I had a contact who maybe could find out—Morris Burlap.

Morris Burlap is in business like me, only he's a theatrical agent, sharp, real sharp. Instead of selling a load of used copper wire, say, or an option on a corner lot in Brooklyn, he sells talent. He sells a bunch of dancers to a hotel in the mountains, a piano player to a bar, a disc jockey or a comic to late-night radio. The reason he's called Morris Burlap is because of the heavy Harris tweed suits he wears winter and summer, every day in the year. They reinforce the image, he says.

I called him from a telephone booth near the entrance and filled him in on the giveaway show. "Now, what I want to find out—"

"Nothing to find out," he cut in. "There's no such show, Bernie."

"There sure as hell is, Morris. One you haven't heard of."

"There's no such show. Not in the works, not being rehearsed, not anywhere. Look: before a show gets to where it's handing out this kind of dough, it's got to have a slot, it's got to have air time all bought. And before it even buys air time, a packager has prepared a pilot. By then I'd have gotten a casting call—I'd have heard about it a dozen different ways. Don't try to tell me my business, Bernie: when I say there's no such show, there's no such show."

So damn positive he was. I had a crazy idea all of a sudden and turned it off. No. Not that. No.

"Then it's a newspaper or college research thing, like Ricardo said?"

He thought it over. I was willing to sit in that stuffy telephone booth and wait: Morris Burlap has a good head. "Those damn documents, those receipts, newspapers and colleges doing research don't operate that way. And nuts don't either. I think you're being taken, Bernie. How you're being taken, I don't know, but you're being taken."

That was enough for me. Morris Burlap can smell a hustle through sixteen feet of rockwool insulation. He's never wrong. Never.

I hung up, sat, thought. The crazy idea came back and exploded.

A bunch of characters from outer space, say they want Earth. They want it for a colony, for a vacation resort, who the hell knows what they want it for? They got their reasons. They're strong enough and advanced enough to come right down and take over. But they don't want to do it cold.

You know, a big country wants to invade a small country, it doesn't start until there's at least a riot on the border. It gives them a legal leg. Even a big country needs a legal leg.

All right. These characters from outer space, maybe all they had to have was a piece of paper from just one genuine, accredited human being, signing the Earth over to them. No, that couldn't be right. *Any* piece of paper? Signed by *any* Joe Jerk?

I jammed a dime into the telephone and called Ricardo's college. He wasn't in. I told the switchboard girl it was very important: she said, all right, she'd ring around and try to spot him.

All that stuff, I kept thinking, the Golden Gate Bridge, the Sea of Azov—they were as much a part of the hook as the twenty-for-a-five routine. There's one sure test of what an operator is really after: when he stops talking, closes up shop and goes away.

With Eksar, it had been the Earth. All that baloney about extra rights on the Moon! They were put in to cover up the real thing he was after, for extra bargaining power.

I go out to buy a shipment of small travel alarm clocks that I've heard a jobber is stuck with. Do I start arguing about the price of clocks? I do not. I tell the jobber I want to buy a truckload of folding ladies' umbrellas, maybe a couple of gross of alarm clocks, say travel alarms if he's got a nice buy in them, and can he do me any good in the men's wallet line?

That's what Eksar had worked on me. It was like he'd made a special study of how I operate. From me alone, he had to buy.

But why me?

All that stuff on the receipt, about my equity, about my professional capacity, what the hell did it mean? I don't own Earth; I'm not in the planet-selling business. You have to own a planet before you can sell it. That's law.

So what could I have sold Eksar? I don't own any real estate. Are they going to take over my office, claim the piece of sidewalk I walk on, attach the stool in the diner where I have my coffee?

That brought me back to my first question. Who was this "they"? Who the holy hell were "they"?

The switchboard girl finally dug up Ricardo. He was irritated. "I'm in the middle of a faculty meeting, Bernie. Call you back?"

"Just listen a second," I begged. "I'm in something, I don't know whether I'm coming or going. I've got to have some advice."

Talking fast—I could hear a lot of big-shot voices in the background—I ran through the story from the time I'd called him in the morning. What Eksar looked like and smelled like, the funny portable color TV he had, the way he'd dropped all those Moon rights and gone charging off once he'd been sure of the Earth. What Morris Burlap had said, the suspicions I'd been building up, everything. "Only thing is," I laughed a little to show that maybe I wasn't really serious about it, "who am I to make such a deal, huh?"

He seemed to be thinking hard for a while. "I don't know, Bernie, it's possible. It does fit together. There's the UN aspect."

"UN aspect? Which UN aspect?"

"The UN aspect of the situation. The—uh—study of the UN on which we collaborated two years ago." He was using double-talk because of the college people around him. But I got it. I got it.

Eksar must have known all along about the deal that Ricardo had thrown my way, getting rid of old, used-up office equipment for the United Nations here in New

York. They'd given me what they called an authorizing document. In a file somewhere there was a piece of paper, United Nations stationery, saying that I was their authorized sales agent for surplus, second-hand equipment and installations.

Talk about a legal leg!

"You think it'll stand up?" I asked Ricardo. "I can see how the Earth is second-hand equipment and installations. But surplus?"

"International law is a tangled field, Bernie. And this might be even more complex. You'd be wise to do something about it."

"But what? What should I do, Ricardo?"

"Bernie," he said, sounding sore as hell, "I told you I'm in a faculty meeting, damn it! A *faculty* meeting!" And he hung up.

I ran out of the drug store like a wild man and grabbed a cab back to Eksar's hotel.

What was I most afraid of? I didn't know, I was so hysterical. This thing was too big-time for a little guy like me, too damn dangerously big-time. It would put my name up in lights as the biggest sellout sucker in history. Who could ever trust me again to make a deal? I had the feeling like somebody had asked me to sell him a snapshot, and I'd said sure, and it turned out to be a picture of the Nike Zeus, you know, one of those top-secret atomic missiles. Only this was worse: I'd sold out my whole goddamn world. I had to buy it back—I had to!

When I got to Eksar's room, I knew he was about ready to check out. He was shoving his funny portable TV in one of those cheap leather grips they sell in chain stores. I left the door open, for the light.

"We made our deal," he said. "It's over. No more deals."

I stood there, blocking his way. "Eksar," I told him, "listen to what I figured out. First, you're not human. Like me, I mean."

"I'm a hell of a lot more human than you, buddy boy."

"Oh, sure. You're a custom-built Cadillac and I'm a four-cylinder factory job. But you're not from Earth—

that's my point. My point is why you want Earth. You can't personally need a—"

"I *don't* need it. I'm an agent. I represent someone."

And there it was, straight out, you are right, Morris Burlap! I stared into his fish eyes, practically pushing into my face. I wouldn't budge an inch if he killed me. "You're an agent for someone," I repeated slowly. "Who? What do they want Earth for?"

"That's their business. I'm an agent. I just buy for them."

"You work on a commission?"

"I'm not in business for my health."

You sure as hell aren't in it for your health, I thought. *That cough, those tics and twitches*— Then I realized what they meant. This wasn't the kind of air he was used to. Like if I go up to Canada, right away I'm down with diarrhea. It's the water or something.

The dirt on his face was a kind of suntan oil! A protection against our sunlight. Blinds pulled down, face smeared over—and dirt all over his clothes so they'd fit in with his face.

Eksar was no bum. He was anything but. I was the bum. Think, Bernie, I said to myself. Think and hustle and operate like you never did before in your whole life. This guy took you, and big!

"How much you work on—ten percent?" No answer: he leaned his chest against mine, and he breathed and he twitched, he breathed and he twitched. "I'll top any deal you have, Eksar. You know what I'll give you? Fifteen percent! I'm the kind of a guy, I hate to see someone running back and forth for a lousy ten percent."

"What about ethics?" he said hoarsely. "I got a client."

"Look who's bringing up ethics! A guy goes out to buy the whole damn Earth for twenty-seven hundred! You call that ethics?"

Now he got sore. He set down the grip and punched his fist into his hand. "No, I call that business. A deal. I offer, you take. You go away happy, you feel you made out. All of a sudden, here you are back, crying you didn't mean it, you sold too much for the price. Too bad! I got ethics: I don't screw my client for a crybaby."

"I'm not a crybaby. I'm just a poor shnook trying to scratch out a living. But who are you? You're a big-time operator from another world with all kinds of gimmicks going for you, buttons you can press, angles I can't even begin to figure."

"You had these angles, these gimmicks, you wouldn't use them?"

"Certain things I wouldn't use, certain things I wouldn't do. Don't laugh, Eksar, I mean it. I wouldn't hustle a guy in an iron lung no matter how much of a buck was in it. And I wouldn't hustle a poor shnook with a hole-in-the-wall office and leave him looking like he's sold out his entire planet."

"Sold out isn't the word for it," he said. "That receipt you signed will stand up anywhere. We got the legal machinery to make it stand up, and we got other machinery, too, planet-size machinery. Once my client takes possession, the human race is finished, it's *kaput*, gone with the wind, forget about it. And you're Mr. Patsy."

It was hot in that hotel room doorway, and I was sweating like crazy. But I was feeling better. First that ethics pitch, now this routine of trying to scare the hell out of me. Maybe his deal with his client wasn't so good, maybe something else, but one thing I knew—Eksar wanted to do business with me. I grinned at him.

He got it. He changed color a little under all that dirt. "What's your offer, anyway?" he asked, coughing. "Name a figure."

"Well, I'll admit you're entitled to a profit. That's only fair. Let's say thirty-one hundred and five. The twenty-seven you paid, plus a full fifteen percent. Do we have a deal?"

"Hell no!" he screamed. "On all three deals, you got a total of thirty-two hundred and thirty dollars out of me—and you're offering thirty-one hundred five to buy it back? You're going down, buddy, you're going down instead of up! Get out of my way—I'm wasting time."

He turned a little and pushed me out of the way. I banged across the corridor. He was *strong*! I ran after him to the elevator—that receipt was still in his pocket.

"How much *do* you want, Eksar?" I asked him as we

were going down. Get him to name a price, then I can bargain from it, I figured.

A shrug. "I got a planet, and I got a buyer for it. You, you're in a jam. The one in a pickle is the one who's got to tickle."

The louse! For every one of my moves, he knew the countermove.

He checked out and I followed him into the street. Down Broadway we went, people staring at a respectable guy like me walking with such a Bowery-type character.

I threw up my hands and offered him the thirty-two hundred and thirty he'd paid me. He said he couldn't make a living out of shoving the same amount of money back and forth all day.

"Thirty-four, then? I mean, you know, thirty-four fifty?"

He didn't say anything. He just kept walking.

"You want it all?" I said. "Okay, take it all, thirty-seven hundred—every last cent. You win."

Still no answer. I was getting worried. I had to get him to name a figure, any figure at all, or I'd be dead.

I ran in front of him. "Eksar, let's stop hustling each other. If you didn't want to sell, you wouldn't be talking to me in the first place. You name a figure. Whatever it is, I'll pay it."

That got a reaction. "You mean it? You won't try to chisel?"

"How can I chisel? I'm over a barrel."

"Okay. It's a long, long trip back to where my client is. Why should I knock myself out when I can help somebody who's in trouble? Let's see—we need a figure that's fair for you and fair for me and fair all around. That would be—oh, say, sixteen thousand."

So there it was. I was booked for a thorough bath. Eksar saw my face and began laughing. He laughed himself into a coughing fit.

Choke, you bastard, I thought, *choke! I hope the air of this planet poisons you. I hope you get gangrene of the lungs.*

That sixteen thousand figure—it was exactly twice what I had in the bank. He knew my bank account cold, up to the last statement.

He knew my thoughts cold, too. "You're going to do business with a guy," he said, between coughs, "you check into him a little."

"Tell me more," I said sarcastically.

"All right. You got seven thousand, eight hundred and change. Two hundred more in accounts receivable. The rest you'll borrow."

"That's all I need to do—go into hock on this deal!"

"You can borrow a little," he coaxed. "A guy like you, in your position, with your contacts, you can borrow a little. I'll settle for twelve thousand. I'll be a good guy. Twelve thousand?"

"Baloney, Eksar. You know me so well, you know I can't borrow."

He looked away at the pigeon-green statue of Father Duffy in front of the Palace Theater. "The trouble is," he said in a mournful voice, "that I wouldn't feel right going back to my client and leaving you in such jam. I'm just not built that way." He threw back his twitching shoulders—you knew, he was about to take a beating for a friend, and he was proud of himself. "Okay, then. I'll take only the eight thousand you have and we'll call it square."

"Are you through, you mother's little helper you, you Florence Goddamn Nightingale? Then let me set you straight. You're not getting any eight thousand out of me. A profit, yes, a little skin I know I have to give up. But not every cent I own, not in a million years, not for you, not for Earth, not for anybody!"

I'd been yelling, and a cop walking by came in close for a look. I thought of calling out "Help! Police! Aliens invading us!" but I knew it was all up to me. I calmed down and waited until he went away, puzzled. But the Broadway we were all standing on—what would it look like in ten years if I didn't talk Eksar out of that receipt?

"Eksar, your client takes over Earth waving my receipt—I'll be hung high. But I've got only one life, and my life is buying and selling. I can't buy and sell without capital. Take my capital away, and it makes no difference to me who owns Earth and who doesn't."

"Who the hell do you think you're kidding?" he said.

"I'm not kidding anybody. Honest, it's the truth. Take

my capital away, and it makes no difference if I'm alive or if I'm dead."

That last bit of hustle seemed to have reached him. Listen, there were practically tears in my eyes the way I was singing it. How much capital did I need, he wanted to know—five hundred? I told him I couldn't operate one single day with less than seven times that. He asked me if I was really seriously trying to buy my lousy little planet back—or was today my birthday and I was expecting a present from him? "Don't give your presents to me," I told him. "Give them to fat people. They're better than going on a diet."

And so we went. Both of us talking ourselves blue in the face, swearing by everything, arguing and bargaining, wheeling and dealing. It was touch and go who was going to give up first.

But neither of us did. We both held out until we reached what I'd figured pretty early we were going to wind up with, maybe a little bit more.

Six thousand, one hundred and fifty dollars.

That was the price over and above what Eksar had given me. The final deal. Listen, it could have been worse.

Even so, we almost broke up when we began talking payment.

"Your bank's not far. We could get there before closing."

"Why walk myself into a heart attack? My check's good as gold."

"Who wants a piece of paper? I want cash. Cash is definite."

Finally, I managed to talk him into a check. I wrote it out; he took it and gave me the receipts, all of them. The twenty for a five, the Golden Gate Bridge, the Sea of Azov—every last receipt I'd signed. Then he picked up his little satchel and marched away.

Straight down Broadway, without even a good-by. All business, Eksar was, nothing but business. He didn't look back once.

All business. I found out next morning he'd gone right to the bank and had my check certified before closing time. What do you think of that? I couldn't do a damn thing: I was out six thousand, one hundred and fifty dollars. Just for talking to someone.

Ricardo said I was a Faust. I walked out of the bank, beating my head with my fist, and I called up him and Morris Burlap and asked them to have lunch with me. I went over the whole story with them in an expensive place that Ricardo picked out. "You're a Faust," he said.

"What Faust?" I asked him. "Who Faust? How Faust?"

So naturally he had to tell us all about Faust. Only I was a new kind of Faust, a twentieth-century American one. The other Fausts, they wanted to know everything. I wanted to own everything.

"But I didn't wind up owning," I pointed out. "I got taken. Six thousand one hundred and fifty dollars worth I got taken."

Ricardo chuckled and leaned back in his chair. "O my sweet gold," he said under his breath. "O my sweet gold."

"What?"

"A quotation, Bernie. From Marlowe's *Doctor Faustus*. I forget the context, but it seems apt. *'O my sweet gold.'* "

I looked from him to Morris Burlap, but nobody can ever tell when Morris Burlap is puzzled. As a matter of fact, he looks more like a professor than Ricardo, him with those thick Harris tweeds and that heavy, thinking look. Ricardo is, you know, a bit too natty.

The two of them added up to all the brains and sharpness a guy could ask for. That's why I was paying out an arm and a leg for this lunch, on top of all my losses with Eksar.

"Morris, tell the truth. You understand him?"

"What's there to understand, Bernie? A quote about the sweet gold? It might be the answer, right there."

Now I looked at Ricardo. He was eating away at a creamy Italian pudding. Two bucks even, those puddings cost in that place.

"Let's say he was an alien," Morris Burlap said. "Let's say he came from somewhere in outer space. Okay. Now what would an alien want with U.S. dollars? What's the rate of exchange out there? How much is a dollar worth forty, fifty light years away?"

"You mean he needed it to buy some merchandise here on Earth?"

"That's exactly what I mean. But what *kind* of merchandise, that's the question. What could Earth have that he'd want?"

Ricardo finished the pudding and wiped his lips with a napkin. "I think you're on the right track, Morris," he said, and I swung my attention back to him. "We can postulate a civilization far in advance of our own. One that would feel we're not quite ready to know about them. One that has placed primitive little Earth strictly off limits—a restriction only desperate criminals dare ignore."

"From where come criminals, Ricardo, if they're so advanced?"

"Laws produce lawbreakers, Bernie, like hens produce eggs. Civilization has nothing to do with it. I'm beginning to see Eksar now. An unprincipled adventurer, a starman version of those cutthroats who sailed the South Pacific a hundred years or more ago. Once in a while, a ship would smash up against the coral reefs, and a bloody opportunist out of Boston would be stranded for life among primitive, backward tribesmen. I'm sure you can fill in the rest."

"No, I can't. And if you don't mind, Ricardo—"

Morris Burlap said he'd like another brandy. I ordered it. He came as close to smiling as Morris Burlap ever does and leaned toward me confidentially. "Ricardo's got it, Bernie. Put yourself in this guy Eksar's position. He wraps up his space ship on a dirty little planet which it's against the law to be near in the first place. He can make some half-assed repairs with merchandise that's available here—but he has to buy the stuff. Any noise, any uproar, and he'll be grabbed for a Federal rap in outer space. Say you're Eksar, what do you do?"

I could see it now. "I'd peddle and I'd parlay. Copper bracelets, strings of beads, dollars—whatever I had to lay my hands on to buy the native merchandise, I'd peddle and I'd parlay in deal after deal. Until I'd run it up to the amount I needed. Maybe I'd get my start with a piece of equipment from the ship, then I'd find some novelty item that the natives would go for. But all this is *Earth* business know-how, *human* business know-how."

"Bernie," Ricardo told me, "Indians once traded pretty little shells for beaver pelts at the exact spot where the stock exchange now stands. Some kind of business goes on in Eksar's world, I assure you, but its simplest form would make one of our corporate mergers look like a game of potsy on the sidewalk."

Well, I'd wanted to figure it out. "So I was marked as his fish all the way. I was screwed and blued and tattooed," I mumbled, "by a hustler superman."

Ricardo nodded. "By a businessman's Mephistopheles fleeing the thunderbolts of heaven. He needed to double his money one more time and he'd have enough to repair his ship. He had at his disposal a fantastic sophistication in all the ways of commerce."

"What Ricardo's saying," came an almost soft voice from Morris Burlap, "is the guy who beat you up was a whole lot bigger than you."

My shoulders felt loose, like they were sliding down off my arms. "What the hell," I said. "You get stepped on by a horse or you get stepped on by an elephant. You're still stepped on."

I paid the check, got myself together and went away.

Then I began to wonder if maybe this was really the story after all. They both enjoyed seeing me up there as an interplanetary jerk. Ricardo's a brilliant guy, Morris Burlap's sharp as hell, but so what? Ideas, yes. Facts, no.

So here's a fact.

My bank statement came at the end of the month with that canceled check I'd given Eksar. It had been endorsed by a big store in the Cortlandt Street area. I know that store. I've dealt with them. I went down and asked them about it.

They handle mostly marked-down, surplus electronic equipment. That's what they said Eksar had bought. A walloping big order of transistors and transformers, resistors and printed circuits, electronic tubes, wiring, tools, gimmicks like that. All mixed up, they said, a lot of components that just didn't go together. He'd given the clerk the impression that he had an emergency job to do—and he'd take as close as he could get to the things he actually needed. He'd paid a lot of money for freight charges: delivery was to some backwoods town in northern Canada.

That's a fact, now, I have to admit it. But here's another one.

I've dealt with that store, like I said. Their prices are the lowest in the neighborhood. And why is it, do you think, they can sell so cheap? There's only one answer: because they buy so cheap. They buy at the lowest prices; they don't give a damn about quality: all they want to know is, how much mark-up? I've personally sold them job-lots of electronic junk that I couldn't unload anywhere else, condemned stuff, badly wired stuff, stuff that was almost dangerous—it's a place to sell when you've given up on making a profit because you yourself have been stuck with inferior merchandise in the first place.

You get the picture? It makes me feel rosy all over.

There is Eksar out in space, the way I see it. He's fixed up his ship, good enough to travel, and he's on his way to his next big deal. The motors are humming, the ship is running, and he's sitting there with a big smile on his dirty face: he's thinking how he took me, how easy it was.

He's laughing his head off.

All of a sudden, there's a screech and a smell of burning. That circuit that's running the front motor, a wire just got touched through the thin insulation, the circuit's tearing the hell out of itself. He gets scared. He turns on the auxiliaries. The auxiliaries don't go on—you know why? The vacuum tubes he's using have come to the end of their rope, they didn't have much juice to start with. *Blooie!* That's the rear motor developing a short-circuit. *Ka-pow!* That's a defective transformer melting away in the middle of the ship.

And there he is, millions of miles from nowhere, empty space all around him, no more spare parts, tools that practically break in his hands—and not a single, living soul he can hustle.

And here am I, walking up and down my nine-by-six office, thinking about it, and *I'm* laughing my head off.

Because it's just possible, it just could happen, that what goes wrong with his ship is one of the half-dozen or so job-lots of really bad electronic equipment that I personally, me, Bernie the Faust, that I sold to that surplus store at one time or another.

That's all I'd ask. Just to have it happen that way.

Faust. He'd have Faust from me then. Right in the face, Faust. On the head, splitting it open, Faust.

Faust he wants? *Faust* I'd give him!

A ROSE FOR ECCLESIASTES

BY ROGER ZELAZNY (1937-   )

THE MAGAZINE OF FANTASY AND SCIENCE FICTION
NOVEMBER

As I write this headnote it's early November, and I just returned from the World Fantasy Convention in Tuscon where I had the great pleasure of spending part of one evening with Roger Zelazny, and he was just as intelligent and interesting as his fiction. He roared through the 1960s with some of the most remarkable science fiction ever seen—books like This Immortal *(1966),* The Dream Master *(1966; what a year!),* Lord of Light *(1967),* Isle of the Dead *and* Damnation Alley *(both 1969). His remarkable career continues to this day, including noteworthy collaborations with writers as different as Philip K. Dick, Fred Saberhagen, and Robert Sheckley.*

"A Rose for Ecclesiastes" is a stunning story of renewal that remains one of this fine author's most impressive works.

I

I was busy translating one of my *Madrigals Macabre* into Martian on the morning I was found acceptable. The intercom had buzzed briefly, and I dropped my pencil and flipped on the toggle in a single motion.

"Mister G," piped Morton's youthful contralto, "the old man says I should 'get hold of that damned conceited rhymer' right away, and send him to his cabin. Since there's only one damned conceited rhymer . . ."

"Let not ambition mock thy useful toil." I cut him off.

319

So, the Martians had finally made up their minds! I knocked an inch and a half of ash from a smoldering butt, and took my first drag since I had lit it. The entire month's anticipation tried hard to crowd itself into the moment, but could not quite make it. I was frightened to walk those forty feet and hear Emory say the words I already knew he would say; and that feeling elbowed the other one into the background.

So I finished the stanza I was translating before I got up.

It took only a moment to reach Emory's door. I knocked twice and opened it, just as he growled, "Come in."

"You wanted to see me?" I sat down quickly to save him the trouble of offering me a seat.

"That was fast. What did you do, run?"

I regarded his paternal discontent:

Little fatty flecks beneath pale eyes, thinning hair, and an Irish nose; a voice a decibel louder than anyone else's. . . .

Hamlet to Claudius: "I was working."

"Hah!" he snorted. "Come off it. No one's ever seen you do any of that stuff."

I shrugged my shoulders and started to rise.

"If that's what you called me down here—"

"Sit down!"

He stood up. He walked around his desk. He hovered above me and glared down. (A hard trick, even when I'm in a low chair.)

"You are undoubtedly the most antagonistic bastard I've ever had to work with!" he bellowed, like a belly-stung buffalo. "Why the hell don't you act like a human being sometime and surprise everybody? I'm willing to admit you're smart, maybe even a genius, but—oh, hell!" He made a heaving gesture with both hands and walked back to his chair.

"Betty has finally talked them into letting you go in." His voice was normal again. "They'll receive you this afternoon. Draw one of the jeepsters after lunch, and get down there."

"Okay," I said.

"That's all, then."

I nodded, got to my feet. My hand was on the door-knob when he said:

"I don't have to tell you how important this is. Don't treat them the way you treat us."

I closed the door behind me.

I don't remember what I had for lunch. I was nervous, but I knew instinctively that I wouldn't muff it. My Boston publishers expected a Martian Idyll, or at least a Saint-Exupéry job on space flight. The National Science Association wanted a complete report on the Rise and Fall of the Martian Empire.

They would both be pleased. I knew.

That's the reason everyone is jealous—why they hate me. I always come through, and I can come through better than anyone else.

I shoveled in a final anthill of slop, and made my way to our car barn. I drew one jeepster and headed it toward Tirellian.

Flames of sand, lousy with iron oxide, set fire to the buggy. They swarmed over the open top and bit through my scarf; they set to work pitting my goggles.

The jeepster, swaying and panting like a little donkey I once rode through the Himalayas, kept kicking me in the seat of the pants. The Mountains of Tirellian shuffled their feet and moved toward me at a cockeyed angle.

Suddenly I was heading uphill, and I shifted gears to accommodate the engine's braying. Not like Gobi, not like the Great Southwestern Desert, I mused. Just red, just dead . . . without even a cactus.

I reached the crest of the hill, but I had raised too much dust to see what was ahead. It didn't matter, though; I have a head full of maps. I bore to the left and downhill, adjusting the throttle. A crosswind and solid ground beat down the fires. I felt like Ulysses in Malebolge—with a terza-rima speech in one hand and an eye out for Dante.

I rounded a rock pagoda and arrived.

Betty waved as I crunched to a halt, then jumped down.

"Hi," I choked, unwinding my scarf and shaking out

a pound and a half of grit. "Like, where do I go and who do I see?"

She permitted herself a brief Germanic giggle—more at my starting a sentence with "like" than at my discomfort—then she started talking. (She is a top linguist, so a word from the Village Idiom still tickles her!)

I appreciate her precise, furry talk; informational, and all that. I had enough in the way of social pleasantries before me to last at least the rest of my life. I looked at her chocolate-bar eyes and perfect teeth, at her sun-bleached hair, close-cropped to the head (I hate blondes!), and decided that she was in love with me.

"Mr. Gallinger, the Matriarch is waiting inside to be introduced. She has consented to open the Temple records for your study." She paused here to pat her hair and squirm a little. Did my gaze make her nervous?

"They are religious documents, as well as their only history," she continued, "sort of like the Mahabharata. She expects you to observe certain rituals in handling them, like repeating the sacred words when you turn pages—she will teach you the system."

I nodded quickly, several times.

"Fine, let's go in."

"Uh—" She paused. "Do not forget their Eleven Forms of Politeness and Degree. They take matters of form quite seriously—and do not get into any discussions over the equality of the sexes—"

"I know all about their taboos," I broke in. "Don't worry. I've lived in the Orient, remember?"

She dropped her eyes and seized my hand. I almost jerked it away.

"It will look better if I enter leading you."

I swallowed my comments, and followed her, like Samson in Gaza.

Inside, my last thought met with a strange correspondence. The Matriarch's quarters were a rather abstract version of what I imagine the tents of the tribes of Israel to have been like. Abstract, I say, because it was all frescoed brick, peaked like a huge tent, with animal-skin representations like gray-blue scars, that looked as if they had been laid on the walls with a palette knife.

The Matriarch, M'Cwyie, was short, white-haired, fif-tyish, and dressed like a Gypsy queen. With her rainbow of voluminous skirts she looked like an inverted punch bowl set atop a cushion.

Accepting my obeisances, she regarded me as an owl might a rabbit. The lids of those black, black eyes jumped upwards as she discovered my perfect accent. —The tape recorder Betty had carried on her interviews had done its part, and I knew the language reports from the first two expeditions, verbatim. I'm all hell when it comes to picking up accents.

"You are the poet?"

"Yes," I replied.

"Recite one of your poems, please."

"I'm sorry, but nothing short of a thorough translating job would do justice to your language and my poetry, and I don't know enough of your language yet."

"Oh?"

"But I've been making such translations for my own amusement, as an exercise in grammar," I continued. "I'd be honored to bring a few of them along one of the times that I come here."

"Yes. Do so."

Score one for me!

She turned to Betty.

"You may go now."

Betty muttered the parting formalities, gave me a strange sidewise look, and was gone. She apparently had expected to stay and "assist" me. She wanted a piece of the glory, like everyone else. But I was the Schliemann at this Troy, and there would be only one name on the Association report!

M'Cwyie rose, and I noticed that she gained very little height by standing. But then I'm six-six and look like a poplar in October: thin, bright red on top, and towering above everyone else.

"Our records are very, very old," she began. "Betty says that your word for their age is 'millennia.' "

I nodded appreciatively.

"I'm very eager to see them."

"They are not here. We will have to go into the Tem-ple—they may not be removed."

I was suddenly wary.

"You have no objections to my copying them, do you?"

"No. I see that you respect them, or your desire would not be so great."

"Excellent."

She seemed amused. I asked her what was funny.

"The High Tongue may not be so easy for a foreigner to learn."

It came through fast.

No one on the first expedition had gotten this close. I had had no way of knowing that this was a double-language deal—a classical as well as a vulgar. I knew some of their Prakrit, now I had to learn all their Sanskrit.

"Ouch and damn!"

"Pardon, please?"

"It's non-translatable, M'Cwyie. But imagine yourself having to learn the High Tongue in a hurry, and you can guess at the sentiment."

She seemed amused again, and told me to remove my shoes.

She guided me through an alcove . . .

. . . and into a burst of Byzantine brilliance!

No Earthman had ever been in this room before, or I would have heard about it. Carter, the first expedition's linguist, with the help of one Mary Allen, M.D., had learned all the grammar and vocabulary that I knew while sitting cross-legged in the antechamber.

We had no idea this existed. Greedily, I cast my eyes about. A highly sophisticated system of esthetics lay behind the decor. We would have to revise our entire estimation of Martian culture.

For one thing, the ceiling was vaulted and corbeled; for another, there were side-columns with reverse flutings; for another—oh hell! The place was big. Posh. You could never have guessed it from the shaggy outsides.

I bent forward to study the gilt filigree on a ceremonial table. M'Cwyie seemed a bit smug at my intentness, but I'd still have hated to play poker with her.

The table was loaded with books.

With my toe, I traced a mosaic on the floor.

"Is your entire city within this one building?"

"Yes, it goes far back into the mountain."

"I see," I said, seeing nothing.

I couldn't ask her for a conducted tour, yet.

She moved to a small stool by the table.

"Shall we begin your friendship with the High Tongue?"

I was trying to photograph the hall with my eyes, knowing I would have to get a camera in here, somehow, sooner or later. I tore my gaze from a statuette and nodded, hard.

"Yes, introduce me."

I sat down.

For the next three weeks alphabet-bugs chased each other behind my eyelids whenever I tried to sleep. The sky was an unclouded pool of turquoise that rippled calligraphies whenever I swept my eyes across it. I drank quarts of coffee while I worked and mixed cocktails of Benzedrine and champagne for my coffee breaks.

M'Cwyie tutored me two hours every morning, and occasionally for another two in the evening. I spent an additional fourteen hours a day on my own, once I had gotten up sufficient momentum to go ahead alone.

And at night the elevator of time dropped me to its bottom floors. . . .

I was six again, learning my Hebrew, Greek, Latin, and Aramaic. I was ten, sneaking peeks at the *Iliad*. When Daddy wasn't spreading hellfire brimstone, and brotherly love, he was teaching me to dig the Word, like in the original.

Lord! There are so many originals and so *many* words! When I was twelve I started pointing out the little differences between what he was preaching and what I was reading.

The fundamentalist vigor of his reply brooked no debate. It was worse than any beating. I kept my mouth shut after that and learned to appreciate Old Testament poetry.

—*Lord, I am sorry! Daddy—Sir—I am sorry —It couldn't be! It couldn't be. . . .*

On the day the boy graduated from high school, with

the French, German, Spanish, and Latin awards, Dad Gallinger had told his fourteen-year-old, six-foot scarecrow of a son that he wanted him to enter the ministry. I remember how his son was evasive:

"Sir," he had said, "I'd sort of like to study on my own for a year or so, and then take pre-theology courses at some liberal arts university. I feel I'm still sort of young to try a seminary, straight off."

The Voice of God: "But you have the gift of tongues, my son. You can preach the Gospel in all the lands of Babel. You were born to be a missionary. You say you are young, but time is rushing by you like a whirlwind. Start early, and you will enjoy added years of service."

The added years of service were so many added tails to the cat repeatedly laid on my back. I can't see his face now; I never can. Maybe it is because I was always afraid to look at it then.

And years later, when he was dead, and laid out, in black, amidst bouquets, amidst weeping congregationalists, amidst prayers, red faces, handkerchiefs, hands patting your shoulders, solemn faced comforters . . . I looked at him and did not recognize him.

We had met nine months before my birth, this stranger and I. He had never been cruel—stern, demanding, with contempt for everyone's shortcomings—but never cruel. He was also all that I had had of a mother. And brothers. And sisters. He had tolerated my three years at St. John's, possibly because of its name, never knowing how liberal and delightful a place it really was.

But I never knew him, and the man atop the catafalque demanded nothing now; I was free not to preach the Word. But now I wanted to, in a different way. I wanted to preach a word that I could never have voiced while he lived.

I did not return for my senior year in the fall. I had a small inheritance coming, and a bit of trouble getting control of it, since I was still under eighteen. But I managed.

It was Greenwich Village I finally settled upon.

Not telling any well-meaning parishioners my new address, I entered into a daily routine of writing poetry and teaching myself Japanese and Hindustani. I grew a fiery beard, drank espresso, and learned to play chess. I wanted to try a couple of the other paths to salvation.

After that, it was two years in India with the Old Peace Corps—which broke me of my Buddhism, and gave me my *Pipes of Krishna* lyrics and the Pulitzer they deserved.

Then back to the States for my degree, grad work in linguistics, and more prizes.

Then one day a ship went to Mars. The vessel settling in its New Mexico nest of fires contained a new language. —It was fantastic, exotic, and esthetically overpowering. After I had learned all there was to know about it, and written my book, I was famous in new circles:

"Go, Gallinger. Dip your bucket in the well, and bring up a drink of Mars. Go, learn another world—but remain aloof, rail at it gently like Auden—and hand us its soul in iambics."

And I came to the land where the sun is a tarnished penny, where the wind is a whip, where two moons play at hot rod games, and a hell of sand gives you the incendiary itches whenever you look at it.

I rose from my twistings on the bunk and crossed the darkened cabin to a port. The desert was a carpet of endless orange, bulging from the sweepings of centuries beneath it.

"I a stranger, unafraid—This is the land—I've got it made!"

I laughed.

I had the High Tongue by the tail already—or the roots, if you want your puns anatomical, as well as correct.

The High and Low Tongues were not so dissimilar as they had first seemed. I had enough of the one to get me through the murkier parts of the other. I had the grammar and all the commoner irregular verbs down cold; the dictionary I was constructing grew by the day, like a tulip, and would bloom shortly. Every time I played the tapes the stem lengthened.

Now was the time to tax my ingenuity, to really drive the lessons home. I had purposely refrained from plunging into the major texts until I could do justice to them. I had been reading minor commentaries, bits of verse, fragments of history. And one thing had impressed me strongly in all that I read.

They wrote about concrete things: rock, sand, water, winds; and the tenor couched within these elemental symbols was fiercely pessimistic. It reminded me of some Budhist texts, but even more so, I realized from my recent *recherches*, it was like parts of the Old Testament. Specifically, it reminded me of the Book of Ecclesiastes.

That, then, would be it. The sentiment, as well as the vocabulary, was so similar that it would be a perfect exercise. Like putting Poe into French. I would never be a convert to the Way of Malann, but I would show them that an Earthman had once thought the same thoughts, felt similarly.

I switched on my desk lamp and sought King James amidst my books.

Vanity of vanities, saith the Preacher, vanity of vanities; all is vanity. What profit hath a man . . .

My progress seemed to startle M'Cwyie. She peered at me, like Sartre's Other, across the tabletop. I ran through a chapter in the Book of the Locar. I didn't look up, but I could feel the tight net her eyes were working about my head, shoulders, and rapid hands. I turned another page.

Was she weighing the net, judging the size of the catch? And what for? The books said nothing of fishers on Mars. Especially of men. They said that some god named Malann had spat, or had done something disgusting (depending on the version you read), and that life had gotten underway as a disease in inorganic matter. They said that movement was its first law, its first law, and that the dance was the only legitimate reply to the inorganic . . . the dance's quality its justification,—fication . . . and love is a disease in organic matter—Inorganic matter?

I shook my head. I had almost been asleep.

"M'narra."

I stood and stretched. Her eyes outlined me greedily now. So I met them, and they dropped.

"I grow tired. I want to rest awhile. I didn't sleep much last night."

She nodded, Earth's shorthand for "yes," as she had learned from me.

"You wish to relax, and see the explicitness of the doctrine of Locar in its fullness?"

"Pardon me?"

"You wish to see a Dance of Locar?"

"Oh." Their damned circuits of form and periphrasis here ran worse than the Korean! "Yes. Surely. Any time it's going to be done I'd be happy to watch."

I continued, "In the meantime, I've been meaning to ask you whether I might take some pictures—"

"Now is the time. Sit down. Rest. I will call the musicians."

She bustled out through a door I had never been past.

Well now, the dance was the highest art, according to Locar, not to mention Havelock Ellis, and I was about to see how their centuries-dead philosopher felt it should be conducted. I rubbed my eyes and snapped over, touching my toes a few times.

The blood began pounding in my head, and I sucked in a couple deep breaths. I bent again and there was a flurry of motion at the door.

To the trio who entered with M'Cwyie I must have looked as if I were searching for the marbles I had just lost, bent over like that.

I grinned weakly and straightened up, my face red from more than exertion. I hadn't expected them *that* quickly.

Suddenly I thought of Havelock Ellis again in his area of greatest popularity.

The little redheaded doll, wearing, sari-like, a diaphanous piece of Martian sky, looked up in wonder—as a child at some colorful flag on a high pole.

"Hello," I said, or its equivalent.

She bowed before replying. Evidently I had been promoted in status.

"I shall dance," said the red wound in that pale, pale cameo, her face. Eyes, the color of dream and her dress, pulled away from mine.

She drifted to the center of the room.

Standing there, like a figure in an Etruscan frieze, she was either meditating or regarding the design on the floor.

Was the mosaic symbolic of something? I studied it. If it was, it eluded me; it would make an attractive bathroom floor or patio, but I couldn't see much in it beyond that.

The other two were paint-spattered sparrows like M'Cwyie, in their middle years. One settled to the floor with a triple-stringed instrument faintly resembling a *samisen*. The other held a simple woodblock and two drumsticks.

M'Cwyie disdained her stool and was seated upon the floor before I realized it. I followed suit.

The *samisen* player was still tuning it up, so I leaned toward M'Cwyie.

"What is the dancer's name?"

"Braxa," she replied, without looking at me, and raised her left hand, slowly, which meant yes, and go ahead, and let it begin.

The stringed-thing throbbed like a toothache, and a tick-tocking, like ghosts of all the clocks they had never invented, sprang from the block.

Braxa was a statue, both hands raised to her face, elbows high and outspread.

The music became a metaphor for fire.

Crackle, purr, snap . . .

She did not move.

The hissing altered to splashes. The cadence slowed. It was water now, the most precious thing in the world, gurgling clear then green over mossy rocks.

Still she did not move.

Glassandos. A pause.

Then, so faint I could hardly be sure at first, the tremble of the winds began. Softly, gently, sighing and halting, uncertain. A pause, a sob, then a repetition of the first statement, only louder.

Were my eyes completely bugged from my reading, or was Braxa actually trembling, all over, head to foot?

She was.

She began a microscopic swaying. A fraction of an inch

right, then left. Her fingers opened like the petals of a flower, and I could see that her eyes were closed.

Her eyes opened. They were distant, glassy, looking through me and the walls. Her swaying became pronounced, merged with the beat.

The wind was sweeping in from the desert now, falling against Tirellian like waves on a dike. Her fingers moved, they were the gusts. Her arms, slow pendulums, descended, began a counter-movement.

The gale was coming now. She began an axial movement and her hands caught up with the rest of her body, only now her shoulders commenced to writhe out a figure-eight.

The wind! The wind, I say. O wild, enigmatic! O muse of St. John Perse!

The cyclone was twisting around those eyes, its still center. Her head was thrown back, but I knew there was no ceiling between her gaze, passive as Buddha's, and the unchanging skies. Only the two moons, perhaps, interrupted their slumber in that elemental Nirvana of uninhabited turquoise.

Years ago, I had seen the Devadasis in India, the streetdancers, spinning their colorful webs, drawing in the male insect. But Braxa was more than this: she was a Ramadjany, like those votaries of Rama, incarnation of Vishnu, who had given the dance to man: the sacred dancers.

The clicking was monotonously steady now; the whine of the strings made me think of the stinging rays of the sun, their heat stolen by the wind's halations; the blue was Sarasvati and Mary, and a girl named Laura. I heard a sitar from somewhere, watched this statue come to life, and inhaled a divine afflatus.

I was again Rimbaud with his hashish, Baudelaire with his laudanum, Poe, De Quincy, Wilde, Mallarme and Aleister Crowley. I was, for a fleeting second, my father in his dark pulpit and darker suit, the hymns and the organ's wheeze transmuted to bright wind.

She was a spun weather vane, a feathered crucifix hovering in the air, a clothes-line holding one bright garment lashed parallel to the ground. Her shoulder was bare now, and her right breast moved up and down like a moon in the sky, its red nipple appearing momently above a fold and vanishing again. The music was as formal as Job's argument with God. Her dance was God's reply.

The music slowed, settled; it had been met, matched, answered. Her garment, as if alive, crept back into the more sedate folds it originally held.

She dropped low, lower, to the floor. Her head fell upon her raised knees. She did not move.

There was silence.

I realized from the ache across my shoulders, how tensely I had been sitting. My armpits were wet. Rivulets had been running down my sides. What did one do now? Applaud?

I sought M'Cwyie from the corner of my eye. She raised her right hand.

As if by telepathy the girl shuddered all over and stood. The musicians also rose. So did M'Cwyie.

I got to my feet, with a charley horse in my left leg, and said, "It was beautiful," inane as that sounds.

I received three different High Forms of "thank you."

There was a flurry of color and I was alone again with M'Cwyie.

"That is the one hundred-seventeenth of the two thousand, two hundred-twenty-four dances of Locar."

I looked down at her.

"Whether Locar was right or wrong, he worked out a fine reply to the inorganic."

She smiled.

"Are the dances of your world like this?"

"Some of them are similar. I was reminded of them as I watched Braxa—but I've never seen anything exactly like hers."

"She is good," M'Cwyie said. "She knows all the dances."

A hint of her earlier expression which had troubled me . . .

It was gone in an instant.

"I must tend my duties now." She moved to the table and closed the books. "M'narra."

"Good-bye." I slipped into my boots.

"Good-bye, Gallinger."

I walked out the door, mounted the jeepster, and roared across the evening into night, my wings of risen desert flapping slowly behind me.

II

I had just closed the door behind Betty, after a brief grammar session, when I heard the voices in the hall. My vent was opened a fraction, so I stood there and eavesdropped:

Morton's fruity treble: "Guess what? He said 'hello' to me awhile ago."

"Hmmph!" Emory's elephant lungs exploded. "Either he's slipping, or you were standing in his way and he wanted you to move."

"Probably didn't recognize me. I don't think he sleeps any more, now he has that language to play with. I had night watch last week, and every night I passed his door at 0300—I always heard that recorder going. At 0500 when I got off, he was still at it."

"The guy *is* working hard," Emory admitted, grudgingly. "In fact, I think he's taking some kind of dope to keep awake. He looks sort of glassy-eyed these days. Maybe that's natural for a poet, though."

Betty had been standing there, because she broke in then:

"Regardless of what you think of him, it's going to take me at least a year to learn what he's picked up in three weeks. And I'm just a linguist, not a poet."

Morton must have been nursing a crush on her bovine charms. It's the only reason I can think of for his dropping his guns to say what he did.

"I took a course in modern poetry when I was back at the university," he began. "We read six authors—Yeats, Pound, Eliot, Crane, Stevens, and Gallinger—and on the last day of the semester, when the prof was feeling a little rhetorical, he said, 'These six names are written on the century, and all the gates of criticism and hell shall not prevail against them.'

"Myself," he continued, "I thought his *Pipes of Krishna* and his *Madrigals* were great. I was honored to be chosen for an expedition he was going on.

"I think he's spoken two dozen words to me since I met him," he finished.

The Defense: "Did it ever occur to you," Betty said, "that he might be tremendously self-conscious about his appearance? He was also a precocious child, and probably never even had school friends. He's sensitive and very introverted."

"Sensitive? Self-conscious?" Emory choked and gagged. "The man is as proud as Lucifer, and he's a walking insult machine. You press a button like 'Hello' or 'Nice day' and he thumbs his nose at you. He's got it down to a reflex."

They muttered a few other pleasantries and drifted away.

Well bless you, Morton boy. You little pimple-faced, Ivy-bred connoisseur! I've never taken a course in my poetry, but I'm glad someone said that. The Gates of Hell. Well now! Maybe Daddy's prayers got heard somewhere, and I am a missionary, after all!

Only . . .

. . . Only a missionary needs something to convert people *to*. I have my private system of ethics, and I suppose it oozes an ethical by-product somewhere. But if I ever had anything to preach, really, even in my poems, I wouldn't care to preach it to such low-lifes as you. If you think I'm a slob, I'm also a snob, and there's no room for you in my Heaven—it's a private place, where Swift, Shaw, and Petronius Arbiter come to dinner.

And oh, the feasts we have! The Trimalchio's, the Emory's we dissect!

We finish you with the soup, Morton!

I turned and settled at my desk. I wanted to write something. Ecclesiastes could take a night off. I wanted to write a poem, a poem about the one hundred-seventeenth dance of Locar; about a rose, following the light, traced by the wind, sick, like Blake's rose, dying. . . .

I found a pencil and began.

When I had finished I was pleased. It wasn't great—at least, it was no greater than it needed to be—High Martian not being my strongest tongue. I groped, and put it into English, with partial rhymes. Maybe I'd stick it in my next book. I called it *Braxa*:

*In a land of wind and red, where the icy evening
of Time freezes milk in the breasts of Life, as
two moons overhead—cat and dog in alleyways
of dream—scratch and scramble agelessly my
flight . . .*

This final flower turns a burning head.

I put it away and found some phenobarbitol. I was
suddenly tired.

When I showed my poem to M'Cwyie the next day,
she read it through several times, very slowly.

"It is lovely," she said. "But you used three words
from your own language. 'Cat' and 'dog,' I assume, are
two small animals with a hereditary hatred for one another. But what is 'flower?' "

"Oh," I said. "I've never come across your word for
'flower,' but I was actually thinking of an Earth flower,
the rose."

"What is it like?"

"Well, its petals are generally bright red. That's what
I meant, on one level, by 'burning heads.' I also wanted
it to imply fever, though, and red hair, and the fire of
life. The rose, itself, has a thorny stem, green leaves,
and a distinct, pleasing aroma."

"I wish I could see one."

"I suppose it could be arranged. I'll check."

"Do it, please. You are a—" She used the word for
"prophet," or religious poet, like Isaias or Locar.
"—and your poem is inspired. I shall tell Baxa of it."

I declined the nomination, but felt flattered.

This, then, I decided, was the strategic day, the day
on which to ask whether I might bring in the microfilm
machine and the camera. I wanted to copy all their texts,
I explained, and I couldn't write fast enough to do it.

She surprised me by agreeing immediately. But she
bowled me over with her invitation.

"Would you like to come and stay here while you do
this thing? Then you can work night and day, any time you
want—except when the Temple is being used, of course."

I bowed.

"I should be honored."

"Good. Bring your machines when you want, and I will show you a room."

"Will this afternoon be all right?"

"Certainly."

"Then I will go now and get things ready. Until this afternoon . . ."

"Good-bye."

I anticipated a little trouble from Emory, but not much. Everyone back at the ship was anxious to see the Martians, poke needles in the Martians, ask them about Martian climate, diseases, soil chemistry, politics, and mushrooms (our botanist was a fungus nut, but a reasonably good guy)—and only four or five had actually gotten to see them. The crew had been spending most of its time excavating dead cities and their acropolises. We played the game by strict rules, and the natives were as fiercely insular as the nineteenth-century Japanese. I figured I would meet with little resistance, and I figured right.

In fact, I got the distinct impression that everyone was happy to see me move out.

I stopped in the hydroponics room to speak with our mushroom master.

"Hi, Kane. Grow any toadstools in the sand yet?"

He sniffed. He always sniffs. Maybe he's allergic to plants.

"Hello, Gallinger. No, I haven't had any success with toadstools, but look behind the car barn next time you're out there. I've got a few cacti going."

"Great," I observed. Doc Kane was about my only friend aboard, not counting Betty.

"Say, I came down to ask you a favor."

"Name it."

"I want a rose."

"A what?"

"A rose. You know, a nice red American Beauty job—thorns, pretty smelling—"

"I don't think it will take in this soil. *Snif, sniff.*"

"No, you don't understand. I don't want to plant it, I just want the flower."

"I'd have to use the tanks." He scratched his hairline

dome. "It would take at least three months to get you flowers, even under forced growth."

"Will you do it?"

"Sure, if you don't mind the wait."

"Not at all. In fact, three months will just make it before we leave." I looked about at the pools of crawling slime, at the trays of shoots. "—I'm moving up to Tirellian today, but I'll be in and out all the time. I'll be here when it blooms."

"Moving up there, eh? Moore said they're an in-group."

"I guess I'm 'in' then."

"Looks that way—I still don't see how you learned their language, though. Of course, I had trouble with French and German for my Ph.D., but last week I heard Betty demonstrate it at lunch. It just sounds like a lot of weird noises. She says speaking it is like working a *Times* crossword and trying to imitate birdcalls at the same time."

I laughed, and took the cigarette he offered me.

"It's complicated," I acknowledged. "But, well, it's as if you suddenly came across a whole new class of mycetae here—you'd dream about it at night."

His eyes were gleaming.

"Wouldn't that be something! I might, yet, you know."

"Maybe you will."

He chuckled as we walked to the door.

"I'll start your roses tonight. Take it easy down there."

"You bet. Thanks."

Like I said, a fungus nut, but a fairly good guy. My quarters in the Citadel of Tirellian were directly adjacent to the Temple, on the inward side and slightly to the left. They were a considerable improvement over my cramped cabin, and I was pleased that Martian culture had progressed sufficiently to discover the desirability of the mattress over the pallet. Also, the bed was long enough to accommodate me, which was surprising.

So I unpacked and took sixteen 35mm. shots of the Temple, before starting on the books.

I took 'stats until I was sick of turning pages without

knowing what they said. So I started translating a work of history.

"Lo. In the thirty-seventh year of the Process of Cillen the rains came, which gave rise to rejoicing, for it was a rare and untoward occurrence, and commonly construed a blessing.

"But it was not the life-giving semen of Malann which fell from the heavens. It was the blood of the universe, spurting from an artery. And the last days were upon us. The final dance was to begin.

"The rains brought the plague that does not kill, and the last passes of Locar began with their drumming. . . ."

I asked myself what the hell Tamur meant, for he was an historian and supposedly committed to fact. This was not their Apocalypse.

Unless they could be one and the same . . . ?

Why not? I mused. Tirellian's handful of people were the remnant of what had obviously once been a highly developed culture. They had had wars, but no holocausts; science, but little technology. A plague that did not kill . . . ? Could that have done it? How, if it wasn't fatal?

I read on, but the nature of the plague was not discussed. I turned pages, skipped ahead, and drew a blank.

M'Cwyie! M'Cwyie! When I want to question you most, you are not around!

Would it be a *faux pas* to go looking for her? Yes, I decided. I was restricted to the rooms I had been shown, that had been an implicit understanding. I would have to wait to find out.

So I cursed long and loud, in many languages, doubtless burning Malann's sacred ears, there in his Temple.

He did not see fit to strike me dead, so I decided to call it a day and hit the sack.

I must have been asleep for several hours when Braxa entered my room with a tiny lamp. She dragged me awake by tugging at my pajama sleeve.

I said hello. Thinking back, there is not much else I could have said.

"Hello."

"I have come," she said, "to hear the poem."

"What poem?"

"Yours."

"Oh."

I yawned, sat up, and did things people usually do when awakened in the middle of the night to read poetry.

"That is very kind of you, but isn't the hour a trifle awkward?"

"I don't mind," she said.

Someday I am going to write an article for the *Journal of Semantics*, called "Tone of Voice: An Insufficient Vehicle for Irony."

However, I was awake, so I grabbed my robe.

"What sort of animal is that?" she asked, pointing at the silk dragon on my lapel.

"Mythical," I replied. "Now look, it's late. I am tired. I have much to do in the morning. And M'Cwyie just might get the wrong idea if she learns you were here."

"Wrong idea?"

"You know damned well what I mean!" It was the first time I had an opportunity to use Martian profanity, and it failed.

"No," she said, "I do not know."

She seemed frightened, like a puppy being scolded without knowing what it has done wrong.

I softened. Her red cloak matched her hair and lips so perfectly, and those lips were trembling.

"Here now, I didn't mean to upset you. On my world there are certain, uh, mores, concerning people of different sex alone together in bedrooms, and not allied by marriage. . . . Um, I mean, you see what I mean?"

"No."

They were jade, her eyes.

"Well, it's sort of . . . Well, it's sex, that's what it is."

A light was switched on in those jade lamps.

"Oh, you mean having children!"

"Yes. That's it! Exactly."

She laughed. It was the first time I had heard laughter in Tirellian. It sounded like a violinist striking his high strings with the bow, in short little chops. It was not an altogether pleasant thing to hear, especially because she laughed too long.

When she had finished she moved closer.

"I remember, now," she said. "We used to have such rules. Half a Process ago, when I was a child, we had such rules. But"—she looked as if she were ready to laugh again—"there is no need for them now."

My mind moved like a tape recorder played at triple speed.

Half a Process! HalfaProcessa-ProcessaProcess! No! Yes! Half a Process was two hundred-forty-three years, roughly speaking!

—Time enough to learn the 2224 dances of Locar.

—Time enough to grow old, if you were human.

—Earth-style human, I mean.

I looked at her again, pale as the white queen in an ivory chess set.

She was human. I'd stake my soul—alive, normal, healthy. I'd stake my life—woman, my body . . .

But she was two and a half centuries old, which made M'Cwyie Methuselah's grandma. It flattered me to think of their repeated complimenting of my skills, as linguist, as poet. These superior beings!

But what did she mean "there is no such need for them now"? Why the near-hysteria? Why all those funny looks I'd been getting from M'Cwyie?

I suddenly knew I was close to something important, besides a beautiful girl.

"Tell me," I said, in my Casual Voice, "did it have anything to do with 'the plague that does not kill,' of which Tamur wrote?"

"Yes," she replied, "the children born after the Rains could have no children of their own, and—"

"And what?" I was leaning forward, memory set at "record."

"—and the men had no desire to get any."

I sagged backward against the bedpost. Racial sterility, masculine impotence, following phenomenal weather. Had some vagabond cloud of radioactive junk from God knows where penetrated their weak atmosphere one day? One day long before Shiaparelli saw the canals, mythical as my dragon, before those "canals" had given rise to some correct guesses for all the wrong reasons, had Braxa been alive, dancing, here—damned in the womb since blind Milton had written of another paradise, equally lost?

I found a cigarette. Good thing I had thought to bring ashtrays. Mars had never had a tobacco industry either. Or booze. The ascetics I had met in India had been Dionysiac compared to this.

"What is that tube of fire?"

"A cigarette. Want one?"

"Yes, please."

She sat beside me, and I lighted it for her.

"It irritates the nose."

"Yes. Draw some into your lungs, hold it there, and exhale."

A moment passed.

"Ooh," she said.

A pause, then, "Is it sacred?"

"No, it's nicotine," I answered, "a very *ersatz* form of divinity."

Another pause.

"Please don't ask me to translate 'ersatz.' "

"I won't. I get this feeling sometimes when I dance."

"It will pass in a moment."

"Tell me your poem now."

An idea hit me.

"Wait a minute," I said; "I may have something better."

I got up and rummaged through my notebooks, then I returned and sat beside her.

"These are the first three chapters of the Book of Ecclesiastes," I explained. "It is very similiar to your own sacred books."

I started reading.

I got through eleven verses before she cried out, "Please don't read that! Tell me one of yours!"

I stopped and tossed the notebook onto a nearby table. She was shaking, not as she had quivered that day she danced as the wind, but with the jitter of unshed tears. She held her cigarette awkwardly, like a pencil. Clumsily, I put my arm about her shoulders.

"He is so sad," she said, "like all the others."

So I twisted my mind like a bright ribbon, folded it, and tied the crazy Christmas knots I love so well. From

German to Martian, with love, I did an impromptu
paraphrasal of a poem about a Spanish dancer. I thought
it would please her. I was right.

"Oooh," she said again. "Did you write that?"

"No, it's by a better man than I."

"I don't believe you. You wrote it."

"No, a man named Rilke did."

"But you brought it across to my language. Light
another match, so I can see how she danced."

I did.

"The fires of forever," she mused, "and she stamped
them out, 'with small, firm feet.' I wish I could dance
like that."

"You're better than any Gypsy," I laughed, blowing it
out.

"No, I'm not. I couldn't do that."

"Do you want me to dance for you?"

Her cigarette was burning down, so I removed it from
her fingers and put it out, along with my own.

"No," I said. "Go to bed."

She smiled, and before I realized it, had unclasped the
fold of red at her shoulder.

And everything fell away.

And I swallowed, with some difficulty.

"All right," she said.

So I kissed her, as the breath of fallen cloth extinguished the lamp.

III

The days were like Shelley's leaves: yellow, red,
brown, whipped in bright gusts by the west wind. They
swirled past me with the rattle of microfilm. Almost all
the books were recorded now. It would take scholars
years to get through them, to properly assess their value.
Mars was locked in my desk.

Ecclesiastes, abandoned and returned to a dozen
times, was almost ready to speak in the High Tongue.

I whistled when I wasn't in the Temple. I wrote reams
of poetry I would have been ashamed of before. Eve-
nings I would walk with Braxa, across the dunes or up
into the mountains. Sometimes she would dance for me;

and I would read something long, and in dactylic hexameter. She still thought I was Rilke, and I almost kidded myself into believing it. Here I was, staying at the Castle Duino, writing his *Elegies*.

> *. . . It is strange to inhabit the Earth no more,*
> *to use no longer customs scarce acquired,*
> *nor interpret roses . . .*

No! Never interpret roses! Don't Smell them (sniff, Kane!), pick them, enjoy them. Live in the moment. Hold to it tightly. But charge not the gods to explain. So fast the leaves go by, are blown . . .

And no one ever noticed us. Or cared.

Laura. Laura and Braxa. They rhyme, you know, with a bit of a clash. Tall, cool, and blonde was she (I hate blondes!), and Daddy had turned me inside out, like a pocket, and I thought she could fill me again. But the big, beat word-slinger, with Judas-beard and dog-trust in his eyes, oh, he had been a fine decoration at her parties. And that was all.

How the machine cursed me in the Temple! It blasphemed Malann and Gallinger. And the wild west wind went by and something was not far behind.

The last days were upon us.

A day went by and I did not see Braxa, and a night. And a second. A third.

I was half-mad. I hadn't realized how close we had become, how important she had been. With a dumb assurance of presence, I had fought against questioning roses.

I had to ask. I didn't want to, but I had no choice.

"Where is she, M'Cwyie? Where is Braxa?"

"She is gone," she said.

"Where?"

"I do not know."

I looked at those devil-bird eyes. Anathema maranatha rose to my lips.

"I must know."

She looked through me.

"She has left us. She is gone. Up into the hills, I suppose. Or the desert. It does not matter. What does anything matter? The dance draws to a close. The Temple will soon be empty."

"Why? Why did she leave?"

"I do not know."

"I must see her again. We lift off in a matter of days."

"I am sorry, Gallinger."

"So am I," I said, and slammed shut a book without saying "m'narra."

I stood up.

"I will find her."

I left the Temple. M'Cwyie was a seated statue. My boots were still where I had left them.

All day I roared up and down the dunes, going nowhere. To the crew of the *Aspic* I must have looked like a sandstorm, all by myself. Finally, I had to return for more fuel.

Emory came stalking out.

"Okay, make it good. You look like the abominable dust man. Why the rodeo?"

"Why, I, uh, lost something."

"In the middle of the desert? Was it one of your sonnets? They're the only thing I can think of that you'd make such a fuss over."

"No, dammit! It was something personal."

George had finished filling the tank. I started to mount the jeepster again.

"Hold on there!" he grabbed my arm.

"You're not going back until you tell me what this is all about."

I could have broken his grip, but then he could order me dragged back by the heels, and quite a few people would enjoy doing the dragging. So I forced myself to speak slowly, softly:

"It's simply that I lost my watch. My mother gave it to me and it's a family heirloom. I want to find it before we leave."

"You sure its not in your cabin, or down in Tirellian?"

"I've already checked."

"Maybe somebody hid it to irritate you. You know you're not the most popular guy around."

I shook my head.

"I thought of that. But I always carry it in my right pocket. I think it might have bounced out going over the dunes."

He narrowed his eyes.

"I remember reading on a book jacket that your mother died when you were born."

"That's right," I said, biting my tongue. "The watch belonged to her father and she wanted me to have it. My father kept it for me."

"Hmph!" he snorted. "That's a pretty strange way to look for a watch, riding up and down in a jeepster."

"I could see the light shining off it that way," I offered, lamely.

"Well, it's starting to get dark," he observed. "No sense looking any more today.

"Throw a dust sheet over the jeepster," he directed a mechanic.

He patted my arm.

"Come on in and get a shower, and something to eat. You look as if you could use both."

Little fatty flecks beneath pale eyes, thinning hair, and an Irish nose; a voice a decibel louder than anyone else's. . . .

His only qualification for leadership!

I stood there, hating him. Claudius! If only this were the fifth act!

But suddenly the idea of a shower, and food, came through to me. I could use both badly. If I insisted on hurrying back immediately I might arouse more suspicion.

So I brushed some sand from my sleeve.

"You're right. That sounds like a good idea."

"Come on, we'll eat in my cabin."

The shower was a blessing, clean khakis were the grace of God, and the food smelled like Heaven.

"Smells pretty good," I said.

We hacked up our steaks in silence. When we got to the dessert and coffee he suggested:

"Why don't you take take the night off? Stay here and get some sleep."

I shook my head.

"I'm pretty busy. Finishing up. There's not much time left."

"A couple of days ago you said you were almost finished."

"Almost, but not quite."

"You also said they'll be holding a service in the Temple tonight."

"That's right. I'm going to work in my room."

He shrugged his shoulders.

Finally, he said, "Gallinger," and I looked up because my name means trouble.

"It shouldn't be any of my business," he said, "but it is. Betty says you have a girl down there."

There was no question mark. It was a statement hanging in the air. Waiting.

Betty, you're a bitch. You're a cow and a bitch. And a jealous one, at that. Why didn't you keep your nose where it belonged, shut your eyes? Your mouth?

"So?" I said, a statement with a question mark.

"So," he answered it, "it is my duty, as head of this expedition, to see that relations with the natives are carried on in a friendly, and diplomatic, manner."

"You speak of them," I said, "as though they are aborigines. Nothing could be further from the truth."

I rose.

"When my papers are published everyone on Earth will know that truth. I'll tell them things Doctor Moore never even guessed at. I'll tell the tragedy of a doomed race, waiting for death, resigned and disinterested. I'll tell why, and it will break hard, scholarly hearts. I'll write about it, and they will give me more prizes, and this time I won't want them.

"My God!" I exclaimed. "They had a culture when our ancestors were clubbing the saber-tooth and finding out how fire works!"

"*Do* you have a girl down there?"

"Yes!" I said. Yes, *Claudius! Yes, Daddy! Yes, Emory!* "I do. But I'm going to let you in on a scholarly scoop now. They're already dead. They're sterile. In one more generation there won't be any Martians."

I paused, then added, "Except in my papers, except on a few pieces of microfilm and tape. And in some poems, about a girl who did give a damn and could only bitch about the unfairness of it all by dancing."

"Oh," he said.

After awhile:

"You *have* been behaving differently these past couple months. You've even been downright civil on occasion, you know. I couldn't help wondering what was happening. I didn't know anything mattered that strongly to you."

I bowed my head.

"Is she the reason you were racing around the desert?"

I nodded.

"Why?"

I looked up.

"Because she's out there, somewhere. I don't know where, or why. And I've got find her before we go."

"Oh," he said again.

Then he leaned back, opened a drawer, and took out something wrapped in a towel. He unwound it. A framed photo of a woman lay on the table.

"My wife," he said.

It was an attractive face, with big, almond eyes.

"I'm a Navy man, you know," he began. "Young officer once. Met her in Japan.

"Where I come from it wasn't considered right to marry into another race, so we never did. But she was my wife. When she died I was on the other side of the world. They took my children, and I've never seen them since. I couldn't learn what orphanage, what home, they were put into. That was long ago. Very few people know about it."

"I'm sorry," I said.

"Don't be. Forget it. But"—he shifted in his chair and looked at me—"if you do want to take her back with you—do it. It'll mean my neck, but I'm too old to ever head another expedition like this one. So go ahead."

He gulped his cold coffee.

"Get your jeepster."

He swiveled the chair around.

I tried to say "thank you" twice, but I couldn't. So I got up and walked out.

"Sayonara, and all that," he muttered behind me.

"Here it is, Gallinger!" I heard a shout.

I turned on my heel and looked back up the ramp.

"Kane!"

He was limned in the port, shadow against light, but I had heard him sniff.

I returned the few steps.

"Here what is?"

"Your rose."

He produced a plastic container, divided internally. The lower half was filled with liquid. The stem ran down into it. The other half, a glass of claret in this horrible night, was a large, newly opened rose.

"Thank you," I said, tucking it into my jacket.

"Going back to Tirellian, eh?"

"Yes."

"I saw you come aboard, so I got it ready. Just missed you at the Captain's cabin. He was busy. Hollered out that I could catch you at the barns."

"Thanks again."

"It's chemically treated. It will stay in bloom for weeks."

I nodded. I was gone.

Up into the mountains now. Far. Far. The sky was a bucket of ice in which no moons floated. The going became steeper, and the little donkey protested. I whipped him with the throttle and went on. Up. Up. I spotted a green, unwinking star, and felt a lump in my throat. The encased rose beat against my chest like an extra heart. The donkey brayed, long and loudly, then began to cough. I lashed him some more and he died.

I threw the emergency brake on and got out. I began to walk.

So cold, so cold it grows. Up here. At night? Why? Why did she do it? Why flee the campfire when night comes on?

And I was up, down, around, and through every chasm, gorge, and pass, with my long-legged strides and an ease of movement never known on Earth.

Barely two days remain, my love, and thou hast forsaken me. Why?

I crawled under overhangs. I leaped over ridges. I scraped my knees, an elbow. I heard my jacket tear.

No answer, Malann? Do you really hate your people

this much? Then I'll try someone else. Vishnu, you're the Preserver. Preserve her, please! Let me find her.

Jehovah?

Adonis? Osiris? Thammuz? Manitou? Legba? Where is she?

I ranged far and high, and I slipped.

Stones ground underfoot and I dangled over an edge. My fingers so cold. It was hard to grip the rock.

I looked down.

Twelve feet or so. I let go and dropped, landed rolling.

Then I heard her scream.

I lay there, not moving, looking up. Against the night, above, she called.

"Gallinger!"

I lay still.

"Gallinger!"

And she was gone.

I heard stones rattle and knew she was coming down some path to the right of me.

I jumped up and ducked into the shadow of a boulder.

She rounded a cut-off, and picked her way, uncertainly, through the stones.

"Gallinger?"

I stepped out and seized her shoulders.

"Braxa."

She screamed again, then began to cry, crowding against me. It was the first time I had ever heard her cry.

"Why?" I asked. "Why?"

But she only clung to me and sobbed.

Finally, "I thought you had killed yourself."

"Maybe I would have," I said. "Why did you leave Tirellian? And me?"

"Didn't M'Cwyie tell you? Didn't you guess?"

"I didn't guess, and M'Cwyie said she didn't know."

"Then she lied. She knows."

"What? What is it she know?"

She shook all over, then was silent for a long time. I realized suddenly that she was wearing only her flimsy dancer's costume. I pushed her from me, took off my jacket, and put it about her shoulders.

"Great Malann!" I cried. "You'll freeze to death!"

"No," she said, "I won't."

I was transferring the rose-case to my pocket.

"What is that?" she asked.

"A rose," I answered. "You can't make it out much in the dark. I once compared you to one. Remember?"

"Ye-Yes. May I carry it?"

"Sure." I stuck it in the jacket pocket.

"Well? I'm still waiting for an explanation."

"You really don't know?" she asked.

"No!"

"When the Rains came," she said, "apparently only our men were affected, which was enough. . . . Because I—wasn't—affected—apparently—"

"Oh," I said. "Oh."

We stood there, and I thought.

"Well, why did you run? What's wrong with being pregnant on Mars? Tamur was mistaken. Your people can live again."

She laughed, again that wild violin played by a Paginini gone mad. I stopped her before it went too far.

"How?" she finally asked, rubbing her cheek.

"Your people live longer than ours. If our child is normal it will mean our races can intermarry. There must still be other fertile women of your race. Why not?"

"You have read the Book of Locar," she said, "and yet you ask me that? Death was decided, voted upon, and passed, shortly after it appeared in this form. But long before, the followers of Locar knew. They decided it long ago. 'We have done all things,' they said, 'we have seen all things, we have heard and felt all things. The dance was good. Now let it end.' "

"You can't believe that."

"What I believe does not matter," she replied. "M'Cwyie and the Mothers have decided we must die. Their very title is now a mockery, but their decisions will be upheld. There is only one prophecy left, and it is mistaken. We will die."

"No," I said.

"What, then?"

"Come back with me, to Earth."

"No."

"All right, then. Come with me now."

"Where?"

"Back to Tirellian. I'm going to talk to the Mothers."

"You can't! There is a Ceremony tonight!"

I laughed.

"A ceremony for a god who knocks you down, and then kicks you in the teeth?"

"He is still Malann," she answered. "We are still his people."

"You and my father would have gotten along fine," I snarled. "But I am going, and you are coming with me, even if I have to carry you—and I'm bigger than you are."

"But you are not bigger than Ontro."

"Who the hell is Ontro?"

"He will stop you, Gallinger. He is the Fist of Malann."

IV

I scudded the jeepster to a halt in front of the only entrance I knew, M'Cwyie's. Braxa, who had seen the rose in a headlamp, now cradled it in her lap, like our child, and said nothing. There was a passive, lovely look on her face.

"Are they in the Temple now?" I wanted to know.

The Madonna-expression did not change. I repeated the question. She stirred.

"Yes," she said, from a distance, "but you cannot go in."

"We'll see."

I circled and helped her down.

I led her by the hand, and she moved, as if in a trance. In the light of the new-risen moon, her eyes looked as they had the day I met her, when she had danced. I snapped my fingers. Nothing happened.

So I pushed the door open and led her in. The room was half-lighted.

And she screamed for the third time that evening:

"Do not harm him, Ontro! It is Gallinger!"

I had never seen a Martian man before, only women.

So I had no way of knowing whether he was a freak, though I suspected it strongly.

I looked up at him.

His half-naked body was covered with moles and swellings. Gland trouble, I guessed.

I had thought I was the tallest man on the planet, but he was seven feet tall and overweight. Now I knew where my giant bed had come from!

"Go back," he said. "She may enter. You may not."

"I must get my books and things."

He raised a huge left arm. I followed it. All my belongings lay neatly stacked in the corner.

"I must go in. I must talk with M'Cwyie and the Mothers."

"You may not."

"The lives of your people depend on it."

"Go back," he boomed. "Go home to *your* people, Gallinger. Leave *us!*"

My name sounded so different on his lips, like someone else's. How old was he? I wondered. Three hundred? Four? Had he been a Temple guardian all his life? Why? Who was there to guard against? I didn't like the way he moved. I had seen men who moved like that before.

"Go back," he repeated.

If they had refined their martial arts as far as they had their dances, or, worse yet, if their fighting arts were a part of the dance, I was in for trouble.

"Go on in," I said to Braxa. "Give the rose to M'Cwyie. Tell her that I sent it. Tell her I'll be there shortly."

"I will do as you ask. Remember me on Earth, Gallinger. Good-bye."

I did not answer her, and she walked past Ontro and into the next room, bearing her rose.

"Now will you leave?" he asked. "If you like, I will tell her that we fought and you almost beat me, but I knocked you unconscious and carried you back to your ship."

"No," I said, "either I go around you or go over you, but I am going through."

He dropped into a crouch, arms extended.

"It is a sin to lay hands on a holy man," he rumbled, "but I will stop you, Gallinger."

My memory was a fogged window, suddenly exposed to fresh air. Things cleared. I looked back six years.

I was a student of Oriental Languages at the University of Tokyo. It was my twice-weekly night of recreation. I stood in a thirty-foot circle in the Kodokan, the *judogi* lashed about my high hips by a brown belt. I was *Ikkyu*, one notch below the lowest degree of expert. A brown diamond above my right breast said "Jiu-Jitsu" in Japananese, and it meant *atemiwaza*, really, because of the one striking-technique I had worked out, found unbelievably suitable to my size, and won matches with.

But I had never used it on a man, and it was five years since I had practiced. I was out of shape, I knew, but I tried hard to force my mind *tsuki no kokoro*, like the moon, reflecting the all of Ontro.

Somewhere, out of the past, a voice said, "*Hajime*, let it begin."

I snapped into my *neko-ashi-dachi* cat-stance, and his eyes burned strangely. He hurried to correct his own position—and I threw it at him!

My one trick!

My long left leg lashed up like a broken spring. Seven feet off the ground my foot connected with his jaw as he tried to leap backward.

His head snapped back and he fell. A soft moan escaped his lips. *That's all there is to it,* I thought. *Sorry, old fellow.*

And as I stepped over him, somehow, groggily, he tripped me, and I fell across his body. I couldn't believe he had strength enough to remain conscious after that blow, let alone move. I hated to punish him any more.

But he found my throat and slipped a forearm across it before I realized there was a purpose to his action.

No! Don't let it end like this!

It was a bar of steel across my windpipe, my carotids. Then I realized that he was still unconscious, and that this was a reflex instilled by countless years of training. I had seen it happen once, in *shiai*. The man died because he had been choked unconscious and still fought on, and his opponent thought he had not been applying the choke properly. He tried harder.

But it was rare, so very rare!

I jammed my elbows into his ribs and threw my head back in his face. The grip eased, but not enough. I hated to do it, but I reached up and broke his little finger.

The arm went loose and I twisted free.

He lay there panting, face contorted. My heart went out to the fallen giant, defending his people, his religion, following his orders. I cursed myself as I had never cursed before, for walking over him, instead of around.

I staggered across the room to my little heap of possessions. I sat on the projector case and lit a cigarette.

I couldn't go into the Temple until I got my breath back, until I thought of something to say.

How do you talk a race out of killing itself?

Suddenly—

—Could it happen? Would it work that way? If I read them the Book of Ecclesiastes—if I read them a greater piece of literature than any Locar ever wrote—and as somber—and as pessimistic—and showed them that our race had gone on despite one man's condemning all of life in the highest poetry—showed them that the vanity he had mocked had borne us to the Heavens—would they believe it—would they change their minds?

I ground out my cigarette on the beautiful floor, and found my notebook. A strange fury rose within me as I stood.

And I walked into the Temple to preach the Black Gospel according to Gallinger, from the Book of Life.

There was silence all about me.

M'Cwyie had been reading Locar, the rose set at her right hand, target of all eyes.

Until I entered.

Hundreds of people were seated on the floor, barefoot. The few men were as small as the women, I noted.

I had my boots on.

Go all the way, I figured. *You either lose or you win— everything!*

A dozen crones sat in a semicircle behind M'Cwyie. The Mothers.

The barren earth, the dry wombs, the fire-touched.
I moved to the table.

"Dying yourselves, you would condemn your people,"
I addressed them, "that they may not know the life you
have known—the joys, the sorrows, the fullness. —But
it is not true that you all must die." I addressed the
multitude now. "Those who say this lie. Braxa knows,
for she will bear a child—"

They sat there, like rows of Buddhas. M'Cwyie drew
back into the semicircle.

"—my child!" I continued, wondering what my father
would have thought of this sermon.

". . . And all the women young enough may bear children. It is only your men who are sterile. —And if you
permit the doctors of the next expedition to examine you,
perhaps even the men may be helped. But if they cannot,
you can mate with the men of Earth.

"And ours is not an insignificant people, an insignificant place," I went on. "Thousands of years ago, the
Locar of our world wrote a book saying that it was. He
spoke as Locar did, but we did not lie down, despite
plagues, wars, and famines. We did not die. One by one
we beat down the diseases, we fed the hungry, we fought
the wars, and, recently, have gone a long time without
them. We may finally have conquered them. I do not
know.

"But we have crossed millions of miles of nothingness.
We have visited another world. And our Locar had said,
'Why bother? What is the worth of it? It is all vanity,
anyhow.'

"And the secret is," I lowered my voice, as at a poetry
reading, "he was right! It *is* vanity; it *is* pride! It is the
hubris of rationalism to always attack the prophet, the
mystic, the god. It is our blasphemy which has made us
great, and will sustain us, and which the gods secretly
admire in us. —And the truly sacred names of God are
blasphemous things to speak!"

I was working up a sweat. I paused dizzily.

"Here is the Book of Ecclesiastes," I announced, and
began:

" 'Vanity of vanities, saith the Preacher, vanity of
vanities; all is vanity. What profit hath a man . . .' "

I spotted Braxa in the back, mute, rapt.

I wondered what she was thinking.

And I wound the hours of night about me, like black thread on a spool.

Oh it was late! I had spoken till day came, and still I spoke. I finished Ecclesiastes and continued Gallinger.

And when I finished there was still only a silence.

The Buddhas, all in a row, had not stirred through the night. And after a long while M'Cwyie raised her right hand. One by one the Mothers did the same.

And I knew what that meant.

It meant no, do not, cease, and stop.

It meant that I had failed.

I walked slowly from the room and slumped beside my baggage.

Ontro was gone. Good that I had not killed him. . . .

After a thousand years M'Cwyie entered.

She said, "Your job is finished."

I did not move.

"The prophecy is fulfilled," she said. "My people are rejoicing. You have won, holy man. Now leave us quickly."

My mind was a deflated balloon. I pumped a little air back into it.

"I'm not a holy man," I said, "just a second-rate poet with a bad case of hubris."

I lit my cigarette.

Finally, "All right, what prophecy?"

"The Promise of Locar," she replied, as though the explaining was unnecesary, "that a holy man would come from the Heavens to save us in our last hours, if all the dances of Locar were completed. He would defeat the Fist of Malann and bring us life."

"How?"

"As with Braxa, and as the example in the Temple."

"Example?"

"You read us his words, as great as Locar's. You read to us how there is 'nothing new under the sun.' And you mocked his words as you read them—showing us a new thing.

"There has never been a flower on Mars," she said, "but we will learn to grow them.

"You are the Sacred Scoffer," she finished. "He-Who-Must-Mock-in-the-Temple—you go shod on holy ground."

"But you voted 'no,' " I said.

"I voted not to carry out our original plan, and to let Braxa's child live instead."

"Oh." The cigarette fell from my fingers. How close it had been! How little I had known!

"And Braxa?"

"She was chosen half a Process ago to do the dances—to wait for you."

"But she said that Ontro would stop me."

M'Cwyie stood there for a long time.

"She had never believed the prophecy herself. Things are not well with her now. She ran away, fearing it was true. When you completed it and we voted, she knew."

"Then she does not love me? Never did?"

"I am sorry, Gallinger. It was the one part of her duty she never managed."

"Duty," I said flatly. . . . Dutydutyduty! Tra-la!

"She has said good-bye; she does not wish to see you again.

". . . and we will never forget your teachings," she added.

"Don't," I said, automatically, suddenly knowing the great paradox which lies at the heart of all miracles. I did not believe a word of my own gospel, never had.

I stood, like a drunken man, and muttered "M'narra."

I went outside, into my last day on Mars.

I have conquered thee, Malann—and the victory is thine! Rest easy on thy starry bed. God damned!

I left the jeepster there and walked back to the *Aspic*, leaving the the burden of life so many footsteps behind me. I went to my cabin, locked the door, and took forty-four sleeping pills.

But when I awakened I was in the dispensary, and alive.

I felt the throb of engines as I slowly stood up and somehow made it to the port.

Blurred Mars hung like a swollen belly above me, until it dissolved, brimmed over, and streamed down my face.

IF THERE WERE NO BENNY CIMOLI

BY PHILIP K. DICK (1928-1982)

GALAXY SCIENCE FICTION
DECEMBER

One of the best things to happen in the science fiction field in the last few years is the incredible attention and praise "enjoyed" (it would be better if he were alive to hear/see it) by Philip K. Dick. His best works are now available from several publishers; TOTAL RECALL (based on "We Can Remember It for You Wholesale") was a smash box office hit; and Richard Bernstein in THE NEW YORK TIMES BOOK REVIEW devoted several thousand words to his importance to popular culture in the United States.

Mr. Bernstein pointed out that the "new" concept of Virtual reality was something that Phil Dick built a career on, and "If There Were No Benny Cimoli" is as perfect an example of the real, the unreal, and the maybe real as he ever produced at the shorter lengths. I also liked it because I like to believe that Benny Cemoli is the cousin of the old Brooklyn Dodger reserve outfielder Gino Cemoli.

Scampering across the unplowed field, the three boys shouted as they saw the ship; it had landed, all right, just where they expected, and they were the first to reach it.

"Hey, that's the biggest I ever saw!" Panting, the first boy halted. "That's not from Mars; that's from farther. It's from all the way out, I know it is." He became silent and afraid as he saw the size of it. And then, looking up into the sky, he realized that an armada had arrived, exactly as everyone had expected. "We better go tell," he said to his companions.

Back on the ridge, John LeConte stood by his steam-powered, chauffeur-driven limousine, impatiently waiting for the boiler to warm. Kids got there first, he said to himself with anger. Whereas I'm supposed to. And the children were ragged; they were merely farm boys.

"Is the phone working today?" LeConte asked his secretary.

Glancing at his clipboard, Mr. Fall said, "Yes, sir. Shall I put through a message to Oklahoma City?" He was the skinniest employee ever assigned to LeConte's office. The man evidently took nothing for himself, was postively uninterested in food. And he was efficient.

LeConte murmured, "The immigration people ought to hear about this outrage."

He sighed. It had all gone wrong. The armada from Proxima Centauri had after ten years arrived and none of the early-warning devices had detected it in advance of its landing. Now Oklahoma City would have to deal with the outsiders here on home ground—a psychological disadvantage which LeConte felt keenly.

Look at the equipment they've got, he thought as he watched the commercial ships of the flotilla begin to lower their cargos. Why, hell, they make us look like provincials. He wished that his official car did not need twenty minutes to warm up; he wished—

Actually, he wished that CURB did not exist.

Centaurus Urban Renewal Bureau, a do-gooding body unfortunately vested with some enormous inter-system authority. It had been informed of the Misadventure back in 2170 and had started into space like a phototropic organism, sensitive to the mere physical light created by the hydrogen-bomb explosions. But LeConte knew better than that. Actually the governing organizations in the Centaurian system knew many details of the tragedy because they had been in radio contact with other planets of the Sol system. Little of the native forms on earth had survived. He himself was from Mars; he had headed a relief mission seven years ago, had decided to stay because there were so many opportunities here on Earth, conditions being what they were . . .

This is all very difficult, he said to himself, as he stood waiting for his steam-powered car to warm. *We* got here first, but CURB does outrank us; we must face that awkward fact. In my opinion, we've done a good job of rebuilding. Of course, it isn't like it was before . . . but ten years is not long. Give us another twenty and we'll have the trains running again. And our recent road-building bonds sold quite successfully, in fact were oversubscribed.

"Call for you, sir, from Oklahoma City," Mr. Fall said, holding out the receiver of the portable field phone.

"Ultimate Representative in the Field John LeConte here," LeConte said into it loudly. "Go ahead; I say go ahead."

"This is Party Headquarters," the dry official voice at the other end came faintly, mixed with static, in his ear. "We've received reports from dozens of alert citizens in Western Oklahoma and Texas of an immense—"

"It's here," LeConte said. "I can see it. I'm just about ready to go out and confer with its ranking members, and I'll file a full report at the usual time. So it wasn't necessary for you to check up on me." He felt irritable."

"Is the armada heavily armed?"

"Naw," LeConte said. "It appears to be comprised of bureaucrats and trade officials and commercial carriers. In other words, vultures."

The Party desk-man said, "Well, go and make certain they understand that their presence here is resented by the native population as well as the Relief of War-torn Areas Administrating Council. Tell them that the legislature will be called to pass a special bill expressing indignation at this intrusion into domestic matters by an intersystem body."

"I know, I know," LeConte said. "It's been all decided; I know."

His chauffeur called to him, "Sir, your car is ready now."

The Party desk-man concluded, "Make certain they understand that you can't negotiate with them; you have no power to admit them to Earth. Only the Council can do that and of course it's adamantly against that."

LeConte hung up the phone and hurried to his car.

*   *   *

Despite the opposition of the local authorities, Peter Hood of CURB decided to locate his headquarters in the ruins of the old Terran capital, New York City. This would lend prestige to the CURBmen as they gradually widened the circle of the organization's influence. At last, of course, the circle would embrace the planet. But that would take decades.

As he walked through the ruins of what had once been a major train yard, Peter Hood thought to himself that when the task was done he himself would have long been retired. Not much remained of the pre-tragedy culture here. The local authorities—the political nonentities who had flocked in from Mars and Venus, as the neighboring planets were called—had done little. And yet he admired their efforts.

To the members of his staff walking directly behind him he said, "You know, they have done the hard part for us. We ought to be grateful. It is not easy to come into a totally destroyed area, as they've done."

His man Fletcher observed, "They got back a good return."

Hood said, "Motive is not important. They have achieved results." He was thinking of the official who had met them in his steam car; it had been solemn and formal, carrying complicated trappings. When these locals had first arrived on the scene years ago *they* had not been greeted, except perhaps by radiation-seared, blackened survivors who had stumbled out of cellars and gaped sightlessly. He shivered.

Coming up to him, a CURBman of minor rank saluted and said, "I think we've managed to locate an undamaged structure in which your staff could be housed for the time being. It's underground." He looked embarrassed. "Not what we had hoped for. We'd have to displace the locals to get anything attractive."

"I don't object," Hood said. "A basement will do."

"The structure," the minor CURBman said, "was once a great homeostatic newspaper, *The New York Times*. It printed itself directly below us. At least, according to the maps. We haven't located the newspaper yet; it was customary for the homeopapes to be buried a mile or so down. As yet we don't know how much of this one survived."

"But it would be valuable," Hood agreed.

"Yes," the CURBman said. "Its outlets are scattered all over the planet; it must have had a thousand different editions which it put out daily. How many outlets function—" He broke off. "It's hard to believe that the local politicos made no efforts to repair any of the ten or eleven worldwide homeopapes, but that seems to be the case."

"Odd," Hood said. Surely it would have eased their task. The post-tragedy job of reuniting people into a common culture depended on newspapers, ionization in the atmosphere making radio and TV reception difficult if not impossible. "This makes me instantly suspicious," he said, turning to his staff. "Are they perhaps not trying to rebuild after all? Is their work merely a pretense?"

It was his own wife, Joan, who spoke up. "They may simply have lacked the ability to place the homeopapes on an operational basis."

Give them the benefit of the doubt, Hood thought. You're right.

"So the last edition of the *Times*," Fletcher said, "was put on the lines the day the Misadventure occurred. And the entire network of newspaper communication and news-creation has been idle since. I can't respect these politicos; it shows they're ignorant of the basics of a culture. By reviving the homeopapes we can do more to reestablish the pre-tragedy culture then they've done in ten thousand pitiful projects." His tone was scornful.

Hood said, "You may misunderstand, but let it go. Let's hope that the cephalon of the pape is undamaged. We couldn't possibly replace it." Ahead he saw the yawning entrance which the CURBmen crews had cleared. This was to be his first move, here on the ruined planet, restoring this immense self-contained entity to its former authority. Once it had resumed its activity he would be freed for other tasks; the homeopape would take some of the burden from him.

A workman, still clearing debris away, muttered, "Jeez, I never saw so many layers of junk. You'd think they deliberately bottled it up here." In his hands, the suction furnace which he operated glowed and pounded as it absorbed material, converting it to energy, leaving an increasingly enlarged opening.

"I'd like a report as soon as possible as to its condition," Hood said to the team of engineers who stood waiting to descend into the opening. "How long it will take to revive it, how much—" He broke off.

Two men in black uniforms had arrived. Police, from the security ship. One, he saw, was Otto Dietrich, the ranking investigator accompanying the armada from Centaurus, and he felt tense automatically; it was a reflex for all of them—he saw the engineers and the workmen cease momentarily and then, more slowly, resume their work.

"Yes," he said to Dietrich. "Glad to see you. Let's go off to this side room and talk there." He knew beyond a doubt what the investigator wanted; he had been expecting him.

Dietrich said, "I won't take up too much of your time, Hood. I know you're quite busy. What is this, here?" He glanced about curiously, his scrubbed, round, alert face eager.

In a small side room, converted to a temporary office, Hood faced the two policemen. "I am opposed to prosecution," he said quietly. "It's been too long. Let them go."

Dietrich, tugging thoughtfully at his ear, said, "But war crimes are war crimes, even foul decades later. Anyhow, what argument can there be? We're required by law to prosecute. Somebody started the war. They may well hold positions of responsibility now, but that hardly matters."

"How many police troops have you landed?" Hood asked.

"Two hundred."

"Then you're ready to go to work."

"We're ready to make inquiries. Sequester pertinent documents and initiate litigation in the local courts. We've prepared to enforce cooperation, if that's what you mean. Various experienced personnel have been distributed to key points." Dietrich eyed him. "All this is necessary; I don't see the problem. Did you intend to protect the guilty parties—make use of their so-called abilities on your staff?"

"No," Hood said evenly.

Dietrich said, "Nearly eighty million people died in the Misfortune. Can you forget that? Or is it that since they were merely local people, not known to us personally—"

"It's not that," Hood said. He knew it was hopeless; he could not communicate with the police mentality. "I've already stated my objections. I feel it serves no purpose at this late date to have trials and hangings. Don't request use of my staff in this; I'll refuse on the grounds that I can spare no one, not even a janitor. Do I make myself clear?"

"You idealists." Dietrich sighed. "This is strictly a noble task confronting us . . . to rebuild, correct? What you don't or won't see is that these people will start it all over again, one day, unless we take steps now. We owe it to future generations. To be harsh now is the most humane method, in the long run. Tell me, Hood. What is this site? What are you resurrecting here with such vigor?"

"*The New York Times,*" Hood said.

"It has, I assume, a morgue? We can consult its back-log of information? That would prove valuable in building up our cases."

Hood said, "I can't deny you access to material we uncover."

Smiling, Dietrich said, "A day-by-day account of the political events leading up to the war would prove quite interesting. Who, for instance, held supreme power in the United States at the time of the Misfortune? No one we've talked to so far seems to remember." His smile increased.

Early the next morning the report from the corps of engineers reached Hood in his temporary office. The power supply of the newspaper had been totally destroyed. But the cephalon, the governing brain-structure which guided and oriented the homeostatic system, appeared to be intact. If a ship were brought close by, perhaps its power supply could be integrated into the newspaper's lines. Thereupon much more would be known.

"In other words," Fletcher said to Hood, as they sat with Joan eating breakfast, "it may come on and it may not. Very pragmatic. You hook it up and if it works you've done your job. What if it doesn't? Do the engineers intend to give up at that point?"

Examining his cup, Hood said, "This tastes like authentic coffee." He pondered. "Tell them to bring a ship in and start the homeopape up. And if it begins to print, bring me the edition at once." He sipped his coffee.

An hour later a ship of the line had landed in the vicinity and its power source had been tapped for insertion into the homeopape. The conduits were placed, the circuits cautiously closed.

Seated in his office, Peter Hood heard far underground a low rumble, a halting, uncertain stirring. They had been successful. The newspaper was returning to life.

The edition, when it was laid on his desk by a bustling CURBman, surprised him by its accuracy. Even in its dormant state, the newspaper had somehow managed not to fall behind events. Its receptors had kept going.

CURB LANDS, TRIP DECADE LONG, PLANS CENTRAL ADMINISTRATION

Ten years after the Misfortune of a nuclear holocaust, the intersystem rehabilitation agency, CURB, has made its historic appearance on Earth's surface, landing from a veritable armada of craft—a sight which witnesses described as "overpowering both in scope and in significance." CURBman Peter Hood, named top coordinator by Centaurian authorities, immediately set up headquarters in the ruins of New York City and conferred with aides, declaring that he had come "not to punish the guilty but to reestablish the planetwide culture by every means available, and to restore . . .

It was uncanny, Hood thought as he read the lead article. The varied news-gathering services of the homeopape had reached into his own life, had digested and then inserted into the lead article even the discussion between himself and Otto Dietrich. The newspaper was—had been—doing its job. Nothing of news-interest escaped it, even a discreet conversation carried on with no outsiders as witnesses. He would have to be careful.

Sure enough, another item, ominous in tone, dealt with the arrival of the black jacks, the police.

SECURITY AGENCY VOWS "WAR CRIMINALS" TARGET

Captain Otto Dietrich, supreme police investigator arriving with the CURB armada from Proxima Centauri, said today that those responsible for the Misfortune of a decade ago "would have to pay for their crimes" before the bar of Centaurian justice. Two hundred black-uniformed police, it was learned by the *Times*, have already begun exploratory activities designed to . . .

The newspaper was warning Earth about Dietrich, and Hood could not help feeling grim relish. The *Times* had not been set up to serve merely the occupying hierarchy. It served everyone, including those Dietrich intended to try. Each step of the police activity would no doubt be reported in full detail. Dietrich, who liked to work in anonymity, would not enjoy this. But the authority to maintain the newspaper belonged to Hood.

And he did not intend to shut it off.

One item on the first page of the paper attracted his further notice; he read it, frowning and a little uneasy.

CEMOLI BACKERS RIOT IN UPSTATE NEW YORK

Supporters of Benny Cemoli, gathered in the familiar tent cities associated with the colorful political figure, clashed with local citizens armed with hammers, shovels, and boards, both sides claiming victory in the two-hour melee which left twenty injured and a dozen hospitalized in hastily erected first-aid stations. Cemoli, garbed as always in his toga-style red robes, visited the injured, evidently in good spirits, joking and telling his supporters that "it won't be long now" an evident reference to the organization's boast that it would march on New York City in the near future to establish what Cemoli deems "social justice and true equality for the first time in world history." It should be recalled that prior to his imprisonment at San Quentin . . .

Flipping a switch on his intercom system. Hood said, "Fletcher, check into activities up in the north of the county. Find out about some sort of a political mob gathering there."

Fletcher's voice came back, "I have a copy of the *Times*, too, sir. I see the item about this Cemoli agitator. There's a ship on the way up there right now; should have a report within ten minutes." Fletcher paused. "Do you think—it'll be necessary to bring in any of Dietrich's people?"

"Let's hope not," Hood said shortly.

Half an hour later the CURB ship, through Fletcher, made its report. Puzzled, Hood asked that it be repeated. But there was no mistake. The CURB field team had investigated thoroughly. They had found no sign whatsoever of any tent city or any group gathering. And citizens in the area whom they had interrogated had never heard of anyone named "Cemoli." And there was no sign of any scuffle having taking place, no first-aid stations, no injured persons. Only the peaceful, semi-rural countryside.

Baffled, Hood read the item in the *Times* once more. There it was, in black and white, on the front page, along with the news about the landing of the CURB armada. What did it mean?

He did not like it at all.

Had it been a mistake to revive the great, old, damaged homeostatic newspaper?

From a sound sleep that night Hood was awakened by a clanging from far beneath the ground, an urgent racket that grew louder and louder as he sat up in bed, blinking and confused. Machinery roared. He heard the heavy rumbling movement as automatic circuits fitted into place, responding to instructions emanating from within the closed system itself.

"Sir," Fletcher was saying from the darkness. A light came on as Fletcher located the temporary overhead fixture. "Thought I should come in and wake you. Sorry, Mrs. Hood."

"I'm awake," Hood muttered, rising from the bed and putting on his robe and slippers. "What's it doing?"

Fletcher said, "It's printing an extra."

Sitting up, smoothing her tousled blond hair back, Joan said, "Good lord. What about?" Wide-eyed, she looked from her husband to Fletcher.

"We'll have to bring in the local authorities," Hood said. "Confer with them." He had an intuition as to the nature of the extra roaring through the presses at this moment. "Get that LeConte, that politico who met us on our arrival. Wake him up and fly him here immediately. We need him."

It took almost an hour to obtain the presence of the haughty, ceremonious local potentate and his staff member. The two of them in their elaborate uniforms at last put in an appearance at Hood's office, both of them indignant. They faced Hood silently, waiting to hear what he wanted.

In his bathrobe and slippers Hood sat at his desk, a copy of the *Times*'s extra before him; he was reading it once more as LeConte and his man entered.

NEW YORK POLICE REPORT
CEMOLI LEGIONS ON MOVE TOWARD CITY,
BARRICADES ERECTED
NATIONAL GUARD ALERTED

He turned the paper, showing the headlines to the two Earthmen. "Who is this man?" he said.

After a moment LeConte said, "I—don't know."

Hood said, "Come on, Mr. LeConte."

"Let me read the article," LeConte said nervously. He scanned it in haste; his hands trembled as he held the newspaper. "Interesting," he said at last. "But I can't tell you a thing. It's news to me. You must understand that our communications have been sparse, since the Misfortune, and it's entirely possible that a political movement could spring up without our—"

"Please," Hood said. "Don't make yourself absurd."

Flushing, LeConte stammered, "I'm doing the best I can, summoned out of my bed in the middle of the night."

There was a stir, and through the office doorway came the rapidly moving figure of Otto Dietrich, looking grim. "Hood," he said without preamble, "there's a *Times* kiosk near my headquarters. It just posted this." He held up a copy of the extra. "The damn thing is running this off and distributing it throughout the world, isn't it? However, we have crack teams up in that area and they report absolutely nothing, no roadblocks, no militia-style troops on the move, no activity of any sort."

"I know," Hood said. He felt weary. And still, from beneath them, the deep rumble continued, the newspaper printing its extra, informing the world of the march by Benny Cemoli's supporters on New York City—a fantasy march, evidently, a product manufactured entirely within the cephalon of the newspaper itself.

"Shut it off," Dietrich said.

Hood shook his head. "No. I want to know more."

"That's no reason," Dietrich said. "Obviously, it's defective. Very seriously damaged, not working properly. You'll have to search elsewhere for your worldwide propaganda network." He tossed the newspaper down on Hood's desk.

To LeConte, Hood said, "Was Benny Cemoli active before the war?"

There was silence. Both LeConte and his assistant Mr. Fall were pale and tense; they faced him tight-lipped, glancing at each other.

"I am not much for police matters," Hood said to Dietrich, "but I think you could reasonably step in here."

Dietrich, understanding, said, "I agree. You two men are under arrest. Unless you feel inclined to talk a little more freely about this agitator in the red toga." He nodded to two of his police, who stood by the office doorway; they stepped obediently forward.

As the two policemen came up to him, LeConte said, "Come to think of it, there was such a person. But—he was very obscure."

"Before the war?" Hood asked.

"Yes." LeConte nodded slowly. "He was a joke. As I recall, and it's difficult . . . a fat, ignorant clown from some backwoods area. He had a little radio station or something over which he broadcast. He peddled some sort of anti-radiation box which you installed in your house, and it made you safe from bomb-test fallout."

Now his staff member Mr. Fall said, "I remember. He even ran for the UN Senate. But he was defeated, naturally."

"And that was the last of him?" Hood asked.

"Oh yes," LeConte said. "He died of Asian flu soon after. He's been dead for fifteen years."

In a helicopter, Hood flew slowly above the terrain depicted in the *Times* articles, seeing for himself that there was no sign of political activity. He did not feel really assured until he had seen with his own eyes that the newspaper had lost contact with actual events. The reality of the situation did not coincide with the *Times*'s articles in any way; that was obvious. And yet—the homeostatic system continued on.

Joan, seated beside him, said, "I have the third article here, if you want to read it." She had been looking the latest edition over.

"No," Hood said.

"It says they're in the outskirts of the city," she said. "They broke through the police barricades and the governor has appealed for UN assistance."

Thoughtfully, Fletcher said, "Here's an idea. One of us, preferably you, Hood, should write a letter to the *Times*."

Hood glanced at him.

"I think I can tell you exactly how it should be worded," Fletcher said. "Make it a simple inquiry. You've followed the accounts in the paper about Cemoli's movement. Tell the editor"—Fletcher paused—"that you feel sympathetic *and you'd like to join the movement*. Ask the paper how."

To himself, Hood thought, In other words ask the newspaper to put me in touch with Cemoli. He had to admire Fletcher's idea. It was brilliant, in a crazy sort of way. It was as if Fletcher had been able to match the derangement of the newspaper by a deliberate shift from common sense on his own part. He would participate in the newspaper's delusion. Assuming there was a Cemoli and a march on New York, he was asking a reasonable question.

Joan said, "I don't want to sound stupid, but how does one go about mailing a letter to a homeopape?"

"I've looked into that," Fletcher said. "At each kiosk set up by the paper there's a letter-slot, next to the coin-slot where you pay for your paper. It was the law, when the homeopapes were set up originally, decades ago. All we need is your husband's signature." Reaching into his jacket, he brought out an envelope. "The letter's written."

Hood took the letter, examined it. So we desire to be part of the mythical fat clown's throng, he said to himself. "Won't there be a headline reading CURB CHIEF JOINS MARCH ON EARTH CAPITAL?" he asked Fletcher, feeling a trace of wry amusement. "Wouldn't a good, enterprising homeopape make front-page use of a letter such as this?"

Obviously Fletcher had not thought of that; he looked chagrined, "I suppose we had better get someone else to sign it," he admitted. "Some minor person attached to your staff." He added, "I could sign it myself."

Handing him the letter back, Hood said, "Do so. It'll be interesting to see what response, if any, there is." Letters to the editor, he thought. Letters to a vast, complex, electronic organism buried deep in the ground, responsible to no one, guided solely by its own ruling circuits. How would it react to this external ratification of its delusion? Would the newspaper be snapped back to reality?

It was, he thought, as if the newspaper, during these years of its enforced silence, had been dreaming, and now, reawakened, it had allowed portions of its former dreams to materialize in its pages along with its accurate, perceptive accounts of the actual situation. A blend of figments and sheer, stark reporting. Which ultimately would triumph? Soon, evidently, the unfolding story of Benny Cemoli would have the toga-wearing spellbinder in New York; it appeared that the march would succeed. And what then? How could this be squared with the arrival of CURB, with all its enormous inter-system authority and power? Surely the homeopape, before long, would have to face the incongruity.

One of the two accounts would have to cease—but Hood had an uneasy intuition that a homeopape which had dreamed for a decade would not readily give up its fantasies.

Perhaps, he thought, the news of us, of CURB and its task of rebuilding Earth, will fade from the pages of the *Times*, will be given in a steadily decreasing coverage each day, farther back in the paper. And at last only the exploits of Benny Cemoli will remain.

It was not a pleasant anticipation. It disturbed him deeply. As if, he thought, we are real only so long as the *Times* writes about us; as if we were dependent for our existence on it.

Twenty-four hours later, in its regular edition, the *Times* printed Fletcher's letter. In print it struck Hood as flimsy and contrived—surely the homeopape could not be taken in by it, and yet here it was. It had managed to pass each of the steps in the pape's processing.

Dear Editor:
    Your coverage of the heroic march on the decadent plutocratic stronghold of New York City has fired my enthusiasm. How does an ordinary citizen become a part of this history in the making? Please inform me at once, as I am eager to join Cemoli and endure the rigors and triumphs with the others.
                                        Cordially,
                                        Rudolf Fletcher

Beneath the letter, the homeopape had given an answer; Hood read it rapidly.

Cemoli's stalwarts maintain a recruiting office in downtown New York; address, 460 Bleekman St.,

New York 32. You might apply there, if the police haven't cracked down on these quasi-legal activities, in view of the current crisis.

Touching a button on his desk, Hood opened the direct line to police headquarters. When he had the chief investigator, he said, "Dietrich, I'd like a team of your men; we have a trip to make and there may be difficulties."

After a pause Dietrich said drily, "So it's not all noble reclamation after all. Well, we've already dispatched a man to keep an eye on the Bleekman Street address. I admire your letter scheme. It may have done the trick." He chuckled.

Shortly, Hood and four black-uniformed Centaurian policemen flew by copter above the ruins of New York City, searching for the remains of what had once been Bleekman Street. By the use of a map they managed after half an hour to locate themselves.

"There," the police captain in charge of the team said, pointing. "That would be it, that building used as a grocery store." The copter began to lower.

It was a grocery store, all right. Hood saw no signs of political activity, no persons loitering, no flags or banners. And yet—something ominous seemed to lie behind the commonplace scene below, the bins of vegetables parked out on the sidewalk, the shabby women in long cloth coats who stood picking over the winter potatoes, the elderly proprietor with his white cloth apron sweeping with his broom. It was too natural, too easy. It was *too* ordinary.

"Shall we land?" the police captain asked him.

"Yes," Hood said. "And be ready."

The proprietor, seeing them land in the street before his grocery store, laid his broom carefully to one side and walked toward them. He was, Hood saw, a Greek. He had a heavy mustache and slightly wavy gray hair, and he gazed at them with innate caution, knowing at once that they did not intend him any good. Yet he had decided to greet them with civility; he was not afraid of them.

"Gentlemen," the Greek grocery store owner said, bowing slightly. "What can I do for you?" His eyes roved speculatively over the black Centaurian police uniforms, but he showed no expression, no reaction.

Hood said, "We've come to arrest a political agitator. You have nothing to be alarmed about." He started toward the grocery store; the team of police followed, their side arms drawn.

"Political agitation here?" the Greek said. "Come on. It is impossible." He hurried after them, panting, alarmed now. "What have I done? Nothing at all; you can look around. Go ahead." He held open the door of the store, ushering them inside. "See right away for yourself."

"That's what we intend to do," Hood said. He moved with agility, wasting no time on the conspicuous portions of the store; he strode directly on through.

The back room lay ahead, the warehouse with its cartons of cans, cardboard boxes stacked up on every side. A young boy was busy making a stock inventory; he glanced up, startled, as they entered. Nothing here, Hood thought. The owner's son at work, that's all. Lifting the lid of a carton, Hood peered inside. Cans of peaches. And beside that a crate of lettuce. He tore off a leaf, feeling futile and—disappointed.

The police captain said to him in a low voice, "Nothing, sir."

"I see that," Hood said, irritably.

A door to the right led to a closet. Opening it, he saw brooms and a mop, a galvanized pail, boxes of detergents. And—

There were drops of paint on the floor.

The closet, sometime recently, had been repainted. When he bent down and scratched with his nail he found the paint still tacky.

"Look at this," he said, beckoning the police captain over.

The Greek, nervously, said, "What's the matter, gentlemen? You find something dirty and report to the board of health, is that it? Customers have complained— tell me the truth, please. Yes, it is fresh paint. We keep everything spick and span. Isn't that in the public interest?"

Running his hands across the wall of the broom closet,

the police captain said quietly, "Mr. Hood, there was a doorway here. Sealed up now, very recently." He looked expectantly toward Hood, awaiting instructions.

Hood said, "Let's go in."

Turning to his subordinates, the police captain gave a series of orders. From the ship, equipment was dragged, through the store, to the closet; a controlled whine arose as the police began the task of cutting into the wood and plaster.

Pale, the Greek said, "This is outrageous. I will sue."

"Right," Hood agreed. "Take us to court." Already a portion of the wall had given way. It fell inward with a crash, and bits of rubble spilled down onto the floor. A white cloud of dust rose, then settled.

It was not a large room which Hood saw in the glare of the police flashlights. Dusty, without windows, smelling stale and ancient . . . the room had not been inhabited for a long, long time, he realized as he warily entered. It was empty. Just an abandoned storeroom of some kind, its wooden walls scaling and dingy. Perhaps before the Misfortune the grocery store had possessed a larger inventory. More stocks had been available then, but now this room was not needed. Hood moved about, flashing his beam of light up to the ceiling and then down to the floor. Dead flies, entombed here . . . and, he saw, a few live ones which crept haltingly in the dust.

"Remember," the police captain said, "it was boarded up just now, within the last three days. Or at least the painting was just now done, to be absolutely accurate about it."

"These flies," Hood said. "They're not even dead yet." So it had not even been three days. Probably the boarding up had been done yesterday.

What had this room been used for? He turned to the Greek, who had come after them, still tense and pale, his dark eyes flickering rapidly with concern. This is a smart man, Hood realized . We will get little out of him.

At the far end of the storeroom the police flashlights picked out a cabinet, empty shelves of bare, rough wood. Hood walked toward it.

"Okay," the Greek said thickly, swallowing. "I admit it. We have kept bootleg gin stored here. We became scared. You. Centaurians—" He looked around at them all with fear. "You're not like our local bosses; we know them, they understand us. You! You can't be reached. But we have to make a living." He spread his hands, appealing to them.

From behind the cabinet the edge of something protruded. Barely visible, it might never have been noticed. A paper which had fallen there, almost out of sight; it had slipped down farther and farther. Now Hood took hold of it and carefully drew it out. Back up the way it had come.

The Greek shuddered.

It was, Hood saw, a picture. A heavy, middle-aged man with loose jowls stained black by the grained beginnings of a beard, frowning, his lips set in defiance. A big man, wearing some kind of uniform. Once this picture had hung on the wall and people had come here and looked at it, paid respect to it. He knew who it was. This was Benny Cemoli, at the height of his political career, the leader glaring bitterly at the followers who had gathered here. So this was the man.

No wonder the *Times* showed such alarm.

To the Greek grocery store owner, Hood said, holding up the picture, "Tell me. Is this familiar to you?"

"No, no," the Greek said. He wiped perspiration from his face with a large red handkerchief. "Certainly not." But obviously, it was.

Hood said, "You're a follower of Cemoli, aren't you?"

There was silence.

"Take him along," Hood said to the police captain. "And let's start back." He walked from the room, carrying the picture with him.

As he spread the picture out on his desk, Hood thought, It isn't merely a fantasy of the *Times*. We know the truth now. The man is real and twenty-four hours ago this portrait of him hung on a wall, in plain sight. It would still be there this moment, if CURB had not put in its appearance. We frightened them. The Earth people have a lot to hide from us, and they know it. They are taking steps, rapidly and effectively, and we will be lucky if we can—

Interrupting his thoughts, Joan said, "Then the Bleekman Street address really was a meeting place for them. The pape was correct."

"Yes," Hood said.

"Where is he now?"

I wish we knew, Hood thought.

"Has Dietrich seen the picture yet?"

"Not yet," Hood said.

Joan said, "He was responsible for the war and Dietrich is going to find it out."

"No one man," Hood said, "could be solely responsible."

"But he figured largely," Joan said. "That's why they've gone to so much effort to eradicate all traces of his existence."

Hood nodded.

"Without the *Times*," she said, "would we ever have guessed that such a political figure as Benny Cemoli existed? We owe a lot to the pape. They overlooked it or weren't able to get to it. Probably they were working in such haste; they couldn't think of everything, even in ten years. It must be hard to obliterare *every* surviving detail of a planetwide political movement, especially when its leader managed to seize absolute power in the final phase."

"Impossible to obliterate," Hood said. "A closed-off storeroom in the back of a Greek grocery store . . . that was enough to tell us what we needed to know. Now Dietrich's men can do the rest. If Cemoli is alive they will eventually find him, and if he's dead—they'll be hard to convince, knowing Dietrich. They'll never stop looking now."

"One good thing about this," Joan said, "is that now a lot of innocent people will be off the hook. Dietrich won't go around prosecuting them. He'll be busy tracking down Cemoli."

True, Hood thought. And that was important. The Centaurian police would be thoroughly occupied for a long time to come, and that was just as well for everyone, including CURB and its ambitious program of reconstruction.

If there had never been a Benny Cemoli, he thought

suddenly, it would almost have been necessary to invent him. An odd thought . . . he wondered how it had happened to come to him. Again he examined the picture, trying to infer as much as possible about the man from this flat likeness. How had Cemoli sounded? Had he gained power through the spoken word, like so many demagogues before him? And his writing . . . Maybe some of it would turn up. Or even tape recordings of speeches he had made, the actual *sound* of the man. And perhaps video tapes as well. Eventually it would all come to light; it was only a question of time. And then we will be able to experience for ourselves how it was to live under the shadow of such a man, he realized.

The line from Dietrich's office buzzed. He picked up the phone.

"We have the Greek here," Dietrich said. "Under drug-guidance he's made a number of admissions; you may be interested."

"Yes," Hood said.

Dietrich said, "He tells us he's been a follower for seventeen years, a real old-timer in the Movement. They met twice a week in the back of his grocery store, in the early days when the Movement was small and relatively powerless. That picture you have—I haven't seen it, of course, but Stavros, our Greek gentleman, told me about it—that portrait is actually obsolete in the sense that several more recent ones have been in vogue among the faithful for some time now. Stavros hung on to it for sentimental reasons. It reminded him of the old days. Later on when the movement grew in strength, Cemoli stopped showing up at the grocery store, and the Greek lost out in any personal contact with him. He continued to be a loyal dues-paying member, but it became abstract for him."

"What about the war?" Hood asked.

"Shortly before the war Cemoli seized power in a coup here in North America, through a march on New York City, during a severe economic depression. Millions were unemployed and he drew a good deal of support from them. He tried to solve the economic problems through an aggressive foreign policy—attacked several Latin American republics which were in the sphere of influence of the Chinese. That seems to be it, but Stavros is a bit hazy about the big picture . . . we'll have to fill in more from other enthusiasts as we go along. From some of the younger ones. After all, this one is over seventy years old."

Hood said, "You're not going to prosecute him, I hope."

"Oh, no. He's simply a source of information. When he's told us all he has on his mind we'll let him go back to his onions and canned applesauce. He's harmless."

"Did Cemoli survive the war?"

"Yes," Dietrich said. "But that was ten years ago. Stavros doesn't know if the man is still alive now. Personally I think he is, and we'll go on that assumption until it's proved false. We have to."

Hood thanked him and hung up.

As he turned from the phone he heard, beneath him, the low, dull rumbling. The homeopape had once more started into life.

"It's not a regular edition," Joan said, quickly consulting her wristwatch. "So it must be another extra. This is exciting, having it happen like this; I can't wait to read the front page."

What has Benny Cemoli done now? Hood wondered. According to the *Times*, in its misphased chronicling of the man's epic . . . what stage, actually taking place years ago, has now been reached? Something climactic, deserving of an extra. It will be interesting, no doubt of that. The *Times* knows what is fit to print.

He, too, could hardly wait.

In downtown Oklahoma City, John LeConte put a coin into the slot of the kiosk which the *Times* had long ago established there. The copy of the *Time*'s latest extra slid out, and he picked it up and read the headline briefly, spending only a moment on it to verify the essentials. Then he crossed the sidewalk and stepped once more into the rear seat of his chauffeur-driven steam car.

Mr. Fall said circumspectly, "Sir, here is the primary material, if you wish to make a word-by-word comparison." The secretary held out the folder, and LeConte accepted it.

The car started up. Without being told, the chauffeur drove in the direction of Party headquarters. LeConte leaned back, lit a cigar and made himself comfortable.

On his lap, the newspaper blazed up its enormous headlines.

CEMOLI ENTERS COALITION UN GOVERNMENT; TEMPORARY CESSATION OF HOSTILITIES

To his secretary, LeConte said, "My phone, please."

"Yes, sir." Mr. Fall handed him the portable field phone. "But we're almost there. And it's always possible, if you don't mind my pointing it out, that they may have tapped us somewhere along the line."

"They're busy in New York," LeConte said: "Among the ruins." In an area that hasn't mattered as long as I can remember, he said to himself. However, possibly Mr. Fall's advice was good; he decided to skip the phone call. "What do you think of this last item?" he asked his secretary, holding up the newspaper.

"Very success-deserving," Mr. Fall said, nodding.

Opening his briefcase, LeConte brought out a tattered, coverless textbook. It had been manufactured only an hour ago, and it was the next artifact to be planted for the invaders from Proxima Centaurus to discover. This was his own contribution, and he was personally quite proud of it. The book outlined in massive detail Cemoli's program of social change; the revolution depicted in language comprehensible to school children.

"May I ask," Mr. Fall said, "if the Party hierarchy intends for them to discover a corpse?"

"Eventually," LeConte said. "But that will be several months from now." Taking a pencil from his coat pocket, he wrote in the tattered textbook, crudely, as if a pupil had done it:

DOWN WITH CEMOLI

Or was that going too far? No, he decided. There would be resistance. Certainly of the spontaneous, schoolboy variety. He added:

WHERE ARE THE ORANGES?

Peering over his shoulder, Mr. Fall said, "What does that mean?"

"Cemoli promises oranges to the youth," LeConte explained. "Another empty boast which the revolution never fulfills. That was Stavros's idea . . . he being a grocer. A nice touch." Giving it, he thought, just that much more semblance of verisimilitude. It's the little touches that have done it.

"Yesterday," Mr. Fall said, "when I was at Party headquarters, I heard an audio tape that had been made. Cemoli addressing the UN. It was uncanny; if you didn't know—"

"Who did they get to do it?" LeConte asked, wondering why he hadn't been in on it.

"Some nightclub entertainer here in Oklahoma City. Rather obscure, of course. I believe he specializes in all sorts of characterizations. The fellow gave it a bombastic, threatening quality . . . I must admit I enjoyed it."

And meanwhile, LeConte thought, *there are no war-crimes trials.* We who were leaders during the war, on Earth and on Mars, we who held responsible posts—we are safe, at least for a while. And perhaps it will be forever. If our strategy continues to work. And if our tunnel to the cephalon of the homeopape, which took us five years to complete, isn't discovered. Or doesn't collapse.

The steam car parked in the reserved space before Party headquarters; the chauffeur came around to open the door, and LeConte got leisurely out, stepping forth into the light of day, with no feeling of anxiety. He tossed his cigar into the gutter and then sauntered across the sidewalk, into the familiar building.

This volume brings to an end the series of retrospective "best of the year" books that Isaac Asimov and I started in 1979. Both of us felt that it was the most important anthology project either of us ever worked on. It was due to end with this volume, the twenty-fifth in the series, because 1963 was the last year before Don Wollheim and Terry Carr began their series (first published at Ace and then continued by Don himself at DAW) of "best of the year" collections—their volume, entitled WORLD'S BEST SCIENCE FICTION: 1965, covered what they considered the best sf of 1964.

I point this out because Isaac died in April 1992, at the age of 72. By the time this book is published you will have read much about his wonderful career and the impact he had on his millions of readers, and I won't add to that here. I would like to say, however, that Isaac was a good friend of Don and Elsie Wollheim for more than fifty years, and that Elsie, Betsy Wollheim, and Sheila Gilbert join me in mourning his passing.

I know that I will never have a better or more loyal friend.

Good-bye, Isaac. We all miss you very much.

DAW
Science Fiction at Its Best

W. Michael Gear

Forbidden Borders

He was the most hated and feared power in human-controlled space—
and only he could become the means of his own destruction....
- [ ] **REQUIEM FOR THE CONQUEROR (#1)** UE2477—$4.99
- [ ] **RELIC OF EMPIRE (#2)** UE2492—$5.99

Cheryl J. Franklin

The Network/Consortium Novels:

- [ ] **THE INQUISITOR** (UE2512—$5.99)

Would an entire race be destroyed by one man's ambitions— and one
woman's thirst for vengeance?

Betty Anne Crawford

- [ ] **THE BUSHIDO INCIDENT** (UE2517—$4.99)

In the future in which Japan economically dominates the Earth, the
past and the present are constantly being "rewritten" by their paid
Historians. But So Pak, son of Earth's finest Historian, seeks another
path—the path of "freedom." Seeking to learn the truth about two lost
mining expeditions, he launches a mission on the starship *Bushido*. But
someone is determined that neither So Pak nor the *Bushido* will ever
return to Earth.

DAW

Attention:

DAW COLLECTORS

Many readers of DAW Books have written requesting information on early titles and book numbers to assist in the collection of DAW editions since the first of our titles appeared in April 1972.

We have prepared a several-pages-long list of all DAW titles, giving their sequence numbers, original and current order numbers, and ISBN numbers. And of course the authors and book titles, as well as reissues.

If you think that this list will be of help, you may have a copy by writing to the address below and enclosing one dollar in stamps or currency to cover the handling and postage costs.

DAW Books, Inc.
Dept. C
375 Hudson Street
New York, NY 10014-3658